EYES IN THE SHADOWS

HITMEN OF ULYSSES BOOK 1
L.M. WHITELEY

CONTENT WARNING

This book is a dark romance intended for mature audiences with an antihero who does bad things and a heroine who falls for him anyway. It contains themes and scenes that may be distressing to some readers, including:

- Stalking

- Graphic violence done to and by main characters

- Gun-related content

- Death, murder and organized crime

- Threats of harm

- Dynamics of dubious consent

- Explicit sexual content

Your mental health matters. Reader discretion is advised.

Dedication

To fans of John Wick, anyone who knows about the government cheese caves, and anyone who took a chance on an unknown author and picked this up. Thank you.

1

ELEANOR

<hr>

I guess it'll be like an adventure...

I don't live in a good part of town.

I may be poor, but I'm not stupid. I know that the guys meeting on the corner at 2 AM are making some kind of illegal exchange. I know that the bar across the street from me has gang affiliations, and not just because of how weird everyone got when I tried to get a beer there after my shift once. I know that the women out on the street dressed in spandex are coatless in January in New Jersey because they don't want to cover up what's for sale. I know there's a reason that the only bench on my block without graffiti is the one with the picture of smiling realtor and biggest slumlord around, Jay Rossi.

I don't know for sure the reason, but I know there is one. And I suspect it's related to the rumors I hear about how he's involved in some shady shit.

Calling Ulysses a city is a bit of a stretch, but it's big enough and close enough to create a New York City-Philadelphia triangle that means we get what spills out past the boundaries. It's got your requisite strip malls with liquor stores, tattoo parlors, cheap stuff outlets, and Chinese food restaurants, strip clubs standing alone on the side of the road, and parks where no one walks at night without a good reason or pepper spray. It's also got gated communities, neighborhoods with town homes, hospitals, museums, libraries, churches, and a community college.

Like most urban-adjacent places, the wealth distribution in Ulysses is wild. I'm in a rent-controlled apartment building near the city center, and just a few miles away is an area full of mansions so enormous and beautiful, all I can think about when I see them is how long it must take to clean one of those bad boys.

Seriously, if you go top to bottom, I bet by the time you reach the first floor you'd have to start over again.

But I'm so far away from Mansion Row that I can't picture myself ever stepping foot in one. Again, this is the wrong side of town. So, it's not really surprising when I find a note taped to my apartment door about evacuating our units so they can fumigate the building. It's not even that surprising to read the words "out of control" and "poses a health risk" to describe the infestation.

What is surprising is the lack of notice. We have to vacate tomorrow morning by 10 AM and can't return until Friday morning at 8 AM, a full three days later. There's a half-assed apology for the short notice and something about a $5 gift card for the inconvenience that I know for a fact the property manager, Ed, will pretend to forget about if anyone approaches him for it. I think he knows most people won't fight him for $5 if he doubles down on the ignorance act.

I glance each way down the hallway and confirm that the other doors have the same note, and shove my key into the lock with a sigh.

I'm comfortable in the middle apartment on the top floor. Sure, my walls are so thin that I can hear the Paulsons arguing about how opening their marriage is going way better for her than it is for him, and it's sweltering in the winter when the heat seeps in through the wall from ancient Mrs. Parker's apartment on my other side. She's a half-blind Louisiana transplant who can't handle the snow. They're fine neighbors otherwise, and they keep to themselves. The people on the other side of the hall—3D through F—are much the same.

One of the most tried-and-true methods for staying out of trouble in a neighborhood like mine is to keep your head down.

I pull off my hat and scarf immediately upon crossing the threshold and toss them onto the end table next to the couch like they've done me a disservice. I run warm, so while the wool helps keep out biting wind and the cute pattern of honeybees makes me feel whimsical and stylish, half the time it's too much. I usually warm up enough from my walk home from the restaurant that my bangs are plastered to my forehead by the time I get to the top of the second staircase.

My bag falls over onto the entry table with a heavy thunk, scattering the few items I carry everywhere—wallet, keys, phone, lip balm, pepper spray—and I write it off as something to take care of later. I cross the small living space to throw open my window, nearly bumping into the ugly wooden coffee table I found next to a dumpster.

The view is nothing to write home about, mostly some buildings across the street with first-floor businesses and apartments above. The bar directly facing us, The Lucky Goat, is one of the few places on the block with signs of life at this hour. A few people are smoking outside the door, and I can hear the muffled music and chatter.

I shuck off my coat, which joins the ranks of the scarf and hat, and head to the kitchen to grab a beer. It's a sad state of affairs in the "space saver" fridge, with three IPAs left in the six-pack, a thawed package of salmon filets, a few lemons huddled together in the back corner, an experimental batch of homemade yogurt and several half-empty sauce bottles. The lack of freezer space is really the only thing I let myself be annoyed about with this apartment. I abhor food waste, so I only shop on my day off and try to use everything up by mid-week. It's getting to be that time.

Trying to enjoy the cold beer in spite of the chill outside, I sit down in the wobbly chair at the table that bisects the single space into a kitchen and a living room. My dining room, I often joke.

It's not much, but it's cozy. I've got a futon that doubles as my bed, facing a small TV that I never turn on because I don't want to pay for cable or streaming services, a bright rug that the previous tenant left, some light-blocking curtains I make sure to draw every night so I can sleep in late enough to offset an 11 PM shift conclusion, and colorful drawings from my niece and nephew on the walls.

Hunger gnaws at my belly, and I check my phone screen. It's been a long time since shift meal, and I have too much energy to sleep for a while yet. So, though I've been on my feet, preparing food for seven hours, I grab everything edible from the fridge and a box of pasta from my cupboard.

30 minutes later, I text my friend, Harrison, in 3E, and the response bubbles are instantaneous, so I don't even bother putting my phone down.

Lemon yogurt salmon and pasta?

I'll bring dessert.

I've always loved feeding people. Stuck back in a kitchen, working mostly on prep and final assembly, there's a divide between me and the customer. I don't get to see people's reactions when they try something for the first time. I don't get to watch their enjoyment. I don't get to learn from my mistakes directly.

For a while, I've entertained the idea of starting a business and becoming a personal chef for one of those people who live over on Mansion Row. But no one hires a personal chef with no education or credentials. So, I bust my ass in the third nicest restaurant in town, pad my resume and experiment on my own time and dime.

There's a cursory knock before the door opens, revealing Harrison in the doorway. He holds up a tin of cookies in lieu of a greeting. I eye the note on the top of the container as I approach.

"Double chocolate chip, huh? How'd you swing that?" I whistle, knowing they've got $20 of the good Dutch chocolate in them. In spite of what Harrison thinks, I can taste the difference.

He hands me the box, then pulls the sleeves of his bulky sweater down over his thin forearms to protect against the cold air wafting through my apartment. "As usual, by doing my job. She's convinced that what I do is some sort of IT magic, but she just kicked the power cord out of the socket again. I think she thinks double chocolate is my favorite."

I grin to myself, recognizing a flirting attempt from a shy girl when I hear one. Harrison is cute in a nerdy-guy way—about my height at 5'9" with dark skin and eyes and a friendly smile. He's rail thin, which makes his afro seem even more voluminous, and leans towards a button-downs-and-chunky-knits style that gives off student teacher vibes.

"Why don't you just tell Stacey that you don't want them?" I ask as I move over to the window to shut it so he's more comfortable.

Harrison has used the words "trigger food" to describe cookies in the past, which I take to mean that he has a complex relationship with food totally different from my own. I've never asked, and he's never expanded on it, which is fine by me because I'd rather not get involved in a conversation about weight or body image with someone whose life experiences are all on the opposite side of the scale.

The sound of paper tearing makes me turn to see Harrison tugging at the fumigation notice as he steps inside and closes my front door behind himself.

"Because if I tell her I don't want them, she'll stop," he replies simply. I only laugh, so he expands, "I don't want her to think I don't want them. I like that she makes them for me."

"That's sweet." I smile. Their delicate, cautious courtship gives me such vicarious delight. I love love.

"God, it smells amazing in here. I gotta admit, when you said yogurt and pasta, I was pretty skeptical. Whenever you get your own restaurant, you need to put someone else in charge of naming dishes."

I hand him a plate. It's a calculated exchange, perhaps over-thought on my part. I fill my plate first, then sit facing away as he takes as much or as little as he wants with no judgment on my part.

He takes the chair across from me and lays the paper in his hand on the table on top of a small pile of mail. He gestures to it with his chin as he carefully twirls the pasta around his fork. "So, what are you going to do for the next three days?"

I don't answer right away. Instead, I watch as he takes the first bite, trying not to look too eager and weird, and I smile in satisfaction when his eyes close with bliss.

"Good?" I verify, knowing it is.

"So good."

I pick up my fork and break off a bite of fish to top the swirl of pasta. It's got a great balance of flavors—tangy and rich from the yogurt, with plenty of complementary spices. And the salmon is perfectly done, if I do say so myself.

"Um, I'm really not sure. I haven't had much time to think about it since I got home. Kind of makes me wish my parents hadn't moved to Florida last year. What are you going to do?"

"I'll probably just post up in the library—if I can get there early enough, I can grab one of the study rooms with a door that locks. I've got class anyway, so it'll be nice to be so close to campus. I'll have to sleep sitting up, but it's better than spending money I don't have on a hotel room."

I wince as that one hits a little too close to home. "Maybe I'll see if Rachel's wife is okay with me crashing on their couch," I say, not overly thrilled by that option.

The sous chef at Bistro Jacques, Rachel, is friendly enough, though I wouldn't call us friends. Her wife, Eliza, came to our Christmas party a few weeks ago. Eliza got drunk and confessed that she'd been nervous to meet me because of how much Rachel talked about me, but then she saw me in person and knew she had nothing to worry about.

I mean, I don't look much like wiry, petite, bottle-blonde, Jersey-Italian Mrs. Eliza Lee, so if Rachel's got a type, I'm clearly not it. And I definitely don't like Rachel like that, but still. Ouch.

"It's so annoying. This shitty building gets bugs, and we have less than 12 hours to figure out where to stay and shower and eat for three whole days... And five bucks? What a slap in the face," he grumbles, carefully twirling up another tidy bite.

"Yeah, I'd say I can't believe how short notice it is..." we exchange a look and Harrison chuckles, "but I think we both can believe it."

"Ed probably forgot to put up the notice until today," Harrison suggests, and I have to admit that it sounds very likely. "You should just come to the library with me."

"For three days?" I say, unable to stop from wrinkling my nose. "Trust me, we're not that close. You really don't want to know what I'll smell like after three days in a small room with no shower."

He breezes past my self-deprecation. "They just opened that new gym over on Rider Street, and with the New Year they're running all kinds of specials. If we both sign up for a free-month trial pass, we can shower there."

I pause, trying to consider it but not getting very far. "As much as I appreciate the offer, I'm not 20 years old and I can't sleep sitting up. You see, young man, when you're approaching 30, you start getting this thing called back pain."

He pretends wide-eyed wonder. "Tell me more of this back... pain? Is that why you have to wear those?"

I follow his line of sight down to my rubber clogs. I lift my legs and turn my ankles to allow the light to catch on the little decorative buttons I've placed in some of the holes. "Don't tell me you're a Croc hater."

"I assume no one actually buys them. I figure, you reach a certain age, and a package just shows up at your door with a pair of reading glasses from the pharmacy and the ugliest shoes in the world."

My lips twitch. "I don't need the readers yet, but these bad boys are comfortable. Great for arch support."

"Even if they are—"

"They are."

With a huff of a laugh, he tries again. "Even if they are, it's like 20 degrees outside and they have holes."

"Hence, the thick socks."

He tries not to laugh again and fails under the weight of my superior sarcastic deadpan, choosing to cover his eyes instead. "Don't your socks get wet?"

"I avoid the snow piles."

"You're what, 29?"

"28 for a while yet." My tone is somewhat sharp—I get to joke about being old, he doesn't get to call me old.

He holds up his hands in a conciliatory gesture. "Apologies. All I'm sayin' is, you're 28 and you're wearing shoes just for their arch support?"

"Hey, it's not pretty, but this is what you get when the adults in your life start calling you an old soul at eight years old." I grab my phone and hurriedly type a few things into the search bar. "Which is why I refuse to sleep at the library. Want to split a motel room? Looks like the Super Dreams has availability for three nights for $120 before fees. I'll do 70-30 with you."

"They'll need to fumigate again with what we bring back," he says, frowning with distaste.

I can't disagree. Any motel room that's $40 a night around here is the kind of place where you bring your own cleaning wipes and shower shoes, and pray the stains on the rug aren't blood. Or at least that the police solved the case.

It's the only place around here cheap enough that I could afford it on my own, but I'd feel a lot safer with Harrison snoring in the other double bed. "80-20?"

He sighs and takes another bite, chewing slowly. "I guess it'll be easier than trying to sneak my sleeping bag into the library. I still think we should shower at that fancy new gym."

I wince, swiping through the pictures that the management at Super Dreams really thought would help sell the rooms. One of the pictures has a small mirror lying on the table in the little sitting area—at least someone remembered to wipe off the lines of coke for the photo. Another photo has a bedspread with some fairly obvious stains.

"Can't argue with you there. Maybe we should bring our own sheets."

"Good idea. I guess it'll be like an adventure."

"Yeah, because I *love* those," I reply wryly.

I've lived in the same crappy apartment, worked the same crappy job for years. I haven't been on a vacation since my parents took me when I was a kid.

My life may seem small and boring, but I like it. It's easy. Predictable. Safe.

Harrison grins. "You need something to shake things up every once in a while."

2

MAC

⸺◦⸺

Leave no trace—a motto beloved by snipers and national park enthusiasts alike.

According to the residents file that the oily property manager, Ed Something, gave me, the tenant of 3B is Eleanor Wilson. I blow out a breath as I lift my knuckles against the thick wood, preparing to lay on the charm. The old bags really love the Southern accent, and I've never met a woman named Eleanor under the age of 75.

So, even though it's 10 AM on a Tuesday, I fully expect the apartment to be occupied. Old usually means retired, bored, opinionated, and generally a pain in my ass for this kind of thing.

As if to prove my point, a head pops out from the apartment next door. The woman is so myopic that her glasses are half an inch thick, and the halo of gray curls is too perfect not to be a wig. She looks me up and down, taking in the gray jumpsuit. "You here about them bugs?" she asks in a thick Cajun accent.

"Yes, Ma'am." I push the fake frames I'm wearing up my nose to draw more attention to them.

She startles at the twang in my voice, but it's quickly replaced by irritation. "I don't got nowhere to go, me."

"We're awful sorry for the short notice, Ma'am. Between you and me, this is one of the worst cases I've ever seen. You've never seen a nest this size. Another couple'a days and we would've had to condemn."

Her eyes widen behind the lenses, though still appearing comically small in her face. "No," she cries as she looks around nervously and scratches her arm, like she can feel the nonexistent bugs. "You serious? Hmm. I s'pose I can figure somethin' out. You don't start sprayin' nothin' 'til I leave, you. Uh?"

I nod, an answer to the creative noise that represents a question. "I'm getting everyone out first."

She shuffles back into her apartment, and the door slams.

I'm not concerned. I've got hours until the real action starts, and this is the last floor I have to clear out. Alice Parker isn't the first resident to put up something of a fight, but no one really wants to stick around and see the kind of bugs that would make an exterminator nervous. They just want to grumble and make it clear they're not happy about being put out last minute like this.

I knock and after a moment, I hear something crash inside followed by, "I'm coming! I'm coming!"

I almost snort as there's another loud crash, a yelp of pain and a loud curse, and then the door swings open in front of me.

Well, shit. Eleanor Wilson is not 75.

She is lush. And just my fucking type.

She's holding her left elbow in her right hand, and it pushes her breasts together in a way that makes my mouth go dry. She's wearing some kind of sleeping outfit, and I can see all of her long, thick legs in those shorts. Her wavy dark hair is mussed, and her bangs are flipped up in the middle. She's pretty tall for a woman, standing just under my chin in lovely, arched bare feet, and she's so fucking soft. Even her face has a rounded jaw, full lips, heavy-lidded blue eyes...

Those eyes scan me with a blank lack of recognition, traveling to my face, then down my body. I see pink appear on her cheeks as she subtly moves her arms to cover more of her unmistakable breasts, and I find myself grinning a little at her reaction.

I'm used to people staring, normally finding it more irritating than anything else, since being noticed is the very last thing I need in my line of work. It's helpful when it comes time to blow off some steam by getting someone under me, but a damn nuisance when I'm trying to be functional instead of just decorative.

But I'm tall, stacked and have a face more than a few mamas could love, so I do understand it. And I know I've got a memorable face, so I wear the huge, thick-framed glasses so people will remember that instead of other identifiable details.

However, irritation is not what I'm feeling under my skin as this little piece gives me the thorough once-over. Her perusal stops at my nametag.

"Mac?" Understanding, then embarrassment, twists across her face. "You're the exterminator. Oh God, I'm so sorry. I got in late, and I forgot to set my alarm, and I don't wake up until 10 most days... I swear I'll be out of your hair in two minutes."

Trying to hide my grin at her apology-fueled explanation, I glance over her shoulder. There's an overturned chair next to a duffel bag in the center of the floor, which has clothes haphazardly sticking out. She's got the curtains drawn, so it's dark—curtains are good—and I can see that the windows take up most of the opposite wall. That's also good.

"That's all right, Miss... Wilson," I say, pretending to read her name off my clipboard. I lay on the southern accent thick, and I tell myself it's so the story about me stays consistent. But really, it's so I can see those eyes perk up with interest. These northerners love a Southern transplant. "We are sorry for the inconvenience. You have somewhere to go, I hope?"

"Oh, yeah, a friend and I are going to stay at the Ritz-Carlton."

I cock my head, slow to catch the joke when she laughs, but I grin back anyway because that damn smile is infectious. I try not to watch how the laughter makes her chest shake under the flimsy tank top.

"God, I wish. No, we're staying at Super Dreams," she admits with a shrug.

Now, I frown. That place is... seedy. I don't like the idea of her being in one of those dirty rooms surrounded by drug deals, pay for the night encounters and possible homicide. I know for a fact that the night manager keeps track of which rooms have young women staying alone. "One of your downstairs neighbors mentioned they're staying at the SeaBreeze Inn; maybe they have a vacancy?"

"It's too far. I don't have a car; I need to be able to walk to work." With a little sigh, she shakes her head.

She turns and I almost groan. The view from the back is... better. Those shorts are made of something so thin that I can see everything. Every. Damn. Thing. She's not wearing panties. I move my clipboard to cover the front of my jumpsuit, watching as her hips swing and jiggle as she hurries.

I want to follow her inside so badly, but I can't. It's not what an exterminator would do. An exterminator would ensure she was leaving on schedule and go back to his truck to get his supplies. But I don't want to leave. I want more time to interact with her. So, I lean against the doorjamb, filling the space with my shoulders and height. I watch her whirling-dervish routine, grabbing items from the floor and sofa and tossing them haphazardly into the open duffel.

"I really will just be a minute. I'm so sorry; I know you're just trying to do your job."

"Stop apologizing. I'm the one kicking you out of your apartment; I appreciate the hustle. What brought you back so late, if you don't mind me asking?"

She throws a quick look my way, flushes again, and grabs something out of a drawer to throw into her bag. "Work. I don't finish at the restaurant until 10:30 or 11 most nights."

"Which restaurant? I'm new in town and I'd take a recommendation." Maybe I'll make a chance-meeting happen when this is all over.

"Bistro Jacques. It sounds French until you realize that the guy who owns it is named Jack and he's about as South Jersey as they get." Her head whips back around to me, eyes wide like she realizes she's said something wrong—talking me out of going instead of talking me into it. "The food is really good, though. You should totally check it out."

"Maybe I will."

She disappears into the bathroom, and I hear the fan come on as she flicks on the light. Seconds later, she's back out, arms full of towels and bottles and a pink floral travel bag.

"Um, so all my stuff is okay, right? The chemicals or whatever won't hurt anything?"

"The gas will be long gone by the time you get back. As long as you don't leave anything alive, you're good to go."

She pauses, cocking her head at me. "What about a sourdough starter? That's alive."

I balk. "Uh... What is that, exactly?"

Her eyes widen with excitement as she explains it to me. "It's like my pet. It's wild yeast that I use to make bread. Never mind, that paper said any food in the fridge would be okay," she brushes it off, heads into the kitchen, grabs a jar off the counter and shoves it into the back of the refrigerator.

Then, she throws on her coat over her pajamas, shoves her feet into some ugly rubber clogs, and grabs the duffel. Realization hits me a second too late. I shift to the side as she approaches to block her exit. "Now, hold on, Eleanor. I can't let you leave like that. That's not what you wear to the restaurant, is it?" And I'll be damned if any of those lowlifes out there get an eyeful of those legs.

I know she hears the heated interest in my voice, because that blush starts creeping down her cheeks towards her ears. Her head drops, and she bites her lip and wraps the coat around herself tighter.

"How about if I start in," I pretend to check my watch, when really, I'm just picturing taking ahold of that lip in my own teeth, "10 minutes. Get dressed before you go."

"You're sure?"

"Positive. I should go start on my paperwork, anyway. It was nice meeting you, Eleanor."

"Ellie," she says somewhat shakily. "People call me Ellie."

"It's a beautiful name; people should spend the extra time to say the whole thing," I flirt.

She bites her lip. "Thanks. It was nice to meet you too, Mac," she says, smiling and glancing again at the name tag.

It's a nickname, and the tag was Wes's idea of a joke, but now I can't stop thinking about her saying my name over and over—screaming it, whimpering it, gagging on it.

Fuck. I've got a job to do.

At least now I know where I'm setting up. And it's not just because her view is perfect—all these top units on this side have a sightline to both the bar across the street and the warehouse on the outskirts of town—but it has the added benefit of being hers. And probably not smelling like mothballs.

I shake it off as I move to another door. The rest of the top floor is empty, so I make my way back down the stairwell at the end of the hall and stop to check on the few other stragglers. When I'm done, I stride out to the Harry's Bugs-B-Gon van parked on the street in front of the dilapidated brick building. The B is in the shape of an ant. It's little touches like that that give us credibility.

The inside of the van is another world entirely, full of monitors built into an impressive display, control panels connected with zip-tied wires, black cases of weapons, cameras, and a pop-out tabletop with a man hunched over his laptop. Wesley barely turns his head when I slide in through the front, still in setup mode. That picture never gets old, all six-ish feet of him hunched over the tiny screen, balancing on the small, round stool seat.

"Found your vantage point, then?" he asks in his deep baritone. His British accent curls around his r's and lifts his vowels. We're way past me ribbing him for it, and I'm just glad he has one of those posh accents and not the ones where it sounds like they're trying to talk around a mouthful of mud. At least I can understand him.

"Yup."

He nods and types something into his laptop. I reach around him for my duffel and the case next to it. I freeze as I see the familiar, stupid ant silhouette on the side of my nondescript black case. "Did you... did you put a fucking sticker on my rifle?"

The edges of Wes's lips curl up, and he doesn't look away from his screen. "It sells the story. Anyone who sees that will assume it's just full of bug bombs."

I glare at him and try to lift the corner of it with my thumbnail. Fortunately for Wes, it comes up easily and in one piece. "They would have assumed that from the uniform, clipboard and van. Don't touch my guns," I growl.

He just grins. The smarmy fuck.

"You don't want to start this shit with me, Short Round. I know where you keep your physical backups."

Calling Wesley "Short Round" is almost laughably inaccurate—he's more like a tattooed Indiana Jones on steroids—but I like to take every opportunity to remind him that I've got a couple of inches on him.

"You don't know the combination to the safe," he replies, unfazed.

"I'll scratch Dimitri's throwing knives and tell him it was you."

I have him then. His eyes flick to me, and he swallows. He opens his mouth, presumably to stick his foot back in it, but I cut him off. "Don't. Touch. My. Guns."

He holds up his hands in a conciliatory gesture and turns it into a stretch, leaning back over the chair. "Think we'll get what we need tonight?" he asks as I unzip the case and check the pieces inside for signs of tampering.

"Probably, if they're as eager for the sale as it sounds. Dimitri's setting up the perimeter at the warehouse?"

"He's on his way," Wes nods, reaching across the counter into a bag of jerky. I recognize the label instantly and reach forward to swipe it out of his hands.

"I'm never leaving my stuff in the van with you again," I grumble.

His laughter follows me out, abruptly ending as I slam the van door shut. I'm hoping for another sign of Eleanor as I look down the street and step into the mailroom/entryway, but my watch tells me that her 10 minutes were up 20 minutes ago and there's no doubt in my mind that blushing, overly-apologetic Eleanor is a rule-following submissive at heart.

Which is good. I'm not a fan of brats.

I make my way back up the stairwell, pausing at each floor to verify that everyone is gone. Only lonely Mrs. Parker from 3A is still inside, descending the stairs so carefully with her carpet bag that she actually appears to be moving backwards. I sigh, set down my gear, and escort her out. Then I lock the doors behind her.

I hate dealing with tenants. It always sucks when we can't find an empty building for cover and have to go to plan B. But plan B isn't hard to execute; all it takes is a few well-placed cockroaches and an intercepted phone call to the exterminator. I've got some empty bug bombs I'll set up on my way out to sell it.

One of the reasons being an exterminator makes a great cover is that it's one of the few things that will clear out a whole building for more than a day. We need everyone gone because if I'm somehow spotted, or the building is compromised during the mission, no one will be around to see anything. It keeps people safe.

The other reason is that the building manager has to give you copies of all the keys to all the units.

I set my cases down outside the door of 3B, put the key into the lock, and push inside. The first thing I notice is that she's picked up the mess. She did a lot in 10 minutes—turned her bed into a couch, put away the rest of the clothes hanging out of drawers, and cleared away the dishes that had been sitting out. The place is clean, if bursting with so much stuff I'm not sure she's ever heard of the concept of minimalism.

My chest puffs out as I inhale deeply. There's a hint of that old-building smell under layers of other scents, like cleaning products and candle wax. But it also smells like some kind of flowers and a distinctly feminine musk that I know is what she'd smell like if I woke up next to her. It's sharp and sweet and bitter and subtle.

I set down my bags by the window and draw the curtains closed. They're the thick, light-blocking kind and dark. No one will see the end of my gun poking through in the dark unless they know exactly where to look, and they look hard. They certainly won't be able to see my silhouette behind it. It's perfect.

I grab ahold of one of the chairs at the pathetic little dining table and start to drag it over to the window to get set up, then stop with a frown. It creaks and wiggles in my hand. No fucking way this thing is going to hold me. I eye the other chair at the table, but it doesn't look much better. So, I drag the futon over and perch on the arm.

Some time later, I've got the scope and tripod assembled, all my gear has been checked and the line of communication with my team is open. This has officially become a waiting game. I stand, stretch and take a look around. My first stop is the TV remote. I click it on and get nothing but static, no matter which buttons I press. Fucking perfect.

A few hours later, the sun has set at the ripe hour of 4 PM like it does here in the winter, and I'm numb with boredom and sick of my phone screen. So, I decide to snoop.

I grab a framed photo of two little kids off the table behind where the couch was. It's recent, judging from the Disney characters they picked for their Halloween costumes. I eye the terrible drawings taped to the opposite wall. Are those her kids?

Nah. It's a studio. What would you do with two kids in a studio? There'd be more signs of them—toys, small clothes, that sort of thing.

The other pictures are of an elderly couple at the beach, some college-aged girls with their arms around each other, and some candids of the same people. One particularly old one is of two little girls—one with thick, straight bangs, smiling with her eyes closed and missing a front tooth and one, slightly taller, holding a black cat hostage in her inexpert grip.

Other than the one with two little girls—her bangs are almost the same—Eleanor isn't in any of the pictures, and I frown.

I move into the cramped kitchen next, opening cabinets and seeing more appliances than I was aware existed. Her fridge is fairly empty except for a few containers of what must be leftovers, and I'm sorely tempted to steal one of those IPAs, but I refrain. Top cabinets are pretty ordinary with glasses, plates and... hello...

More spices than I've ever seen in my entire life fill one cupboard to bursting. It doesn't even close all the way, something I'd initially assumed was just yet another quirk of this shithole studio apartment.

I pick up a few I recognize—garlic, onion, salt—but my eyes widen at some. The fuck is gochugaru? I open it, give a heavy sniff, and cap it quickly enough that I don't get snot inside the bottle when I sneeze.

Okay, I'm really starting to like this chick. She likes it spicy.

My stomach growls, reminding me it's been approximately three hours since I last ate. I'm always hungry, a side effect of a high metabolism needing 4k calories a day to maintain muscle mass at my size. My duffel is half beef jerky and packaged salty snacks, but now… I'm kind of curious about those leftovers. She did say she works at a restaurant. I assumed she meant as a server, but maybe I'm wrong.

I grab one, pull the lid off and a delicate—if fishy—smell wafts out. Oh shit, is that salmon?

This is a bad idea, I tell myself as I toss the container in the microwave. Her fridge is empty, so she'll notice that the leftovers are gone. But as the pasta heats up, and the scent fills the air, my mouth waters and I silence the part of my brain that reminds me of the motto beloved by snipers and national park enthusiasts alike: leave no trace.

I audibly moan at the first bite. Wes and Dimitri aren't exactly putting time in to meal prep, and I barely know my way around a microwave. Sure, we appreciate a good meal, but the food-is-fuel approach has gotten us all this far. Dimitri even did his little OCD calculations to figure out optimum nutritional requirements for us all, and has the same groceries delivered every week. Eggs. Chicken. Broccoli. Lettuce.

I'm so sick of fucking salad and grilled chicken breast.

Movement across the street on my monitor catches my eye, and I shove another forkful in my mouth as I cross the room in two strides. "Status?" I say into the earpiece.

"I am here," comes Dimitri's deep Russian voice over the mic. *"I have a corner booth on the southeast side, close to the kitchen."*

"I've got a visual," I say, pressing a few buttons and smoothing out the image so I can see the Russian more clearly through the grimy windows of The Lucky Goat. The guy is fucking huge—his legs barely fold under the table, and looks like he's having a terrible time. I almost laugh as the first girl approaches in spite of his mean mug. "Good luck with blondie."

He grunts, annoyed, and I see him wave her off and take a swig of his beer.

As I finish the salmon pasta, I reflect on the job. We've only been here about a month, and that was all it took to figure out the exact pickup and drop points for the weapons shipments. If all goes well, we'll get everything we need tonight for the hit tomorrow. I'm not on deck tonight; I'm a contingency for the man on the ground.

Dimitri's meeting with Rossi's guys goes well, and the drop is set for tomorrow night.

He often poses as a buyer for this kind of thing. His size makes him believable as a thug, and his accent is so thick that people make their own assumptions about who he works for. Wes arranges the meetup, Big D shows up, and no one asks too many questions. When pressed, he told me once that he just rattles off the names of his extended family back home. Nine times out of ten, the other guys just pretend to know who he's talking about to save face. That last time, Dimitri's knives come out to play.

There really is no doubt in my mind that Jacob Rossi is our guy, even if we've only dealt with his underlings and he's kept his face out of it so far. Public record alone told us he's a real wife-beating, tax-evading, steal-from-the-poor piece of shit. Couldn't cut it in New York, had to bring his brand of corruption here to be a big fish in a small pond.

But we don't cut corners. We'd all agreed, even before the first job, that we wouldn't skip the important first step that we call "Beyond a Reasonable Doubt." Plus, anything we learn while we watch just helps us formulate our airtight plan for taking them out.

Recon is 90% of the battle. You can't just kill a kingpin. They've got seconds, thirds, fourths in command. You take out the top guy, chances are one of them is going to step in and pick up right where the boss left off. Or, they'll make it real inconvenient for us by trying to avenge their leader or some shit. So, if the goal is stopping the smuggling operation, we need to take them all out. The research makes the hit—which only ever really takes a few minutes, in the end—go smoothly.

It'll be a long two days, but it'll be worth it. I stand and stretch, then bring the empty container over to the sink. At least I have space to move around—I'd go insane stuck in that cramped van like Wes. Though, he'll head home tonight. Dimitri, too. It's easier for me just to stay put. The more trips in and out, the higher the risk I'm seen.

I'm sorely tempted to pull out this couch and lay down where she does. Use her pillow. Roll in her sheets.

But I don't. Because I've got a shred of impulse control left, apparently. I don't wear scented deodorant or aftershave as a rule, but I don't have to smell like Old Spice to leave something behind that she'd perceive. Then there's the hair, fibers, etc. I'm careful. Fastidious, usually.

So, why do I want her to know I was here?

That same instinct telling me to eat her leftovers tells me to do it—sleep in her spot, leave part of myself behind so this place is marked, claimed, owned. Like it belongs to me and, by extension, so does she.

3

ELEANOR

You know, in some ways, I'm kind of like an exterminator.

For two days, I've been clumsy and distracted, thinking about that exterminator. Mac.

There must be some biological imperative women have that makes us weak-kneed around tall men. Tall, muscly, gorgeous men who have great smiles and seem confident but not arrogant. And I'm such a sucker for a guy in glasses...

He'd been so nice about how late I was getting out of his way, hadn't acted annoyed that I kept him from starting on time. And he'd stuck around almost like... like he wanted to talk to me. He'd laughed at my cheesy joke about the Ritz. Even the way he'd said "get dressed," like it was an order, like he was so used to people doing what he said, that it didn't even occur to him that he was telling me what to do. And the way he'd stared at my legs...

What the hell is a man with a face like that doing killing bugs for a living? He should be somewhere more people get to see him—plastered across billboards in his underwear or acting opposite some equally gorgeous woman in a romcom.

With a face like that, I could get over the gross job.

God, I'm getting so far ahead of myself, I'm 10 years down the road, married and watching our kids run around in mini gray jumpsuits that match his.

For the hundredth time, I replay what I remember of our interaction. He'd told me not to rush, asked if I had somewhere to stay, asked for a restaurant recommendation because he's new to the area...

Yeah, Eleanor. He's way into you.

I thunk my head against my cubby.

Who am I kidding? He was just being polite. Professional. Friendly at most. He called my *name* beautiful, not me; and maybe it gave me butterflies because I've never really liked my nicknames, but he didn't know that. He'd stared because I was half naked, in my pajamas. I'd probably shocked him, answering the door like that—and if he'd been interested, he would have asked for my number.

Besides, guys who look like him never show a genuine interest in me. Someone with a face and body like that has options. Why would a man settle for ground beef when he had the option of a steak? Not that there's anything wrong with ground beef—who doesn't love a good burger?

Now I'm hungry. And my metaphor is falling apart.

I reach for the gauze wraps and Band-Aids from the kit on the shelf. Once the cut on my finger is dealt with, I grab a pair of black disposable gloves from the wall-mounted dispenser and tug them on as I head back into the fray. The dull roar of pots clanging on the stove, knives hitting cutting boards, flames spewing from the salamander oven, and people shouting at one another comes into sharp focus as I reenter the kitchen from the breakroom. Wednesday nights aren't normally such a shitshow, but we had a walk-in table of 12.

"You're cut, Ellie," Chef Robert barks.

I whip my head around, knowing he's talking about the schedule and not my finger. I can tell from the intensity in his deep-set, bloodshot blue eyes that he's in a mood. His chef hat is askew, and there's visible sweat on his face running down into the crease of his neck.

"What? But I still need to finish the risotto—"

He levels a finger at me. "That's the second day in a row you bled on my floor, and table five just sent back their scallops, hold the tomato compote. Does this look like you held the tomato fuckin' compote?" he shouts angrily, tossing the perfectly plated dish into the trash. The whole thing.

I jump as the plate breaks at the bottom of the trashcan. The kitchen chatter dies down, and the sound of sizzling food becomes the loudest thing in the room. My face heats in shame, especially now that we have an audience, and I mumble, "No, chef."

"I checked the ticket. Hannah rang it in right, so this is your fuck-up. You're being careless. Get the hell out of my kitchen." He gives me his back.

I want to argue, but I know from experience that it would make things worse. I can't have him sending me home without pay for a week again, not when I have a surprise three-day motel stay to cover 80% of. I sigh angrily and spin on my heel, tearing the gloves back off.

The door to the breakroom swings behind me, and I hear him yell, "Get back to work!" at the gawkers. The kitchen symphony begins again in earnest as I rip off my apron, wad it up and toss it into my cubby. I sit heavily in the closest chair and drop my head into my hands.

This day sucks. And to top it all off, I feel the awful, familiar, burning tingle on my left knee. Idly, I reach down and rub the area through my pants, trying to relieve the itch without scratching the skin. I knew a flare-up was coming—the stress of vacating my apartment and a few bad days at work, and bam. That's really all it takes, especially in winter. And in my haste to leave yesterday morning, I left my psoriasis cream in the bathroom cabinet.

Screw this. Chef Robert just added two hours to my day off. I'm not spending any more of it here, feeling sorry for myself in this room that smells like sweaty shoes and grease from the fryer.

I grab my stuff, clock out, and am swinging on my coat before I even make it to the back entrance. The door is propped open with a brick that I ensure stays in place as I walk through.

The small figure leaning against the wall between the opening and the dumpster startles me, but only for an instant. She's much smaller than me, but every line of Rachel is no-nonsense—from the blunt, short cut of her straight dark hair that's held back in a plain black bandanna, to the frameless glasses that make her small eyes appear smaller, to the block lettering of her name on the button-free chef coat she chose. Her warm complexion shines in the pale light of the alley, managing to look creamy instead of washed out like mine. Those good genes.

"Hey, Rach," I greet.

She holds out the crumpled pack of cigarettes to me, a cursory gesture. I wave my hand, declining. Her eyes catch on the bandage. "How's the finger?"

I glance down. The size of the bloodstain visible through the Band-Aid hasn't changed much in the past minute, so I know it's stopped bleeding. "I'll live."

"He was way out of line—you can't send someone home for a knife slip."

"Well, I'm sure you heard about the tomato compote fiasco," I mutter, and she huffs a laugh at my sarcasm. "I'd be surprised if the whole restaurant doesn't know."

She shakes her head. "He acts like he's got a Michelin star or some shit. Yes, chef," she mimics in an exaggerated high pitch. "And that hat? Give me a fucking break."

I sniff as the cold makes my nose run. "He's just trying to elevate the environment. Prove he's got standards or something."

"He's a misogynistic asshole on an ego trip who gets off making his staff jump through hoops. I keep telling Jack that he's going to lose the few good people we have if he doesn't put a leash on him." She takes a huge drag and switches her hold on the butt so she's gripping it with her thumb and index finger.

I lean against the building next to her, wrapping my coat around myself tighter as the wind whips through the alley. "Or he could just make you head chef," I venture.

Rachel is level-headed and wouldn't create nearly such a toxic work environment. She doesn't have quite the same creative eye, but she's got a great palate and a knack for knowing when the fish guy is trying to sell us old sea bass.

She glances sideways at me. As the only women in the kitchen, we share a bond. As the only other woman in the kitchen, we both feel a little threatened by the other—probably me more than her, since she outranks me. But still, it's a male-dominated industry, and this restaurant is more of a boy's club than others. We have a tenuous truce, and it feels stronger whenever we're commiserating about the glass ceiling over our heads.

"You think Rob would share the kitchen with me?" she shakes her head. "They'd have to fire him, and Jack's not gonna do that. They go down the shore together every other weekend in the summer."

I sigh. Sounds like sous chef isn't going on my resume any time soon.

"What are you doing here, Ellie?" she asks, not unkindly, blowing smoke out of the corner of her mouth. It swirls back around us in the wind, stinging my nose. I know she doesn't mean the alley, even before she adds, "You're too good to be on the line as long as you have."

The compliment warms me and brings a soft smile to my face. But self-doubt is icy, right on its heels, and I heave a sigh. "I've been asking myself the same thing," I admit. "I've learned a lot here, but I don't think I really want to be head chef. And not just here, I mean anywhere—I don't think I can deal with that much stress."

She looks at the cigarette in her fingers and flicks the ash off the end. I wish I smoked. This would be the perfect conversation to have while sharing a pack. I haven't tried it, mostly because I'm worried about liking it. It seems like a slippery slope. Plus, it's an expensive habit.

"So, what're you gonna do, then? There's only so many places to go in this industry, you know?"

"I just want... I want to cook on my terms, on my time, and see people enjoy what I make for them. Somewhere without all the noise and drama."

Rach coughs out a laugh. "Sounds too calm for me. I live for the rush; it's like pure adrenaline."

"I wish I felt that way," I admit. "I thought something was wrong with me at first because I didn't. I didn't realize it wasn't normal to feel like I'd run a marathon when I got home most nights. Not that I'd know what that actually feels like..."

She laughs, and it's a commiserative noise because neither does she with her pack-a-day lungs. After one more long drag, her break is over, so she stamps out the cherry until it becomes indistinguishable from the other, older cigarette litter at our feet.

"Well, don't wait too long to make a move. You'll either burn out or get stuck," she says, then regards me with a little nudge of her elbow. "You okay?"

"I'm fine. Tomorrow's my day off, so I'll see you Friday." I'm a little pissed that I can't veg on my couch in my underwear—and I'm certainly not touching anything in our motel room with my bare skin if I can help it—but a day off is a day off. Maybe I'll go to the small local movie theater. They only play indie film festival contenders, usually with subtitles, which I find distracting. But it's something to do.

Rach heads back inside, and I hike my purse up on my shoulder. Without her presence, even though I'm six inches taller than her, the alley is just a long, dark, narrow space with way too many shadows. I feel exposed, like someone is watching. I reach inside my purse and grip the pepper spray as I make my way to the street.

It's only 8:30, so though it's pitch black, the street is bustling with activity in a way it isn't at 11 PM. I release my death grip on the small canister and grab my phone instead. After this day, I need a caloric coma.

I text Harrison.

> Got off early. Did you eat yet? I'm thinking Chinese. My treat.

> If you can bring it here. I've got a paper due tomorrow that I forgot about.

I make a sympathetic face. He'll probably have to pull an all-nighter.

> I can do that.

> You're the best. Chicken with steamed broccoli, brown rice.

Man, I wish my Chinese food itch could be scratched by something that full of fiber.

It's like thinking the word *itch* causes the reaction. My knee starts burning again, and I stop, stepping off to the side so I'm not in anyone's way, to reach down and rub it again. God, I want to scratch it. It's becoming more persistent, and I know I won't be able to sleep without some relief.

Cortisone creams only do so much. What I really need is the expensive prescription tube in my cabinet.

I pull my phone back out to dial my favorite—aka, the closest—Chinese restaurant, but pull up the browser instead. I type my question into the search bar and scroll through the top few suggested websites.

The internet is in general agreement that the chemicals used by exterminators can take anywhere from 24 to 72 hours to do their thing, and they tent the building to trap the vapors. Apparently, the fumigant evaporates six hours after the tent is removed, and it's safe to go back inside after that.

Hmm. I know we're not supposed to come back until Friday morning, but maybe it's just overkill so no one gets sued? And I'm going to pass right by it to get the food... If the building is tented, that would be obvious, right? If the tent is still up, I'll just stop at the pharmacy that's on the way and make do with the over-the-counter stuff.

With renewed purpose, I head toward my apartment. It's only a few blocks, and I'm nervous yet optimistic as my building comes into view. I could really use a win.

And luck is on my side! There's no tent that I can see.

I scan the building. It looks so odd, completely dark like this—empty and kind of spooky. Usually at least one or two people have their lights on all night. I stop when my eyes reach the top floor, picking out my middle unit.

That's weird. I could have sworn that I remembered to open my curtains. I always do before I leave for the day, otherwise my apartment gets musty. Well, I had been a tad rushed on my way out... exhibit A: forgot my meds.

The front door is blocked off with caution tape, and there's a sign posted that I can see from where I am that says "Notice" in big block lettering. But I wasn't going to use the front door anyway—since I'm technically not allowed in the building yet, I'm going to be sneaky. I go around to the back, where I know the security cameras are just for show, and check the door. It's not even blocked off, which feels like a good sign that it's safe to enter.

The hallway is so echo-y and creepy in the dark; it feels wrong to go traipsing around at full volume. I close the door quietly. When I'm not met with any strange smells, or weird feelings from inhaling the wrong fumes, I decide that 72 hours was definitely overkill. And frankly, that pisses me off.

Of course, not being sued takes priority over getting everyone back in the building. It's just our homes and livelihoods…

I get to the top floor, pleased that it doesn't put me out of breath. I guess that's what happens when you come home before the point of complete exhaustion at a physically taxing job.

My keyring isn't fussy since I don't have a car and I haven't been anywhere cool enough in the world to justify the purchase of keychains to mark the memory. I find the only key easily, shove it into the lock, throw open the door and flip on the light, just as a loud bang permeates the stillness inside.

I freeze.

There's a man.

There's a man in my apartment.

My heart stutters, and fear like I've never known grips me, locking me in place. My muscles seize, and the blood drains from my face.

He turns, wide eyed, and my memory sparks. I know that face. I've been thinking about it nonstop for two days. He's not in his gray onesie, but the face poking out over his black long-sleeved shirt is unmistakable, if incomprehensible. Even without his thick-rimmed glasses, I know.

It's Mac.

My instant reaction is a knee-jerk apology. "Oh, I'm sorry, I'm just…" I trail off as my brain fully catches up. I'm no expert, but that's some kind of long-barreled gun standing on a tripod, pointed out my window. That popping sound must have been… Oh God. "You're not an exterminator."

"You're not supposed to be here."

It's like the sound of his voice is what breaks me from the spell my fear casts on me. Everything happens at once. Mac curses and launches himself away from the window. I turn on my heel and reach for the doorway, but I only get two steps past the threshold before something huge and heavy hits me from behind and we go crashing into the opposite wall. But my head doesn't smack the plaster, because Mac's beefy palm is wrapping around my mouth, cutting off my scream, and then I'm being dragged backwards.

The light is off again, so when the door closes, we're in complete darkness.

I fight, pumping my legs and jerking my torso against the iron grip wrapped around me. I scream again hoarsely, and the sound is muffled by his hand.

"Shh! Shh—shut up!"

It happens so fast that I can't keep up. One second, I'm flailing around like a madwoman and the next, I'm on the ground. A heavy weight comes down on top of me, and my arms are pulled behind my back. I hear the sharp, plastic *zzzzzip* of a zip-tie, and suddenly I can't get my wrists apart. Once more, and my legs are immobile.

"Don't make me shoot you," Mac growls.

I clamp my lips together, though a pathetic whimpering noise still escapes my throat. He stands fluidly and crosses back over to the window. "I'm here," I hear him say, like he's reentering a room.

Uh, yeah, I know that... we're the only ones in here...

"No, it's—fuck. Fuck! Okay, on it."

I officially know he's not talking to me.

There's a loud pop that makes me jump, then fear freezes my throat back up and the noises I'm making stop. Another pop, and the tears start falling silently from my cheeks to puddle on the laminate as I let my forehead rest on the floor. I'm going to die. He really is going to shoot me, right after he's done shooting those other poor people.

"One in the stairwell," he says. "I've got the guy on the roof. Come on, fucker... Just stick your head out, come on..." a few seconds later there's another pop and Mac releases a heavy breath. Then another curse. "The car turned around. Get out of there. I know. I know! I'll stay here and keep an eye. I know. Over and out."

For a few seconds, the only sound in the room is my wet, musical, shaky breaths. I don't dare lift my head or move in any way—I don't want to remind him I'm here. Not that he'd forget... But maybe if I don't put up a fight, if I don't do anything stupid, he won't shoot me next.

I hear the floorboards creak as he gets up, then I feel Mac standing over me and I shrink into myself. It's maybe not as much bravado as I'd like to believe I'd have, facing death, but at least I don't pee myself? It doesn't feel like much of a win when I'm just going to end up dead anyway.

But the bullet doesn't come. Instead, I feel his arm work its way between me and the ground, and I'm jerked back. I grunt as the pressure on my stomach forces the air out of my lungs, then shriek as I'm airborne.

He lifts me from the waist, tucking me against his side, and carries me over to the couch with a grunt of his own. I have enough deeply held body stigma that, instead of just being afraid, I also distantly wonder how strong he must be to lift my dead weight off the floor... He drops me on the couch and I bounce on the cushion before falling back against my zip-tied hands.

"Sit. Stay," he orders.

What's next? Roll over? Speak? This motherfucker.

I keep my chin tucked, and after a few more shaky breaths that actually manage to level out my heart rate, I start stealing glances at him. There's not much I can do, all trussed up like a damn turkey, but cooperating seems like my best bet for survival. And if I do live, I want to make sure I remember enough to give an accurate description to the police.

He's too much—he's too big, his voice is too deep, his presence is too immense for my poor little apartment. This tiny room feels immeasurably smaller, like his head almost touches the ceiling and he could span the room if he stretched out both arms.

His utter masculinity feels completely out of place in such a jarring way, it's uncomfortable. Not that I've never had a man here, though it has been a while...

I give up on subtlety and turn and face him fully, craning my head back to get another good look at his features. There's a glow coming from whatever screen he's got, so I can see in spite of the darkness. My eyes must have adjusted.

God, why did a man so fine have to end up being a killer?

He's got stubble covering his jaw, but it's obvious that the line of it is strong and prominent. Full lips with a deep Cupid's bow are stretched tight in an anxious frown. His cheeks are hollow, carving up to the curve of cheekbones set under warm, chocolate brown eyes. I couldn't see his hair earlier under the hat, but I can see it now, cut in one of those short-in-the-back-longer-on-top styles men get and a warm, light brown color.

He knows I'm looking at him, but he doesn't look up from the scope to say, "You know, in some ways, I'm kind of like an exterminator."

I look back down at my lap and squeeze my eyes shut.

Fuck. This is so bad.

4

MAC

———◆◇◆———

I know she's going to like me.

What a fucking debacle.

Actually, debacle doesn't cover it. Clusterfuck is something closer to the truth.

If anyone else in the building had come, or if she'd come even an hour earlier or later, none of this would have happened. It's like everything aligned to work out as terribly as possible. I don't know what to make of that. But I am from the Southeast, and everyone knows a Baptist loves a sign.

I grind my jaw as I watch through the scope. Rossi's men are running around the exterior of the warehouse, searching for threats, but I know Dimitri has slipped into the shadows by now. After it's clear Rossi's big, black SUV isn't coming back, I turn to her.

"Why did you come back, Eleanor? You weren't supposed to be here." She presses her lips together and turns her head away from me, so I bark, "Answer me."

"I forgot my medication," she says in a soft, sad voice. It wavers, betraying her fear.

"What kind?" She winces, and I try to soften my voice, even though it's hard when my heart is still pounding from the adrenaline rush of being caught. "Are you sick?"

She closes her eyes and lets her head hang a little. "Nothing more life-threatening than this."

Something stirs, and it's almost like relief. That she isn't sick? Yeah, I'm not letting myself go there… I refocus on the scene at the warehouse.

It takes a little while for the excitement to die down. A cleaning crew is sent in so quickly, I honestly have to marvel at Rossi's team's coordination. I can track their movement through the windows, catching flashes of their white plastic suits. In fact, they're so efficient there's no way they're not professional cleaners—likely contracted by Rossi. Which is just as well, because they're cleaning up the bodies that have my holes in their skulls, too.

It's always nice not to have to deal with local law enforcement. I'm so far away, and resources in most cities are so limited, there's no way they'd pinpoint where I shot from. But if they did find the bodies, and if their coroner is good, it would be obvious the bullet came from a long-distance rifle from the damage. Luckily for us, coroner is an elected position here, and the mayor's nephew needed a job after graduating last in his class at med school. No one even ran against the guy with the mayor's last name and full endorsement.

But they're long gone—bodies cleared, bleach poured, weapons hidden—before the cops do their drive-by. I'd heard a few shots go off while I'd been wrestling with Eleanor, so it's no surprise someone called it in. It's why Dimitri uses knives and I've got a suppressor on my rifle.

When it's clear they're not coming back tonight, I face my intriguing little problem.

I move and sit down on the coffee table across from her, boxing her in with the cage of my body, elbows resting on knees, letting my size intimidate her. It creaks underneath me, protesting my weight. She shrinks back, an instinctual physical reaction to my bulk and perceived threat, but she meets my eye and—holy hell—there is plenty of fire burning. My little temptress is spittin' mad.

This oughtta be fun.

"How did you get in? I've had eyes on the street, and I checked all entry points."

She straightens and fixes me with a look, transparently deciding whether or not to lie. I know this reaction—she's calculating the odds of someone else coming along so she can call for help. After a second, the intention drains from her face, either because others are unlikely to get in the same way she did, or she's realized any potential rescuer would just be in danger, too.

She wiggles a little, moving her arms as if checking the integrity of the zip ties, and winces. "The back door sticks. It feels locked from the inside, but you just have to jiggle the handle up and down."

Option two, then. Interesting. It usually goes the other way. Most people, tied up and backed into a corner, will happily drag others into the same shit if it means they might get out of it.

I stand and walk into the kitchen and start opening drawers. I tap the bud in my left ear. "Yo, Wes, you free for a walkabout?"

The crisp, clear baritone rings back immediately. *"All quiet on my end. What's up?"*

"I need you to barricade the back door of my 20." I open and close another drawer, causing silverware to clang together noisily.

"Erm... you can't?"

"I've got a..." I throw Eleanor a look over my shoulder and take a hard swallow, "situation. I can't leave."

"A situation?" he repeats slowly, as if hearing the word for the first time. *"You want to expand on that a bit, mate?"*

"Not really. It's locked down for the moment; I'll debrief when I get back." I get to the last drawer and finally find what I need.

There's a pause, and I can practically hear the gears in his mind turning. He's too smart for his own good sometimes. *"This have anything to do with you going MIA back there? Dimitri got shot. He's pissed."*

I know from the way Wes said it that D's not too badly hurt, so I huff a sigh. "He's always pissed when he gets shot. Look, I'll explain later," I growl. "Just get the door."

"Roger that."

I tap the bud again, cutting the line, and reach into the drawer.

"Someone you know was shot? Is that who you shot?" Her question cuts off quickly as she sees the knife in my hand. A little noise of terror escapes her lips, and she starts trying to back away. "P-please, don't—"

I make a pit stop at my bag and grab the lengths of rope I always carry. As I sit back down on the coffee table, I lay the coils across my knee for easy access. "Lean forward."

She sucks in air on a wet sob. "Please," she whispers.

My heart jerks in my chest, and I want to be able to tell her that she doesn't need to be afraid of me. But I know I can't. I need her to be a little afraid of me because I can't leave yet and I can't have her trying to escape. "You're uncomfortable. Lean forward, I'm going to cut off the zip ties."

Her teary eyes narrow in suspicion. There's the sound of a double buzz, a text notification most likely, that I know isn't from my always-on-silent phone. But it came from somewhere behind me, so I know she doesn't have it, which means it's not really a priority.

"The rope is softer; it won't bite into your skin as much."

As if the confirmation that I'm not just letting her go is enough to convince her to trust me, she does as I ask. She twists her torso to bring her arms around so I can easily reach her hands. The skin at her wrists is all red, and I kick myself for cinching the ties so tight. I place my hand around her throat as I reach around her with the knife.

She goes rigid against me, but takes the threat for what it is, and doesn't try to fight. My hand cools against her soft skin, feeling the fluttering pulse and labored breathing. Giving in to my baser urges, I give her a small squeeze that has her sucking in a breath before I release.

Her cheeks are pink when she turns back to face me, and I lift a brow. Very interesting. Is it possible she's feeling me right now, in spite of all that healthy, logical fear response? Now that gives me some hope. Maybe my frightened little temptress is a bit of a freak.

"You want to take off your coat so you're not too hot?"

"I, ah—yeah... okay."

I keep a careful eye on her as she shucks the sleeves down and lays the coat next to her on the couch.

"Hands in front."

I tie her hands, then wrap another around her arms and chest, then I just have to sit back and admire it for a second. Because the way that rope looks on her is too fucking good. As she tests out the tightness, it shifts over her skin and digs into that soft, creamy flesh... I wasn't just being nice when I offered to let her take off her coat. I can see down the V of her T-shirt now, and those breasts are just begging to be let out. I haven't done much rope play before, but I'm suddenly more interested in picking up the technique than ever.

Her next question is something of a surprise. Normally a hostage blurts out, 'are you going to kill me' like they'll believe the answer. It's usually a little while before it occurs to them to ask questions about their captor instead of about their situation. Not Eleanor.

"Your name isn't really Mac, is it?"

I wonder if she wants to know so she can give a name to the police or if she's curious about me. "Yes, and no."

She huffs out a breath. "I'm not really sure why I thought you'd answer that," she admits aloud, her tone rueful.

I grin. "What else you got?"

"You don't wear glasses, do you?"

I chuckle. No reason to pretend now. I tossed those useless things into my bag as soon as I was alone; they just get in the way of the scope.

You can't get through advanced sniper training without 20-20 vision. "Nope."

There's another loud double buzz from the other side of the room, and my eyes flick over to the purse lying on the floor that she'd lost in our struggle.

"Did you..." she trails off, then her eyes lock onto something behind me. Her tone shifts, becoming almost accusatory, "Did you eat my salmon?"

I spin a little, seeing the last container still sitting out on the counter. I'd decided around lunchtime that I was in deep enough at this point that it didn't matter if I ate the last serving. I grin again, and then, because she's getting a little too comfortable, lift the knife and stab downwards into the coffee table in a swift, powerful motion.

"Sure did. And it was delicious."

She gasps, eyes wide as she stares at the handle, now sticking out at a sharp, upright angle from the wood. "I can't believe you just did that," she mumbles after she recovers from the shock.

"This table is falling apart—"

"The knife, not the table!" she cries, forgetting herself again. "You probably ruined the tip!"

I really try not to smile, because I think it's giving her the wrong impression, but I can't help it. "I'm going to keep you," I decide.

The indignant expression wipes from her face. "W-what?"

The buzzing of her phone is more persistent now, as well as evenly spaced. A phone call. I let her question hang in the air as I walk over and pick up the bag, dig out the phone, and read the screen. "Harrison? Who's that?"

Her face twists back up with fear and concern. "N-no one."

"Passcode?" Defeated, she recites her PIN, and I slide my finger across the screen to answer it. "Hello?"

"El—wait, whoa, who's this? Why are you answering Ellie's phone?"

I scowl at her as I mute the call. "You have five seconds to tell me who he is and why he's calling you or I'll just find out who he is myself and take care of him."

"Is she okay?" the grating male voice drifts out from the speaker. "What's going on?"

She winces. "Harrison is my neighbor. We're staying together at the motel while—" she looks around, and decides not to bring it up, "I told him I was going to get us something to eat, but I came here first. He doesn't know I'm here. Please don't hurt him!"

I put a finger to my lips, to which she jerks a nod in understanding, and unmute the call. "Eleanor changed her mind about the motel; she's going to stay with me until they're done fumigating."

"Who are you?" the guy asks, not quite suspicious. More curious.

"I'm her boyfriend."

Eleanor makes a choked noise, and the guy has the audacity to laugh. I let my silence hang in the air as a warning to both of them. She clams up instantly, looking away, and after a few seconds, the laughter in his voice drops. "Wait, seriously? She... ah, she never mentioned."

"I'm hurt," I intone, more to her. She scowls at the cushion next to her, not turning my way.

"Uh, sorry, man," the guy says awkwardly. "Well, tell her I said have fun, I guess. And since she was supposed to bring food back with her and instead just abandoned me here, tell her she owes me dinner."

"I'm not going to do that, and she doesn't," I say, my voice lowering in anger.

I can practically hear the fucker's heart racing in fear. "Oh... o-okay. Uh, bye."

"Harrison said to have fun," I say after I end the call and pocket the device. "Some friend. He doesn't seem too concerned that you're not the one who picked up your phone."

"In this case, that's probably a good thing for him," she mumbles, staring with resignation at the pocket where her phone disappeared. It looks like she's staring at my package, and my cock nearly twitches at the thought.

"Probably true. That happen a lot? Lots of guys picking up your phone for you?"

I know I sound jealous, but I can't fucking help myself. I've been watching as her chest expands with each breath, pressing the rope into her upper arms and breasts, and pressure is pounding in my head and in my dick. The thought that she's got other guys is... aggravating. At least this Harrison character doesn't seem like he's one of them.

"Do I really have to answer that?" she asks.

I close my eyes and exhale loudly as I bring up a hand and try to rub the tension out of the back of my neck. I know I'm being crazy—too possessive, too much—so I need to back off. "No." But then I see her eyes follow the movement of my arm, locking in on the triceps bulging through my shirt, and I change my mind. "Yes."

Her eyes cut to the ceiling, and she shakes her head a little, like she doesn't want to say it. "You're the first."

Satisfaction swells in my veins, and because I know I should be more concerned about that reaction than I am, I decide to give her some space. I move back over to my setup, and crouch around the other side so I can keep both the viewfinder and her in my line of sight.

"Tell me something," I say conversationally. I just want to keep talking to her. I know she's going to like me. She already sort of does—I can tell—but the situation doesn't really lend itself to romance. "Why aren't you in any of those photos, darlin'?"

She turns her head in the direction of my gesture, fixing on the row of frames standing on the couch table. "Um, I don't know. I guess I'm usually the one taking them," she says, looking down.

I don't like that for some reason. It strikes me as a bit sad that she's always the one behind the camera. Even sadder if the reason is that she doesn't like photos of herself, the way I know some people don't. She's a woman who should be photographed, and those photos should be framed and put on a shelf to look at often.

Movement catches in the corner of my eye. She shifts on the couch, moving closer to the arm. I keep half an eye on her—if she thinks she's being sneaky in her attempt to break free, she's adorably wrong—but it soon becomes obvious that escape isn't her goal. She starts rubbing her knee against the arm of the couch.

"You got an itch?"

"No," she replies too fast for it to be honest.

"Should I repeat the question?" I ask pointedly.

Her shoulders sag a little. "It's... I have psoriasis. I had a flare-up at work... that's why I came back tonight. I was coming for the cream they prescribed me. I should have just picked up some cortisone."

"That would have been much smarter," I admonish, though I can't bring myself to regret her bad decision.

"I know," she says miserably. "It's just that sometimes it itches so bad that it hurts, and I can't get any relief, and I can't sleep—"

I smile, amused that the over-explaining tic has returned. "Where is it?"

"What? You're going to—you... uh," she stops at my pointed look. "It's in the cabinet in the bathroom. It's the only thing in there."

I find it easily enough, grabbing the twisted metal tube and then pausing on my way out to rectify the fact that I left the toilet seat up. I'm uncapping the cream when I stride back in, heading for the couch this time. "Where do you need it? Your knee?"

"I... you don't have to do that."

I sit next to her, and she immediately slides away. I pat my thigh. "Legs."

"What's happening right now?"

She's going to let me take this opportunity to get my hands on her; that's what's happening. "That wasn't a request, Eleanor." When she still doesn't do as I instructed, I grab underneath her ankles and pull her legs as one restrained unit up into my lap.

"Please don't," she says as I work the left foot hole underneath the zip tie I'd left there.

I'm satisfied when I don't see the same rawness around her ankles that circled her wrists. Her legs are winter-bleached and stubbly, but the skin is just as silky and smooth as I remember it looking when she was wearing those tiny shorts.

Now that we're closer, the air between us fills with her scent. She smells exactly like I knew she would. Her fragrance is a mix of a background of conflicting florals from her lotions and hair products, tangy sweat, various food smells, and something uniquely her own. It's round, feminine, and mouthwatering. Just like her.

And then I realize I'm smelling her.

I've lost my goddamn mind.

I let my fingertips brush against her as I hike up the fabric of her sweatpants, going maybe a little too slowly for her comfort. But then she shivers a little and presses her thighs together. I watch her work down a swallow and her eyes half-close as she zeroes in on my touch. Her lips part.

She's getting fucking turned on.

And blood rushes to my cock. Jesus Christ. Knowing she wants me, too... I'm on the verge of making my own very bad decision. Well, another one, anyway.

"This is too weird," she whispers.

I don't think it was really for me, but I have to agree with her assessment. I'm a fucking sniper—calm and collected is in the job description—but she's getting under my skin.

As I get the pant leg up over her knee, she squirms a little, and the friction really doesn't help my resolve. "Stop," I grind out, gripping both her legs tighter. "You're going to be a good girl and let me do this."

Her eyes meet mine, and the rawness I see there makes me want to dive right into her. I want to drown myself in those clear blue pools, lose myself in those pillowy lips, suffocate in the softness of her until I forget how hard I have to be.

"Why?" she rasps.

It's not 'why should I do what you say?' but it's a lot of other things. A 'why me,' a 'why is this happening,' definitely a 'why are you doing this,' and maybe even a 'why do I feel this way.'

"Because," I say, mentally finishing with *you're mine.*

It's an odd thought, not one I've ever really had before, and I'm not so far gone that I can objectively recognize it as one I shouldn't say out loud. She doesn't know me. I don't know her, even though I feel like I do. But that's only because I've been in her apartment for two days, going through her stuff.

That has to be it.

I can easily see the flare-up she was talking about. The skin is angry, inflamed, patchy red with little white bumps. It's probably killing her right now. She shrinks away when I get the pants up high enough. I reach out to run my fingertips over it, hoping the cool touch will soothe her.

"No, don't—don't touch it," she says.

I jerk my hand back, like I've been burned. "Does it hurt?"

"No, I..." her face flushes. "People just usually think it's gross. Never mind."

To prove I'm not like those fucking *people,* I squirt out a fair amount of the thick white cream, wanting to leave enough that it provides the relief so she doesn't need to scratch. When I start rubbing it in, she inhales sharply and makes a little noise of relief.

It's a nice moment, even though she's tied and not on my lap willingly. I briefly allow myself to forget that my position is home invader and not guest.

"Are you going to let me go? I won't say anything," she says softly.

I glance at her. She's not lying, not really, but she will forget this promise. I'll have to make sure she keeps it. "I know."

She trembles as my hand slides up the outside of her thigh. She's got great legs. Powerful. Strong. I reach her hip and curse softly as it fills my hand. Her stomach tightens. I squeeze, and her body gives way to me immediately, bending under my grip. Just how I fucking like.

"Mac," she whispers. Her blue eyes are round, and her brows are slashed up in apprehension. I can see the conflict on her face. She may want it, but not like this. "You didn't hurt me. You cut off the zip ties; you put on my medicine for me. You... you're not going to hurt me."

Hurting her is not what I had in mind. But I understand what she's saying. It's not the right time. I won't make her admit that she wants me. Yet. She can have that small dignity for now.

"I'm not," I agree, and place her feet back on the floor.

"Thank you."

I just huff a laugh in response—imagine someone thanking you for not touching them against their will after you break into their house, tie them up and kill three people right in front of them. I check my watch and see that it's well after midnight. "You should go to sleep. It'll be better that way."

"Can you... loosen the rope? I know you won't take it off, but I don't think I'll be able to sleep with it digging in like this. I can't really feel my hands."

I look down, and they're not discolored in the least, so I know she's trying to play me. But I do remove the rope around her torso because I was always going to. I leave her hands and feet tied.

She leans against the arm of the couch and closes her eyes. She starts pretending to be asleep around 2 AM and really falls asleep an hour later. For a second, her trust makes me mad. She shouldn't trust me. She shouldn't let her guard down enough to fall asleep around me. I'm a killer.

I watch her for a while after her breathing evens out, her sooty lashes brushing against her cheeks lightly as her eyes move rapidly behind the closed lids. Her chest expands and contracts, her face smooths out, and she looks so... peaceful. She looks delicate and innocent, like something to be protected.

And I intend to.

While she sleeps, I sneak through the apartment. I make a mental note to thank Wes for insisting we all carry a few basic pieces of tech with us on every mission, and leave a few listening devices in places no one would think to look. I want to leave a camera, but I'm not that kind of monster. Well... not so far, anyway.

At least I don't have to wipe away the evidence of myself the way I normally would. Saves me some time on my way out. As my last move, I scrawl out a note on the back of one of the paper bills sitting in a pile on the kitchen table and place it next to the knife. I leave that stuck in the table so she can easily cut herself free when she wakes up.

5

DIMITRI

I have not stayed alive so long by ignoring my own shortcomings

I explode into the first-floor bathroom, nearly shattering the glass mirror on the back of the door. I rip the shirt over my head and use my left hand to pull my right deltoid forward so I can see the damage. Blood forms rivers down my arm, pooling between thick muscle and staining the skin bright red. I hear it dripping onto the floor.

Fuck. It needs at least four stitches.

Grumbling to myself in my mother tongue, I open up the medicine cabinet. The first-aid bag takes up so much room in the built-in space, we had to remove the shelves. It is equipped with more than your average kit; I grab the silver box that has the sterile needles in plastic packaging.

I should make James stitch it for me for several reasons—I am not left-handed, he has the steadiest hands, and he is the reason I got fucking shot in the first place—but he likely will not return soon enough.

I grip the edges of the sink as a wave of dizziness overtakes me. It is just a graze; the pain barely registered, but blood loss and shock are not weaknesses I can train out of myself. But I can treat it and prevent the shock, so I bring the complete kit with me into the kitchen.

The kitchen, much like the rest of this rental house, is huge, ostentatious and made of cold stone and glass. Its luxury is not the quiet kind, but it has its perks. The fully loaded gym downstairs is one of them.

I navigate around the large middle counter, pausing to rinse the blood from my hand in the built-in sink. I look up at the opposite wall as I let the water flow over my skin. Dark as it is, the large wall of windows shows only the light inside and my own reflection back, making me uneasy that I cannot see out into the expanse of open yard behind the mansion. But the perimeter is not only secure, it is easily securable. I made sure of that before I allowed Wesley to sign the lease.

The refrigerator and freezer stand in the middle of a wall of cabinets with no handles, their dark finish the same, making them almost indistinguishable. I grab an unmarked glass bottle from the freezer, uncork it with my teeth and take a deep drink. The taste is familiar, smooth, and I welcome the burn in my throat.

I let my stomach settle around the alcohol, take one more drag, and breathe out in relief as my face warms. My hand grips the neck of the bottle, and I lift to pour some of it on my wound—force of habit—before I remember this is not the field. The kit has disinfectant; I do not need to waste the best potato vodka from my home country.

To offset the dehydrating effect of alcohol, I pour a glass of water and take it with me to sit at the ornate glass table near the windows that easily fits 10. After some spritzes of hydrogen peroxide and a few minutes applying pressure over a gauze pad, the bleeding slows enough so I can work. The first stitch is the hardest, mostly a mental hurdle, easier done with a little liquid bravery.

This injury is infuriating. It is infuriating because it was avoidable. The gunman met his own untimely end with a knife to the throat, but James could have easily picked him off long before he had the chance to aim his gun at me.

Though, truthfully, he was in my line of sight the whole time, and within knife-throwing distance. Maybe it is not completely James's fault.

I have not stayed alive so long by ignoring my own shortcomings, few as they are. The truth is, I have gotten complacent knowing he has my back. But the trouble is, I need to be able to trust my team. A man is only as good as his word in our line of work, and James said he would clear the second floor.

I hear the front door open and the Englishman call into the house, "Dimitri?"

"Here," I respond, pulling the string through the last stitch I will have to make. I work the curved needle under the suture to tie it off, a difficult task with fingers slippery from blood.

Wesley walks into the kitchen with his usual carefree manner, laptop tucked under his arm. That thing is a permanent fixture, an extension of his body in a way similar to my knives. He stops by the refrigerator, and I glance his way to see his stare locked on the pile of bloody gauze in front of me at the table.

He is deadly enough—we have sparred plenty of times for me to know that he deserves my respect—but he spends less time using those sparring skills he practices. His work is mostly done with the blue light of his screen reflecting on his face while he makes this technology bend to his will. It is truly a sight.

And he is many things, including a crucial member of our small team, but I am never quite sure if 'good with blood' is one. We have been on enough missions at this point that he should be used to the sight of me cleaning myself up.

I hear the soft clack as the laptop hits the surface of the counter, then see him rest his upper body on his forearms as they strain against his shirt. He was not exactly scrawny before, but he has put on some muscle since we formed our team. Those ridiculous tattoos that wind down his arms are slightly distorted from the thicker limbs and veins. I credit myself for this. As James is closer to my size, he has always been a stronger fighter than Wesley, but it is still my job as the strongest of us to push the others.

"Can't be that bad if you're still sitting upright," Wesley says with a smile curling his lips.

He smiles too much, like a woman or a child. It made me suspicious when we first met. James too, though I think that is just an American thing.

"A scratch," I grumble, clipping the string and placing the medical scissors back in the metal box.

"That's good to hear."

"I should not be scratched at all," I point out. Our research was thorough, and the meeting and setup went according to plan, so the execution should have been easy. "What happened? Where is he?"

"You know I don't like to speculate..."

I glare at him as I tear a piece of tape with my teeth, then place it over the edge of the gauze pad. "Tell me."

"I think someone walked in on him. *Exterminus interruptus*, as it were."

I curse. "How could this have happened?"

"Well," he begins, pushing himself up off the counter, "we don't *know* that it did."

I eye him. Wesley's unwillingness to speak in absolutes or believe assumptions is one of his most frustrating qualities in conversation. An asset when he is triple-checking everyone's work, though. "But you think he was compromised?"

"I do."

I swallow some of my anger and shift in my chair to face him more fully, now that the wound is taken care of. "Does he need backup?"

"He said he was handling it."

Good. I would not bother concerning myself with it, then. "We lost Rossi. We need to regroup. We are back on our first square."

"Square one," Wesley corrects.

"That is what I said."

His lips twitch, and he grabs his laptop. "I'll put out some feelers and see if I can find anything that'll help us nail down their next move."

That is a fine, cautious approach, but I know a few likely scenarios. "He will either go into hiding, if he does not care about seeming brave, or they will believe that I was acting alone. Either way, they will move their operation."

"I'll create a flag for your picture in all the usual places, in case they put out a hit."

I nod, approving of this plan. "James will watch for the new location. It is the least he can do to clean up his mess. Will you be telling the General?" I ask as an afterthought.

The man who brought us together, each of us with our own specific set of skills that work together so nicely. The man who sends the details for the jobs, and takes a cut off the top for his service. The man who communicates almost exclusively with Wesley. I know so little of this man.

"This isn't Charlie's fucking Angels, mate. The General doesn't give a good goddamn about screw-ups, as long as we get it right in the end."

I nod. This is as I would expect, but I cannot have one setback making my team look bad. "I will be downstairs. If I am not back in two hours, call for an IV delivery."

I grab two water bottles out of the fridge and make my way down to the gym in the basement. There is a sauna, which will be good for the cold shock setting in.

The heat of the sauna helps with the shivering, but does little to help my anger.

A month of work down the drain. I will have to take some time to recover from this injury, and even after I heal, we will have to rework our strategy. Too many of Rossi's men have seen my face.

Nothing makes me angrier than not being able to do my job because of stupidity. Whatever happened, I hope James confronts his errors. There is no doubt in my mind that this fuckup was someone's error, and I know it was not mine. I will not work with people who do not learn from their mistakes.

6

ELEANOR

— ◇ —

I'm not upset about the right stuff.

I wake in a panic from a bad dream that slips away as soon as I try to grab onto it. It takes me a second to register that I'm lying on my side on the couch, and my right hand has gone numb from the pressure of sleeping on my shoulder. I look down, see the rope, and it all comes flooding back in.

Mac. The gun. Being tied up and terrified. Him saying he's going to keep me. His hand inching up my leg...

Stop, Eleanor. Don't think about that.

I sit up with some difficulty. I can tell from the light quality in the room that morning has come, and I know Mac is gone without even needing to check. I can... feel it. I do still look around, though, and everything looks just how I left it. The tripod and his bag are gone.

There are a few tells, proving that it wasn't all just a nightmare. The takeout containers that had my leftovers in them are sitting face down on a towel next to the sink, and the knife is still deeply embedded into the pine table. Grumbling, I reach forward with both hands and grip the handle, having to give it a surprisingly significant jerk to get it out. The motion jostles a piece of paper on the table, which then falls to the floor, but I ignore it for now. Instead, I examine the tip of the knife, which had better not be bent...

It's only duller now, mercifully. And since that means I have to re-sharpen it anyway, I decide to use it to saw through the rope. One look at that complicated knot and I know my teeth won't do the trick.

I have to awkwardly angle the blade back and be extra careful not to cut myself, but even so, cutting through all the fibers takes way longer than I expect. Eventually, I free myself and let the ropes fall away as I rub the skin gently, massaging the blood back into the area.

I bend forward and grab the paper off the floor. At first, I think it's just my electric bill, but when I turn it over, my stomach drops at the cramped, half-cursive handwriting that I've never seen before.

Keep the curtains closed. Stay inside until Friday. I'm watching.

My heart pounds heavily and loudly, making my blood roar in my ears and bringing a flush to my face. He can see me somehow. Or, he's watching the building. Either way, it's like adding a *to be continued* to the end of this story.

And it's a horror story. So why does a small part of me thrill in the fact that it's not over?

Okay, not going there... he broke in. Held me hostage. Made me think he was going to kill me.

I suddenly feel unprotected and unsafe in my apartment. I'm all alone in this building, apparently confined to my room, and I'm pretty sure that he took my phone. No one knows where I am except him, and he has the key to my place. How else could he have gotten in?

I leap up and grab the bottom corner of the couch. It's the heaviest thing in my apartment that I can move, and the door swings inward. I pull it over and then shove it flush against the wall. It's not the best solution, especially for later when I'll wish I had somewhere to sleep, but it does make me feel a little better. First thing Friday morning when we're allowed back in, I'm going to Ed to get my locks changed.

It occurs to me that I don't know for sure he took my phone, so I start looking around. I even rifle through my drawers when it's obvious that it's not sitting out anywhere. But there are only so many places in a studio to put things, so I run out of places to look pretty quickly. I almost cry in frustration. I'd just finished paying that thing off. A two-year payment plan for a cell phone was bad enough.

Great. Now I'm stranded in my apartment until tomorrow with no phone, no one to talk to, and no way to mindlessly entertain myself. God, you never realize how critical that small rectangle of metal and glass has become in your life until you're forced to try to live without it. I don't even feel like I'm on my phone all the time—my screen-time usually sits somewhere around one to two hours per day—but evidently, it's still a crutch.

I spend an hour honing and resharpening my knife, mostly as something mindless to do with my hands, but also because it feels like a bloodthirsty thing to do, and that settles some of my fear, minting it into cold, metallic anger.

Then, I do what I usually do when I have the time and energy to kill. I go into the kitchen to start some projects.

I feed my starter. Then I take everything out of everything until the counters, table, and floor are covered with boxes, bags, jars, and cartons. Then, I start cleaning. I wipe, I disinfect, I scrub. I check expiration dates and create a *Use Now* pile.

When everything is returned to its place, I cook. I mix together a sourdough loaf. I combine the freezer-burned bags of vegetables and sausage with the nearly expired cans of beans and the half an onion going soft that was hiding in the back of the crisper into a soup. Then, I make a casserole. Then a galette. Then another casserole.

Suddenly, I'm out of ingredients, but I've got a freezer packed with leftovers—gifts for a future me, too tired to do anything after her shift but throw something in the microwave.

It occurs to me distantly, though I have no way to check without my phone, that this is a pretty standard response to a traumatic event. What starts out as a distraction—a way to occupy my mind with something that soothes me, like food preparation—becomes my sole focus. I can be in total control of this. I can choose to add something or not. I decide the flavors. I say how long it cooks.

I clean the rest of the apartment as the sourdough loaf finishes in the oven. The day creeps away, and I have to stop when I can't see much anymore. I'm too afraid to turn on the light, so I sit in the middle of the freshly scrubbed floor and wish my brain was as tired as my body now is so I could just sleep and escape all the thoughts that way.

But I'm wired. And I need something to do that won't require me to turn on the light. I don't have a laptop because I haven't needed a computer since school and I can do pretty much everything I need to on my phone these days, but I have the most basic model of e-reader available and a library full of high fantasy, smut, and cookbooks.

I give a fantasy book a try first—dragons and fairies feel like the right thing to take me away—but I can't get into it. Their problems seem too foreign, too unreal. I want their fantastical adventures when I'm sick of my own boring existence.

But I also can't focus on the cookbooks. Most cookbooks aren't meant to be read front to back, and it's frustrating when you read something and your first reaction is to go try to make it, but you can't because you're completely out of ingredients.

I hesitate before selecting what I hope will be an innocuous enough romance, but the second the chemistry starts between the main characters, my mind wanders. The feel of his fingers on my leg. The commanding way he acted, bossing me around about the flare-up on my knee. The possessive way he talked about me to Harrison.

I shouldn't like that he did that.

I let the e-reader fall into my lap and stare, unseeing, at the blackout curtains. And as I sit, as I finally slow to a stop, everything comes flooding in. I wait for the tears, but they don't come. I'm upset, sure, but I'm also frustrated that I'm not upset about the right stuff.

I deserve this cry. I deserve to feel safe in my own home. I deserve to self-soothe after being scared out of my mind.

So why does it feel more like I want to cry because I lost something? Like my feelings are hurt? Like I'm mourning a relationship that never even started and was never going to be? Like some part of me—so deep down I could convince myself it didn't exist—thought maybe I had a chance with him?

Because he touched me. And I let him. And, *God help me*, I liked it.

Ugh. Am I that starved for attention and touch? No. He was fucking with me. Keeping me off balance, keeping me scared and submissive. Threatening me with... rape...

I brush my fingers against my hip, hoping to feel some lingering twinge—something that would remind me of what his hands felt like.

No, that moment... it wasn't a threat. And maybe if I hadn't stopped him, it wouldn't have been totally on my terms, but it really wouldn't have been rape either. At one point, when he was leaning over me, staring at my body with such hunger and focus, I was so wet that I ached with it.

I wanted him to kiss me, to take me. I wanted him to devour me.

I wanted to know what it felt like to be the object of desire of a man that powerful and that attractive. And—*fuck him*—he really made me feel like I was.

This really isn't a helpful spiral, though I suppose if it were helpful, it wouldn't be called spiraling. I need to do something else. I need to occupy my mind and exhaust myself.

After some debate, I decide to brave the abandoned hallway and stairwell to exhaust myself in the basement gym. Only once I'm dripping in sweat and so tired I can't see straight, I head back upstairs for a fumbled shower in the dark, and a half-assed tooth brushing using my finger while wearing pajamas that are probably inside out. I set the couch cushions on the floor, curl under a blanket, and close my eyes for the worst night's sleep of my life.

The sound of a door slamming shut wakes me, and I realize it must be 8 AM and people are returning. I moan, rolling onto my back and wincing at the stiffness. I am not made to sleep on the floor, even with cushions.

I stretch it out and realize the stiffness is also self-inflicted. Too many squats. I throw open the curtains, blinking at the light, and set about getting the couch back in place. The clock on the microwave confirms my suspicion; it's 8:35. I need to go get my stuff from the motel, and I'm pretty sure that EZ checkout is by 10, so I change into clothes to go outside.

But before I can leave, there's a knock at the door. My heart jumps and I freeze, then roll my eyes at myself. It's not him. Even if he actually were watching—and the more I think about it, the more I have my doubts—he wouldn't be back now that everyone else is, too.

It's Harrison. He looks a bit more rumpled than usual, and he's shifting from foot to foot in an antsy, uncomfortable way. His tone is apprehensive, too. "Hey. I checked us out and packed up your stuff for you."

He hands me my duffel, and I'm almost giddy with appreciation. That was so thoughtful. I take the bag. "Oh my God, thank you, Harrison. You're the best."

"Why didn't you come back for it? Is everything okay? I've been texting you."

"Oh, I lost my phone," I say. It's not technically a lie, but it feels like one. "I was just about to swing by the motel for my stuff... and hey, I'm sorry about bailing—"

I turn to toss the duffel on the ground behind me, and Harrison steps inside and closes the door behind him. "All right, spill."

I feel my stomach drop, my mind instantly spinning with possibilities for how he could know. Logic catches up a second later, and I clear the frog from my throat. "About what?"

"Since when do you have a boyfriend? And why didn't you tell me?" he doesn't sound hurt, but there's an edge to his voice.

I balk, searching for any excuse. Maybe if I turn it back on him, he'll drop it... "It's not like you tell me things about Stacey without me asking. And you didn't ask."

"Because me and Stacey aren't actually a thing yet. There's nothing really to tell," he says, looking away and trying to hide a little smile. "But don't change the subject. I'm asking now—who is he?"

"He's..."

I should have prepared for this question. After Mac's rude handling of the phone call they had, I should have known Harrison would want details. And I really, really don't want to lie to Harrison. But I also know deep down that he'll be in serious trouble if I tell him the truth.

I sigh. "It's complicated. I'm not really sure what happened between us, exactly."

My tone must sound as tired and pathetic as I feel, because I watch the indignation melt out of his body—his shoulders drop, and his frown smooths out. "Hey, I didn't mean... You don't have to tell me anything. But I'm here to talk if you want to, okay?"

I just nod. This conversation feels wrong. It's so normal, so banal. I feel like I'm outside myself looking in, observing who I used to be without experiencing it. I don't feel like the same carefree Eleanor who ribs her neighbor about his love life. I'm Eleanor with a dark secret. I'm Eleanor who's been tied up in my own apartment. I'm Eleanor who's watched a man kill. And—worst of all—I'm Eleanor with complicated, mixed emotions about it all.

"He sounds kind of... never mind."

"No, what?" I prompt.

Harrison lifts a hand to scratch his scalp, and he turns his head away to say, "Well, he wasn't exactly friendly on the phone. Sounds like maybe he's sort of controlling? I say this as your friend; I don't want you to get mixed up in some sort of bad situation."

The edges of my mouth lift in a half-hearted smile. It's too ironic not to acknowledge it, but too fresh to actually be funny. "Thanks, Harrison. You're a good friend."

"Okay, well I've got to get to work. But I meant what I said. Always here to talk."

I nod and usher him out of the apartment. I sit on the couch after he's gone, and seriously consider a nap. I also seriously consider calling out from work. Then I remember I still don't have my phone, and, frankly, I'm not sure I can stand another day like yesterday. At least the restaurant will give me something to throw myself into.

I feel naked, cut off without my phone. I really should go to the police, but it takes me a second to remember where the station is. Then, I groan. I'll have to borrow Harrison's laptop to figure out the route I need and take the bus because it's too far to walk.

As I stare out the window, it suddenly occurs to me that whatever Mac was shooting at, I should be able to see from here. I stand and approach, trying to remember the angle of his setup. I crouch down to the approximate height and look out in the approximate direction, but everything looks normal.

As far as the eye can see—which, admittedly, is maybe not as far as his military-grade equipment—it's all hustling commuters, dogs being walked, kids running around playground equipment, garbage being picked up. Normal city stuff. There's no tape, no police barricades, blocking off the area of a murder.

I remember Mac saying something about a roof, but none of the buildings in my view that have accessible roofs are cordoned off either. If someone had been shot, wouldn't it be more obvious?

Unless it's being covered up.

Maybe I watch too many crime dramas.

7

MAC

———◦◦◦———

Good thing I like 'em a little crazy.

I feel myself smile as she manages her way through her first test—a conversation with that damn insolent, nosy, overbearing neighbor—and passes with flying colors. She didn't even let my name slip.

He has been texting her, like he said. I grab her phone, type in the passcode she gave me, and flip through his messages again.

> How's it going?

> Hope you're having a good time. You coming back tonight?

> Hey, I'm going to leave soon. Want me to check out?

> Should I grab your stuff?

> Hello???

I toss the phone aside with a scowl, and it bounces on the mattress next to me. He's lucky it's all innocent stuff. But I still don't like that he feels like he has a claim on her—that he expects a response, or he gets to know things about where she is and what her plans are.

And he called *me* controlling...

At least I can easily pivot. After Dimitri tore me a new one about my fuck-up, I found a new vantage point in this city's zoning department's bygone attempt at gentrification. They'd allowed several chain hotels to build on the opposite side of town, likely back in the 90s, judging from the worn-down carpet and popcorn ceiling. It's only six stories high, but it's clean, and there's a shower, a bed, and a restaurant on the ground floor. No one will surprise me if I leave the *Do Not Disturb* sign on the handle. And from my room on the top floor, I can watch both the activity at the warehouse and Eleanor.

I'm watching her. Not because I have to, but because I can't stop.

And what a good girl she was. She listened. She didn't leave the building. She kept the curtains closed. But the first thing she did this morning? Opened them and let me in.

I listened to her in her apartment all day yesterday, wishing like hell I didn't have to just listen. The clanging of pots and pans and furious scrubbing told me she was working out the assault on her person with relatively healthy coping mechanisms. I kept waiting for a breakdown of some kind—tears, or something—but it never came.

So, she's either tough as nails, or has a few screws loose.

Good thing I like 'em a little crazy. You can't really be completely ordinary and survive in my world.

I know my focus is torn because it's only once she leaves for her job for the day around 2:30 that I can really settle in and give the warehouse my full attention. It's busy there, but only to the trained eye. They've locked down the perimeter and are trying to move the goods as subtly as possible, a crate at a time. The same cycle repeats for the rest of the day—a van pulls up, disappears around the back, I see two guys moving around inside, and the van comes back around the corner riding a lot lower.

I start itching for another hit of Eleanor after nightfall, but check my watch and see that she's got about two hours left on her shift. So, I decide to get out, stretch my legs.

Rossi's warehouse is pretty deserted, but they did leave the van they've been using parked out back. Very accommodating of them. I place a tracker under the back bumper.

I eye her phone and grab for it. No one has contacted her since Harrison's frantic messages this morning. Her older text chains are people from work, spam, group texts with her family and college friends, more spam, and then a few from people who she only ever texts with to trade birthday wishes. Her emotional support browser tabs are mostly abandoned shopping carts full of clothes and recipe blogs, but there are a few with travel destinations and memes. The incognito tabs, however...

I love being right. She is a freak.

My girl—yeah, "my," I'm way past being normal about this—has a very healthy sexual appetite. She is adventurous and all over the map. Soft and sensual, BDSM, blowjobs, romantic, roleplaying, anal, gay and lesbian... I watch some of the porn she likes and my dick hardens painfully, thinking about her lying in bed with her phone in one hand and the other one working that sweet pussy and clit. I know she'll be mortified when she finds out I know her secret little fantasies, and I can't fucking wait to see that pretty pink blush on her cheeks.

I watch her walk home, shivering in the wind. I hate that her way home takes her through those blocks so late at night. She shouldn't have to risk crossing paths with the crackheads in the alleys and men buying their pleasure on street corners. As she walks, I notice that she clutches something tightly in her bag, and I hope it's a taser or something.

I see her enter her apartment, toss off her winter wear and go to the window. After a second's hesitation, she opens it and stares into the darkness. Her eyes never quite make it to where I'm watching from, but they're scanning like they're looking for me.

I eat my takeout when she sits down with her microwaved leftovers, like we're having dinner together. She flits around the apartment, disappears behind the wall that I know leads to the bathroom, and emerges half an hour later, hair wet and dressed for bed. She closes the window, locks and chains the door—*good girl*—and pulls out her couch-bed. I wait for her to close the curtains. She doesn't.

The next day is exactly the same. Bad guys move their stuff, Eleanor goes to work. Some maintenance guys come to her door in the morning, which puts me immediately on edge, but they are in and out in a matter of hours and I can hear that they don't even really pay her any attention.

Silly girl. Like a new lock is going to keep me out. I'm glad if it makes her feel safer, though.

The next day, she's off work. I know because I checked the restaurant website and saw that they're closed on Sundays. I get out to stretch my legs again and check in on the warehouse, which seems to be empty now. Then—wouldn't you know it?—I find myself on her street.

This is stalker behavior. Some might even go so far as to say obsessive. I know that. But frankly, it's my job—it's what I know how to do. And unlike in my job, I'm really just keeping an eye on her. It's a dangerous world with dangerous people, myself included. But I'm not going to hurt her. I'm looking out for her.

It's not exactly like she's given me any indication that I'm welcome in her life, except... well, I told her I was watching. And she keeps opening her curtains. It really fucking feels like it's for me.

And maybe I'm reading into it, but unfortunately for her—and now, I guess, me—she's cute as hell. And wholesome as fuck.

She starts her day off sitting in the corner of a cafe, nursing a fancy latte and a croissant. Then, she goes to the fucking farmers' market. She brings her own bags and chats with literally every vendor. On her way out, she stops and stares at the bouquets of flowers with a sad, longing sort of smile but doesn't buy any.

Halfway home, she stops at a budget cell service store. I know it's a company that leeches onto larger company's towers and, as a result, tends to drop calls on its customers. She should have something better.

Her phone is burning a hole in my pocket. I should return it. It's old, and the glass on the back is covered in spiderweb cracks. She really should have something better, but at least this one will do for now. I've already cloned it anyway.

I pull my hat down lower over my brow as I use the key I never returned to access the back stairwell of her apartment building. I narrowly avoid a run-in with one of the neighbors I'd had to convince to leave the building that day, but I make it to the top floor without drawing any notice.

Getting past her new lock is child's play—a matter of the right tools and a basic knowledge of how tumbler locks work—and it concerns me how easy it is. At least when she's home, she uses the chain, too.

I step inside and gently close the door. Not much has changed, except everything is a bit neater now, and the scent of pine cleaning solution is stronger, stinging my nose. I want to stick around, but I know she's on her way home and this is a huge risk anyway. So, I don't dawdle. I wedge her phone into the back of the couch so she'll assume I never took it, and straighten the pillow.

Fabric catches my eye, something stuck in between the back of the couch and the bottom cushions. I give it a tug and see that it's that flimsy tank top she was wearing when we first met. I lift it to my nose and inhale her, feeling stirrings in my gut and finding that I like the smell even better now that I've been deprived of it for several days.

Not really giving it a second thought, I wad it up and stick it in my back pocket. Then I slip out as carefully as I entered.

That night, while she's sitting on the couch with her e-reader, I send her a text that would look just like spam from an unknown number. I know the exact moment that double buzz sounds—both because it's fucking loud, even through the muffled listening devices, and because her head whips up. She twists in her seat, looking around, then leaps up and starts frantically digging through the couch, ripping it apart.

When she finds it, she squeals in excitement and hugs it to her chest. Then, after a second, she looks at it and then down at where she was sitting with a slight frown.

"I pulled these cushions off already," she mutters to herself.

Whoops.

But the next second, she dismisses her totally justified wariness. *"Must've missed it somehow."*

My pulse cools it as she lets me off the hook. Damn, am I getting sloppy? She scrolls for a while, catching herself up and checking her messages. If she thinks it's odd that her notification screen didn't have Harrison's frantic messages, she doesn't show it.

I eat dinner with her again and turn out my lights when she does. Before climbing into bed, I go around for a last check on my equipment and to set up the programs that will notify me if there's movement on the truck. Just as I'm about to turn in, I hear it.

Is she... are those moans? Of pleasure?

I straighten and press the headphones more tightly over my ears.

"Please," she whimpers. *"Please, Mac..."*

I go hard as a fucking diamond.

I barely breathe, listening so hard to the soft wet noises of her body and the sighs of pleasure and delight. It's the "oh fuck," that has me scrambling across the room and grabbing the pants I'd worn earlier in the day. Roughly, I yank the pajama top out of the pocket and fall onto my ass on the edge of my bed.

Dirty fuck that I apparently now am, I close my eyes, breathing in her scent and listening to her moans. I palm my cock through the hole in my boxers, holding tight and trying to sync the strokes with her breathing. It's like she's right fucking here, writhing under me, tits bouncing, head thrown back in ecstasy. I can almost picture her body jolting as I snap my hips against hers, bury myself deep and feel her cunt spasm around me.

She'd be so tight. It would feel so fucking good. I grip myself harder.

I'd bring her to the edge—that place where pain meets sweet pleasure and they twist around each other almost cruelly. She'd be so pretty tied up, at my mercy, finally admitting to herself how much she wants to do what I say. How much she wants me.

Because now I know. I know what she sounds like. I've heard those soft moans and whimpers that prove she likes it just a little rough. I already know what she sounds like when she whispers the word, "please."

When she says my name again, I come all over my hand, shooting further than normal, managing to actually hit myself in the chest with it. I pant, and wipe at the cum with her pajama shirt, needing our scents to be commingled. And then, like I never even fucking came in the first place, my cock starts to tighten again, hardening in my hand.

I need more. More of her.

As her panting gets faster, I know she's right there. I want to be there to give her what she needs so badly.

I wish I were a better man. A better man would walk away. She deserves that small, peaceful life she built, if that's what she wants. I can't give her that. What kind of stability can a hitman offer? I'll be putting her in danger.

But the voice of reason is too easy to ignore.

Because I want her. And now I know she wants me too, in spite of everything.

So now... all bets are off.

8

ELEANOR

Really fucking creepy.

It takes several days before I'm not looking over my shoulder everywhere I go. A week before I feel like myself again. I never make it to the police station—not really sure what I'd say. And the longer I wait, the more ridiculous the story starts to sound, even to me.

A man broke in, and I think I heard him kill someone. I don't know anything about him, except that his name might or might not be Mac and that he doesn't *wear glasses. I don't know anything about who he killed, or even for sure if he did kill someone because I didn't see it. But he tied me up and applied my psoriasis cream against my will.*

Yeah, right.

Still, I keep a critical eye out, scan local news, listen to chatter in the restaurant and streets. Nothing. No one is talking about any local murders, and that feels too conspicuous to be a fluke.

But life goes on, and the world keeps spinning.

I just wish I could stop thinking about him, stop fantasizing about him. In my head, he never stopped when I told him to. In my head, he peeled down my sweatpants and bent me over the arm of that sofa and just absolutely filled me with what he was hiding in that bulge in his pants...

At least I found my phone—it gives me something to do to keep my mind busy in the long mornings before work. And the timing was lucky, too, because I'd just been about to get another one when I realized I'd left my ID at home. My bank account is thrilled.

My next day off finds me at home, contemplating the list of foreign films currently playing near me, when there's a knock at the door. I'm still in my pajamas, so I check the peephole because I really try not to make the same mistake twice.

There's an unfamiliar woman in the hallway. She's got flowers in one hand and a small package in the other, and her ugly brown polo is clearly a uniform. *Zippy Delivery* is embossed on her chest.

"Who is it?"

"I've got a delivery for Eleanor Wilson?"

"Just a second." Even though this pajama top covers much more than my other one—which I think maybe the laundry goblins ate—I go into the bathroom and put on my old, tattered terry-cloth robe. I unchain and open the door.

"Eleanor Wilson?" she asks again, like she didn't get the confirmation she needed the first time.

I nod, a little breathlessly. "That's me."

She hands me the shoebox-sized package, and I turn it over in my hands. It's got some weight, and rustles in a satisfying way when shaken, but it's a plain brown box with nothing on it. No shipping address or payment label. Weird. I didn't order anything.

Then, she extends her other arm and hands me the flowers.

"Oh, these are for me, too?" I ask, shocked.

"Yup," she says, snapping her gum and grabbing the clipboard out from under her armpit.

They're so gorgeous, I'm stunned for a second. The colors are bright—oranges, reds, pinks, purples—and it looks so perfect that I'm afraid to do anything with it. Even the wrapping looks expensive, with thick brown paper tied with twine. No cheap plastic sleeves here. I don't know a thing about flowers, and I don't see anything I recognize, except roses. I lean down and press my nose against the bouquet, as one does, and pull away a little disappointed. It doesn't smell like much, just fresh and green and very faintly of roses.

There's a card poking out the top with writing only on one side, a message that doesn't make any sense to me.

I'm sorry.

Who is? About what?

Disappointment surges. "Oh, these must be for someone else…"

The woman looks up from arranging the paperwork on her clipboard. "I work for the delivery company, not the flower shop. You'll have to take it up with them. Sign here."

Well, the card has an embossed logo on the top. If they're local, maybe I can call them and let them at least know that their delivery missed its mark. I place the package and flowers down on the kitchen counter so I can take the clipboard and pen, draw a squiggle on the line as meaningless as my signature would have been, and close the door.

The flowers are making me grin like a schoolgirl with a crush, so even though they're not for me, I'm going to pretend they are. I'm keeping them.

I give them another sniff, just in case I missed a scent the first time. Nothing. I almost feel robbed of a quintessential part of the receiving-flowers experience. Especially since this is my first time. I just assumed roses smelled a lot more like… well, roses. This scent is nothing like the body products that claim the name.

I've never gotten flowers before, but I have seen movies. In the movies, they always put them in water. But because I've never gotten flowers before, I don't have a vase. I don't even have an excess of clean drinking glasses. However, I do work in a kitchen, so I always have an excess of something else.

I grab a deli cup and unwind the thick paper from around the bouquet. The sight of the beautiful flowers in the cheap plastic is almost painfully ridiculous. But even though it makes me laugh at myself, I have to admit that the deli cup is a nice touch. It feels more like me.

I take a butter knife to the box next. Inside, nestled in some recycled cardboard packaging material, is something about the size and shape of a hardback book, wrapped in thick black paper with a white silk bow. I frown, confused. Black and white doesn't exactly scream holidays, but maybe it's a belated Christmas present? But who could it be from? I already received the e-gift cards from my parents and the Christmas card with flight vouchers in it from my sister so I could come visit her and the kids. No one at the restaurant knows where I live, and Harrison and I don't exchange gifts because we both agreed we're too poor.

I untie the bow and unwrap the paper, then I drop it with a gasp. It hits the packaging material with a soft swish, and I back away a few steps.

It's a picture. In a frame. Of me.

The image is blurry, like it's been zoomed in or taken from very far away, and I'm in the very center of a black circle with crossing lines, like crosshairs or a target. I'm smiling with my eyes closed, head tilted up to soak in the sunlight. I'm wearing my pajamas and, though it's blurry, I recognize the vague shapes in the background as the refrigerator and cabinets of my own kitchen.

Chills erupt under my skin. The pounding of my heartbeat is so intense it almost hurts.

With shaking hands, I pick the frame back up, and something falls into the packaging below. It's a note. Scrawled on a yellow Post-it note in that same cramped scribble I have memorized is, *Now you have one of yourself.*

He has been watching me, just like he promised.

I press my lips together and look up at the window. The curtains are open, so he might be watching, even now. I don't remember standing there, smiling in the sunlight this morning, but I was wearing these pajamas. Was this taken today?

My phone buzzes, making me jump, and my stomach tries to fall further out my butt. It couldn't be... No way... Swallowing, I inch towards the couch where I left my phone. And the relief is so acute it's almost painful when I see my sister's face on the caller ID screen.

"Hey, Melissa," I greet her. I sound out of breath, and I know it's my racing heart.

"Hey, you! How have you been?"

I slump onto the couch, dropping the picture into my lap. "Oh, you know... same old."

"Cooking, reading, working?"

I laugh a little because I usually really am that predictable. This would be the first time we've spoken in the past five years where anything really different has happened, and I can't even tell her about it. "Eat, sleep, repeat."

"Bo-ring," she sings.

"Yeah," I agree, staring down at the picture frame in my lap. I didn't notice before when I was busy freaking out about what was inside it, but the frame is silver, and hefty. It's plain, but in a way that looks expensive. It's the kind of frame Melissa put her wedding portrait in.

My sister never really calls me to talk about me, though, so I throw that ball back to her. "But what about you? How's Nick? How are the kids?"

"Nick is fine, whatever. He's doing well in some fantasy draft or something, and it's all he fucking talks about. Avery is great, they just had a trip to the zoo with her class, so she's in her 'I'm going to be a vet' era, which is adorable. She's telling me all these things she's learning about lions and hippos. It's so fun watching her get excited about stuff.

"And Warren's front tooth just fell out, and he informed me that he knows the tooth fairy isn't real because some kid named Jeff told him. So now I have to go find some kid named Jeff and kick a 6-year-old's ass."

I laugh. "It's only right. He can't be allowed to keep spreading those lies. Just make sure it's the right kid named Jeff."

I can hear the smile in her voice. "Good call. And as for me..."

As she regales me with tales of a new breakfast she's been making on repeat that she's loving and how annoyed she is about a promotion that should have been hers going to someone else, I quietly have a crisis.

He's watching me. He watches me. He's been watching me.

I keep waiting for the fear or panic to set in. I keep thinking it's going to freak me out, make me want to throw closed the curtains and hide in the dark forever.

Why the hell doesn't this bother me like it should?

What has he even seen? I don't sleep with the curtains open, or change in front of the window. At most, he's seen me pick my nose or itch my ass, which—while private—aren't exactly earth-shattering.

Which just begs the question: why? Why is he watching me? It makes sense he would be keeping tabs on me right after that night—he would have wanted to make sure I didn't tell anyone about what I'd seen—but I would think that it's been obvious for a while that I'm not going to be a problem.

So, why? It's not like I'm all that interesting, as Melissa so generously pointed out.

As my sister switches topics to her last run-in with Avery's hot teacher, I look down at the picture again. I should throw it away. My fingers tighten around the edge, and I get up off the couch and head towards the kitchen trash can, shoved against the wall near the fridge. I stand over it, but can't bring myself to let go.

When Melissa pauses for breath, I jump in. "Mel, what would you do if someone sent you something kind of creepy and stalkerish? Would you throw it away?"

"Yes," she replies instantly.

"But what if... you don't want to?"

She sighs, and I swear I can practically see her switching her phone to the other ear in frustration as one of her kids—not sure which, they're both equally loud—screams in the background. "Why do I feel like there's a right answer but you're not giving me the context I need to get there?"

I hesitate. Do I chance it? I desperately want to tell someone, and surely Melissa, who's miles away in Pittsburgh, is safe from any potential repercussions. It's not like she'd be able to do anything on her end anyway. "Well, there is one thing—"

"No, no! Paul, gah! Bad dog! Ellie, I need to call you back. My asshole dog just took a dump in the middle of the floor."

I snort, like I always do at the mention of Paul the Asshole, as he's fondly known. She puts the phone down, but forgets to hang up, so I hear her voice trail off as she admonishes him and her kids chant in sing-song voices, "asshole, asshole." With one last chuckle, I hang up for both of us.

And fall right back into my spiral.

If the package was from him, that must mean the flowers are, too. I look over at them, biting my lip against a smile. He sent me flowers? Why would he do that? Then I remember the note and wipe away the expression completely.

I'm sorry, it says. He's sorry?! For what, being a total creep?

Suddenly, I'm sick of this. Sick of questions with no answers. Sick of this note crap only going one way.

I place the frame carefully on the edge of the windowsill, facing my picture inward. The only blank paper I have is an almost used up yellow legal pad that I don't remember buying, but it'll do. I write big, in sharpie, pressing the tip a little too hard to the paper in my anger. Then, I tape my note to the window above the picture so the arrow I drew is pointing right at it.

Really fucking creepy.

9

ELEANOR

<hr>

What kind of twisted game is he playing?

Satisfied with a job well done, I head towards the shower. Before I get too far, my phone starts buzzing again, and I grab it from the pocket of my robe, figuring it's Melissa calling to finish our discussion. Which is honestly a bit out of character for her—she usually forgets to call me back.

But the name on the screen baffles me. Grandpa? My last grandfather died nine years ago, and he never even got a cell phone.

"Uh... hello?"

"Really fucking creepy, am I?" There's amusement in the deep timbre of his voice, and it sends an immediate shiver down my spine as my stomach clenches. But not in fear. My stupid adrenaline response seems to be broken.

Mac. He's calling me? He put his number in my phone? How did he... when did he...

I inhale, and it breaks in my throat, making me sound afraid. I try for some false bravado to save face. "You realize I have your phone number now, and I could easily take that to the police?"

"How do you know I'm not with the police?"

I hesitate for a second. There's no way... "Are you?"

"No," he says with a totally unbothered laugh. The noise sluices across my skin like hot water, leaving a trail of goosebumps. "And even if I believed you were going to, it wouldn't matter. It's a burner."

I hesitate. The dozens of questions that were swirling around in my head that only he could answer are suddenly, inconveniently gone. I look up at the window, like I'm looking at him. Then, realizing that I probably actually am looking at him, I retreat to the bathroom. It feels like leveling the playing field—now we both can't see each other.

I nearly groan. That's really not a normal reaction. None of this is normal.

"This is... This is the strangest thing that's ever happened to me," I grumble.

"What, getting a call from your favorite grandpa?"

I wince, wishing I didn't want to laugh at that.

The way his voice wraps around me, the rasp of it, the very subtle twang—way more subtle now than it was initially—the confidence in his tone... I wish there was a way to bottle up how the sound of him makes me feel.

The full-body flush, not the self-doubt.

I close my eyes and let my head fall back against the bathroom door. "Why are you doing this? What do you want from me?"

"I want you..." The pause is pregnant. I almost gasp, thinking that's all he's going to say, when he finishes, "to tell me what you want."

I ignore how my heart sinks that his sentence didn't end in the middle. Wait, what? Tell him what I want? What kind of twisted game is he playing? "What do you mean?"

He doesn't expand; the silence just stretches between us.

"Why were you in my apartment?"

"To kill someone," he answers immediately.

Wow. I really wasn't expecting him to answer that one. The honesty is somehow both chilling and refreshing at the same time—a testament both to the horrific nature of the truth and to how much I hate being lied to. "Just one? You shot more than once. How many did you kill?"

"Are you asking for my stats?"

My stomach drops—that feels like a confirmation of my suspicions. This wasn't a one-off; he's a certified, cold-blooded killer. "Why?" I ask softly.

"There's a lot of different answers to that question. The shortest one is, it's what I do."

I chew on my lip. I have no idea what to do with that one. "Does that mean it's a career, or a calling?"

He laughs. "Clever. Bit of both."

"And me? What do I have to do with all this?"

"That part's up to you now, darlin'. You know how to reach me."

The line goes dead, and I stare at my phone, completely flabbergasted and flustered. How did I get the chance to talk to him and end up learning nothing?! I mean, I guess I learned he's not with law enforcement—*which I knew*—and that he's a killer—*which I also knew*—and that I'm so attracted to him that even his voice made me wet—*which I also fucking already knew.*

With a sigh that turns into a little scream of frustration, I toss the phone. Literally the only new piece of information I have is his phone number, which could be construed as learning something. But his cryptic parting words keep playing back in my mind as I disrobe and turn on the water for my shower.

What part of this is up to me? The part where he's sending me ominous gifts? The part where he's putting his contact in my phone without my permission? The part where he watches through my window? How is being stalked within my control?

The time spent under the spray of the shower eventually calms me, and I step out, resolved not to let this consume the rest of my entire day.

I get dressed, go to that weird movie theater, and let the teenager who runs the ticket booth pick something for me. Then I lose myself in a tub of buttered popcorn, subtitles, and confusing subplots for two hours.

It's just starting to get dark when I get back, and my stomach gurgles as I climb the stairs. I press my hand to it, full of regret. Ugh, I shouldn't have eaten all the popcorn, but something about sitting in the dark, eyes glued to a big screen, makes it impossible to stop before you reach the bottom of the tub.

When I reach my floor, I stop dead just outside the stairwell. There are two guys at my door, neither of whom I recognize, but my heart kicks into double time as I see the black uniform on the one with his back to me.

Shit. It's the cops.

The other guy doesn't seem to be wearing a police uniform, but they're standing so close and talking, so they have to be together. I hear him say, "Can't we just..." and he starts pulling open the flap of his leather jacket, looking around sort of furtively. When he sees me, he stops instantly, letting his coat fall back down. Then he smacks the guy in the uniform on the chest and gestures at me with a nod.

The officer turns around. He's about 50, starting to jowl out, and has a clean-cut look to him. "Hello, Ma'am. My name is Officer McCloskey, and this is Detective O'Malley," he gestures to the guy in plainclothes standing behind him.

I glance up at the detective, take in his square jaw and piercing eyes and decide he'd be handsome, if not for the weird vibes he's giving off. He seems incredibly intense, focused on me in a way that doesn't feel in alignment with Officer McCloskey's calculatedly friendly, plastered-on smile. The visible gun in his holster under his leather jacket doesn't exactly help me feel more at ease.

"Is this you? 3B?"

I nod.

"We have a couple of questions for you, if you have a few minutes."

I suddenly wish I wasn't clearly just arriving home, because then I could pretend like I was on my way out or something. I decide to try it anyway. "Actually, I was just—"

"This won't take long," he cuts in, and this time the smile falters a bit.

I feel both cornered and blocked from the safety behind my door, but with no good reason to refuse to speak to them—because doesn't that just make me seem suspicious?—I relent. "Of course."

"Were you at home between the hours of 8 PM and 10 PM last Wednesday night?"

Oh my God. Oh my God. Yes. Yes, I was. "Uh... no. We all had to vacate because they were fumigating. I was staying at the... um, the motel. Sweet Dreams."

Officer McCloskey whips out a pad of paper from his little breast pocket and writes something down, then his brows lift. "Super Dreams?"

I swear I'm going to pass out. My heart is hammering in my chest. Can they hear it from there? "Yeah, that one," I say, forcing a laugh. "I always mess that up."

Officer McCloskey exchanges a look with the detective. The guy nods once. "Have you seen this man?" the cop asks, stepping towards me with a picture outstretched in his hand.

I move forward to meet him halfway, and relief floods my system. It's not Mac. The image is grainy, maybe from some kind of security camera from the angle, and the cut of the jaw initially had me worried. Also, the size and shape of him is close to what I remember of my intruder—namely, he's huge and built.

I shake my head, so grateful that I don't have to lie to the police. About this, anyway. "No. Who is he?"

"He's a person of interest in a recent incident. We think someone here might have seen something around that time."

"Why? I mean, I'm sure everyone else here told you that the building was empty. We weren't allowed back until Friday." No lies detected.

The detective speaks for the first time, and his voice is like a pit of gravel in South Jersey. "We have a witness who says a light came on. In this unit." He taps on my door with two blunt fingertips.

My mind blanks, then races too fast for me to grasp any single thought with both hands. Someone saw the light come on. They know someone was here. Do I lie? Do I stick with my story? Or do I try to play it off? What if they check the cameras at the motel and see I wasn't there during that time frame? Will they arrest me for lying? Can I say I was at work? Will they check my story with Harrison? Oh God, what do I do?

"Ma'am?"

I clear my throat, which has gone completely dry. "M-must have been an electricity surge or something. These old buildings are weird like that."

The look he gives me does not in any way assuage my anxiety. I honestly can't tell whether he believes me or not. But I'm in too deep now. No going back. Time to cut and run.

My stomach lets out a loud popcorn-digesting gurgle that sounds bad enough that it gives me an idea. "Is that everything? I'm sorry, officer, but I'm really not feeling well."

His eyes trace the sweat beading on my forehead and what is probably a ghostly white pallor from fear. He nods and flips his little notebook closed, and his eyes flick side to side, looking at the doors of the other two apartments. "That can be it for now, but we may have some more questions for you. Don't leave town, Ma'am."

I swallow again. "I never do."

I should leave town.

10

MAC

I like how literally he takes the phrase chill out.

Oh, sweet Eleanor. You've done it now.

I make it clear that I'm watching her while she's at home, and I show her how I can see in. She could close her curtains. Could shut me out.

Instead, she communicates with me through them.

I ask her to tell me what she wants. She could tell me to back off. She could tell me to leave her alone, or to stop watching her. It would be rough to hear, but I would honor her wishes.

Instead, she asks me questions about who I am and what I do.

It's time to step up my game. She liked the flowers; I saw her face light up through the window as she arranged them in that plastic cup. My girl clearly enjoys being wooed, maybe even likes feeling chased. I can do romance. Flowers and candy and shit aren't usually my speed—too slow, too indirect—but I'm willing to spend some time courting her. It seems like a good way to offset being really fucking creepy.

I grin at that, because it feels almost like we've got an inside joke now.

She leaves her apartment after a shower, and I assume from her phone activity that she's going to the movies. I resist the urge to follow her into that dark theater where she'll probably be the only person. Getting that close to her isn't safe for her. Not yet, with Rossi's guys still actively looking for us.

Wes found Dimitri's picture circulating in the hitman-for-hire part of the web yesterday. He got it down within a couple of minutes, but plenty of people in those circles know us, and it's honestly a toss-up whether they'd work with us or against us. Even with the gentleman's agreement among hitmen not to shit where you eat, having someone sell your info can often be worse than if they'd just taken the job. Good thing our real identities are so buried.

I check my watch. She'll be at the movies for a few hours, so I'm going to take this opportunity to regroup. It's time to report in for my actual job and take care of some personal stuff.

I climb into the nondescript rental car—dark blue Toyota Corolla, small for me, but just old enough to evade notice—and navigate the roads that have gotten slippery as the daily highs have hovered around 28°F. The city gets worse as I drive, with more and more condemned row-homes and potholes, until suddenly the landscape opens up. Businesses become only one story and have parking lots. Trees line the sides of the road. Large chain superstores become the tallest things around. The abrupt change from poorest-part-of-town to suburbs is almost jarring.

A few more minutes, and I'm turning onto roads that have names like Wisteria Drive and Normandy Lane. Houses space further apart, yards widen, fences go up. I keep driving. Soon, the houses disappear altogether behind long, curving driveways flanked by young trees and walls of evergreen hedges for privacy. Our rental is the last house at the top of a cul-de-sac.

I punch my code into the keypad on the pillar and press my thumb to the print scanner Wes installed. The gate slowly swings outwards towards me. It's part of a 12-foot wrought-iron fence that encircles the entire property, in the middle of which the mega-mansion sits.

That thing is a monstrosity of stone, glass, and wood—four floors with an elevator, 10 bedrooms, 16 bathrooms, full gym with steam bath/sauna and hot tub, mini movie theater with a projector and recliners, chef's kitchen, sunroom full of plants, two-story library with a grand piano, game room... Whoever built it gave themselves no reason to ever leave.

I like a big house, but I'd never even think of doing all this with my money. And I'll admit that it's well designed, but loudly decorated. The people who live here clearly like to surround themselves with things that remind them of just how much money they have. I think I remember Wes saying they're "wintering" in the Caymans.

I set down my bag at the base of one of the sets of stairs that flanks the foyer. I never got the two staircases thing—is one for going up and one for going down?

I head for the kitchen because I'm starved. Wes is sitting at the glass table against the wall of windows with his laptop and an energy drink. He doesn't look up when I enter the room, just continues moving his fingers across the keys almost faster than I can track. "Hey," he greets distractedly.

"Hey, Wes," I say, going to the fridge. It's cavernous, but far from empty. The only trouble is, almost everything in here needs to be cooked to be edible, and I don't have that kind of patience. I peruse the shelves and pull out someone's leftovers. "This yours?"

He doesn't answer, so I peel back the lid and give it a sniff, and it makes me wish I had any other option. But I don't, so I eat the soggy broccoli and unseasoned chicken cold, just to fill the void. Then I move to the coffee machine so I can wash it down.

"What are you doing here?"

I don't need to turn around to know exactly whose angry Russian voice that is. But I do, because I'm not afraid of his ire. "I needed a workout and a change of clothes."

I also need a cup of coffee from this ridiculous Italian machine. I'd knocked it, then I'd tried it. And even though Wes had to translate and then print instructions for us, I don't even care. Hotel coffee tastes like dishwater, and this thing makes real espresso.

Dimitri's frown hardly ever wavers, but it deepens now as he eyes the mug in my hand. The Bear was his code name when I first met him, and it's damn fitting. His size alone would be intimidating enough—topping out at about 6'8" in boots, bulky muscles, long limbs—but add the scar that curls back from his forehead and through his short buzzed black hair, and the icy blue of his eyes that mirrors the coldness in the expression he always wears... he's one hell of a war machine.

But he's not infallible. He crosses his arms over his barrel chest, bringing my attention to the bullet wound near his shoulder—the gauze is gone, so it must be healing well.

"No, you need to fix this situation and find out where they are moving the guns."

"Relax," I say, bringing up a map on my phone. I send the pin to our secure group chat, then re-pocket it. "That's the new place. They moved it quickly."

The new storage location is a literal storage unit. It's past where I can see from my hotel room, on the other side of the city, so I've been away from my room with a view more than I like. But I did my due diligence and surveilled long enough to confirm that it's definitely where they moved it all.

"And it's not going to stay there very long," Wes adds. He jerks his head to the side, cracking his neck and giving us a flash of the ink below his neckline, then pushes his laptop forward and drains the rest of the can next to him. "He got nervous, sold the whole thing for half."

"Half?" Dimitri repeats, nonplussed.

Wes's eyes cut to the left, thinking. "57% of the original asking price."

I whistle. Both at the human calculator and his calculations. "He got really nervous. One buyer?"

Wes nods, then pushes away from the table to make his way to the fridge. He grabs another energy drink.

"Do we know when is pickup?" Dimitri asks. His grammar always slips when he's deep in problem-solving mode.

"Not yet. I've got my spiders on it, so we should know when they set up the details."

I smirk. Wesley's spiders. Spiders. On the web. Internet folk that he trades with in expertise and secrets. He scoffed when I told him he should call them spy-ders, since they're basically sending him intel acquired through dubious means. He said adding a second layer to a pun is overkill.

"Who's the lucky buyer that got the deal of the century?"

Wes shrugs. "Haven't pulled to the end of that thread yet; I'll let you know when I get through the chain of encryptions and dummy accounts."

Dimitri nods, then turns to me. "James, stay on the new location. I want to know who goes in and out, when, what kind of security measures, any movements—"

"The usual," I nod. Normally it chafes at me a little when he acts like he's our commander. But he's injured, his cover is blown, and he's clearly antsy about not being out there. Plus, there's a kind of unspoken agreement between us that Big D calls the shots when he's the one sticking his neck out there.

He sighs, a pained look crossing his face. "I will assist Wesley in monitoring the audio feeds."

"Cheer up, mate!" Wes says cheerily, slapping Dimitri on his good shoulder as he passes by him to settle back down in front of his laptop. "Just think of all the things we'll get to hear people do when they think they're alone."

"It is so boring. All they do is talk to themselves and pass gas," Dimitri grimaces, not even a hint of a smile in spite of the fact that—as we all know—farts are funny. He glances back at me. "You are managing alone?"

"Don't worry about me, I've got a room at the Ritz," I say, using her joke.

Wes snorts.

"And what about the girl?"

I tense. "What girl." It comes out as more of a warning than a question.

Wes's eyebrows shoot up, but Dimitri just forges on right past it. "The one you allowed to compromise our mission, obviously. Has that loose end been tied?"

"I've got it under control."

Dimitri slams both palms onto the counter and growls, "That had better not mean what I think it means. Are you saying she is still alive?!"

"What was I supposed to do? Shoot her?"

"As you have done many times in the past? Yes."

I take a sip of my coffee to appear offhand, but inside I'm fuming. No one will be touching a single hair on her head. "She's not going to be a problem. Believe me."

A stream of angry Russian pours out of Dimitri's mouth, and Wes and I exchange a look. He understands more than I do, but we both understand more than Dimitri thinks. I try not to let on, but it gets hard not to smile at the insult that literally translates to "goat testicles." Russians are so creative.

He switches to English so seamlessly, I almost don't catch it at first. "You try my patience, James."

"How about a little of that trust you're so big on? I say I've got it, and I do. Stop worrying, *babushka*."

He sighs through his nose, glares at me one more time, and crosses the room to exit the kitchen through the double doors out into the cold. Steam rolls off him in coiling waves as he walks around the in-ground pool and disappears into the vast yard.

"I like how literally he takes the phrase chill out," I smirk. Wes makes a noise of agreement, but something about it has me looking over. He's staring. "What?"

"You know I can see when you activate one of my devices, right?" Wes says, those intelligent eyes gleaming with knowing amusement and curiosity.

"Fuck off," I say without any heat.

"Who'd you bug?"

I try not to glower at him. Dimitri doesn't care so much about details until he feels like he has to get involved—he's Mr. Big Picture—but that's not Wes. Everything is a puzzle to him.

And he's too close to the truth—he knows which building I was in, which side I was facing, and that I always go to the top if I can. From there, it's an easy process of elimination to know which apartment. He'll know everything there is to know about her in about an hour. But maybe I can convince him that my reasons are something other than the sordid truth. If it's just the job, maybe he won't dig.

"Well, I let her go. I had to be sure she wouldn't talk."

He blinks. "You sure that's all it is?"

"Gotta say, I'm getting real fuckin' tired of being second-guessed. Just let me do my thing, yeah?"

He lifts his palms. "Fine. Just making sure you know what you're doing."

Too smart for his own damn good. I huff a significantly less dramatic breath than Dimitri did before his exit, and start for the gym. "Come down if you feel like it. I'm going to lift heavy today; I could use a spot."

"Didn't you just finish saying you don't need anyone watching your back?"

"English prick. Shut up and put on some sweats."

A workout, a shower, a change of clothes and I'm a new man. Wes doesn't push me again about Eleanor, and I don't even see Dimitri before I leave.

On my way back downtown, I make a detour—Petra's Petals.

The building is so small; I feel like I should duck when I'm standing inside. It's bursting at the seams with greenery and smells so much it nearly gives me a headache. I walk up to the counter, where a girl with bright green hair and a nose ring is sitting with her booted feet up on the counter, reading a gossip magazine.

When she doesn't look up, in spite of my substantial presence in front of her, I clear my throat. "I'd like to set up a weekly delivery."

She glances up, does a double take, then almost falls out of her chair in her haste to drop her feet to the floor and stand. She preens, thinking she's being subtle—running her hands through her hair and giving it a little fluff in the back, throwing her shoulders back so the deep V of her shirt shows what she's got, chewing on her bottom lip to give it some color. Sure, in another life I'd have been drawn to her plentiful curves and interesting features. Adornments like green hair and a nose ring have historically promised wild sex and a limited interest in attachments.

"How can I help you?" she purrs. I can see the sexual interest in her eyes.

Shit. I shouldn't have come in. She's attracted to me, so she'll remember me. Time to pivot. "My boss would like to set up a weekly bouquet delivery," I amend, irritated. "Something big and bright, but with flowers that don't smell. I was told I couldn't do it over the phone."

Recognition flashes across her face. "Right, you're the guy who called," she breathes, running a hand subconsciously across her chest, letting it settle in the center, gripping her necklace.

Shit, shit. She's the one I talked to on the phone last time. I hold out the prepaid gift card, totally untraceable, and try to seem like I'm in a hurry, using a clipped tone and tapping the plastic against the counter. I can't be rude; that would make me even more memorable. Plus, it's not her fault—I'm not obviously taken, or wearing a ring. Still, her flirting exasperates me.

"Same address and same delivery company as before, please. Here's the card."

She takes it, brushing her fingers against mine very intentionally, and smiles coyly at me. "No other preferences..." her eyes rake down my body, "for the flowers?"

"As long as they don't smell and it looks good, dealer's choice."

As she smiles, the pink tip of her tongue pokes out to swipe across her bottom lip. She bends down and pulls out an order form from the shelf underneath the counter. "That's awesome. We love having creative freedom like that. Fill this out," she says, turning the paper around to me.

I sigh and glance down at the paper. It has too many questions; I need to be in and out. "No, thanks. Just send as many bouquets as the card will pay for, and give yourselves a 20% tip. No note. My boss doesn't want his name on it."

She wavers, the seductress act falling to the wayside as she remembers what she should be doing. She turns the paper back to face her and picks up the pen. "Uh... what about delivery timing?"

"Sundays, doesn't matter when."

"Okay. Wrapped in paper, standard size? Same as last time?"

"Yup. I really have to get going. Is that everything?"

She sighs, like she's mourning the loss of the only interesting thing that's happened to her today. "Yeah. I'll fill this out for you. Thanks for your business; have a nice day."

I book it out of there and shake my head as I get back into the sedan. In another time, I would have eaten up her aggression and obvious flirtations. Now, I place one earbud in, sync it up to the feed in Eleanor's apartment, and listen to my girl milling about as I navigate to the storage facility. I feel a deep satisfaction knowing she's safe at home, even if I don't have eyes on her.

It takes a certain kind of person not to go totally fucking batshit while doing surveillance. Nothing happens for 90% of it, but if you miss that 10% you've totally wasted your time. It's somehow both high-stakes and boring. But I think I've cracked the code for how to stay awake, and it's listening to Eleanor's private life like it's the best fucking podcast I've ever heard.

She has that prick Harrison over for dinner, and I nearly snap the binoculars in my hand. Why does he get to eat her food and enjoy her company? Why is he so special?

After some small talk and friendly banter that better fucking not be flirting, they get into meatier topics. *"I don't think I can live here anymore,"* she says softly.

"Really?" the douchebag asks, mouth full of something. *"Where else would you go?"*

I hear a fork scraping ceramic, and I can picture her pushing her food around on her plate. *"I don't know. I guess I was thinking maybe I'd rent a U-Haul and go stay with my sister and figure it out."*

"Whoa," he says, and I have to agree. I know her sister lives in Pittsburgh, and that's way too fucking far. *"That's not just, 'I think I'll move out of this shitty building,' that's another city. That's a huge change."*

"Yeah, I don't know..." she inhales. *"Maybe it's time for a change."*

There's a heavy pause, and when Harrison speaks again, it's in a soft tone. *"Maybe? Um, Ellie, it doesn't really sound like you have a plan, and that's not like you. Did something happen at work, or... with that guy?"*

I perk up at the mention of me.

"No, he's... things with him are c-complicated. And work is... okay. I do feel like I'm not really getting anywhere there, though."

"Why?"

"Oh, just Chef Robert has really been riding my ass, and I'm starting to wonder why I'm putting all this time in somewhere I don't think I want to be long term."

Chef Robert is about to get a fucking black eye.

"You don't?" Harrison asks, his mouth full again. He sounds distracted, and it's pissing me off. He gets the dinner I wish I had, with the company I'd kill for, and he's not even fucking paying attention?

"I don't know. I've been thinking about trying again with the business plan. I've got more experience now, so maybe people will—"

Movement catches my eye, and I have to zero in my focus, even though it kills me not to really hear the rest of that sentence. She has a business plan. A dream. I want to know about it.

A man in a leather jacket approaches the storage unit, making a beeline for the guy who's sitting by the door on a cheap wooden chair, playing on his phone. He stands when he sees his relief for sentry duty. They grab hands and turn it into a quick, clap-on-the-back type of hug, and chat for a moment. I don't know what they're saying because I don't read lips, but I imagine it's some variation of the small talk we all make with coworkers, if more bad-guy adjacent. Then, the guy in the leather jacket takes the chair, and the other guy heads for the parking lot.

I lean over to record the time of the changing of the guard on the paper in my passenger seat and take a few photos of the new guy's face.

"—well, can't you do that here?" Harrison's asking as I tune back in.

"I guess I don't really feel that safe here anymore," she admits.

That catches my interest, and I can't help but wonder if I have anything to do with it.

"Not because of that guy, or anything, right?"

For the first time, I'm kind of coming around to this douchebag. At least he asks the right questions—the ones *I* want him to.

"No, not because of him." Her tone is so firm, it relieves any lingering doubts. *"It's... um... the city. There's just so much crime,"* she hurriedly adds.

Even if I didn't know it already, this wouldn't sound like the truth to me.

My fingers tighten around the binoculars as hot anger solidifies in my chest. I feel the intense need to let off some aggression, only made worse by the helplessness in not knowing where to direct it.

What's got my girl feeling scared?

11

ELEANOR

Do you have any idea how hard it's been to get you somewhere alone?

I love a 30-day trial period. I always put a note in my phone as soon as I sign up so I remember to cancel before they start charging me some ungodly sum every month. Because this gym? With the cardio equipment that automatically links to your phone, a full-sized pool on the roof and a sauna/steam bath in the locker rooms in the basement? My salary could never.

"And towels go here when you're done with them," the tall, tan, toned blond man says, pointing to a discreet corner structure that has *Used Towels* embossed on the front and a circular hole for easy deposits. He sighs for the fourth or fifth time on our tour, and I get the feeling he couldn't care less if I lived or died.

"Cool, thanks," I say. "Um, I think I can find my way around now, if you want to—"

"Okay, cool." Without another glance in my direction, he strides away. His long legs eat up the rubber flooring, and he disappears through the glass double doors with the gym logo shown in reverse from the back.

And just like that, I'm on my own in the equipment room. It's vast, lined totally in mirrors, and there's a handful of people who look completely focused, like they know exactly what they're doing. The air is filled with the clinking sound of weights hitting weights. A woman walks by, and her eyes briefly scan me.

I want to believe it's to approve of my gym attire, but I know differently, because my set doesn't match like her gorgeous olive-green crop top and leggings. I've got on the bike shorts I wear under every dress and an oversized t-shirt with those weird, small, inexplicable holes that always seem to form on the stomach of my soft shirts. I look down at my shorts and tug them lower on my thighs.

Objectively, I know that people aren't paying attention to me. I know the judgment I think I'm seeing is in my head. I know that no one in the middle of their workout is stopping to wonder who the overweight girl thinks she's fooling. Everyone is way more involved in what they're doing to really notice what anyone else is. Still, I feel gauche and awkward with my free membership in this fancy gym with these people who look like they belong here.

They gave me a locker as part of my temporary membership, and I've already deposited my coat and gym bag. I'm dressed for it and have my water bottle, so there's nothing keeping me from starting my workout except me. So, I head to the treadmills and choose one. It doesn't take long for the endorphins to kick in, and I get into the rhythm of the first workout playlist that Spotify suggests.

When I'm done, I debate taking a shower. They looked so cool during the tour with rainfall heads, but I didn't bring one of my bath sheet towels, and their towels look small. I really hate the feeling of sweat drying on my skin, though, so maybe I can just double up. And I do want to sit in the steam room for a minute; I've never been in one before.

As I descend the main staircase into the first-floor area, I stare at my phone screen. I open a blank new text chat with Grandpa, but like they have so many times this week, my fingers just hover over the screen in uncertainty. I type things, and I delete them. What do you say to the man stalking you?

Hi. So basic. Boring.

Watched anything good lately? What, am I trying to be funny with that?!

I have more questions. Kind of demanding. Would he even want to answer them?

Why am I even considering initiating a conversation?

Because he put the ball in my court. He told me the next move was mine, and I... I want to see him again.

I reach the bottom stair, pause, and type out:

> Thanks for the flowers.

Another bouquet was delivered this morning, even though the other one is still alive. This one has different flowers entirely, but they're still fragrance free. I'm starting to think people are making up the sniffing thing they do—

Someone clips my shoulder from behind, jolting me forward. I catch myself with one hand on the railing and clutch my phone against my chest with the other so it doesn't go flying.

"Sorry!" the girl calls over her shoulder as she makes her way towards the exit.

I look after her, waving to show no harm—okay, she's not even look-ing—and my eye catches on a large man at the check-in desk. It's that detective who was at my door... Detective O'Irish-Sounding? O'Malley, maybe? My heart lurches. What is he doing here? Following me?!

Calm down, Eleanor. I do occasionally run into people I recognize. We live in the same city, and it's not that big of a place. I'm being paranoid. I'm sure a detective can afford to come to a gym like this. He's allowed to go to the same gym as me, just like my gynecologist is allowed to go to the same farmer's market.

Yeah, but my gynecologist can't arrest me for lying to the police.

I decide to give him a wide berth, made easier as he strides away from the desk, off in the opposite direction from where I'm standing. He's not really dressed for the gym, still wearing fancy loafers and a leather jacket, so he sticks out among the gym shorts and tee shirts. But so do most people on their way in. He's probably headed to the men's locker room to change.

I glance back down at the phone screen, and my stomach drops. Oh, no. Oh no, oh no.

The text sent.

This is bad. Is this bad? I did want to reach out; it's like the universe just decided for me. But now that it's out there, the single message on an otherwise blank screen feels desperate and a little pathetic.

What good can come of this? What am I even trying to do here? He's a killer.

A killer who sends me flowers. A killer who—in spite of myself—I'm so curious about, I can't stand it. Maybe he has reasons, something explainable. I want to let him fill in the blanks, let him confirm or correct what I think I know.

I turn the corner on the stairs to finish the half-flight that leads down to the sub-1st floor area with the locker rooms. The men's room is at one end of a narrow hall; the women's on the other. The whole area is blissfully empty, likely because it's a Sunday evening. Most people are at home, spending time with their families and/or getting ready for a long work week ahead of them. But my next day off fell on a Monday this week, so for the first time in a long time, I have two days off in a row, and this feels like the start of my weekend.

Is it normal behavior to take your phone—which is no longer watertight due to an unfortunate incident with gravity and the stairs in my building—into the shower and then also the room full of steam? Especially because if he texts, even though I'll read it immediately, I'm going to make myself wait to reply anyway so I can seem cool and aloof?

Probably not. But I do it anyway.

I wait until the coast is clear to step out of the shower, wrapped in the two overlapping towels, and hurry over to the steam room. It's pretty dark inside with only the one overhead bulb, and the little bit of light scatters from all the water in the air. There's a bench that makes a U shape, hugging the walls opposite the frosted glass door entrance.

I choose the seat in one of the far corners, reveling in the solitude. There's a loud background sound from the spigot intermittently dispensing steam, but otherwise it's kind of peaceful. It's so private. I can't see much further than my outstretched hand in front of me in the misty air. I think people normally sit in here nude.

My phone buzzes. My heart flutters, and I grin like an idiot down at the name flashing across the top. I swipe across the screen and just as I'm about to lift it to my ear, I hear, "Do you have any idea how hard it's been to get you somewhere alone?"

My eyes fly open at the voice. That deep, gravelly tone echoing around me off the tile is instantly recognizable, since I literally just saw him. But I can't really see him now through the steam, except as a vague, dark shape. My heart starts hammering.

"D-detective O'Malley? What—this is the women's room! You can't be in here!" I clutch the towel around my chest and snap my knees together. This feels bad, ominous, and being nearly naked seems like a distinct disadvantage. I glance down at my phone and debate hanging up on Mac to call... who, 911?

"Jesus, you are a creature of habit, ain't ya? You go to work, you go home, same way every time. Public, well-lit route. You probably got pepper spray in that bag you hold so tight, too, huh? If you were a slightly more interesting person, I wouldn't have had to create my own opportunity to talk to you."

"What?" I ask. The air is hot and wet in a way that feels like I should be able to blink away some of the blurriness, but that's not the case. My head feels thick with it. "I'm confused. Um, do you have more questions for me? Did you try reaching me at home?"

"Security cameras already caught me there once."

My stomach sinks. He's not a detective. There's no way even the worst kind of police-brutality offender would try to avoid security cameras and corner a woman, naked and alone. I look back down at my phone screen. The call is active, though I haven't heard him speak. My instinct is to hide it from O'Malley—if that's even his name—because it feels like my last lifeline. I slowly lower the phone to the bench next to me, face down.

"Why wouldn't you want anyone to know—"

I stop mid-sentence with a gasp and try to back up as far as I can as the guy steps close enough for me to see him through the steam. He's fully clothed, and his handsome face is covered in sweat. Oh, and he's got a gun pointed at my chest.

My hands shoot up instantly as fear spikes through me, making them tremble. I'm trapped. He stands between me and the only door and—though it's probably about six feet wide—the room feels too narrow for me to try to get around him.

"Oh my God," I cry, hearing the terror in my tone.

"If you scream, I'll shoot you. Got it?"

Definitely not a cop. My stomach lurches, and I'm sure I'm going to throw up. "S-someone will come in—"

He shakes his head, a slow, nasty smile curving his lips. "Everyone's evacuating. Didn't you hear the fire alarm going off?" His taunting tone makes it clear he was responsible. "Oh, that's right. I cut the line down here."

I'm finding it very hard to look away from the black hole staring me down. I'd never seen a real gun in person up until a little while ago, and now I've seen two. This is the first one that's ever been pointed at me, though, and the panic that's welling in my chest is also clouding my mind. My body isn't accustomed to this kind of rush of adrenaline, and it's making my muscles feel all weird, like jelly. "W-what's—"

"What happens next is up to you. You can either tell me what you know, or I'll be escorting you out the emergency exit into the van waiting for us and we'll go somewhere a lot more private for this chat. I can think of a few ways we can make you talk..." his eyes fall meaningfully down my body, resting on the bare skin of my chest and arms, then legs.

My breath stutters out. The threat of a second location, and whatever he's implying they'll do to me there, is almost more terrifying than the gun. I try not to look down at my phone, not wanting to draw attention to it, but I wonder if Mac is still there. If he's listening. I know it's a long shot... who knows where he is right now? And how could he know where I am?

"Is this about the guy in the picture? I swear, I don't know anything about him!"

"Yeah, but you know something."

I curse myself for being the world's worst liar. I fan myself a little. "God, it's so hot in here..." I breathe.

"Listen, lady. Rossi doesn't fuck around, okay? So, you can either play nice or you'll go down with that Russian fucker when we find him. Because we're going to find him."

"Rossi?" I repeat, baffled. "Like, Jay Rossi?"

"Are you fucking stupid or something?"

There's a rush of cool air, which blows the steam around just enough for me to see the outline of another large person entering the room. O'Malley jerks his head around and manages to get out, "What—" before something wraps around his neck from behind.

In horror, I watch as the thug brings up both hands, clutching the thin line of what looks like wire around his throat with one and turning the weapon upside down to point it behind him with the other.

"Gun!" I shriek.

It's wrenched out of O'Malley's hand, and I hear it clatter to the ground a second later. He's struggling wildly, all jabbing elbows and twisting limbs. The sounds of male grunts of effort and pain cut through the noisy steam spigot, filling the echoing space. Their collective mass goes careening forward, and, running purely on instinct, I dive for the opposite corner of the room to keep out of the way.

I spy the gun through the steam and make a grab for it, just as the wood of the bench cracks and splinters under the weight of whatever fell onto it. My fingers close around the cool handle, and I whirl, just in time to watch O'Malley's eyes close in his beet-red face, and his whole body go limp.

With a forceful grunt, the man underneath O'Malley pushes him off, and his body rolls away.

Of course it's Mac.

"Are you okay?" he asks, getting to his feet with some effort, holding his arm like it's injured. Blood is dripping out of his nose.

Then his eyes drop. And I realize that my towel is gone.

It's like I'm completely frozen and time slows. His eyes widen, then follow a zigzagging path down my body, then up, stopping midway.

"Eleanor," he says, his tone cautious and tight, "hand me the gun."

It's only then that I realize I'm shaking, and I have the gun pointed right at him.

12

MAC

Is it sick that part of me thrills that she's got no other options now?

"Hand me the gun, darlin'," I say again, even gentler this time. I can see that she's shaking from here, and I'm concerned that, for someone who's never really dealt with shock before, it might feel disorienting enough to make her unpredictable. "Or, at least point it somewhere else, yeah?"

"It's heavier than I thought it would be," she says softly, looking down at her hand like she doesn't recognize it. She shakes her head, like she's snapping herself out of it, and extends her arm towards me, palm up.

"Good girl." I breathe out my relief. I wipe her fingerprints away with the bottom of my shirt, just in case. Then, I engage the safety, and tuck it in my waistband so my shirt covers it.

"H-how did you..." she inhales shakily.

"There will be time for questions later," I say. "Are you hurt?"

I scan her body, telling myself it's just to check for injuries, which is a lie. Because she's really, gloriously, goddamn naked. I try to tear my gaze away, but it's hard when every soft, pale, dimpled inch of her is on display in front of me like a fucking buffet for the eyes. I should be a gentleman and get her a towel, but I'm an asshole, so I don't.

I want to memorize it. I've spent so long admiring the small, faraway version of her through my scope that this doesn't feel real, and all I want to do is touch her to make sure it is.

But when she says nothing, I look up and see that she's fixed on the body on the ground, her eyes welling with tears. "Don't look at him. Eyes on me, darlin'." I point with two fingers. "Right here."

Gratifyingly, she does as I say, but starts shivering. As if suddenly realizing just how naked she is, she folds into herself, crossing one leg in front of the other and her arms over her chest; and I finally feel like enough of a schmuck to stop staring and help her out.

I find her towel on the ground near the body. I bend over to scoop it up, ignoring the pain in my side, and drop to one knee in front of her as she sits on the bench. Trying to ignore the feeling of rightness that settles deep in my belly, that she's nude and I'm on my knees in front of her, I drape the towel over her shoulders and grip her upper arms. "Eleanor, I need you to calm down. Breathe. Can you do that for me?"

She nods, not meeting my eye. A deep inhale, a long exhale. A tear falls down her cheek, and I reach up to wipe it away with the tips of my fingers. She flinches a little at the touch.

Rage wells in my chest. I wish I'd had the time to kill him slowly for scaring my girl.

"He's dead, isn't he?" she asks after another two measured breaths.

"Yes." Shit. If she starts freaking out on me—

"You saved me," she whispers. "Thank you."

Well, I wasn't expecting that, but I'll have to bask in the satisfaction later. I'm getting too distracted by her as it is, and we don't have much time.

Fuck. How do I get us out of this one? Thankfully, the gun didn't go off, and strangulation is a relatively clean way to die, but it's only 8 PM. The world is still plenty awake, though it's as dark as midnight in the early night of winter. But people are going to start returning into the building any minute. I need to get him out of here. I need to get *her* out of here.

"Where are your clothes? You need to get dressed. We've gotta get out of here before anyone gets back."

"But..." she begins, flicking her gaze back behind me. "We can't just leave him—"

"Let me worry about it. Go get dressed. Quick as you can. Then I'll figure out how to get us out of here."

Before she stands, she pulls the towel off her shoulders and holds it in front of her body. *Sure, you can be shy now,* I want to tell her. At least I've got that mental image burned into my brain to use later.

I rise from my knees and turn to my problem. I hear her exit the steam room and the wet plopping noises of her feet on the tile floor as she hurries to wherever she stashed her bag.

I sigh and look back down at the body. Even if I didn't have a dislocated shoulder, a bruised rib and a kidney contusion, this guy is probably 250-260. I could do it, but I wouldn't make it look easy. And there's no way I can leave him here. My prints are all over, her prints are all over, and I clocked at least four cameras in public spaces on my way in. I know I didn't avoid them all completely in my rush.

Fuck.

Well, there's nothing for it but to try. I take care of the dislocated shoulder first. Luckily, it's my left again, so relocating it is a matter of some pressure in the right place and bracing myself for the pop. It isn't a bad one, where the arm is completely out of the joint, so the pain is minimal.

After a quick check of his pockets yields a wallet, phone, another hidden gun and a fake detective badge, I get him sitting up. His dead weight is substantial, but manageable at least that far. The only way I'll be able to do this is to get him over my shoulder, but it's going to be really fucking hard to play that one off to the spectators. I'll have to give Eleanor an excuse to tell anyone who sees us. And I'm also concerned about the van he claimed was waiting at the emergency exit. He was probably bluffing, but in my hurry, I didn't check.

"Mac?"

I turn around at the tentative voice. She's got her shirt and shorts on—no bra, and I'd wager no panties either—and her feet have been shoved sockless into some sneakers. "Yeah, baby?" the endearment slips out, but she's too shell-shocked to notice or care.

She looks down at the key around her wrist on one of those coil cord keychains. "How long... um, does it take for a... dead... p-person to start smelling?"

"Depends on the weather conditions, but usually a few days. Why?"

She throws a look over her shoulder. "Think he'd fit in one of these lockers?"

The sly little minx. She's quick on her feet; I'll give her that. It's perfect. I'll call Felix as soon as we're out of here—I know he operates in the area—and his crew can come clean up once the gym closes for the day. "Good idea. See if there's any kind of 'out of order' sign and put it up on the door. Should buy us some time if we run out." I busted through the lock to get in, so that's not an option anymore.

She scurries off to do as I ask, and I grab both his ankles. Dragging is so much easier than carrying. I feel her stare like a physical touch as she watches me pull the body across the floor. She holds the locker open for me as I get him upright inside. It's a tight fit, but I'm not too worried about his comfort.

Once I get him closed in, she steps into the space between me and the metal door to get it locked. I lean down just close enough to get a deep whiff of her hair. The scent of other people's sweat and chlorine in this locker room isn't enough to overpower the sweetness of her. She pulls back, brushing against the entire front of me, and I nearly groan at the contact. Just as she would pull away, I grip her shoulders and keep her pressed to me.

It helps to soothe the part of me that's still so full of white-hot rage at that motherfucker who thought he could threaten—thought he could even fucking *look at*—what's mine. When I think about how much skin she was showing, and how his eyes were on her... I should take them with me as a trophy.

But we don't have time.

I lean down so I can murmur into her ear, if for no other reason than it means I can keep her close a second longer. "Take another deep breath, darlin'. I need you to be ready to walk out of here, looking like nothing's wrong. Can you do that?"

I hear her loud exhale, feel some of the tension leach out of her body. She nods. "I think so."

"Good girl." She shivers against me, and I really, really hope it's because she liked what I said and not because she's going into shock.

But she looks okay for the most part, hair a little mussed and eyes kind of wild with the adrenaline. She winces a little when she looks at my face, then darts away before I can say anything. When she returns, she's got a wet paper towel. "Your nose," she says, handing it to me.

Another point to Eleanor.

I wipe the blood off my upper lip, and when she nods in approval, I pocket the towel with my DNA and I tug her behind me as I ease open the door. The buzzing of the fire alarm has stopped, and I hear voices above us. Relief washes over me—they just started letting people back in. We slip into the hall.

She's power-walking, and her head keeps whipping side to side like she's keeping watch for someone about to jump out or spot us. It's nice, but my carefully honed senses will do just fine for us, and she looks really goddamn conspicuous.

When she starts yanking on her jacket, I grab onto her hand to stop her before she can start climbing the stairs. Her eyes go wide in surprise as I pull her into my side so I can lean close and mutter, "You need to be better about hiding things with your face. Now, smile at me like I just said something sweet and play along."

There's an instant when I pull away where I can read her face like an open book, and what I see is as humbling as it is arousing. Desire, wariness, trust, concern, fear, resolve...

"You're being so brave, Eleanor," I murmur, swiping across the top of her hand with my thumb.

She smiles, and even though I know I just told her to, it really feels genuine. I pull her against me, drape my arm over her shoulders, step up, and say, "I'm thinking pizza tonight if you don't feel like cooking."

She matches my pace, but falters for an instant at the unexpected topic. "Oh. Yeah, pizza would be fine."

"And I think there's another episode of that show you were telling me about."

I tighten my arm around her as I feel her instinct to walk faster as we reach the top stair and people's heads turn in our direction. "Uh... that cooking show? The competition one?"

I want to laugh, because I did put her on the spot, so I shouldn't be surprised that's what she came up with, but I just grin. "I'll agree to it on one condition."

"Yeah?"

I can see the front desk in my periphery, and the people just getting back to work aren't paying us any mind. "That we watch all the Mission Impossible movies this weekend, even the new one."

The face she makes in response is genuine. "What? Are you serious?"

I laugh and push against the handle, biting back a noise as the weight of the door against my recently dislocated shoulder sends hot pain down my arm. I step to the side so she can go ahead of me, and take her bag as she passes. I swing it over my shoulder and reach ahead of her to open the second set of glass doors.

The cold air bites into any exposed skin that's still clammy from the warm, wet locker room, and it feels like pure freedom. I hear Eleanor fill her lungs with the same emotion. The lights are on in the lot, casting large circles of safety at regular intervals. It's nearly empty, though, and clearing out. The only movement I see is a woman getting into her car in the second row, and another car turning out of the lot.

When she starts heading to the left, I grab her hand and pull her back towards me. "Nope. This way; I'm at the back of the lot."

"But I live—"

I lower my voice, just in case. The last thing I need is someone seeing and overhearing some massive dude kidnapping a struggling woman in the gym parking lot in the dark. "You're coming with me, darlin'."

"What? Why?"

I glance at her with a raised brow. Why? She can't be serious. Like I'd let her go home. Like I'm ever fucking letting her out of my sight again. "He wasn't really a cop."

"Yeah, no shit!"

"He knew where you live and he was following you, which means they know you're involved, so you're not safe. You need to come with me," I say slowly, and watch as the understanding settles across her face. It spreads into dread and fear a second later, and she nods urgently at me.

Is it sick that part of me thrills that she's got no other options now? That she's finally forced to submit to the inevitability of this—us. Because she'd finally reached out, finally texted me, finally opened that door. But now I get to expedite this.

Because I've been craving her like an addict in need of a fix. Slow and indirect is going, well... it's too damn slow and indirect. I need all of her, as fast as I can get it.

13

MAC

◆◇◆

The casual use of the word "we," like we're in this together

She follows meekly, standing back and watching silently as I toss her bag into the trunk and go around to open the passenger door for her. I don't miss the way she reacts with surprise to the gesture.

When I climb into the driver's seat, I'm gratified to see that she's already buckled in. But she's reaching into her pocket, and I spot the top of the screen as it lights up. "Don't make me take that from you," I warn. "Leave it in your pocket, at least for now, okay?"

She frowns at me, but pushes the phone back where it was and rests her hands on her thighs.

I'm not trying to be a controlling asshole, but until we can talk and she understands what kind of danger she really is in, I need her to find another way to calm that anxiety than scrolling through her phone. It's not that I don't trust her; she just doesn't know what any of this means for her going forward. What she can and can't do.

"What's going on?" she asks, like she's been saving it for a moment alone. "What did you mean 'they know' I'm involved? Who are *they*? What am I involved in?"

"Just give me two minutes, darlin'. I'm going to call someone to take care of that guy, and it'll be better if he doesn't know anything about you. Okay?" I trust Felix, but only the smallest bit further than I can throw him. And that's nowhere near how close I'd let him come to my girl.

She nods, taking the message to keep silent. As I settle into my seat, I pull the dead man's gun from my waistband and lean across her to shove it in the glove compartment. Then, I throw the car into reverse and pull out my phone. As I start for the home base, I speed dial my fixer.

"Mac, my man," Felix greets me, and I can hear the smile in his voice. "How's one of my favorite customers?"

"About to become better."

"All business, huh? Fine by me. Whatchu need, *amigo*?"

"I need a discreet rush on a cold one." I rattle off the address of the gym as we pull onto the main street and start making our way out of the city. I keep Eleanor in my periphery and one eye on the rearview to make sure we're not being followed, which doesn't leave a lot to pay attention to the road. Good thing driving under pressure is one of my skills.

"Ladies locker 28, as of," I check my watch, never trusting the clock on a dash, "11 minutes ago. He's a big fucker, so send guys. And I want the *ojos, comprende*?"

Felix whistles in respect—he has always appreciated a bit of drama, so a request to bring me the eyes of a dead man is right up his alley. "What'd he do to you?"

"Looked at someone he shouldn't have."

"Shiiit. Like, a lady someone?"

Appreciates drama was perhaps too generous. Fucking nosy is more like it.

"Just send me a bill," I grit out through my teeth.

"Can do, *chico*. It's gonna be quite the roll."

"I only pay for the best," I remind him. Felix and his team are quick, quiet and careful. And he's got enough powerful people in his pocket for one hell of a contingency plan. He takes his payments in money or I-O-U's, and the more powerful and well-connected the client, the less physical currency they pay for Felix's services. I prefer cash; I've got plenty, and I'm not a fan of owing favors.

I hang up, then hang a left at the light that indicates we've officially left city limits. The coast is clear—we're not being followed.

"Okay," I tell her. "Here's a CliffsNotes to save us some back and forth. I'll answer whatever you still got after. Sound good?"

She eyes me warily, trying to hide her surprise. "Yeah, okay."

"That man worked for Jacob Rossi, a businessman, landlord—"

"I know who he is," she interrupts.

"—murderer, wife-beater, thief, gun-smuggler and all-around dick," I finish, eyeing her. She swallows audibly. "I—we—were running a mission to take him and most of his guys out before they could sell their most recent shipment of AK-47s, explosives and other automatic weapons."

"So, you're trying to tell me that you're a sniper with a moral code?" she replies, boiling it down to its essence as she inhales shakily and turns to look out the window. "Give me a break."

If anyone else said that, I could easily brush it off. I need her to understand. I need her to believe me... but I also need her to be a little bit afraid so she'll stay vigilant and be careful. "Morality has nothing to do with it, but yeah, they're scum. So, my job was to put him down. But you walked in on me, the mission went sideways, and now Rossi is out for blood. I don't know how they found out about you, but they must have."

"Someone saw the light come on in my apartment that night," she says, and her voice is so small, it hurts.

Of all the piss-poor luck... That light couldn't have been on for more than a minute. I'll have to ask how she knows when it's my turn for questions. But right now, she gets her answers because she's been through a lot and she's taken it all on the chin.

"No matter what that guy said, he was going to kill you—if you'd talked or if you hadn't, it wouldn't have mattered. They were looking for information on, well, me basically. Me and my associates.

"We're bad people, Eleanor. We kill people. We tried to kill him, and we failed. So now Rossi is going to try to kill us. And you're in the middle of it. So, I'm taking you back to my place." I finish with a little sigh. I want to reach out and take her hand, but she lifts them from her lap to cross her arms over her chest.

Her eyes narrow at me. "Nice speech. How do I know that it's not all just a bunch of lies?"

"I won't lie to you. I only did that one time when you thought I was an exterminator."

Her mouth falls open. "That *one* time? That was a... a whole thing! It doesn't count as one lie!"

"Why not?"

She ticks them off as her eyes flash with the kind of vitality I haven't seen since before the sauna. It fires me up, too. "Because the uniform was a lie, the hat was a lie, those glasses were a lie, the words out of your mouth about being an exterminator were a lie. Everything about that interaction was a lie—except, apparently, your name? Which I really cannot fathom."

I can safely assume she heard some of my exchange with Felix, then.

This temper is good. Anger, I can deal with. It's the cold, afraid, timid Eleanor that worries me. "Okay, how about this: I haven't lied since then. And I won't, that's a promise."

She heaves a sigh. Her stare is burning a hole into the side of my face, but I keep my eyes forward. If I turn, I'm not going to be able to stop myself from pulling over. If I pull over, I'm not going to be able to stop myself from touching her. And she probably doesn't want me touching her right now. Not yet.

"How did you know where I was? How did you get here so fast?"

I didn't expect to have to curse my promise not to lie so quickly, but here we are. "I followed you." When she says nothing to that, just sucks her bottom lip into her mouth to chew on it, I continue with the story, "I saw him pull into the lot after you, wait in his car, then go in after you'd been in there a while. I thought he looked familiar. I called to check on you."

"You really did save me," she says, almost as if to herself. "Why?"

Why? She wants to know why? I shake my head a little. "I'm not ready to answer that." It's not technically a lie—*she's* not ready for me to answer that, so I'm not ready for it either.

The truth is, I've decided she's mine to protect. But women don't often take kindly to obsessive, possessive declarations before you've even learned each other's last names.

Her shoulders slump and her hands fall back into her lap. I eye the one closest to me, itching to take it, but I make myself use both hands for my next turn to give them something else to do. "Now, my turn. How did you know that someone saw the light?"

"It's what they said when they came to my door. He was pretending to be a detective."

"They?"

"Um, the guy you just... um... him, and there was an officer there, too. Really Irish name... McCloskey, I think."

I frown. Why hadn't I heard any of it? "They came to your door? When?"

"Um, Thursday. I went to the movies and when I got back, they were standing there"—makes sense, they were outside the apartment, out of range of the bugs—"and asked me if I was home that night and showed me a picture of some guy I didn't know. Said he was a person of interest or something." She winces. "I, ah, don't think I did a very good job lying. I was really freaked out."

"What made you think the other guy was a cop?"

"He was in the full uniform and... I dunno, he sounded really convincing. Had one of those little notepads and used all the lingo I hear on cop dramas. Hey, wait. I just remembered: back in the sauna, that guy said something about how he didn't want to get caught on the security cameras of my building again."

"Yeah?" I ease to a stop at the last light right before I start the maze of back roads through the 'burbs.

"Well, you've been there, right? Should we be worried that someone might have seen you—"

Maybe it's the relief in realizing her concern is solely that I might be in danger of getting caught. Maybe it's the casual use of the word "we," like we're in this together, like we have been since we hid that body in the locker room. Maybe it's that she just looks so damn gorgeous—strong, resilient, earnest—in spite of the fear, and I can't believe I get to have her in front of me, within touching distance like this.

I reach over and cup the back of her neck, pulling her roughly forward to meet my lips halfway. She's stiff at first, stunned, but then she relaxes and melts into me. The contact is a spark, just the start of a fire that runs hot through my veins. Her lips are so fucking soft, so pliable, so warm...

As much as I want to deepen it, I don't. Someone honks behind us. I pull away and notice that the light is green, so I make my turn.

"Listen to me, darlin'. If you're ever approached by the police in the future, I want you to ask for their name and badge number and then get somewhere safe until you can call into the station and verify their information. Worst-case scenario, it'll irritate the hell out of some sheriff trying to get you for speeding, but it may save your life someday. It's too easy to impersonate an officer, and the cops generally make people nervous enough that they usually just cooperate. It's the perfect disguise for one of those guys." And me.

She nods, a silent promise as she looks deep in thought, filing that information away. "Have you ever pretended to be a cop?"

Doesn't miss a beat, does she? "Yes."

I nearly grimace as she starts chewing that lip again, looking thoughtful. This is going to be a long fucking drive.

14

ELEANOR

You saved me; I saved you. We're square.

My hands are practically shaking with the effort not to lift my fingers to my lips, to trace where his just were. The skin tingles. When I wet my lips with my tongue, I can taste him—tangy, salty and a little minty. My stomach is full of fluttering butterflies, and they're all going fucking crazy for Mac.

But now he's sitting there, all cool and calm, like nothing even happened. Like he didn't just kiss me. And then he said that stuff about not trusting the police and asking for badge numbers... was it just to make me stop talking and pay attention? I feel like I have whiplash.

I glance around me as the comfort and security of my apartment feel miles away. I wish I knew where we were going, or how long we'd be there, or if I could go back and get anything. If this is going to be more than a few days, maybe Harrison can—

I gasp, realizing. "Oh my God, do you think Harrison is in danger?"

His hands tighten on the wheel until it makes a little squeaking noise, and his knuckles turn white. His jaw flexes. "What?" he bites out.

I shrink away a little at the aggressive reaction. "You said my apartment wasn't safe, and he lives in the same building and we're friends—"

"He's on the wrong side, so they won't assume he knows anything," he clips.

"Oh, okay." That's a relief.

"Unless they think you're more than friends," he adds, lips thin with displeasure.

"Why would they?"

"Why else is his the first name on your lips after *I* kiss you?"

I start, completely shocked. Was that what that little testosterone show was all about? Whatever beef he's got with Harrison? I almost roll my eyes. "One kiss and you've got some sort of jealous claim on me, huh?"

He smiles, and it's not very kind. It's full of self-satisfaction and male pride. "Like that one kiss didn't leave you hot and bothered. Would you stop me, darlin', if I did it again?"

Of course not. He knows it; I know it. Doesn't make him any less of a dick for pointing it out. I cross my arms.

"That's what I thought," he says, smirking.

It feels like he's making fun of me now, even though I can't really put my finger on why. And it stings more than I'd care to admit. He's not a good guy; he's reminded me of that several times. Why would I think he cares about my emotions?

Because I'm an idiot, that's why. I have this whole made up scenario in my head. It's a fantasy world I created, where he watches me and follows me and sends me gifts because he *likes* me. God, I need a fucking straitjacket. Or a reminder that having these inexplicable feelings for someone I don't know, who's very dangerous, is a terrible idea.

"Why are you here to kill Rossi?"

"I told you; he's going to sell those—"

"No, I mean, why are *you* going to kill him?"

"I kill a lot of people, darlin'. It's what I do. And I get paid a lot of money for it."

I close my eyes. There it is. There's my reality check. "How many people have you killed? Five? Ten?" I demand before I lose my nerve.

"Eleanor—"

"Dozens?"

His face screws up in a look that's half resignation, half cringe.

"More?" I breathe, my lower lip wobbling. What started as an antagonistic line of questioning got real a little too quickly.

"Probably more in the hundreds at this point. I haven't really kept track."

"You don't keep track?!" I squeak out. I'm not really sure why that detail makes the fact that he's killed so many people worse, but it does. Like it's just further proof that human life means nothing to this man. He clearly feels no remorse.

"Yeah, well..." he huffs a sigh and runs a hand through his hair. "One man dying is a tragedy. A hundred is a statistic."

My blood runs cold. "Did you just quote Stalin?"

His eyes cut briefly to me before returning to the road as he turns into a neighborhood, and he actually fucking smirks. "Paraphrased."

Oh God. He is a psychopath. I can't believe I let my little fantasy go so far. I'm such an idiot.

Well, for whatever reason, this psychopath hasn't shown much interest in killing me, so there's that. That means that for right now he's my best bet for surviving whatever situation this is. Because I'm severely out of my element, I'm trusting his guidance. I can't go home. I don't know how to disappear from anyone looking for me. I don't know how to fight off anyone who might attack me...

He eases the car to a stop at an intersection where the homes are bigger than my entire apartment building. "There's one more thing I need to know before we get there, darlin'. Why didn't you go to the police? After I let you go."

I almost snort, angry as I am at myself. "And say what exactly? That a man broke into my apartment, tied me up and I watched as he shot people through my window with a sniper rifle?"

He glances at me from the edge of his vision, and his expression is tense, guarded, but curious. "Exactly that, yeah."

I turn to him full-on and scowl. "Because that is crazy. That sounds crazy. Even if they took me seriously, I had no proof and no real information for them. And I'm not an idiot, Mac. I followed the local news afterwards; I know there's a reason I never heard about a shooting or a murder. Someone covered it up, or the police never even knew about it to begin with. And if it's being covered up and I'm the one who reports it... I don't know, it just seems like a bad idea to be on the bad side of someone who has a sniper after them."

I am trying to convey that while I'm not strictly on his side, I'm also not a threat. It feels right to try to show the psychopath who doesn't blink at murder that you're not a threat. After a few seconds of studying my face, during which I suck in a breath and wait for his reaction, he barks a laugh, and I feel my chest contract.

"If there's one thing I like in a woman, it's a strong sense of self-preservation."

I inhale again, more shakily this time, and look back out the window, trying to focus on anything other than what he's giving me. Because he says I've got a strong sense of self-preservation, but the way I reacted to that kiss... the way I can't help but notice his chest pressing against his shirt—a shirt that is already straining against broad muscles—as he laughs, and the smile curling those lick-able lips, and the sparkle in his brown eyes as he looks at me now...

Yeah, I wouldn't call this level of attraction to a literal murderer something that is in my own best interest.

"And if there's two things... a strong sense of self-preservation and a great ass," he says with a wink, making a little clicking noise with his tongue.

My heart flutters. Is he... does that mean he thinks my ass is great? Or is he trying to fluster me again, throw me off? It's like the second I decide to build some emotional distance, he dials up the charm. It's too coincidental not to be a manipulation.

But, a small voice argues... he stared back in the sauna. It wasn't a quick glance, the surprised, automatic reaction of someone unexpectedly confronted with a full-frontal. It wasn't a mildly-disappointed-yet-still-half-interested look, like a stranger from a dating app taking what they can get for the night. It was a stare with open, fully masculine appreciation.

I just wish I had any clue what to do about it.

"My ass is pretty great," I agree, crossing my arms over my chest.

He inhales noisily through his nose, and I feel his eyes on me, even though I'm not looking. It brings a rush of goosebumps to the surface, and I try to hide the little shiver. "The third thing would be confidence. That's so fucking hot."

At that, I do turn back, suspicious that he's needling me again. "Sounds like I'm just ticking all your boxes then, huh? Too bad nothing about you is on the list of things *I* like in a man."

I'm lying through my teeth, of course. I can literally see four things I like very much from here, and they're called face, hair, body, and sense of style. Not to mention the growly possessiveness that makes my lady bits do a river dance. And, as fucked up as it might be, knowing he's as good with a gun as he is with his hands... well, that doesn't suck for him either.

"Nothing?" he repeats, surprise in his tone. "Not even *my* ass?"

God, how I want to take a bite out of that ass. But I shake my head. "Nope."

"What about the southern charm? The handsome yet rugged smile? The biceps?"

"Kind of outweighed by the murdering and stalking."

His grin is easy, confident. "If I'm just some asshole, why did you protect me back there? You could have run, but you stayed and helped. The locker thing was your idea," he reminds me needlessly.

"Tit for tat. You saved me; I saved you. We're square."

"Oh, darlin', if you think that makes us square, you've got another thing coming."

Well, that's ominous. I rack my brain, trying to think of another time he's saved me. I narrow my eyes at him. "I'm not really sure what else I could possibly owe you for. You're the one who put me in danger, you know."

"We're here."

I turn my head forward and immediately gape, seeing some sort of palace. It's dark, but from the way the fence extends into that darkness I know it just keeps going. The yard is huge, with old hardwood trees partially obscuring the front yard. The house is up-lit with those fancy lights, and so far away from the gate that it almost appears small, but I know that's a trick of the eye. There are too many windows, too much stone and stucco for it to be anything other than massive.

He leans out his side of the car far enough to press his thumb against what must be some kind of fingerprint thingy because it makes the gate in front of us creep slowly open. That security detail feels high-tech and impressive, and for a moment, I actually feel a little safer because of it. Then I remember security keeps things out *and* in.

It occurs to me that he never really said he was bringing me here to keep me safe. It was implied, sure, but the words... Did he ever say the actual words?

The gate closes behind us with a resounding click, and fear worms its way back into my belly.

15

MAC

❦

She's... non-negotiable.

We're square.

She doesn't know the half of it. Not only have I repeatedly put her in danger, listened to her private life, and spied on her without her knowledge, but now I've put a target on her back.

No, we'll never be square. I'll never make it up to her.

Truth be told, I like the idea of being in her debt, almost like it means she has to stick around so I can work on the deficit. And because I'm a real asshole, I also like that she assumed I meant she's in *my* debt. It feels like a power balance I can use to my advantage. It feels like it proves she knows I can protect her.

She's right. Can and will.

I take her bag from the trunk and place my free hand on her lower back to escort her to the front door. Something happened when we passed through the gate—her body language changed. She seems jumpier, and I don't like it, so I want her within easy reach.

"This is your place?" she asks, wonder in her voice as her neck tilts back and she locks eyes on the crystal chandelier hanging between the dual staircases.

I almost wince, seeing the marble floor and gold accents for the first time again through her viewpoint. It's so over-the-top, but I wasn't the decorator. "It's a rental."

"Oh," she says softly. "That's... not better."

"It was the only available short-term rental that wasn't a one-bedroom apartment," comes Wes's dry, amused tone from around the corner. He walks into the entryway, laptop balanced on one forearm, and extends his hand to her without so much as a glance my way. "I'm Wesley."

She takes his hand, and I realize suddenly that I'm on edge—tense about them meeting. Wesley is what girls might consider a bit of a heart-throb, with his British accent and aw-shucks demeanor coupled with a well-honed body. But her eyes only scan him briefly in curiosity, and my hackles lower.

"Mac didn't mention a roommate."

"Then Dimitri will be an even bigger surprise," Wes replies mildly, and I want to throttle him because I'm pretty sure he meant it as a pun. I mean, there's a reason we call him Big D. "May I take your coat?"

It's on the tip of my tongue to stop her, but she's already handing him her things, completely blithe, and leveling a look my way that is adorable, if accusatory. "Two roommates?"

It would take a practiced eye—or knowing him as well as I do—to see Wes pocket her phone as he makes a show of folding the corners of her jacket on a hanger, fluffing it, and placing the hanger delicately in the closet.

"Wonderful to meet you, Eleanor," he says, striding towards one of the studies on this floor where I know he's made his little cave.

"You too... wait, did I tell him my name?" she asks, half to me and half to herself.

I curse inwardly. No, she didn't. Which means that he already knows about her. Which means he probably has known about her since Thursday, when I not-so-successfully threw him off the trail. Fucking Wesley.

I leave her bag at the bottom of the stairs and usher her directly into the kitchen, partly because it's where I normally head when I walk through the door and partly because it's a good neutral spot to leave her while I eat crow and clean up my own mess. Her head bounces around, side to side, trying to take in the grandeur all at once. When we enter the kitchen, she stops dead, eyes locked on the high-end appliances.

"Can I get you anything? A glass of water?"

She hesitates, and I see the inner struggle flitting across her expressive face. "Do you have anything stronger? I did help you hide a body today."

"Um, I've got some beer, and Wesley keeps bottles of champagne—"

"Stronger?"

"Dimitri's got some sort of small-batch, homemade potato vodka."

She blows out a breath and turns watery blue eyes on me. "Think he'd share?" Her voice is thin, and she sniffles after she asks the question.

I balk. I didn't realize how close she was to breaking down. Those damn hackles raise again, and I'm an instant away from declaring how I'll make sure she gets whatever she wants, whenever she wants. "Yeah. Sit over there; let me get you a glass."

"Thanks," she whispers, all but collapsing into the chair that sits at the head of the huge table.

I pull a lowball glass from the cabinet and Dimitri's unmarked swing-top bottle out of the freezer. I bring her both, set them down on the table near her and crouch in front of her. If she were shorter, we'd be at eye level. But she's not, so I have to tilt my head up a bit.

"James," comes the deep, accented voice. "Come. Now."

I glance up, and Eleanor twists in her seat to see Dimitri's massive form filling the doorway. She goes rigid and gasps.

Yeah, his size and mean, scarred face have that effect on people.

"I've got to go have a chat with my... roommates. Will you be okay here for a few minutes?"

Her eyes cut to me. "Will I?"

I tense. Her tone is part challenge, and as much as that fucking stirs my blood, it's also part question. "Eleanor—"

"Just go. I'm... I'll be fine." With grim resolve and shaking hands, she reaches for the bottle of vodka. She pours a finger, pauses, and pours a second.

Okay, yeah, I'll give her that one, but if she thinks she can get drunk and close me out, she'll be learning her lesson when I get back. I've noticed she responds well to a firm hand, coupled with a reminder of our sexual chemistry, so I indulge. I stand, then lean in to invade her space. When she shifts away, I place a hand on each arm of her chair and corner her against the back of it.

"Be a good girl for me and stay here. I'll be right back."

Since she has nowhere further to back away, she can't escape the quick kiss to her cheek.

As I stride out of the kitchen, I throw a look over my shoulder and see her gulp down at least a shot's worth of vodka.

Wes repurposed the formal study into a symphony of electronic whirring and humming computer fans. The mahogany desk in the center of the room boasts several huge monitors and enough computing juice to keep him flush in bitcoin, if he cared to mine for it. He told me once it was boring.

He's sitting at his desk, and Dimitri walks over to stand behind him, arms folded. It's like being sent to the principal's office for fighting all over again. They both look up when I close the door behind me, but Wes is the first to speak.

"What the hell are you doing here with Eleanor Wilson, 1226 Second Ave, Apartment 3B, 28 years old, blue eyes, 5'9", line cook at Bistro Jacques, account balance of $407?"

And that's why piquing his curiosity is so dangerous. He probably knew that within 15 minutes. "So what, now we can't even have girls over?" I aim for levity, but neither of them looks very impressed.

"Of course we cannot," Dimitri snaps. "But even so, she is not a girl—she is *the* girl. From the night of the mission failure."

I'm not sure if he put it together or Wes told him, but there's no use denying it now. I sigh. "She is. I've been... keeping tabs on her."

"What about her has you so ass over tit, Mac? Couldn't be her credit score," Wes says, pulling a face. "Oof, 525."

"Now you're showing off," I grumble.

"No, I'm showing *you* how easy it was to find her. She can't be here, you know that."

My hands curl into fists because he's saying all the things that I haven't been letting myself think. "Her safety was compromised. Rossi sent a fixer after her."

"Jesus Christ," Wes mutters as Dimitri curses in Russian.

Dimitri looks up at me, and I scowl at the look in his eye. "Don't say it—"

"If Rossi has her information, her safety is a lost cause. She knows too much."

"No." I shake my head.

He taps the glass on the top of the desk emphatically with two fingers. "You brought her here. She has seen our faces, knows our names. So now she *really* knows too much, and that is your fault."

"No!" I growl. "We can... I'll keep her here until the job is done."

"And then what?" Dimitri scoffs. "You will let her go? What if she involves the police?"

"She won't go to the cops. She could have already, and she didn't."

"Even if that's true," Wes cuts in, and his reasonable tone is so fucking grating. "You know you can't just cut her loose after the job is done. Not with what Rossi already knows about her."

I shake my head and cross my arms. "Once we take them all out, the city will be empty—"

"Unless the supplier comes looking for anyone who knows information about their deaths. She is like a bright sign that says, 'easy target.' They will find her," Dimitri points out harshly.

My stomach drops at the possibility that soft, compassionate, lovely Eleanor might end up in enemy hands. I can't picture her being interrogated, being broken... I won't go there. "She'd never betray me—us, I mean."

"We're not saying she'd want to, but... She has a family," Wes said, spinning his laptop and showing me an old picture on her social media, holding a tiny baby, with the caption *Aunt Eleanor, Reporting for Duty!* "She's got weaknesses for them to exploit."

"So, what? You want me to just kill her?" Dimitri and Wes exchange a look, and I uncross my arms and lean forward, preparing for battle. "If anyone so much as lays a hand on her, they lose that hand."

"You cannot compromise this whole mission for—"

I cut Dimitri off with a swipe of my arm through the air. "I'm not discussing her termination. I'll take her somewhere else if you want me to, but we all know it'll be less secure. And the more time I have to spend keeping her safe, the less time I'll have to cover your asses. You feel me?"

"Mac," Wes tries, after exchanging a look with Dimitri that's all betrayal and disappointment. He hides it, but he's too expressive to do it well—he didn't expect me to pick her over them. "Do you even know her? Who could she possibly be to you after two weeks?"

"She's... non-negotiable. I'll take complete responsibility for her."

Dimitri mutters something in Russian about security risks, and Wes turns his laptop back around and starts clacking away. "Maybe there's something I can do—wipe her from the internet, give her a new identity. We'll have to relocate her after all this, obviously. And she will have to stop being Aunt Eleanor if she wants to keep her family safe."

Relief floods my system, and I let my shoulders drop. It's not ideal, maybe—most people would object to being picked up and moved somewhere far away against their will—but it's better than the alternative. Alive is good. Alive means I can make sure she's safe; it means I get to keep her...

But she'll hate me. I'll be the guy who ruined her life. The guy who made her leave her home, leave her job and friends, and made her cut ties with her family...

But she'll be alive.

"Wipe her for now. Her family is far enough away that it'll buy us some time."

"Until the fixer Rossi had on her fails to report in," Dimitri points out. "Tell me you at least took care of that."

"I called in a cleaning crew on my way out. They're probably there now," I add, glancing at my watch. Then, I dig in my pocket and toss the contents onto the desk. "His phone and wallet."

I've never been more glad to have my own fixer than I am now—nothing would have inspired less confidence in my ability to handle this than needing to ask one of them for help retrieving the body.

Wes sighs, reaching for the items I brought. "That's something at least. It'll buy us a few days if I can mimic his check-ins."

Dimitri is still grinding his jaw. "Wesley should be focusing on the drop so we are prepared, not protecting some girl. This is unacceptable, James. You have put us all at risk and broken our trust. If we fail—"

"When have we ever failed?"

"If we fail, this will be our last job," Dimitri finishes. "I will not work with someone who puts a woman that he does not know before his team."

Wesley's head is down, looking through the wallet, but his eyebrows shoot up at the declaration. I second his shock, and an uncomfortable sort of helpless frustration curls my hands into fists. I fucking hate an ultimatum, but I suppose I just did the same thing.

I want to say he's being unreasonable, but the truth is I know where he's coming from. The work we do is too dangerous not to trust each other. "We won't fail."

"And you will be responsible for her. If she is staying here, she must be completely locked down. She may not go in or out, no phone, no internet, no nothing."

I nod, swallowing the snark just like Dimitri is swallowing his pride. Of course I know how to lock someone down—I don't need him telling me—but I also don't want him thinking he needs to keep an eye on her or tell her himself.

"So, erm, speaking of focusing on the drop," Wes interjects, cutting the tension, "I just got a ping off one of my spiders. The pickup is set—midnight next Sunday."

"Good." Dimitri clips out. He sighs and scrubs a hand over his buzzed hair, scratching the scalp audibly. "We should review James's surveillance information and decide what our plan will be."

"Just let me get Eleanor sorted," I say.

I expect him to bristle at the mention of her and any further delays because of her, and my anger rises in my throat, ready to defend. But he just nods again. "Yes. And I am too angry to be thinking clearly, so I will be using the punch-kick bag."

"Punching bag," Wes corrects.

"That is what I said. Meet back here in two hours." Dimitri crosses the room and exits, leaving the door wide open to signal the meeting is officially over, according to him.

Wes eyes me, and I feel the urge to apologize to him in a way that Dimitri's rage never prompts. "You know it's not like that, right? I'm not choosing someone I barely know, I'm... I won't let you guys down, but I can't let her get hurt. It's a really fucking hard place to be."

"Oh, I get it now."

"The fuck does that mean?"

He grins, then sits back in his chair and links his arms behind his head. "It means... she's cute, Mac."

A pressure is lifted off my chest at his implied forgiveness. "Get fucked," I say, but then register what I said. "But don't even think about touching her, pipsqueak."

His voice follows me to the door. "All I'm saying is, if you do end up getting us all killed, at least she was hot, yeah?"

I flip him the bird on my way out.

16

ELEANOR

You lookin' to get chased, darlin'?

My face feels warm after that first gulp of vodka hits my stomach, so I slow down for the rest of the glass. I'm not much of a drinker, and I don't want to completely lose my faculties. Mac might be keeping me safe (?) here, but he's clearly not the only killer under this roof. I shiver at the memory of the scary, scarred man with the thick Russian accent. Wesley seemed nice, at least. Cool tats, too.

I take another sip and notice that my hands are a little steadier now. I'm not sure how much time passes as I stare, seeing nothing, but eventually I realize that the wall of windows next to me is letting some of the cold pass through the glass. I'm shivering; so, I toss back the rest of the vodka and stand to get the blood moving.

God, this kitchen.

It's the size of my apartment, first of all, which probably isn't saying that much. I doubt there's a single room in this house that isn't. The room has one of those no-clutter, clean lines, modern/minimalist designs. The top-of-the-line appliances gleam spotlessly from the perfect kitchen triangle they create. Two sinks—one just for prep on the island—two dishwashers, a huge, funky light fixture spanning the width of an enormous island...

Chef Robert was bragging once about remodeling his home and made a joke that the fancier the kitchen, the harder it is to find the garbage. I look around at identical cabinets without handles—I wouldn't even know where to start looking—and decide this probably puts his to shame. No stashing the trash in a corner or under the sink here.

I run my hand across the counter and shake my head. Marble. When will rich people stop using porous stones for kitchen surfaces? Grease doesn't care that it costs $35K; it'll ruin it just the same without regular preventative maintenance.

I walk around, letting my fingers trail over the tops of the stools, which appear to be some kind of polished natural-edge wood. I peek into the bathtub-sized stainless-steel sink and find nothing but a shiny surface. No dishes.

And the stove... Oh my God.

60 inches wide, dual-fuel, six full-sized burners with built-in griddle and grill, two ovens and a touch panel that is probably the most intimidating thing I've ever seen in my life.

I think I just came.

Then, I gasp suddenly, seeing the espresso machine.

I hear a low, angry exclamation in a language I don't understand behind me. When I turn, that huge, scarred, menacing-looking guy is grabbing the vodka from the table where I left it and shooting me a glare.

I gulp. Apparently, Dimitri doesn't like to share.

"S-sorry," I manage.

It does nothing to mollify him. With steps so heavy they make the glasses in the cupboards behind me tinkle as they tremble against each other, he stalks around the island. I fall back up as he comes closer, but he stops and disappears behind one of the long cabinet doors briefly. When he shuts it, I see he's gotten a water bottle out. The vodka is tucked under his arm.

His eyes scan me, head to toe, and he shakes his head dismissively and turns around.

A breath of relief spills from my lips, as indignation refills my lungs. I'm not sure why I care about his approval, considering he might as well have the word *Murderer* tattooed across his forehead from the way menace fills the air around him. Plus, now that I've gotten another look at him, I'm pretty sure he's the guy from that grainy picture Officer McCloskey showed me. Which means he's as deep in this world as any of the rest of them.

But the awareness of being judged by a stranger is deeply ingrained, and its effects are cumulative, even if the moments themselves pass quickly.

"Whatcha up to, darlin'?"

I jump, startled, and the way my heart continues to hammer at the sound of Mac's deep voice? I have to get that under control. But he's not making it easy. His long-sleeved shirt is just loose enough that it still stretches against his torso, making it look broad and flat, but I lose the taper of his hips. The sleeves are pushed over his elbows, and his hands are stuck into his pockets. That's some serious forearm-porn. And his black pants hug his thighs, and he's doing that leaning thing against the doorframe...

He seems more relaxed now than he was before he left me in here, though I can't quite put my finger on why.

I bend down to scratch my knee idly, then look away, letting my hand rest on the marble. "Just looking around. This kitchen is... wow."

"I knew you'd like it."

I tap my fingers a few times, suddenly antsy in my attempt not to feel any sort of way about that. "What chef wouldn't? It's a dream."

"Are you hungry? I'm not sure what we have—"

"No." The burning feeling behind my eyes makes me want to rub them. "I'm tired. Can we go—I mean, can you show me somewhere I can sleep? I don't know what time it is, but... wait." I pat the pockets of my shorts and look around the kitchen, just to be sure I didn't leave it at the table or something. "Where's my phone? Oh, right. Coat pocket."

"About that," Mac begins ruefully, lifting his eyebrows. He pushes off the wall and steps towards the island. "Some rules while you're here. Safe house rules."

"Okay," I say hesitantly.

"You can't leave."

"For how long?"

I watch his jaw work a little before he replies, "Until I say it's safe. As long as it takes."

Translating that vague Mac speak... "So, I can't go to work?"

He shakes his head.

"I'm going to lose my job." I should be more upset at the prospect of losing my job. I could take a week off, probably, but only because it's the off season now. And they wouldn't hold my spot for me any longer than that. They need all their kitchen hands too much.

He shrugs. "But you won't lose your life."

Fair point. "Okay. What else?" At the questioning expression, I just sigh. "You said rules; that was just one—stay here until you say I can leave."

He advances around the counter, and I take a step in the opposite direction, keeping it between us. "No contact with anyone. You can't have your phone; it'll be turned off, in a box we have that blocks any trackers or anything that might be on it."

I press my lips together. "People will be worried about me—people at work, Harrison, my sister... maybe my parents, depending on how long I'm gone."

There's a glint in his eye when I bring up Harrison's name that almost makes me want to do it again just to see how he'll react. "I'll have Wes send them an email from your account on an untraceable IP that you're taking a vacation and you'll be off-grid. Anything you want to add that might help sell it?"

I consider that. It's going to sound strange no matter what they say—I don't take vacations; everyone knows that. He takes another step, and so do I. "When we were little, my parents took us camping in West Virginia. I remember it being really remote."

He nods. His step is slower this time, and I let his weight shift before I match it with my own. "That works. Service is bad in the mountains."

I swallow. "Anything else? Am I confined to my room, or am I supposed to avoid windows—"

"Eleanor, why are you backing away from me? You lookin' to get chased, darlin'?"

A thrill zings through my belly, but I spit, "Because you're following me? I really don't want you to chase me."

He smiles slowly, flashing those white teeth. "I seriously doubt that."

My heart starts pounding, heavy and fast. The urge for fight or flight is strong, and it's only the knowledge that there is a 0% chance that I'm faster than him that glues me in place. I'm not quite sure how to get out of this thing I've apparently started, either, except that I've noticed he backs off when I submit—it's not the fear he likes, it's the defiance I show when he's expecting fear.

I look down when he takes another step, letting him know he's won. "I'm really tired," I say. It's not the most prevalent feeling in my body right now, but it is true.

He finishes closing the distance between us, but the predatory look has been subdued. "Then, let's get you to bed. You're not confined to your room, and you don't have to avoid windows. We're tucked away in here; that's why it's safe."

He places his hand at the small of my back and starts gently leading me out towards the foyer.

"Oh, before I forget, that guy who came in here before, Dimitri?"

"Did he say something to you?" Mac asks, a hard edge to his voice.

I bite my lip and shake my head. "No, I think he was the one in the photo they showed me—those pretend cops, I mean. He was wearing a hat in the picture, so I couldn't see that scar he has, but I'm pretty sure it was him."

I feel him tense, even through the minimal contact of his hand. "It's good that you told me. We'll look into if that other guy actually was a cop. You said his name was McCloskey?"

I nod.

I have to try to keep my jaw off the floor as we walk back into the grand entrance. My sneakers keep making little squeaking noises against the polished floors, and I'm reminded of just how out of place I must look in my dirty gym clothes. And that I'm not wearing a bra... I glance down. Oh my God, I'm officially three for three.

All three of the hottest men I've ever seen in my life met me for the first time with my nipples visible through my shirt.

Well... not much I can do about that now.

We reach the stairs, and I make a move to grab my gym bag, but Mac beats me to it.

"So, your name is James?" I ask to fill the silence as he gestures to the staircase and lets me go ahead of him. He swings my gym bag over his shoulder and follows me.

"James Mackenzie. Mac."

"Got it. Do you like James, or—"

"I'll answer to whatever you want to call me, darlin'. Mac is how you met me; Mac works for me."

I find it a little strange that he doesn't prefer one or the other, but decide not to press.

When I'd stop at the top of the staircase, Mac keeps pushing me along, up another flight that curls around the corner. At the top of the second set of stairs, he gestures to the left. All the lights come on like they're on motion detecting sensors as we continue down a hallway so long, we must be headed for The East Wing or something equally as ridiculous. The house is dead silent, and it feels totally empty, especially all the way up here.

Eventually, he stops and opens a bedroom door. Unlike everywhere else, he has to flip the light on in here.

"This is..." I trail off, stepping into the room and taking in the massive bed that dominates one side of the room, the plush white carpet, the reading nook, the double doors that lead out to a fucking balcony, the en suite bathroom just past the massive walk-in closet, the matching glass bedside tables with... wait, personal stuff? A charging cable, a stack of books, a bottle of ibuprofen, a box of tissues... "Is this your room?"

"It is."

"Okay, so where am I sleeping?"

"Here," he says, like that was obvious.

"Oh, come on," I complain. My vagina likes this idea a bit too much, spasming with need at the thought of this kind of forced proximity. "There must be a dozen bedrooms in this place—"

"10."

"Surely, one of them—"

"You live in my house, you're gonna sleep in my bed."

My breath breaks in my throat as a shiver crawls under my skin, making my nipples tingle and ache. That tone, that don't-argue-with-me statement, that hungry look in his eyes—it all almost makes me think he really does want me in his bed. Legitimately.

I want to scream in frustration. Why is he making this so hard on me? I cross my arms. "I thought you were some kind of Southern gentleman. Chivalrous, even."

"I am," he protests, crossing the room to place my bag on the cozy chair in the corner. "I saved your life."

"You endangered it!" I shout, losing my cool for a second. "I've lived in Ulysses my whole life, and a thug has never followed me into the sauna before."

"That you know of," he scoffs.

I scowl at him, and suddenly everything comes pouring out. "I'm an overweight line cook with no boyfriend and, like, two friends—one of whom is my sister. All I have to my name is a bunch of expensive kitchen gadgets and a pile of debt from the college I never even finished. My life is so small and I'm so unremarkable that it's almost impressive. Don't pretend like anyone would have noticed me if it weren't for this mess you dragged me into, because no one ever has before."

He bristles, shooting me a sideways glance. "I did."

"I caught you shooting someone out my window! That's not the same—"

"No," he cuts in, and his tone is so firm that I stop. "Before that."

I snort. "Yeah, right."

"You came waltzing up to that door in the tiniest damn shorts I've ever seen, looking up at me with those big blue eyes, bitin' that lip... I almost had you against the wall, then and there."

My breath whooshes out, and I feel warmth spreading in a few places at once—on my cheeks, my chest, and, more urgently, between my legs. Like he knows it, he takes a step towards me, and I make a hasty retreat. "That's..." I clear my throat. "That's not the point."

He grins at the tremor in my voice and moves towards me. "Me wanting to have you flat on your back, screaming my name as you come all over my tongue isn't the point?"

I gasp and stumble away another step. I'm against the wall now, and I curse myself for this little repeat performance from the kitchen. How did I let this happen? "N-no."

"What if you're the one on your knees, then, and I'm pushing all the way to the back of your throat—"

"We're getting way off topic," I breathe as he boxes me in. He places his hands on either side of my head, and I'm surrounded by him—his scent, his size, his power.

"Are we? Because I think the point is, I'd never hurt you. Unless you want me to," he adds, nipping my earlobe. I yelp, but it melts into a breathy moan as he scrapes his teeth against the delicate skin under my ear. "But if you ever call yourself unremarkable again, I'll take you over my knee."

My gut spasms so hard it's like I've taken a punch. Heat flares, and the rush of need flooding my system momentarily stuns me.

"I... you..."

Shit, what had I been saying? Another moan slips out as he brushes his chest against mine, stimulating the already-painfully hard tips of my breasts.

"Oh, you like that idea, don't you?"

Out of nowhere, his hand comes to rest on my ass, and he squeezes. It breaks me out of whatever spell he's casting, and I flatten my hands on his chest so I can push. "Mac, please... stop."

He moves away a little, drops his hand, and flashes his teeth. "Darlin', I don't care that you're mad at me for this shit I've gotten you into. You should be. Just don't try to use it as a shield. You can be mad at me, but don't pretend you don't want me. Because I know you do."

Irritation prickles again, and I can mentally take a step back. I'm a quivering mess, so hot I can barely speak, but he's in total control—even breath, relaxed posture. And he's fucking smirking.

"You... asshole!" I hiss. "Is that what all this hot and cold is about? You... touch me, make me think you want me, then you try to scare me away and keep your distance? You want to know you're the one in control? You want me to admit how much I want you? Fine! I want you. Is that what your ego needed? You get off on that?"

He chuckles and leans forward. Suddenly, I feel the warmth of his hand wrapping around my throat. There's no pressure, but it makes me go completely, rigidly still. Still enough that he can bring his face close enough so his lips just brush against mine when he speaks. "Oh, sweet Eleanor. I told you. I know you want me—I don't need to hear it, though I'll admit it's nice. But you don't know half of what you think you do."

I swallow, and the weight of his palm makes me even more aware of how it feels. I can feel the heat of my own breath, bouncing back against my mouth from his nearness. "And what exactly don't I know?"

"It's not my ego you should be worried about; it's my obsession."

"W-what?" I croak.

His thumb starts running up and down the column of my neck, and he pulls back to watch the movement with half-lidded, hypnotized eyes. "This hot and cold, as you called it, is me being a gentleman. It's me respecting your 'no' while, respectfully, trying to get you to admit that 'no' is a 'yes'."

His eyes lift, catching mine. I want to drown in those brown depths.

"Give me an inch, darlin', and I'll have you underneath me so fast your head will spin. Just know once you do, I'm never letting go."

I gasp. My whole body is on fire at that declaration, dark as it is. I feel so completely consumed by this man in this moment; I don't know which way is up or down. It's like my brain shut off, took a back seat to letting my body just... feel the effects he has on me.

"But I'm not a man who takes what isn't freely given."

"What does that mean?"

"It means... I'm going to protect you. And that means you're going to trust that I'm not going to take advantage of you when you've just been held at gunpoint. So, you're going to take a hot shower, put on one of my shirts, get in that bed and go to sleep."

The way the emotions war within me at that suggestion is almost physically too much. The desire to do what he says, the wariness of his unhinged behavior, the excitement of sharing his bed, the comfort of knowing he won't take it further... the sharp disappointment of knowing he won't take it further...

God, Eleanor, pick a damn side.

He releases me, and I shuffle away against the wall until I'm clear of him. Then, with really nothing else to do, I head for the bathroom.

"And Eleanor?"

I turn.

"If you try to lock that door to keep me out, it won't work."

17

ELEANOR

*I'm not sure that whatever's between us is enough
for me to get over that.*

I knew we'd wake up like this. I knew that if I didn't lock the door—or, according to him, even if I did—then the next-morning entanglement would be as embarrassing as it is sexually frustrating.

I just didn't expect to be the one spooning him.

Though, to be fair, as I come to full consciousness, I realize that it's not technically an all-out spooning. My hand is resting on his side just above his hip, my legs are curled in the space behind his knees, and my head is tucked against his back, but my ass is scooted back far enough that we're not quite nestled.

His breathing is deep, even, and I can even hear a faint honk-shoo, so I allow myself the opportunity to stare at the ridged, defined contours of his back. The skin is stretched tight over all that muscle, and mostly hairless. But it isn't exactly smooth, with plenty of freckles, moles, and shiny pink scars. There's a round one near his right shoulder, a long cut that slashes diagonally through his spine, another round one down by his hip, and a tiny crescent moon-shaped one a few inches to the left.

He's clearly been through a lot. I wonder if it ever made him cry. Because I can't seem to.

Last night, I sat on the floor of that cavernous shower with, like, seven shower heads spraying me, and hugged my knees and waited for the tears. I gave up when my ass fell asleep and finished my shower. I used the strange, scentless body wash on the shelf, wrapped myself in a huge fluffy towel, and then I scoped out the bathroom for extras of things like toothbrushes and floss, and found completely bare drawers.

I put my own oversized T-shirt and shorts on afterwards, cringing at the way the pits were still soggy from my workout. But whether or not I can fit into one of his shirts is not really a question I need answered. There isn't much point in trying to have one of those cute, *look how big his shirt is on my tiny body* moments, and I came to terms with that a long time ago.

I sat in the middle of the bed that felt bigger than a king—not that I'd really know; my futon is a queen at best—staring at that closed door, debating turning that lock. In the end, I was too tired to put up a fight or deal with the ominous consequences.

And since I'm not ready to deal with the consequences of him waking and finding me all over him like this, either... Gingerly, I lift my hand and pull away. He barely shifts in response, so I roll onto my back and stare at the crisp white ceiling. I scratch my knee, then do a double take and make a face. Great. Another flare up.

I scooch to the edge of the bed slowly, trying not to jostle him on the memory foam, and creep to the bathroom. I'm so used to the floor creaking under every move I make in my apartment, I'm surprised with how quiet I can actually be.

Since the night before was such an emotional blur, I didn't really register the splendor of the bathroom. Walking in, I gape.

I think I have actually found a room roughly the size of my apartment.

The shower stands next to a large, jetted tub, spanning the whole far side of the room. Apparently, the toilet gets its own little room within the bathroom because, why not? But the other door, when opened, has a stacked washer-dryer unit next to a rack with a robe on a hanger and a fully loaded linen closet. I should have looked in here the night before, because there are baskets with all kinds of helpful toiletries. Well, that's a pleasant surprise.

First, I brush my teeth for a long time at the double vanity, staring blankly into the mirror with built-in back lighting. Then, I go to the duffel I'd left in here in the corner and retrieve my underwear, bra, socks, and the towel I apparently stole from the gym. That joins the clothes I'm wearing in the washer. Then, because it feels like a wastefully small load, I throw in the towel I used last night. And the other one on the rack.

My shower last night had such an unsatisfying conclusion—having to put dirty clothes back on—that I decide to take another. When I step in, the steam that pours out gives me a flashback of the dark hole of a gun barrel poking through the swirling white. But as the dread starts to curl around my guts, I manage to keep it at bay by physically shaking myself out of it.

He's dead. I saw him die.

I grab the robe from the closet and am relieved when it cinches closed. Barely, but it's better than nothing—which is what I'll have for the next hour and a half until my only clothes are clean and dry. And that's a long time to try to hide from Mac in a place where there's nowhere to sit, unless you count the toilet.

I brace myself and open the door. He's on his back, scrolling through his phone with a scowl, the covers slung low over his hips, giving me a truly spectacular view of his chest and abs and biceps...God, there's not a single inch of him that isn't tanned, toned and perfect. He looks over when the door opens, and the scowl melts away.

"Mornin', darlin'."

His voice is scratchy, rubbing against my skin like sandpaper. I reach down to itch my knee, and he tracks the movement. "Morning," I reply softly.

"You finished in the bathroom?"

I nod and quickly move to the other side of the room to stay out of his way. Thankfully—unfortunately?—he's not naked, but boxers don't hide much. I make myself look away, focusing down on the bedside table that was next to where I was lying. Our awkward morning dance doesn't last long as he closes the door.

The urge to pick up my phone is strong, especially in my boredom. And now that I've confined myself to the bedroom for the next 85 minutes until the dryer cycle is done, I'm especially at a loss. I cross the room, curious about the view I couldn't see last night, as I hear the shower turn on.

The grounds—yeah, a yard this big has to be called grounds—are spectacular. There's a dusting of frost on what must be acres and acres of grass, making it look like sparkling waves of blue-green. We're facing the back of the house, because I can see a covered pool below us and a large building to the left of it that must be a pool house. There's some bird activity, but not much other movement than empty tree branches swaying in the wind, and no other wildlife that I can see. I guess deer can't jump a fence this high.

Mac emerges some time later, slipping a watch over his hand and securing it. My mouth goes dry. Not only is watching a man putting on a watch the hottest fucking thing for some reason, he's also in only a towel. I turn firmly back around.

"Oh, we're still doing that, huh?" his voice is thick with amusement.

"Doing what?"

"Pretending you don't want to look."

I don't know what to say to that, so I choose silence. I can't hear him as he moves across the thick carpet, but I do hear the closet door open. And I can hear his voice clearly as he says, "I have a meeting this morning with the team, then I'll probably have to go do some work for a bit. Feel free to explore."

"Okay."

"After your clothes are done."

I roll my eyes. Duh. Like I'd walk around an unfamiliar house in a robe that barely fits me with nothing underneath. "Don't worry, I won't embarrass you by accidentally flashing your roommates."

"That's good, because I'd have to cut out their eyes."

I swallow. I can't tell if that's a joke.

A memory surfaces; *I want the* ojos. I shiver.

"You can explore wherever you want inside the fence—just knock first if a door is closed," he says, coming back out, fully clothed. He's rubbing his hair violently with the towel, so he can't see as I take in and appreciate the sight of him in the daylight, wearing those dark jeans and henley so well.

"Okay."

He crosses the room again, and I hear what I assume is the towel being hung, then he leaves. No goodbye.

Eventually, my clothes are dry, and I can leave the room. I wander slowly through the house, starting at the top. There's a converted attic space above our floor with another bedroom and a bathroom, a kitchenette, and a lounging space with a giant TV and leather reclining couch—like its own little apartment. It all looks completely untouched.

Mac seems to be the only one on the third floor; the other bedrooms have an empty feel to them, and the beds aren't made up with sheets. There's an office, though, and I find a few of what must be Mac's personal electronics and what has to be gun cleaning equipment that I leave the hell alone. The second floor has more shut doors, so I assume both Dimitri and Wesley stay there.

It gets warmer the further down I go. The gym and movie room in the basement genuinely excite me, then I'm distracted by the elevator. I use it to ride back up to the first floor, just because.

And the first floor is just a complete sensory overload. I've never been in a house that has a hallway before. My parents' house was firmly middle class—each room led to another—but this place has so many rooms it needs its own highway to expedite the trip from one end to the other. And while the library, conservatory, dining room and game room are all impressive in their own right, I end up back in the kitchen.

This time, I let myself be nosy. I open cabinet doors and paw through the fridge and freezer. The pantry is so well-stocked and organized, I almost start drooling. They have every gadget I do, plus any I've ever even considered wanting.

The doorbell rings, pausing me in my exploration. I wait for the sound of footsteps—or, in Dimitri's case, stomping—but nothing comes. I'm probably not supposed to answer the door. But I move into the foyer out of sheer curiosity, and peek through the peephole.

I'm confused. No one is there.

It feels off, but it's not like just anyone can get in through that gate, right? Mac needed a fingerprint and a code. And though it feels wrong to answer the door at someone else's house, I'm too curious now. I twist the locks and open the door, really hoping this isn't some kind of trick.

But it's not a trick. It's... a grocery delivery. I glimpse the back of a sedan with Jersey plates disappearing down the driveway and take a step forward to examine the tidy pile. Then, I blow out a breath. This is going to take a few trips.

Some time later, it's all laid out on the countertop and I'm out of breath. And kind of flabbergasted. Six dozen eggs, 15 pounds of chicken breast, a huge box of broccoli, 20 bags of lettuce, four gallons of milk, a bag of onions, a bag of potatoes, 10 pounds of ground beef, some berries, and oranges, plain nonfat Greek yogurt, oatmeal... it's a power lifter's wet dream—all lean protein and fiber.

I have a sinking feeling about the food situation in this house.

"—if something happens, so there is someone in place... ah, good. The groceries have come."

I look up at the sound of what I assume is Dimitri's voice, from the accent. The three of them enter the kitchen, and it shrinks in size as the testosterone fills the space. I'm seriously not sure how three men this good-looking are working together and the job isn't, like, actors or porn stars.

My brain momentarily goes on the fritz at that thought.

Mac smiles at me. "Did you bring all that inside, darlin'? You didn't have to do that."

I shrug, though I secretly thrill at the use of my pet name in front of his friends. "Does this look... right?" While I want to be sure they got everything they wanted, I'm hoping they didn't. Where's the fat, or spice, or acidity? Where's the flavor?

Dimitri's eyes scan the pile, and it doesn't take very long. "Yes. Every week, the same."

"That's so..." I clear my throat, trying to find the right word, "efficient."

I hear a snicker, but I'm not sure whether it's Mac or Wesley. Dimitri turns his stony glare on them. "I know," he replies curtly.

I eye the pile of food, and my fingers itch to do something with it. Not only will it really calm me down to have something to focus on other than my own boredom, but it'll give me a way to contribute. "I can... I mean, do you want me to make you guys some meals?"

"Yes," Mac replies instantly, at the same time Dimitri says, "No."

"Trust me, man, you really want her to," Mac tells the larger guy, clapping him on the shoulder. "She's a chef."

I try to hide how I puff with pleasure at that. It's technically an accurate description of my job, though usually I call myself a line cook. But Mac's total confidence in me, and the way he alludes to my skills eagerly and with pride, makes me all gooey.

"I prefer to know precisely what I am eating," Dimitri argues, but he's not looking at me when he says it.

"Come on, live a little," Mac replies.

As they go back and forth, Wesley weaves around them and the island, grabs an energy drink from the fridge, and starts loading the new pack in. "I'll let them sort it out between themselves, but I'm in either way," he says softly, shooting me a smile. "A real chef, eh? What a treat you are."

I smile back at him and open my mouth to rattle off my credentials, but Mac cuts me off with a growled, "Stop flirting and get back to your cave."

My head whips around, but his ire isn't for me. He's glaring at Wesley.

"I was talking to the lady," Wesley clips back, sending me a surreptitious wink that earns him another displeased noise from across the kitchen.

"I promise it'll be restaurant quality," I say, hoping to tempt Dimitri. It'll be easier to just prep everything instead of leaving some out for him to be stubborn about. "I'll keep it healthy, if that's what you want. I'll be able to do a lot—this is basically a commercial kitchen. Except the knives kind of suck, for some reason."

Dimitri looks at me suspiciously. "Why do they suck?"

"They're just old. Dull."

When he starts muttering in what I'm now sure is Russian and strides from the room, I throw Mac a bewildered look. "What did I say?"

Wesley is the one to answer as he slides the last of his drinks onto the shelf. "You implied there was a knife under his roof that isn't sharp enough to splice a hair. He won't stand for it. Don't be surprised if you come back and every knife has been taken to the grinding stone."

I press my lips together to tamp down on the smile. "That's a bit neurotic."

"You don't know the half."

I feel an arm come around my waist from behind, and I'm stunned as I'm physically blocked from Wesley's line of sight. I didn't even hear Mac move, but here he is, pressing me against the counter and shielding my body with his own.

"Back to your cave," Mac says, his voice settling in a low, threatening register. He's looking at me, staring at my mouth.

"Oh, but I was just about to drag her back there by her hair," Wesley laughs as he walks out.

I want so badly to squirm against him, but I have a feeling that would end poorly for me. I can already feel his pelvis pressing against mine, and just a bit of pressure might be the end of me. So, I stay still, letting him surround me, tilting my head back so much further than I'm used to. I want to protest the manhandling and the crowding, but the dirty truth is... I'm worried if I do, he'll stop.

"I'm not allowed to talk to other men at all, now?" I ask in an accusatory tone. Every deep breath makes my chest brush against his.

"Darlin', say those words you know I want to hear, and you can talk to anyone you want. Are you going to stop pretending?"

I sigh. "Okay, I give up. I'll admit there's something here; you want me, I want you. But you know it can't be that simple for us—for me. This thing you do... I'm not sure that whatever's between us is enough for me to get over that. And I don't know if I can do *just sex*," I finish with a shrug, feeling especially awkward. If we have sex, there's no way I'm not getting my heart broken.

"We're way past just sex," he agrees.

I look down. "So... where does that leave us?"

He takes a pointed step back, looks me up and down, meets my eye, and adjusts the front of his pants. "Just so we're clear, you did this," he says, meaning the hardened bulge. "And once you're mine, you're going to be responsible for your actions when you do. Until then, well... it's just gonna be real hard for me to see you smiling at any other guy, so keep that in mind."

My mouth has gone so dry, I can't even swallow, as my mind immediately creates my very own alternate reality where I drop to my knees to take care of that straining length that's gotten so hard for me.

My face flushes as heat creeps up my neck. "It's like you heard what I said and listened to none of it."

"Oh, I listened, darlin'. You said no; I backed off. Isn't going to stop me from fantasizing," he says with a wink.

He turns around and produces a pad of paper from one of the drawers near the double doors that lead outside. With a flick of his wrist, he tosses it onto the island. "I'm going to send someone to pick up your things so you don't have to wash those clothes every day. And you were scratching this morning, so I'm guessing you need your medication. Make me a list of what you want."

Somewhat thrown off by the abrupt change in temperature of the exchange, I pull the paper closer to me and pick up the pen, then hesitate. "How long do you think I'll be staying?" At his scowl, I quickly add, "just because there's a difference between a night and a week in terms of, you know, things like toiletries and underwear..."

I feel myself blush a little, thinking about what else is in my underwear drawer. Just from being so close to him, I'm definitely in need of a little bit of a release. But if Mac is going to make me share his bed, there's no way in hell I'll be using my vibrator. I'm not tempting fate. Guess we're going old-school, in stolen moments when he's not around.

"There's a possibility this will all be over next Sunday."

So soon? I swallow the jumbled mess of excitement and disappointment that I really don't feel like untangling. I nod and start listing things, adding a buffer for the "possibility" that a week is an underestimate. I feel a twinge of guilt at making some stranger lift my over-packed bags, but I push it aside.

When I'm done, he takes my list, scans it, glances at me with an unreadable expression, and nods. He walks away, and I see him make a note at the bottom of the paper.

As he disappears into the hallway, I hear, "Felix—I know, twice in one week... yeah, you're the luckiest boy in all the land."

18

ELEANOR

No one is wholly good or bad.

By the time it's dark, I've transformed half of the groceries and some pantry items into a few sets of three square meals a day for two people. I had to start from scratch for things like the mayonnaise for chicken salad and an olive oil pastry crust for the quiche, so it took longer than it would have with those shortcuts. I've just gotten dinner started when I'm interrupted.

"What is that? It smells amazing," a posh British voice says. I throw Wesley a glance over my shoulder, smile at the look of pure astonishment on his face, and return my attention to the pan.

"It's literally just onions and garlic," I laugh. It's the perfume of line cooks; everyone's favorite.

"I could smell it all the way from my office. What are you making?"

"Pan seared chicken breast smothered in caramelized onions, baked potatoes and a salad. It's for dinner for, well... the three of us, I guess. I didn't really get the point across earlier with Dimitri, but I kind of meant for this to be my contribution and, like, a thanks for letting me stay and keeping me safe."

He smiles and sets his laptop on the kitchen table. "Well, I think I'll work in here if you don't mind. My office is starting to smell like bollocks."

I laugh. "It's your house, but please, be my guest."

He settles into a chair behind the screen, and I continue sautéing. The silence is comfortable, but I've got too many questions to really let it simmer. And unlike Dimitri's prickliness and Mac's... distractingness... Wesley seems calm and friendly. "You're the one who sent the email for me to my family, right?"

"Last night," he nods.

"Are they in danger because of all this?"

He glances up from his screen briefly. "I doubt it. Your parents are well out of reach in Florida, and your sister, who lives outside Pittsburgh, is far enough."

I wince, but I guess I shouldn't really be surprised he knows where they all live. Anyone who can use my email without needing my password from me probably has skills I can't comprehend. "What does that mean, far enough? Like, they won't bother with her?" Maybe I really should go stay with her for a while after all this.

He clears his throat and sits back in his chair. From that position, I can see more of his throat and chest through the opening of his button-down, and the beginning of the colorful designs etched into his skin.

He taps his finger on the glass thoughtfully a few times. "Let's just say that in the time it would take Rossi to track her down and send someone out there, he'll already be neutralized."

"Neutralized," I repeat on a scoff. "What a synonym. They should hire you to do PR."

He grins, totally unfazed.

"What do you do? Who do you guys actually work for, anyway? Is this a self-employment thing, or..."

"I think I want to hear your theories."

I give the pan a thorough turnover first, then give it my back so I can face him. I want to see his expressions. "Well, I thought at first maybe some sort of military operation. It just doesn't explain the charade."

"The charade?"

"The story with the building fumigation, the costumes, the van—"

"I'll have you know it's called a cover, not a charade. And it's a disguise, not a costume."

I chuckle. "Right, well... it seems to me that the military doesn't need a cover. And if they want someone dead, they can arrest them or send in SWAT, or drop a bomb and pretend it was, what do they call it? A training accident?"

His lips stretch into a smile. "Does Mac know?"

"Know what?"

"That you're a conspiracy theorist?"

I feel my cheeks heat. "I mean, I don't just, like, believe everything I'm told, if that's what you're saying..."

"No, don't be embarrassed—this is going to be so much easier if you are. Because you're right, the corruption is part of the problem—part of the reason we do what we do. Bureaucracy works too slowly, and money walks. The bad guys get away. Sometimes they're even in bed together."

"So, enter the three Musketeers?"

He tilts his head back and laughs with his whole body. "Oh, I like that. New group chat name." He pulls a phone out of his pocket and bends his head over it. "Though, unlike the Musketeers, we do have an employer—someone we answer to. A handler, they call it."

"You're assassins." That feels weird to say out loud.

"Hitmen. Yes. Paid killers. Though personally I like to think of myself as more of a Batman figure—the genius, rich, dashing, heroic type with a preference for vigilante justice."

I turn back around to ponder that under the guise of stirring the onions.

As tempting as it is to embrace the comic book mindset—if for no other reason than it's so much easier—I know real people are more complex than that. No one is wholly good or bad. And while I understand Wesley's point about the injustices and imperfections in our systems, vigilante justice has never quite sat right with me, not when normal people so often become collateral damage.

But at least they're doing something about the corruption and injustices. Something most normal people would never be able to do. Am I just judging from the safety of the sidelines? The high and mighty convictions of someone who'll never have to live with the guilt and psychological damage of taking another life?

Seems to me, people don't just do this kind of thing for no reason. Maybe I haven't given Mac enough of a chance to explain himself. If the why is important too, maybe I should ask for his.

"So, if you're Batman, that makes Mac... like, Hawkeye, I guess?"

Wes tilts his head, thinking. "A dead shot from afar. Yes, I see where you're going with that."

"And Dimitri is... the Hulk? But, like, only the green version."

Wes laughs again. "I'll be quite generous and say part team leader, part green Hulk. He is organized and an ace in a jam."

"So, like, Captain Hulk."

"I like it."

"Well, it does help to think of it that way, I guess. I just hope that doesn't make me civilian casualty #4," I mutter.

"I wouldn't be too worried about that. That's the thing about Mac—he's always watching, always protecting. Once you're in his inner circle, he'll do everything he can to keep you safe. And from what I've seen, you, my dear, *are* the inner circle."

I'm not sure exactly what that means, but I get the gist.

I think I'm starting to understand their dynamic, so the superhero metaphor is good for one thing, at least. Dimitri is kind of like the leader, even with his anger problems, and would be fighting in the thick of it. Wes takes care of the complexities of the technological side of things, and likely packs his own punch if he needs to. Mac watches over them, covers their asses—he's the backup plan, and the element of surprise.

No wonder he was so upset when I interrupted that night. Dimitri was probably the one who got shot.

When dinner is finished, Wes grabs a plate and squirrels it away to his office. I graze on it, kind of wanting to wait for Mac, but not knowing when he'll be back. Dimitri comes into the kitchen, sniffs the air, glowers at the chicken in the pan and starts removing raw ingredients from the fridge. I take that as my cue to leave.

19

MAC

——◆◇◆——

Yeah, darlin'. It's dangerous. But so am I.

> **That's it. I'm marrying her**

He sends a text with a picture of his dinner. I know he's just trying to goad me, but there'd better be some of that left for me when I get back. I swallow the knee-jerk possessive response.

> **What makes you think she'd marry you?**

> **Blackmail. Obviously.**

I roll my eyes. Wes has to re-invite Dimitri to the chat every time we get off topic—luckily, he finds it hilarious instead of tedious. For someone so severe, Dimitri can be pretty dramatic. Once, he joined and immediately left when he saw Wes had added him under the name Papa Bear.

It was just another day in the glamorous life of surveillance duty, watching the guards at a storage unit. Chairs were sat upon. Phones were scrolled. Balls were scratched. Nothing fucking happened.

But at least I got some good shots of the faces of the men on duty. I sent them to Wes, and he added their personal details to the file we've been keeping. It all gets wiped when the job is done, but we're never upset that we had too much information.

I make a pit stop at the address Felix texted me, park next to the car he described in the mostly empty strip mall parking lot, and find Eleanor's bags in the unlocked trunk. There's a paper bag next to them with a little Sharpie doodle of an eyeball. The suitcases go into my trunk, but the paper bag gets placed on the seat next to me. I'm going to need to remember to put them on ice.

More of the house is lit on the third floor than usual, so I know my girl is in our bedroom. The comfort of knowing she's been safe at home—untouchable and getting her scent all over my bed—almost made up for the fact that I had nothing to listen to while I worked today. Almost. It is going to make coming home interesting, though, because I'm so juiced, but she's still playing hard to get.

Once I'm inside, I make a beeline for the source of the amazing smell in the air and find only clean pans laid upside down to dry next to the sink and a spotless stovetop. With a frown, I open the fridge. There are a dozen neatly stacked Tupperware, and I check each one, but can't find the brown onion-y thing Wes sent the picture of. Grumbling, I toss one of the other containers into the microwave and eat the contents standing up. Whatever it is, it's good—damn good—but I'm still pissed.

Jealousy makes my temples pound. I'm going to have to have a chat with her about cooking meals for the other guys and not me. Especially if she's doing it on purpose now, like it seems. I've seen the flash of defiance in her eyes when I remind her it's only a matter of time until she's mine. So, if this is her fucking around, she's about to find out.

I rifle through her bag long enough to find what I want, then I take the stairs two at a time. When I get to the third floor, I slow down to a crawl. Our bedroom door is open, and the hallway is still lit from the motion sensor, so if I'm quiet she won't necessarily know I'm coming. It's almost comically nostalgic—me framing her in my view, her blithely unaware.

My heart pounds as I watch her. She's sitting in the very middle of the bed that she must have made, cross-legged, with a pad of paper in her lap. She chews on her lower lip thoughtfully and crosses out something that she's written. The pen makes a loose rattling noise as she taps it against her knee.

It feels so different now. Before, it was all about being the eyes in the shadows—captivated, covetous, greedy—and now that I have her... well, it's not better. The satisfaction of having her in my bed, the feeling of rightness, that she's where she belongs, is only second to the primal need to be inside her, hearing her cry out my name and knowing that the rest of the house hears it, too.

The noise of nails against skin drags me out of my fantasy, and I remember I have the cure to her suffering.

She looks up when I enter the room. "Hi," she says. Her tone isn't quite what I expect; it's bright and casual. Her eyes scan me, settling on the bags now on the ground at my feet. "Is that my stuff?"

"Yes."

Eager, excited almost, she scrambles off the bed, leaving the paper behind. I glance at it as she kneels down and unzips the first suitcase. It's a meal plan. Hot jealousy climbs back up my throat as I glance over what she's planned to feed everyone but me, and I sit on the bed.

"Mac, what's this?" She pulls the canvas case out of one of the bags and flips it open. Inside, I know she'll find her entire knife drawer. She glances up at me. "These weren't on my list."

I'm impressed. She's good. No hint of unrepentant rebellion, or the overconfidence brats wear when they know they're about to get the punishment they want.

"You said the ones here suck, so I added it. Thought you'd like having your own."

A ghost of a smile traces her lips, and she sets the canvas roll back down. "That was... really thoughtful. Thank you."

I let her dig through the bag a little longer. She pulls out clothes, finds the travel bag of toiletries and unzips it. She frowns as she moves aside the tubes and bottles.

"Looking for this?" I produce the medicated cream from my pocket.

She freezes, seeing it in my hand, the color rising to her cheeks. Now she gets it.

I pat my lap, like I did the first time. "Legs."

Her chest rises and falls. Slowly, she stands and moves towards me and the bed. It fires me up even more that she keeps her eyes locked with mine—a good girl like her should lower her gaze, accept the repercussions with deference.

So, I make a decision. I shake my head as she moves to place her knee next to me. "Shorts off this time."

She pauses, and I wait for the defiance. I wait for her to tell me to kick rocks, to declare that she doesn't need the cream that badly, to call me an asshole for holding her medication over her head. Instead, she looks down, swallows, and hooks her thumbs into either side of the waistband of her shorts. As she pulls them down, I eat up the sight of her exposed skin hungrily, feeling the blood rush and the pressure building in my dick, giving it its own heartbeat. I can only see the very bottom of her pale green underwear below the hem of her shirt, which she tries to tug lower.

I let the tension mount in my silence as she decides how best to follow my order. Does she place her foot on my knee, knowing how it'll open her up? Does she sit back against the pillows so she can keep her legs together, knowing how much easier it'll be for me to get her under me? I'm tempted to let her make the call.

"Sit," I nod next to me, and tap my lap again. "Legs. Don't make me tell you again."

I uncap the tube as the bed dips under her weight. I catch a flash of pale skin, but then she's on her ass, turned around. It was a calculated move on my part—we're sitting far enough that she can't lean against the headboard. She shifts her weight onto her hands and drapes her knees over my lap.

Once there's sufficient cream on my fingers, I grab her opposite ankle with my free hand, locking both legs down. I know she can feel my hard on when she inhales sharply.

As I smear some cream on the area, she relaxes a bit. Enough anyway to focus on other things. "Mac?" she asks, voice small. "Will you tell me... How did you get into this job? What did you do before?"

Her timid curiosity catches me a bit off guard. "Special forces sniper for eight years."

"Hundreds," she says softly, and I know she's remembering before when she asked how many I'd killed. And she's right. Most of that number is from my military days. "What's the pipeline from military to hitman?"

I rub gently, focusing on my task, but the question is a good one. It's one that Wes and Dimitri know the answer to, more or less, but I haven't really talked about it to anyone else before. "They gave the order, I shot. Boom, done. No questions, no opportunity to do any due diligence. If the intel was bad or incomplete, we usually found out too late. It started to... bother me. I wanted to understand, to know what I was doing."

She laughs, and it's so far from the reaction I'm expecting that I look over with a confused frown. "What? You gonna call me an asshole for killing without asking questions?"

"No, it's not that... it's actually, weirdly, I kind of understand. You got out for the same reason I've been thinking about leaving my job. You want to see the impact of what you do and to understand its significance. Don't get me wrong... our jobs have wildly different levels of significance, but, I don't know. It just seems related somehow." She shakes her head, preparing to backpedal. "Maybe that doesn't make any sense, but in my head it does."

I crack a smile. This isn't at all where I expected this conversation to go. I'm glad I let her speak first. "I'm surprised you'd even want to compare what we do like that. You've been pretty clear on your feelings about my job."

"I guess I was just coming to terms with the fact that there really are people out there who kill for money. Maybe I didn't think the why mattered, since the what isn't great. And it didn't help that you're so... so blasé about it. Killing. Death in general."

I hesitate to admit how easy it's gotten because I know that's a fucked-up thing to say. It's a fucked-up thing to feel. And I know she's grappling with some heavy, good-and-bad/right-and-wrong shit right now.

"I'm not trying to be blasé. It's not like I think human life has no value at all... but I guess the way I see it, I've got an opportunity that a lot of people don't have. I get to do something that I'm good at, and it makes the world a little better."

"Killing people makes the world better?"

"Depends on the person, but I think so," I reply honestly, in spite of the skepticism in her voice and written all over that lovely, open face. I cap the tube carefully and toss it onto the bed behind me. She tries to move her legs, but I don't release my grip.

"But don't they have their own lives? Their own families and hopes and dreams?"

"Does having those things make you a good person?"

"Does being a bad person mean you deserve to die?"

I grin, because she comes back with that so fast that it was clearly locked and loaded. She's been thinking about this a lot, which fills me with an odd sort of vindication. "Touché. You're against the death penalty then, I take it."

"I don't know," she admits, dropping her head back between her shoulder blades. "I don't know what to think. I don't think people should be allowed to kill without consequences, but that's also what you're stopping them from doing. Where does it end?"

"It's a lot to take in," I acknowledge, running my hand soothingly up and down her leg. I can feel her skin tense under my hand, and my cock twitches in interest, knowing how easy it would be to just reach up a few more inches and pull down those panties. *Down, boy, we'll get to that in a minute.* "For what it's worth, you're asking good questions. Most people never have to go through a big challenge to their moral code like this."

She barks a laugh with no mirth, head still back. After a second, she lifts it and looks at me down her nose. "You believe in what you do? It... it saves people?"

"Rossi brought in five shipments last year. Those guns make their way to cities and suburbs all over, to the border, to drug lords and hate groups and gangs. Sometimes, they even end up in the hands of a teenager looking to take their rage out on their classmates."

She gasps and straightens, the color draining from her face.

"Rossi doesn't pull the trigger, but he gives them the means. Is the blood still on his hands?"

Her lower lip wobbles, and she sucks it into her mouth. I love how deeply she feels for people, how open her heart is for those she's never met and will never meet.

"I think it is," I continue. "Just like I know that stopping these shipments will prevent a lot of that shit in the future. Sure, the guys with guns to sell will find another way in. They always do. So, we follow the trail Rossi leaves and go after the suppliers next."

"But..." she chews that lip, and I brace myself for her next argument, her next indictment against my character. "Isn't it dangerous?"

Her concern washes over me like a wave, and I nearly sway from the force of it. She's worried about me? I can't help myself. I tuck my hand in between her thighs, dangerously close to a very hot, very wet center. "Yeah, darlin'. It's dangerous. But so am I."

She inhales sharply.

"Now that we got that out of the way..."

I reach forward and grab her right upper arm, then snake the other around her legs and up to her hip. In one synchronized jerking motion, I flip her over and drag her torso towards me. It places that sweet ass right over my lap. Her shirt has ridden up, showing me enough skin to make my palms twitch.

She's surprised enough for a beat that she just lets it happen, but when she feels my arm belt across her back and my other hand follow the curve of her ass, she starts kicking her legs wildly.

"Let's talk about why you made dinner for everyone but me."

20

ELEANOR

Well, I'm not going to get too hung up on that, but that's new.

"W-what?" I gasp, shivering under the warmth of his hand on my butt. "What are you talking about?"

He squeezes my cheek hard, and I whimper. "Wes sent me a picture. I told you that I—"

"I *did* make some for you!" I cry urgently. "I... there was plenty! I left it on the stove."

"Eleanor, don't lie to me. There was nothing in that kitchen."

I can track his movements, from both the pressure against my skin and the scratchiness of the calluses on his palm against my soft cotton underwear. Heat has exploded through me, pooling in an urgent way between my legs. I'm so wet I know it's only a matter of time until he sees what this is doing to me. And from the sharp bulge against my hipbone, I can feel what it's doing to him.

My brain is foggy, too distracted by the way my breasts are pressed hard into the mattress, but I can still remember a few things. It's too weird talking to the headboard, though, so I try looking at him over my shoulder. "Um... maybe Wes came back for seconds? Or, I guess it could have been Dimitri. I didn't make any for him, and I left the kitchen when he walked in."

His hand moves again, squeezing, kneading thick handfuls of flesh so that the bite of pain is quickly replaced by the sensory overload of this massage. "Blaming Dimitri, huh?"

"I—please," I whisper. I squirm, shifting my hips as much as I can, trying to get some pressure where I desperately need the relief.

"Please, what?" he replies.

The depth of his voice makes me press my legs together tighter. There's so much dark intention, so much amused knowledge of exactly what's happening to me, to my body, so much masculine pride in being the cause.

I'm just a jumbled mass of wants. I want him to stop; this is too embarrassing—I'm a fucking adult. And I want him to spank me, because I'm a fucking adult who's never been this horny in her life, but I also want to... deserve it. And I don't, not about this anyway.

Wait. I want to *deserve* a spanking? Well, I'm not going to get too hung up on that, but that's new.

But I also want him to keep going, because what he's doing isn't enough. I want the sting of his hand, the hard length pressing into my hip, the knowledge that he's so consumed by me that he wants complete control.

His fingers dance along the fabric just covering my pussy lips, and I'm undone. I moan and let my head drop onto the soft comforter. This feeling deep inside me is worse than a craving, how it needs him.

"Don't spank me. Please, just... touch me."

He groans, pressing harder into the seam of my panties. I'm sure he's found the moisture. "You understand what you're asking? It won't just be touching, and it's not just sex. We do this; you're mine. You want that?"

I nod, a bit grateful he can't see how much I do, but I do lift my head so my voice isn't muffled by the pillowy blanket. "I'm tired of fighting this—you and me. I may not love what you do, but I don't think you're a bad person. And... I really did make you dinner. I was even going to wait for you so we could eat together."

"Fuck," he murmurs. He slides the arm that was acting like a strap, holding me in place, under my breasts and stands a little to give himself leverage to turn me over and toss me back in a surprisingly fluid motion. He grunts a bit from the effort, but the noise I make of surprise is much louder.

I sit up, not wanting to miss a moment of him, and feel something like self-doubt creep in as I take in the full splendor. He's so tall, so beautifully carved, so powerful. I want to be his, but even more than that, I want him to be mine. The knowledge takes a chunk out of my armor.

"Just try not to break my heart, okay? I don't think I'll survive it." I look away, not really wanting to feel as laid bare as that confession makes me.

"I will never hurt you," he says, enunciating each word. "No one ever will."

I look back up and I can see the promise written all over his face, like it's sealed in blood. My stomach does a little flip, and all that insecurity drains away. He really was serious. He really does want me as badly as I want him.

The knowledge gives me the confidence I need. I lean forward to get my legs under me so I can kneel at the edge of the bed, and he immediately closes the distance. The mattress is thick, and on a platform, so we're close enough in height that he isn't going to have to stoop.

He takes my waist; I wrap my arms around his neck. And we kiss.

It starts gently, softly. His hands grip just above my hips, holding me so we're completely pressed flush—chest to chest. My torso is stretched, and I use one arm to hold my balance and the other to weave my fingers into his soft, silky hair. I tilt my head up, close my eyes, and as his lips brush mine, mine part.

When his fingers tighten, I let mine do the same, grabbing lightly at his hair. His lips are firm, but smooth, and the new growth of his facial hair rasps against the sensitive skin of my face. He tastes like the meatloaf I made earlier, and something almost indescribably human—the salty, earthy, textured sweetness of someone else's mouth.

He slides his tongue just past my lips, then pulls back, and I almost fall forward from the unexpected shift. My shirt is being lifted, so I unwind my arms from his neck and hold them up. It leaves me bare except for my underwear, and his eyes scan the expanse of skin with appreciation. His look is all reverence and eagerness. He runs the backs of his fingers against the curve of my breast, tapping my nipple with the flat part of his fingernail and grinning when I go, "Ah!"

"I hate sports bras," I mutter as an explanation for my nudity, feeling my face heat under his stare. My nipples prickle, hardening with the cool air and my mounting arousal.

"Me too," he replies, so soberly that I laugh.

I play with the bottom of his henley, and meet his eyes with the question. He smiles, reaches up to grab the shirt from behind his neck—why is it so hot when guys do that?—and gives it a tug. I pretend like I'm helping, then finish pulling it inside out for him over his arms.

I run my fingertips across his chest, pausing at a few puckered scars, and trace the outline of each ridge at the top of his abdomen. His muscles contract under my touch, almost like it tickles. His skin is warm and smooth, but there's no give. Not like mine. Even the very strong parts of me, like my legs, don't feel like this, like the wall of muscle is built harder, somehow. At most, I'm firm, not hard. The difference is almost hypnotic; it's so fascinating.

And he's exploring, too. His palms skate across my shoulders, down my arms, but pause as I find his belt buckle. I don't look for permission this time; I just unbuckle, unbutton and unzip. Unlike my second-skin shorts, his pants fall with a little bit of help and gravity. Then we're both just in our underwear, though his black boxers cover quite a bit more.

There's something so intimate about undressing each other, and something so intoxicating about doing it for the first time. I feel like I'm unwrapping a present. My breath is quick, my pulse is racing, my face feels flushed... I reach for his boxers.

I've never looked at a naked man and wondered if it would fit, and frankly I'd hope not. But I'll admit to a bit of apprehension as I reach to tug the fabric over the tent he's made. Because Mac's a large man, so it stands to reason his cock would also be large. And while I know that the human body—especially the vagina, what with childbirth and all that—can take quite a bit, the idea of having to grin and bear it isn't really sexy to me.

As his boxers join his pants and he steps out of them, I'm both relieved he doesn't have some elephant trunk down there, and thoroughly excited by the size. It's just long enough, thick enough and has an upward curve that I know it's going to fill me so good. And if he knows how to use it, it'll hurt just the right amount.

I lick my lips.

"Oh, you've got to be fucking kidding me with that." He steps forward and grabs my waist again. I hold out my arms, thinking to resume where our kiss was cut short, but he pushes my whole body down and diagonally back so I land with a bounce on the mattress on the side of my ass with my legs curled out.

I look up at him quizzically as he wraps his large, warm palm around my ankle and tugs me forward. "You're gonna stare at my dick and lick your lips like you think it's your turn first? Uh-uh. I've been thinking about this for way too damn long."

I giggle as he pulls me towards him until my legs come over the side of the bed. For some reason, I just love that his idea of a "turn" isn't about receiving an orgasm, it's about giving one. He kneels at the edge of the bed, hooking his index fingers through the elastic at my hips, and pulls down the last piece of clothing between us, leaving a path of tingling sensations.

His breath is hot on the inside of my thigh, just before he places a kiss. I feel the scrape of his stubble more than the softness of his lips, but the sound of it, and knowledge that he's on his knees for me, makes me feel cherished.

He splays his hands on the tops of my thighs, jerks my legs apart, and holds me down.

God, I love the manhandling, too.

He doesn't give me any time to be self-conscious about the normal first-time stuff—sights, smells, the other person's opinions—because he just dives right in. Some guys eat you out like they wish they had an extra hand to hold their nose. Mac eats me out like he's savoring the last bit of melted ice cream at the bottom of the bowl. I writhe under him, trying not to buck my hips but unable to stop myself, as he licks around my clit, across it, finally settling on upward strokes that are almost too gentle.

I grab onto the blanket as his fingers join the party, gently stroking along the slick skin, circling my entrance without penetrating it.

"Fuck, that's good," he croons, pulling away and watching my face as he enters me with two fingers.

My hands fly to his head, holding on, as my back arches and I moan loudly. I'm primed, but it's been so long and I feel so full of him so quickly. He resumes working me with his mouth, and his fingers move and curl inside of me, pumping gently. I'm so primed from what feels like days of foreplay, my release builds with unexpected swiftness. Electricity sparks under my skin, sending bolts of lightning to my core. They fizzle around him, collecting against his tongue, and are suddenly sent shooting in every direction.

I cry out, seizing up, tensing and shaking, and he holds me down and rides it out, unrelenting. My vision clouds, turning into black starlight.

The release is acute, bringing prickly tears to my eyes, and there's a roaring in my ears that dulls the wet sounds of his tongue and fingers. I tighten my hold on his hair just as the pleasure turns into something sour.

I'm breathing heavily when he pulls back, my head spinning a little from the intensity.

"You ready, baby?"

I don't even care what for. I nod. I hope he means it's my turn. I can't wait to see what he feels like against my tongue...

He shifts his position on the floor and pulls me towards him, using the backs of my knees for leverage, and I'm suddenly sliding down the side of the bed, grappling for purchase. I land astride him with my knees barely touching the floor.

Well, I wasn't ready for that. "Mac!" I protest, laying my hands on his chest and trying to shove off. There's nowhere to go; the mattress is at my back. "I'm not a lap girl!"

His grip is like iron. "No? But it's my lap and I say you are."

I laugh, but it comes out as an anxious noise. I don't want to sit like this, where I'm forced to look at the contrast between my soft body and his hard one. And it can't be comfortable for his legs or knees. "Stop, I'm too heavy."

"For what?" he asks, leaning back and bringing me with him.

I fall against his chest with a soft oof, and when I try to brace myself on the floor to push up, he locks an arm across my back. "Mac, stop—"

"Darlin', the fact that you think you know better than me about what I can handle is starting to irritate me. Now, are you going to trust me, or are we going to end up right back where we started with you over my knee?"

Though the idea sends a little shiver of need down my spine, I stop struggling. I can't let myself go all the way limp, but I note with some resigned discomfort that his chest is still rising, and his breath doesn't seem too labored.

"Good girl. Didn't want you to get hurt when I did this."

He rolls us, and I'm on my back. My legs are bent, curling around his hips, his pelvis is pressed into mine and his cock is almost perfectly aligned. "Oh. Ohh," I say, inhaling deeply at the thick length, hard as steel, pressing up and sandwiched between us, applying just a bit of friction against my clit.

"Yeah," he murmurs, brushing his lips against my ear. "Oh."

He pushes up on his hands, triceps bulging to support his weight, and widens his stance. My knees splay even more, my legs are draped over his thighs, and he rolls his hips. The head of his cock rubs along my slit, and I whimper.

"Please..."

"I like please. Please is good," he whispers. "I want to hear you beg for it, baby."

I wrap my arms back around his neck as he slides his arms under my shoulders. It puts us chest to chest, so close we're breathing the same air. The intimacy of it is shattering. "Please, Mac, please... I need it. I want you inside of me."

"Fuck, baby," he groans. "Did you think about it? Did you imagine me fucking you while you played with that pretty little pussy?"

"Yes," I answer immediately, honestly. "I wanted you to fuck me so hard and make me feel good. I wanted you to fill me—ah!"

He does. I throw my head back, closing my eyes, as the full, hard length of him sheathes inside me and touches me exactly where I need it. My body adjusts to him, stretching around him deliciously.

"Don't look away from me," he growls.

My eyes fly open in shock, because it wasn't an intentional attempt at escape, and we're locked in. The closeness, the clarity of his eyes and expression, the rawness of not being able to hide anything... I can see every emotion as he responds to mine—the total control, the excitement, the pleasure, and something so deeply possessive that it's almost unsettling. Every slow, deep thrust makes me whimper, and the noises just seem to spur him on.

It's one of the most intense experiences I've ever had.

"Oh my God, Mac," I say, and it's an emotive rasp. "I didn't know it was going to be like this. It's... so much."

"That's right, baby, now you know. You know you're mine," he declares, his voice strained as he pumps himself in and out of me. "You belong to me now."

His weight shifts to one side, and he frees one hand, which then slides up my forearm and comes down next to my head. His fingers entwine with mine, and he presses his weight on it, forcing it into the carpet.

We're holding hands as his lips crash down, his rhythm slowing to allow for a thorough exploration. I match his passion, tasting myself on him this time, touching his tongue with mine and letting myself be caught up in the violence of his desire for me.

I roll my hips with his, finding the right friction in the right place, and I break free of the kiss to cry out in pleasure. He starts thrusting faster, and the sound of skin slapping skin fills the air. I start riding higher and higher, the pressure of each brief contact hitting my clit and giving it just enough to keep me on edge.

"Mine, mine, mine, mine," he grits out, timing it with the pinnacle of each thrust.

His breath starts hitching, and I let go of his neck to wind my arm between us and rub my clit. I want to come together. My timing is a little off; he starts grunting and his face screws up, just as I start to build to that peak. But watching the pleasure pass over his features, knowing I was the orchestrator of it, sends me hurtling off that same edge.

The full weight of his body as his muscles loosen in the post-orgasm state is a lot—he'd really only given me a hint of it. But I run my fingernails up his back, enjoying the feel of him. We both catch our breath, then he rears back and smiles down at me. It's so content and lazily affectionate, I have to smile back.

"Let's go take a shower. I need a break, but I'm not done with you yet."

29

MAC

—◆—

I just needed you to admit it.

I'm home. Eleanor is home. And I'm never leaving.

"I have to ask because it's been bugging me." She turns her head and sniffs the suds left behind by the loofah I'm working on her shoulders. "Where did you get this body wash? Is it prescription? There's just... no smell."

I grin and move the loofah lower down her back. "I prefer to have all my faculties when I need to focus—strong scents are distracting."

"Is that why you... this is silly and maybe I'm reading into it, but did you send me flowers that didn't smell on purpose?"

I'm pleased she got there so fast. "I did. I noticed that you don't wear perfume, so I thought you might also be sensitive to smells."

She tilts her head back, allowing it to fall against my collarbone. The spray hits her chest, and I watch as the water droplets forge a path down, wanting to follow them with my tongue. I bring the sudsy pouf around, running it gently across her belly. She squirms a little at the attention somewhere she's insecure about. But she'll learn—I'll show her there isn't an inch of her I don't want to worship with my mouth.

"It's not like I don't want to smell nice," she says, laying her hands on my forearms as I slide down towards the soft curls between her legs. "It's just kind of a faux pas in the kitchen. You don't want to throw off anyone's taste buds. And then even on my day off I don't because I'm worried it'll stick to my clothes."

"You do smell nice."

"What?" Her voice becomes breathy, distracted, as I inch lower with my soapy, slick fingers. "But, like you just said, I... um, I don't wear perfume."

"If I thought it was perfume, I'd say, 'Your perfume smells nice.' But I said *you* smell nice, darlin'."

"Oh." She gasps as I find her swollen clit. Her fingernails dig into my arm, and her back arches against me, but she's got nowhere to go and I'm not loosening my grip. "Mac, I can't—not again—"

"Yes, again." I stroke the little nub, relishing in every broken inhale, every squirm and tightening of her limbs, every shudder. My dick stirs, interested in another round but still a bit oversensitive and numb at the same time. I'll be ready again soon. In the meantime, I want her to be loose, soft, satiated, and sleepy yet energized, the way only an orgasm can do.

"Come for me, baby," I whisper into her ear. "You can do it. You can be my good girl."

She whimpers, moving her hips in small circles counter to my touch. The whimpers become moans, and her breath starts picking up. I keep my steady, even pace, though the urge to speed up as her body prepares for its climax is hard to fight—I want to get her there faster, but I know it doesn't work that way with women.

I drop my lips onto her shoulder, running them over the smoothness I find. I taste her, nip at the skin, fill my free hand with her breast and give the sensitive tip a little tweak. Every movement, every sound, every sensation of her skin against me... it's all mine.

Her legs start to shake, and I know she's close, so I brace myself in case she loses control of her knees. After a few more strokes, she does, and I'm right there for her. She slumps a little in my arms, slow to get her legs back under her, and makes satisfied little humming noises. When she recovers, she turns around in my arms, hooks an arm around my neck and pulls me towards her.

I love the feel of her stretching against me, breasts pressing into my chest and belly pressing into my cock, and her kiss is equal parts hunger and gratitude. The feel of her desire, knowing she's trying to keep up—match it with mine—makes me want to head straight back to that bed. We have a lot of surfaces to christen.

But her stomach growls as we step out of the shower and I hand her the towel from the hanger. "You're hungry," I observe. "Go put something on, and we'll get some food."

She looks down, winding the towel around herself. "Oh, that's okay. I can just go get something for myself and bring it back up. You already ate—"

"Darlin', I need 4000 calories a day to maintain mass. I could always eat."

"Show off," she mutters.

"Either we both go or I bring something up for you. You choose."

Her lips twitch. "You're going to spoil me."

"That's the plan."

"I'll get dressed." She starts sorting through her clothing in the open suitcase.

I grab the other one and bring it into the closet with me. There's plenty of room for her stuff in this cavernous walk-in. "You can unpack in here tomorrow," I tell her as I grab a clean pair of sweats from one of the drawers. A quick check of my watch tells me it's past 10, meaning Dimitri is in his room for the night and Wes's night is just beginning, so I doubt we'll see him.

I decide to forgo a shirt. I like my girl's eyes on me.

She's sliding the same oversized shirt she's been wearing over her head when I walk back in. I remember those sleep shorts, and I really remember how they look with no panties underneath... like now.

"No."

Her face is surprised as it appears through the hole in her shirt, her hair wild with static, pointing in all directions. She smooths it out of her eyes. "No?"

"I don't want to see those shorts anywhere but in here with the door closed. That view is only for me now. Put on pants."

She looks pointedly at my bare chest, raises an eyebrow and cocks her head.

"I don't know what kind of point you think you're making with that look, but it doesn't matter. Pants, Eleanor."

She presses her lips together against the smile curving at the corners. With a little shake of her head, she crosses the room, bends back down over the suitcase at the waist—on fucking purpose, most likely—and pulls out a pair of sweatpants. With quick, jerking movements, she pulls them on over her shorts and turns back around to me. "Happy?"

My palm twitches against my thigh. "A smart mouth will also get you laid over my knee, darlin'."

Her eyes flash with sexual interest, and she bites her bottom lip. "Lucky me."

She's hungry. She's hungry. She needs food. She'll probably pass out after the next round if I don't let her refuel...

I take a calming breath and open the door. She starts moving towards the stairs, but I catch her hand. If Wes is still settling in, he sometimes travels back and forth between his room and office. "Let's take the elevator."

"I still can't believe there's an elevator." She sighs, shaking her head. "It's so not fair."

I push the button at the end of the hallway, and we hear the gears move. "Why, *not fair*?"

"Because you're living like this while I bust my ass for $40K a year. You probably pay half that in rent for the month in a place like this."

She's not that far off, but I don't remember the exact numbers since Wes takes care of it. "A few million per hit, split three ways... tends to add up." It's really four ways, since the General takes a cut off the top. I won't be able to avoid telling her forever, but she'll be so much safer if she doesn't know about him.

Her eyes widen. "Guess I'm in the wrong industry," she says, her tone somewhat harsh. "So much money to end people's lives."

I probably shouldn't have gotten into the specifics, but my instinct was to share any detail she might want. I'm trying not to keep things from her, and it really didn't occur to me that her reaction would be bitter. "Call it skilled labor and hazard pay."

"Right."

I notice how she tries to stand away from me in the elevator, but I refuse to let her create distance—emotionally, anyway. Still, I try to keep the pressure off the question by watching the buttons light up as we descend. "Was it just being reminded of what I do, or something else?" I ask, referring to her rigid posture next to me.

"It's nothing."

"No, it's not," I say, turning towards her and placing an arm against the open elevator door, barring her exit. "Talk to me."

She sighs again, looking away. "It's... well, all my adult life I've felt like I had to make a choice between pursuing a dream and making ends meet, only to get this far and feel like I chose wrong," as she continues the sentence, her voice wavers. "I sacrificed and scrimped for all those years, and I still picked the wrong dream because I don't even fucking like it anymore. Do you have any idea how... exhausting that is?"

I watch her angrily wipe tears from the corners of her eyes. "I do. Maybe more than you know."

Watery blue eyes flick to me, as if to assess whether or not I'm making fun of her. But truthfully, I'm relieved this seems to be more about the money itself than the fact that I kill people for it. As far as I'm concerned, it's all hers from now on, anyway.

"Really?" she asks.

I nod down at her, and move my arm, lowering it to gesture for her to go first through the door. "I don't know if you know this about the military in general, but it requires a certain suspension of disbelief."

"I can only imagine," she says quietly.

We walk towards the kitchen, and I put my hand on her lower back—to guide her, but mostly to put my hand on her. "The training is one thing—there's a camaraderie with the other cadets, and you don't really know what you're getting into yet. But then I spent years thinking that maybe one more mission... maybe just a little longer, and I'd feel like I was where I was supposed to be, or doing what I was supposed to be doing. No one around me questioned their purpose at all. It's probably why I stayed as long as I did."

She cranes her neck and sends me a look that's full of sympathy and understanding.

"It wasn't years of struggling in poverty or anything, but it was years full of choices that added up to a situation I didn't want to be in. No one to blame but myself, either, so I did... for a while."

"How did you stop?" she asks.

I flick on the lights and move towards the table, ushering her ahead. "I found something else I actually wanted to do and figured out how to leave the past in the past."

She laughs a little. "You make it sound easy."

"It's not, and I don't mean to make it sound like it is. But you get better at it the more you practice."

I pull out the chair and motion to it, but she shakes her head and spins so she can place a light touch to the center of my chest, forcing me down. "No, you sit. You took very good care of me; let me take care of you."

I smile because it feels wrong not to, when my girl is offering to remind me that she's mine. I watch as she works, pulling out a large mixing bowl and whisk, then grabbing some eggs out of the fridge.

"There's so much I still don't know about you," she muses distractedly.

"Like?"

"How old are you?"

"33."

"Oh."

"Oh? You were hoping for more of a May-December thing?"

She smiles, looking down, cracking eggs into the bowl. "No, I just... I'm really bad at guessing people's ages. And you did add yourself as 'grandpa' in my phone."

I laugh at the memory. "Oh, that. It's just a contact name that people wouldn't think to look at closely."

She nods, accepting that, then gets distracted by chopping some vegetables. I let her work, not wanting to split her focus when she's holding a knife. So, I start checking the messages on my phone, and the omelet comes together so quickly that she's sitting at the table before I can even finish typing my email.

"Thank you, darlin'." I tuck in with gusto, noticing how much larger my portion is than hers. It's perfectly cooked, seasoned, and filled with vegetables that are somehow delicious, in spite of their greenness.

"Do you have siblings?" she asks between bites.

"I'm the seventh of eight kids." Her eyes widen, then her smile is wry. "What?"

"Wow. Eight kids. I can't even imagine. That explains why you eat like you're afraid there won't be enough."

I set down my fork and let loose a surprised laugh as I dab the egg off my face with the napkin she brought. "Wouldn't have put that one together, but you're probably right. Nothing was ever mine. It's why

I decided to serve—the military was a way out of rural life. It gave me something my family didn't have, that they couldn't give. And it felt like a better option than settling down, getting married to someone in the area and always wondering how close my family tree actually was to hers."

She snorts. "Did most of your siblings do that—settle down?"

"They all have at least two kids of their own now, except my younger brother. But he's the baby, so he's not leaving home until he's got a boot print on his ass. I usually go home for Christmas, and they all pity me because I haven't found my 'true purpose.'"

"So, your family doesn't know what you do," she surmises.

I shake my head. "They think I'm still in the Marines. My mother tells everyone she knows that her son is saving the nation."

"I mean, technically you still are. Your methods are different..."

"Frankly, they're not even that different," I admit. "But it's safer if they don't know. I have Wes keep an eye on traffic through the major airports near them, but I'm not really too concerned. It's a whole lotta nothin' down there. You have to know where to look to find people in that mess of forests and mountains."

She smiles and finishes her last bite. "So, where do they think all your money comes from?"

"Oh, they don't know anything about it. Except for the kids, I guess. All 19 of my nieces and nephews have accounts in their names that'll get them through college, if they want, and buy their first home. But on the condition that they don't tell their parents where they got the money."

"You don't want your brothers and sisters knowing how rich you are?"

"Nope. Appalachians are a proud people, so they'd expect me to convince them to take my money. I don't really feel like doing that. Besides, I'm not trying to turn my family into the Beverly Hillbillies."

She laughs.

When she tries to protest me taking her plate, I shut it down with, "You cooked, I'll clean." I give everything she used a quick scrub and set it out to dry on top of the other pans, then take her hand to lead her back to the elevator.

It feels like we're a normal, 10-years-married couple as we brush our teeth and climb into bed. She sits up against the headboard, applying more cream that she lost in the shower, and I stretch out next to her on my back, hand on my full stomach, watching.

"Can I ask something a bit... strange?" At my smile and nod, she breathes in deeply and asks, "Have you always been so... possessive? Do you always fall hard?"

I tilt my head. "That's getting dangerously close to talking about exes, darlin', which isn't going to end well for whoever you might have in your past." As long as she never brings it up, I can go right on with my life, pretending they don't exist. Otherwise, her closets might pick up a few real skeletons.

"No," she hurries to assure me, laughing a little. "Don't get me wrong, it's really... flattering. I just—I'm surprised, I guess. You don't even know me that well, but you keep saying that I'm yours. And there's a difference between finding each other attractive—like we both obviously do," she hurries to add, seeing my lifted brow, "—and learning all the stuff that you can like about someone. Not like favorite color; more like the way they interact with the world and how they treat people and what they want from life."

"I do know some of that. You forget—I was watching you." As she nods, the memory flashing across her face in that subtle pink blush, I stretch an arm behind my head. "I also bugged your apartment."

"You what?!" she shrieks.

I chuckle. I knew that would be her reaction, but I'm still amused by it. "Darlin', I followed you. I stalked you for weeks. Why is that the line?"

"Because I... you..." I see her mind race, trying to remember every embarrassing thing she's ever done. Then, realization hits. She suddenly remembers what might be the worst—worse than any of the farting or off-key singing in the shower.

I let the smile spread, slow and intentional, as I sit up and turn around to cage her with my body, one hand planted on the mattress on either side of her. "That's right, Eleanor, I heard my name on those lips that first night, when you fingered that pretty pussy, thinking about me. You didn't know it, but that was the night you became mine."

She swallows, eyes round and slightly accusatory. "So, you knew all along—"

"I told you I didn't need you to tell me you wanted me. I just needed you to admit it. And admit that you wanted to act on it."

"I just..." she trails off, blushing harder. "I didn't realize it was... I mean, I guess I just assumed it wasn't really about me, so much as it was just a quirk of yours. I know some people fall really hard and fast, so I figured—"

I cut her off by gripping her chin and holding her still for a kiss. "Getting dangerously close to calling yourself unremarkable, there, darlin'."

Her eyes flash with heat, blood rushes to my dick, and our conversation is over.

22

ELEANOR

⸻◈⸻

Are we... vibing?

I've never been with someone who wanted so much from me. And it was a release like I've never known, just to give in and let him take it.

Sex has always seemed so transactional. Your pleasure, my pleasure, getting ourselves off and having fun together doing it. Even with guys who stuck around long enough to earn the illustrious title of Boyfriend, sex was, at most, an additional way to connect that felt good.

Sex with Mac is absolutely nothing like that. He acts like everything about me is his. My pleasure is his—his to give, his to take. Hell, with the way he's so attentive, thoughtful and obsessed, so is my heart. I'm not sure I'm even protecting it from him anymore.

Because in truth, that's why I kept my distance. I didn't want to admit to myself that letting him in even a little would blow me wide open. And he's so... much. So much power, and vitality, and intelligence, and physical perfection...

Yeah, I'm doomed. All I can do is hope he meant what he said about never letting me go, or at least that he means to keep me for a little while. Even beyond the next week, which is really my only guaranteed time.

He keeps me up so late that I spend most of the next day snoozing, missing him, and sneaking down to the kitchen in the elevator for snacks. In the late afternoon, I decide to give the well-equipped gym in the basement a try, in spite of the soreness in my legs and core.

It's such a large space, and it feels cavernous as the motion-sensor lights come on. Being alone with so much big equipment is almost intimidating, but it's better than accidentally making eye contact with Dimitri on the inner-thigh machine.

My workout is eerily quiet, since I can't figure out how to work the complicated music system built into the wall, but it leaves me feeling sweaty and accomplished. Afterwards, I shower, spend some time carving out a spot in Mac's closet for my stuff—feeling just a little silly doing it, knowing my days are numbered—and make my way back downstairs to start dinner.

Intentionally, I didn't make too much food when I was meal prepping. I know people get weird about leftovers, and, quite honestly, I wanted to give myself something to do while Mac was gone. But I did make enough to get Mac and Wesley through a couple of days, knowing that I could easily make something ad hoc for myself.

So, when I open the fridge to assess where we stand, I'm completely stunned. All those meals I prepared yesterday are gone. Either I severely misunderstood how much food these guys eat, or... I didn't calculate correctly for the number of people actually eating it. I have a reasonable idea of how much of that grocery order should be left, and a quick check of the remaining chicken and ground beef tells me that my suspicions were right. There's no way Dimitri is cooking for himself.

As if the thought summons the man...

"You," I hear, and whirl with a hand pressed to my chest in fear.

The fear doesn't abate as I see Dimitri's angry face. "Me?"

"You tell me these knives *suck*," he spits, emphasizing the American slang that sounds so strange in his accent. He places a canvas bundle on the counter with a distasteful look my way. "I come, take them to sharpen, only to find you know nothing. These knives are as sharp as you could want. Maybe they are too sharp? Hmm? You cut yourself? This is not my problem."

I'd know that beat-up canvas case anywhere, even if I hadn't just pulled it from my bags the night before. From here, I can even see my initials at the top, written in Sharpie. I'd assumed Mac had taken them to the kitchen for me. Then, when I couldn't find them down here, I assumed I'd simply missed them in our room somewhere.

"No, those are my knives," I say. "Mac had them brought here from my apartment."

He looks down, but his scowl stays firmly affixed, like he doesn't believe me or understand. So, I go to the knife drawer in the island and pull out one of the old, ceramic-coated ones for him. "These are the knives that were here."

He takes it, and recognition dawns on his face. Setting it down, he opens up the canvas case, and picks up my 7" chef's knife—the one Mac stabbed my table with. "These are very nice," he says with some ill-disguised surprise. "Well-balanced."

"Careful, I haven't even used that one since I sharpened it—" I start to protest as he turns it around in his hand, but stop as he holds it with enough confidence that I know he's not going to hurt himself. And when he presses his thumb to the edge of the blade and blood immediately wells, he just lifts his brows in surprise.

"You sharpened this? What did you use?"

Most people don't smile when they cut themselves. And frankly, anything other than a dirty look on his face feels out of place after how surly he's been. I'm more than a little thrown off. "Dual grit whetstone. It takes some time, but... sharp knives are important," I say slowly, defensively.

"I could not agree more." He lifts his head, still smiling faintly, though the gravity in his tone makes it clear he's not being facetious.

"I've cut myself much worse on dull knives."

"That is what I always say."

Encouraged by the change to his demeanor, I show him my index finger, where a scar curves almost all the way around. "Nearly lost this one."

He sets down the chef's knife gingerly—with reverence, almost—and holds out both his palms, then turns them over to show me the backs. They're littered with white raised scars, some small, some longer than an inch. "Training knives mostly, too dull to cut deep and just painful instead. This one, though, was from when I was surprised after just sharpening one. I also use a whetstone."

"It's all I can afford," I admit, smiling a little. Are we... vibing?

"Pah," he dismisses. "Expensive tools are for those who will not bother to learn the skill properly. Good results require patience, always."

Mac enters the kitchen, covered in sweat. I'm a little bummed, since it appears we missed each other in the gym. Then, I shake the emotion from my head. I look like a red-faced, sweaty monster when I work out—he doesn't need to see that just yet. I let my eyes travel the length of him, pausing to admire how much more prominent the veins on his arms seem right now. That post-pump swell is making my mouth water.

His eyes are warm as he beelines right for me and lays a heavy kiss on my lips. When he pulls back, I can see Dimitri has picked the blade back up and is staring down the length with one eye.

"This woman has good sense, James. And good knives."

Mac throws him a glance over his shoulder, then turns back to me with a self-satisfied grin. I want to knock that pretentious smile off his face because it was a compliment for me, no matter how he twists it to make it one about himself. "Mac stabbed my coffee table with that one. Almost ruined the tip."

As Dimitri scowls at him, Mac straightens and shoots me a look of betrayal.

"How could you?" Dimitri asks. "You, of all people, who lets no one touch his weapons."

"They were so expensive, too. I've been collecting for years. German, high carbon steel."

"German?" he repeats disparagingly, immediately setting it back down. "I take back what I said. You have no sense at all."

"What? You *just* said they were well-balanced."

"Japanese, or you are wasting your time and money." He approaches us and whips one out from his belt.

I freeze, and Mac tenses at my side, but the alarm melts quickly into admiration. The blade is short, more like 5", and shaped like a dagger where it's sharp on both sides. It's an instrument of death, with a cutout pattern at the end meant for easy gripping in spite of a bloody handle, and the tip is almost razor-blade sharp, 10° at most.

It's an odd feeling, knowing for sure that I'm looking at a murder weapon.

"Very nice," I breathe, my appreciation honest. I want to touch it, but I'm also a little afraid to ask. And of it.

Mac swats at my ass and steps around to grab water from the fridge. "I'm going to make dinner in a minute," I let him know as I watch him rifling through the drawers for something to eat.

"James, we will review the information from your watch today?"

Mac nods. "I'll drop in after my shower, before dinner."

"Do you want dinner, too?" I ask Dimitri. I try to keep my voice light, like I don't know he's been eating my food already. I want to give him his dignity, so he won't feel backed into a corner about it and turn me down out of spite.

Dimitri narrows his eyes at me, then shakes his head, his face a mask again. "No, thank you."

As soon as Dimitri is out of the kitchen, Mac sets down the bottle he'd just gulped and swoops in on me. I reach up, expecting the embrace, but he uses the firm grip around my waist to lift me up and place my ass on the counter. I squeak, reaching for the edges to steady myself, and widen my legs as he steps between them.

"Hi," he murmurs, staring straight into my eyes. The counters are a little higher than my waist, so this puts us almost level.

"Hi," I whisper back. I grab around his neck and press my torso into him. "How was your day?"

"It fucking sucked because I wasn't inside you."

His mouth claims mine, and there's nothing slow or sweet or gentle about it. The Mac from last night that wanted to savor the moment is gone; this version is raw with the hunger created by having already had a taste. His tongue plunges inside my mouth, and his hands press into the fleshy part between hip and ass, holding me still and tight against him so he can grind his pelvis against the hot, soft center of me. My skin tingles, and I shiver from the heat blooming everywhere in my body.

When he pulls away, I almost whine at the loss.

"I'm going to go take a shower. Care to join me?" he asks, reaching up to cup my jaw and run his finger roughly across my bottom lip.

I smile and touch the pad of the thick digit with my tongue. Then, I pull back. "It's getting late; I should start dinner. And I just took one."

"Take another," he urges, letting his thumb drag his hand across my chin so it can swipe down and circle my throat.

My pulse starts to race, and desire floods my pussy, making the whole area pound in time. He applies pressure with just his fingertips, and moves in again, stealing my breath into his mouth and holding me still with his delicate grip. I'm so consumed, so frenzied, that I'm truly lost to my senses as they fill with him—his scent, his touch, his taste.

He pulls back, rubbing the side of my neck softly. "So? Shower?"

I have to take a couple of deep breaths to recover. Then, I swallow against his hand with some difficulty. "Um, three in one day seems excessive," I reply.

"Three?"

"I plan on taking one later tonight after I show you how much I missed you." I ball the bottom of his shirt in my hands, looking down, transfixed, as it reveals a strip of hard flesh.

He grins. "You missed me, darlin'?"

"Yes, I thought about you all day."

His eyebrows lift, and the look is salacious. His fingers tighten just a hair. In response, I reach up and grip his forearm, feeling those veins under my hand. "And did you touch yourself?" There's no censure or approval. Just curiosity.

"No," I say, and it sounds almost like an admission. He has to know I thought about it, right?

"Good," he replies. His other hand trails over my hip and down my stomach, lightly running down the seam of my leggings. "It means you'll be hot and needy for me."

I moan a little at the feather-light touch. It's nowhere near enough. Once he reaches the approximate area of my entrance, he starts an up-ward stroke, never applying enough pressure. At the top, just where my clitoris is, he changes directions again, back down. I shiver and squirm.

"I bet you're ready now, aren't you, baby? I bet if I checked, you'd be dripping wet, wouldn't you?"

"Please," I cry softly as my eyes drift closed.

"Please, what? Please fuck you here on the counter?"

I just whimper in need because I don't want that—anyone could walk in—but I'm so fucking turned on that I also kind of do. I can't think straight. I know I'd let him if he wanted to. Thankfully, based on previous statements, I'm pretty sure he doesn't.

"One day, maybe," he says, letting me off the hook. "I'll tell you what's going to happen, though. You're going to get down off this counter, go into the bathroom, take off your panties and give them to me. Then, I'm going to go upstairs and take my shower, and you're going to cook us dinner."

Oh, God. He wants my panties? It's so unbelievably fucking hot. And dirty. "What are you going to do with them?" I wrinkle my nose.

"What do you think? I'm going to take the edge off so I can last more than 30 seconds when I finally get inside this sweet pussy later," he says with a little smirk, giving it a light slap that makes me jump and the blood rush to my clit from the gentle impact.

I heave a deep breath. He steps back just far enough that when I slide down off the counter, I end up dragging my whole torso against his, and we both groan a little. I feel his eyes on me as I exit the kitchen. I'm not 100% sure where the bathroom down here is, but I vaguely remember seeing a closed door near the foyer that looked too big to be a closet.

I'm right. I enter the powder room and close the door behind me. The tall mirror over the vanity shows me my wild state, and I laugh a little. A quick splash of water to cool my burning face, wet hands to smooth down my hair, and then I'm following Mac's orders. I give the piece of clothing a preemptive sniff, mostly out of curiosity, and it smells like nothing but clean laundry and tangy desire. And me, I suppose.

I emerge a minute later, underwear in pocket, and hand them to Mac when I see he's still alone in the kitchen. "Will I get these back?"

"Maybe when they lose your scent," he shrugs. "That pajama shirt did after a week or so. You can have it back now. Actually, let me wash it first. It's probably sticky."

My jaw drops. "You stole my pajama shirt? I was looking everywhere for that!"

He winks. "It's under my pillow."

I swat at him as he darts in for a kiss, laughing as he skillfully collects my wrists and holds me still to kiss me properly. Then he strides out of the room, and I'm left to catch my breath. He's such a whirlwind.

As I get started with dinner, I reflect on how strange today was. My life is so suddenly, so drastically different. I had a few moments where panic clawed at my throat—after my workout, when I'd seen the steam bath in the basement, and finding a gun in one of Mac's drawers when putting my clothes away—that reminded me this isn't just some vacation or honeymoon. Those kinds of triggers are probably going to stick with me for a little while, too.

Once the covered dish is in the oven, I wander down the hallway in the direction I always see Wesley coming from. Most of the doors in the hallway are open, except one. I knock and wait until I hear, "Yeah?"

Wesley looks up, then does a double take in surprise. "Oh, hello Eleanor. Is everything all right?"

I let my eyes wander for a few seconds, stunned by the sight of so much tech I don't even recognize. What on earth is that box in the corner, lighting up with rainbow colors? "Uh, yeah... everything is fine. I wanted to come find you because I've been thinking about ways to win over Captain Hulk," I say, returning my focus to Wesley.

At that, he sits back in his chair, crosses his arms, and regards me thoughtfully. "Oh? Do tell."

"I actually think Dimitri is coming around to me. He almost likes me, I can tell."

"Don't take it too personally. He doesn't particularly like me, either," Wesley briefly leans forward to retrieve the energy drink off his desk and take a sip. "Actually, I'm not sure he likes anyone."

I grin. "Well, if this works, I'll share credit with you. Because I have an idea, but I need your help."

His smile is conspiratorial now. "What do you need?"

"About 15 minutes with an internet connection—supervised, of course—and access to your grocery delivery service."

He smiles cheekily, then rubs his hands together. "This is going to be good."

23

MAC

<hr>

This is some of my favorite shit.

My update for the team is fuck-all. Another day spent in the comfort of a cramped sedan, mostly watching people access their units who aren't storing military-grade weaponry. Even the guard fell asleep. I saw a guy go into a unit that was full of mannequins and blow-up dolls, and one older lady added a particularly creepy stuffed fox on a plank of wood to her collection.

After checking in with Dimitri and Wes, Eleanor and I sit down at the table to have dinner together, like a real couple. And even though whatever casserole thing she made is amazing and eating next to her is exactly where I want to be, it still feels like an eternity until I can get her back upstairs. Especially with the added layer of torture, sitting there, knowing she's bare under those leggings. Luckily, Wes takes dish duty.

We pass the first floor, and I see that Dimitri's door is closed, his light is out, and I can hear the faint, uniform sound of his white noise machine. Her ass swings in my face as she climbs the second set of stairs, and it reminds me of something... a bookmarked incognito tab I watched on her phone.

I grin. This is going to be fun.

"Darlin', wait a second," I say. She pauses about halfway up the stairs, turning slightly to face me.

I slide my hands into her hair and cup her head to kiss her. Just a few light touches, a brush of my lips, and then a tightening of my hold in her hair, and she's gasping, grasping the sides of my shirt in her fists and her chest is heaving against mine. My girl does like it a little rough, more hardcore than vanilla. And she really likes being told what to do.

"I figured out how you can earn back those panties. If you still want them back."

She swallows and nods. The innocence shining in her eyes is almost too cute to spoil. Almost.

"Take off your clothes. Right here, right now." Her eyes widen, but I'm not done. "And crawl the rest of the way to the bedroom."

"W-what?" It's barely above a whisper, her tone both scandalized and hopelessly intrigued. "But Dimitri and Wesley—"

"You'd better crawl quickly, then," I say, grinning. If we hear Wesley coming, we'll have time to get out of his sight. Dimitri is in for the night.

I watch her weigh the decision, glancing around and then up at the hallway that's just lit due to our disturbance on the stairs. She bites her lip, presses her legs together, looks back at me, and nods with a little smile of excitement. With quick, shaking fingers, she pulls her sweatshirt up and unhooks her bra, handing each to me, then drops her leggings and steps out.

"I'll get them." I tell her when she goes to stoop for the pants, then I gesture forward with my chin. "Hands and knees, darlin'. Crawl."

Her eyes don't leave mine as she sinks to her knees, falling onto the step above where she's standing. She keeps her back arched and takes a second to orient her movements, then makes her way steadily up, step by step.

I have to bite back a groan, and my dick gets so rock hard it's painful. There are so many parts of her I want to see, to watch, I'm not even sure where to let myself linger. Hips, ass, pussy, legs, feet, arms, breasts, nipples, even her hair spilling over her shoulders and down her back... it all jiggles and swishes and sways, and it's all soft and smooth and round and mine.

She makes it to the top of the stairs and looks over her shoulder to see where I am. Finding me glued to the sight in front of me, her cheeks, already flushed with desire and exertion, darken.

"Good girl. Keep going." It comes out as a rasp.

I follow behind her, and her movements are almost painfully slow, now that we're not on the stairs and it's really just the two of us. She lets her knees skim along the carpet, stretching an arm out and throwing her ass up in the air with each movement forward. I even think I see her pussy clench once or twice. I knew she'd enjoy this as much as me.

When she gets to the door, she stops, throwing me another look over her shoulder. I move around her to open the door and turn on the light. Then, I cross to the far corner of the room and sit in the large chair facing the opening. She's still in the doorway, watching what I do. I settle in, toss my handful of her clothes onto the floor off to the side, spread my legs, and crook two fingers at her.

I can't decide which is a better view—the back, with her ass swaying, the hint of those glistening lips peeking out between her legs, or the front with her breasts rocking back and forth, her eyes locked on me, being able to see the expression on her face. She is totally wrapped up in the moment, so completely transfixed that she's left any and all shame behind. All that's in those beautiful blue eyes is the desire to do what I say and get what she wants.

When she's finally across the room, she slides her hands up my legs, starting all the way at the bottom, at my ankles. She skims my shins, spreads her palms over my knees, gives each thigh a light squeeze, and stops when she's hovering over my crotch. Her hand is so gentle as she caresses the side of my erection through my pants.

"Take it out, baby," I instruct, but it's more like giving her permission because she wants it so badly. It's fucking intoxicating.

"So, we both weren't wearing underwear," she says, finding my naked cock immediately under just the one layer of my sweats. She pulls the waistband down, just enough, and my cock springs free—tall and proud, curving up towards my body.

I don't have to ask or tell. She lowers her head and takes the tip into her mouth. The wet warmth envelops the most sensitive part of me, and I groan. I cup the back of her head, trying to keep from gripping her hair. "Fuuuuck," I hiss out as the gentle sucking causes her head to bob around.

She works lower, taking a bit more into her mouth, letting the spit run down the length and using it to give her hand some lubrication where it circles the rest of my shaft. When she twists it, I let my head fall back. The feel of it is unreal. Just as quickly, I lift my head because I'm not losing another second of the best view in the world.

Her tongue is so smooth and warm as it massages over, around, under. I jerk a little as she finds the most sensitive spot—just under the head, in the back. She takes that as a sign to do it again, then go deeper. I'm lost, my mind swirling somewhere above us, as she finds a steady rhythm, up and down with mouth and hand.

I feel a tightening in my balls, a building, tingling pressure. But I already came once in the shower earlier, and if one more is all I get for tonight, I don't want to shoot it down her willing little throat. Not this time. I tighten my hand in her hair and pull her back. She comes away looking almost upset to be interrupted.

"Up," I say, grabbing her hands and helping her stand, then pulling her into my lap.

I pull my legs together so she can be comfortable while straddling me, and lean back further into the plush double-wide chair so there's plenty of room.

This is some of my favorite shit. I love being mostly clothed while she's so totally bare for me. It's a heady feeling of control, of having the ultimate upper hand. Especially when she's spread open like this, too.

Not quite lined up, she leans forward, pressing her breasts against the ribbed material of my shirt, and finds my mouth. After a sloppy, urgent kiss, I guide her back, help her lift enough to get positioned correctly, and jerk her down hard on my well-slicked cock. She lets out a hoarse cry at the invasion, one stroke filling her to the brim, and I tense my abs, trying to give her even a centimeter more. Her tits bounce, her skin makes a slapping sound against mine, and I watch as my cock goes in and emerges, shiny and coated in a mix of my precum, and her arousal and spit.

"Oh my God," she moans, throwing her head back and rocking up and down. She holds onto my shoulders, her fingertips digging into the ridges between my traps and delts.

She's so tight and warm around me, so much better than my fucking hand and an empty pump onto the wall of the shower. Her weight on my lap, her body in my arms, the scent of her all around me... it's fucking perfect. And she's clearly enjoying setting the pace, finding her pleasure at the bottom of each stroke, full of my cock and able to grind that sensitive little clit against me.

In fact, she's enjoying it so much I'm going to wait until she comes to switch it up on her. I enjoy a good turn on the bottom, but not when I'm desperate like this—like I always seem to be for her. The need to take over and fuck hard burns in the back of my throat. My animal brain wants to take, claim, own, mark...

So, I'm going to help her along. I fill one hand with her thick, soft hip and move the other to give her some more friction where she needs it. Her clit slides along my fingers, and I move them back and forth—slowly, gently, watching her face as I do to see how it affects her.

And she likes it. I watch her eyes half-close, and go distant with focus. Her little whimpers fill the air, and she starts breathing heavier. "That's it, baby," I encourage. "You're doing so well for me. Such a good girl."

I know she's close when she starts throwing her weight a little on the downstrokes, trying to fill herself all the way, get that small dose of pain with her pleasure. Can do. I reach up and give her nipple a tight pinch, and she yelps in surprise, then moans long and loud as her whole body tenses. It's amazing to watch how completely her orgasm overtakes her, but I almost lose sight of her when she tightens—almost unbelievably—around my cock and her fluttering spasms try to coax me over that same edge.

I let her catch her breath for a few seconds, long enough for her to straighten in my lap and smile down at me. Giving her a little slap on one side of her ass, I tense like I want to get up. She masks the disappointment and lifts her leg; once it's clear, I move. I grab her waist and twist her around, draping her over the arm of the chair on her stomach.

"What—" she begins, but I get around behind her and sink my cock in enough that it turns into a groan.

This angle is so much better; it's so much easier to get in as deep as possible, to pull my hips back and snap them forward with all the power I want. She cries out on each thrust, pressed all the way against the immobile side of the furniture. Her breasts are swinging, and she's gripping around the arm.

I take it back. This is the best fucking view. Fuck it, they're all the best.

"Fuck, Mac, fuck..."

"Fuck," I agree, setting a punishing pace that has me spiraling towards the finish line. "Beg me. Beg me for my cum."

She whimpers as I bottom out, and I eat up the noises that are lifting the small hairs on my neck. "Please. Please, Mac," she moans. "Please fill me up. I want your cum."

So, I give it to her. I last a few more strokes, then I'm feeling that tingle through my scalp, the itch running down my spine. It tightens my balls, and the push-pull feeling of the orgasm slams through my dick and into her.

I slump, but take care not to fall on top of her. I'm not trying to force all the air out of her lungs, and she's leaning on her diaphragm. I pull away and sit my sweaty ass back in the chair. She rises up off the arm, wobbling on her knees, and turns a little to face me.

"Come here," I say, moving to the side to make room and holding out my arm.

With a somewhat sleepy smile, she curls up next to me. We're squished, and she's half on top of me. It's perfect. "Was that all okay?" I ask, stroking her hair.

"Hmm?" She tilts her head, leaning her chin on my chest.

"The crawling, the hair pulling, the roughness... I probably should have asked before—"

She smiles. "Well, 'okay' isn't exactly the word I'd use, but yeah. It was okay."

"What word would you use?"

"Fucking hot," she laughs breathlessly. "Not enough. More, please."

"This is going to be fun."

She smiles. "I would have said something if I didn't want to do the crawling thing, or if you were being too rough. I'm a tough girl; I can take it. Oh, and speaking of dirty fantasies..." she says, lifting her arm and showing me the soft flesh of the underside. "I forgot to tell you, but I have one of these birth control implants."

I nod. "I know."

She makes an exasperated noise and swats me on the chest. "Medical records are supposed to be—"

I cut her off with a laugh. "Darlin', I felt it when I was washing you." It may be the only way I didn't invade her privacy, but not because I wouldn't. Because I just hadn't gotten there yet.

"Oh." Her sheepishness is adorable.

"So, what you're saying is, 'Please fill me up again, Mac,'" I say, grinning at her.

Her smile is pure, feminine satisfaction.

24

MAC

❦

It's a conspiracy

It's a long day, but at least there's some action. I'm able to confirm that Rossi's guys are, in fact, getting ready for the drop on Sunday. In addition to the ever-present guard, two other guys show up and go inside the unit, emerging hours later with clipboards. A long-distance zoom with my lens tells me what I already know—it's a pre-sale checklist.

But after another day without so much as a glimpse of his bulletproof SUV, I'm starting to get concerned. Normally, a kingpin likes to periodically remind his minions who's in charge, and he gets involved in the big stuff. A quick sale of this much artillery is pretty big stuff, if you ask me. But Rossi hasn't shown his ugly mug.

I even follow the checklist guy who takes the papers with him, in the hopes that he's bringing it to the boss in person for a review. He doesn't. He goes to the Lucky Goat and settles in on a stool, gluing his eyes to the game on the TV behind the bar and his hand to a glass of whiskey.

So, on my way home, I decide to take a detour. A simple internet search—Wes isn't the only one who knows how to use public access to his advantage—yields me the address I'm looking for. Rossi's monstrosity is twenty miles from Ulysses, so maybe it's less of a detour and more of a hike. But as I suspected, it's completely locked down, which is part of the reason we don't typically hit them at home.

Only a few lights are on inside, and there are several cars parked out front—fancy Italian and German cars, clearly not owned by the help—but I can't spot the black SUV I saw the night of the warehouse debacle. Which doesn't necessarily mean he isn't home; there's a huge garage, too.

I wonder, not for the first time, if he's gone underground until after the sale. It's smart. Cowardly, but smart.

When I get home, I check the bedroom and hear that Eleanor is in the shower. So, I change for a workout. After shredding my pecs and shoulders, greeting my girl and rubbing one out, I head into Wes's cave. Dimitri is sitting on the other side of his desk, and they're chatting about hockey when I arrive. The conversation cuts short, not that I care. The Southeast doesn't have a lot of ice-based sports, so I never really got into it.

Dimitri is all business. "What do we know today?"

Wes takes his turn first. "Well, they've definitely got the law in their pocket." He spins his laptop to show us the officer profile of Christopher McCloskey, including a sealed disciplinary file that shows he's been reprimanded for accepting bribes, selective enforcement, and witness tampering. The dirty-cop trifecta.

"Good to know," Dimitri nods. "I assume you have added him to the file. We may be able to use this."

"Done. I also found your photo again and took it down. That's twice, if anyone's counting."

Dimitri sighs and nods again. "Good catch. Keep watching. And you, James?"

I prop myself against the back of the chair that sits opposite Wes's desk, leaning on both hands. "Looks like the sale is a go. They did inventory today, and they're just guarding the unit now. It's a waiting game until Sunday. I set up a camera before I left—Wes, can you make a program that'll alert us to any movements?"

He shrugs. "Give me an hour."

The job is Rossi, not the weapons, but I know we all feel the same—it's not a true win unless we get those guns off the market. It's usually easier to get it all in one fell swoop, in and out, but that might not be an option this time.

"I think we need to refocus. We should be trying to find Rossi, keeping some eyes on the house. If he's in there, I have a feeling he's just going to stay put. It's fucking Fort Knox. He's even got dogs patrolling the perimeter. Short of blowing it to hell, we're not getting in."

"Can we get eyes inside?" Dimitri asks Wes.

"I can try, depends on his firewall," Wes hedges, scratching the back of his neck. "But I've got people who owe me favors at most of the big network security providers, so I should be able to crack on."

"For now, let us hope he will be at the drop in person. It will still be the cleanest takedown," Dimitri says.

"What if he doesn't show?" Wes asks.

"He cannot stay in his house forever."

Privately, I disagree. He can if his house is anything like ours. "To do this right, we need a 24-hour watch. I'm going to need some help—I'm just one man."

"That is a good plan. I will take nights."

Wes and I turn to look at Dimitri, wearing twin expressions of shock. "What happened to bedtime at 10 o'clock sharp?" Wes asks.

"Yeah, you've never volunteered to throw off your sleep schedule," I echo. The only time I can remember him taking the night shift was when I had a concussion and couldn't stay awake at night.

"That was before."

"Before?" Wes prods.

"Before one of us had something to come home to," he says, fixing me with a look that's part dare, part self-congratulatory. Like he wants me to acknowledge his sacrifice, but I'd better not say anything about it.

Wes's smile is knowing, but he hides it by taking a sip of his drink.

I'm impressed. It didn't take her long to melt Dimitri's outer layer of ice, and that shit's thick—he is from the frozen Motherland, after all. Or maybe it's his version of an apology to me for wanting me to kill her. "Thanks, man. That's really—"

"You still fall asleep on the night watch. You think I do not know?"

Okay, it's not an apology to me. "That was once. Maybe twice. And you know the first time it was because of the concussion."

He snorts. "I will start tonight after some rest. That is all?"

Wes and I exchange a look. "All on my end for now," I say, and Wes nods his agreement. Dimitri stands fluidly and leaves.

"What just happened?" I ask, pointing at the door and Dimitri's pounding steps down the hallway.

Wes chuckles and shakes his head in disbelief. "He doesn't stand a chance. Oh, you hear that timer? I think that means supper is ready."

Eleanor is setting plates down on the table when we enter the kitchen—she must have heard us coming—and Wes sets a hand over his heart. "Only two place settings? But what'll we do with Hawkeye?" he asks in a low, conspiratorial tone, throwing a thumb my way.

She laughs like they've got some sort of fucking inside joke about it and turns back to the island to grab the other plate and the roll of silverware wrapped in a napkin, which she hands him with a smile. "Off you go."

"Yeah, keep smiling, pipsqueak," I call after him as he retreats down the hall. "It'll be dog food from now on."

I settle down at the table and turn my head up as she approaches with silverware for us. "Thank you, darlin', smells delicious."

She smiles proudly, looking down at the meal. "Chicken piccata, homemade pasta, roasted broccoli. I don't know how you guys were eating it steamed; it's so... fibrous," she says, wrinkling that cute nose.

It only took, like, two days of eating her food to question how I was eating any of it before. I'm never going back. My first bite bursts on my tongue with tart, lemon flavor. "Fucking fantastic," I moan.

She's watching me with a keyed-up expression. "Good? Not too salty? I was a little concerned because I'm used to a different kind of kosher salt than what's here—kitchens use Diamond and most home cooks have Morton, so I was worried that the salinity was a little off—"

"It's perfect," I say, cutting her nervous explanation short. The way she glows with satisfaction is enough to convince me that I should make a point to assure her how amazing everything is from now on. I like that look of contentment.

We fall into light conversation as we eat. I'm spearing one of the final few broccoli trees when I remember to update her on the change to my schedule. "Just so you know, I'll be leaving a bit earlier and getting home a bit later for the next couple of days. We're doing surveillance somewhere a little bit further now."

"Oh, okay," she says, looking down at what's left on her plate. "Is it just you doing surveillance?"

"It was before, but Dimitri's helping now." I sit back a little and regard her. "You know, he took the night shift. He's never taken the night shift willingly like that."

She tilts her head. "You said that with a certain emphasis, but I don't think I have enough context to understand exactly what you mean."

"He said he did it so we could be together more, and he's not a man predisposed to being soft or sentimental."

At that, she laughs. "I'd never have guessed," she says, the gentlest of roasts. "That was really nice of him."

"It was. You must have won him over somehow."

"I think it was the knives." She smiles and pushes around the last broccoli piece before spearing it on her fork. "I'm surprised Wesley can't help with your surveillance. Isn't hacking into people's doorbell cameras kind of his wheelhouse?"

I snort. One of his favorite topics. "Do yourself a favor and don't ask Wes about doorbell cameras unless you like anti-establishment and personal privacy rants."

At that, she smiles. "Love 'em. And conspiracy theories."

"Oh, really?" I push my plate away, finished. "Such as?"

"Well, have you heard about all the cheese they're keeping in caves in Missouri? The government bailed out big dairy years ago, and they've just been hoarding, like, a billion pounds of it."

My smile turns doubtful, and I blink at her. "Big dairy? Seriously?"

"It's why there's cheese in so many places it doesn't belong, like stuffed in the crust of a pizza that's already topped with it—government subsidies. It's a conspiracy," she declares, crossing her arms as I chuckle. "I'm gonna find it one day. If I ever go missing, look for me in the gouda."

"I'm going to look this up, you know," I say, wearing a huge, amused grin. "I'm not just going to take you at your word." I totally would.

"Good, you shouldn't. If I had my phone, I'd send you some links."

I laugh. "To answer your original question, no. Wes won't hack doorbell cameras for this kind of thing—Dimitri and I can handle the watch. We need his RAM for more important things most of the time."

"The anti-establishment stuff, I get. But why does he draw the line at doorbell cameras? Don't you guys regularly do stuff that's pretty invasive? And isn't he, like, a hacker? Seems like getting into places he isn't invited is kind of the idea."

I shrug and collect both of our plates to go start washing up. "We all have those lines we won't cross."

Her laugh is more of a bark, like she didn't mean to make the noise out loud and stopped herself. I throw her a look over my shoulder.

"You're telling me there's a line you won't cross?" she asks, raising an eyebrow at me.

I pause, considering. I'd told myself no video inside her apartment was that line. But really, combining looking in through her window and the audio from the bugs kind of made that a moot point. I haven't dug through her past enough to know every single detail, but that's just because she's here with me now, and I don't feel like I have to.

"For some things, maybe. But not when it comes to protecting the things that are mine." I place the plates in the sink and turn around to face her. She's sipping from her water glass. "There's nothing I won't do to protect you, Eleanor. I'm not the good guy, and I don't want you to forget that. I'm the guy that would kill everyone just to save one person, if that one person is you."

From the look on her face, I know she believes me. And I'm heartened by the flash of heat I see, however buried it is behind the discomfort.

"I know," she says quietly. "But I also really hope we never have to put that to the test."

25

ELEANOR

Am I the only one who deserves to live in spite of what I stumbled into?

Wesley told me to go wild when I placed the auxiliary grocery order and wouldn't let me pay him back. But going wild is exactly what I don't want to be accused of when spending someone else's money. And not having to count pennies feels like a luxury I can't trust. So, I tried to be reasonable—only add what we needed. Butter, white wine vinegar, shallots, that kind of thing.

Only to find that Wesley must have added one of every kind of junk food in the store after I left the office.

"You don't know how hard it's been," he says at the look I give him as he gathers all his contraband into his arms. "I'm a growing boy, and Dimitri won't let me have crisps!"

I snort at that. A growing boy? That, there, is a man grown. "Want me to try to make, like, a gourmet nacho cheese corn chip?"

With a gentle shake of his head, he tears open the bag of the real thing. "As much as I appreciate the offer, just let me have my refined sugar and preservatives."

"Fine, but if he finds out, and he thinks it's my fault because I'm the one that wanted to place the order, I'm going to rat you out so fast..."

He squints, then hands me a Dorito with a grave expression. "For your silence."

I take it with a laugh. Nothing crunches or turns your fingers orange quite like the real thing.

Once the groceries are put away, I check the time on the oven's clock and decide to start on my surprise for Dimitri. I'd noticed for the past couple of days that he's been leaving the house to relieve Mac's watch duty at about 6 PM, and I know I need to give myself extra time when trying something for the first time. So, I get started.

The recipe preamble states that pelmeni are a classic Russian comfort dish. There's not much subtlety to the ingredients—ground meat, grated onion, salt, flour, butter—they're just simple things that taste good together. It feels wrong not to add a little something that I know will elevate it, though. So, I tweak a few things—I sauté the onions first, add nutmeg for depth, and grate in some lemon zest.

Assembling the Russian dumplings is easy, if time-consuming. It's a lot like when I was on pasta duty, that year Chef Robert decided to serve house-made tortellini for restaurant week. The afternoon's hours fly by with the repetitive work, and I make a shit ton of pelmeni—they fill several bags that go straight into the freezer with a little prayer that he likes them.

I prepare a few servings' worth and pack them into containers, finishing just before he comes into the kitchen. He's all in black, even his beanie that covers his buzz cut. He has a black duffel that he sets on the island while he reaches into the fridge.

"Hey Dimitri," I greet him, trying to be cool from my position at the stove. It's stew for dinner tonight, and it really doesn't need constant stirring, but I'm nervous.

He nods at me; what I know now to be his version of a greeting.

"So, Mac told me that you took the night shift so we can have time together in the evenings. That was really sweet," I say.

He grunts, more an acknowledgment that I spoke than a response to it.

I swallow. Time to go in for the kill... "Well, to show you my thanks, I made you something to bring with you tonight, in case you get hungry." I turn and grab one of the containers from the counter. I hold out the Tupperware for him, trying not to let my face show the mixture of pride—they turned out good, for a first attempt—and anxious curiosity because he's Russian and he actually knows what it should taste like.

"What is it?" he asks, somehow managing to be both dismissive and suspicious.

"Pelmeni. Am I saying that right?"

"Pelmeni?" he repeats, blinking. He takes the rectangular container and peels back the lid to give it a good sniff.

My breath is literally bated. "You'll have to let me know if they're right, or what I can do better next time. I've never tried to make them before, but I thought that you might like a taste of home—if you even like pelmeni, that is... oh, damn, I probably should have asked—"

He's not even listening. He picks up a dumpling in his fingers, turns it around to examine it, and pops the whole thing into his mouth. Then, his eyes widen.

"Are they okay?"

"Where did you learn to make pelmeni?" he asks.

My breath whooshes out in relief. He didn't exactly say he likes them, but his tone is one of pleasant surprise. "The internet. The recipe I found swore they were authentic."

"My *babushka* made the best," he says vehemently. Then, he looks down and selects another and takes a bite. "These are... different. Not bad. For an American, you did well."

I warm with the praise, however slight it is. It feels like a lot, though, considering the most I've gotten out of him so far is a weird appreciation for how sharp I keep my knives. "I know, fat girl who can cook. What a revelation, huh?"

Dimitri chews thoughtfully. "I understand this is a thing you say to criticize yourself. But in my family, we say that large women make good food and good lovers." He looks down at the half-eaten dumpling. "These are good pelmeni."

There's nothing remotely sexual in his tone, nothing but a factual assessment. Still, I feel my face heat at the frankness of his speech. It didn't even occur to me I was being critical; people usually respond well to self-deprecation and witty observations. I was really just trying to win him over with humor, since he hasn't seemed like my biggest fan. It's my knee-jerk reaction.

"I'm glad you like them."

"I will take the other," he says, holding out his hand expectantly and looking at the second box sitting on the counter.

A thrill of pride spikes through me, and I rush to hand it to him. "There's a bunch in the freezer, too. If you want more, just let me know and I'll prepare them!"

He nods as he puts the containers into his bag. He adds a few bottles of water and, after a sidelong look my way, takes one of the other prepared meals. "Thank you," he says curtly, and leaves.

I'm going to ride the high of that win for the rest of the night.

It's a couple of hours until Mac walks back through the front door. I've been learning his routine over the past few days. Dimitri leaves at 6, Mac gets back at 8, and he always comes to greet me first. Then he changes into sweats, works out, showers, we eat dinner, and then we go have completely mind-blowing sex for, like, two hours. My response to that front door is basically Pavlovian now. The door clicks closed at 8 PM, and I get wet.

But realistically, this is the last night of that. It's Saturday. I know that whatever is going to happen is supposed to go down tomorrow night. After it's over, I'll be able to go home.

My heart sinks.

Wes takes his stew into his office, like usual, so it's just me and Mac at the table. I'm quiet, and Mac notices, but I don't really work up the courage to say anything about it until he's going back for seconds and I'm picking at the last couple of carrots and potatoes in my bowl. "Can I... Is it okay for me to ask you stuff about your work?" I say uncertainly.

"'Course you can ask. I'll tell you whatever I can."

"You're going somewhere further away, and you were doing surveillance alone before and now Dimitri's helping... I assume something changed. Is it just that whatever's going to happen is so soon?"

He sits back, looking thoughtful. "You know, for someone who really doesn't have any details, you've picked up a lot just by observing."

"It's not hard to notice comings and goings—I'm here all the time," I say. I try not to smile because, though it feels like praise, it's fundamentally about that thing we've been ignoring. The looming, abrupt conclusion to this honeymoon phase. "You don't have to tell me anything if you don't want to or you can't—"

"No, it's not that. You just haven't asked. But if you want to know, I'll tell you. Simple as that. I'm just trying to figure out how far back to go to give you the context you need."

I smile a little at the implicit trust. For my part, I was pretty intentionally staying out of it. Asking feels like opening a door that can't be closed—I'll know about the lives about to end, the danger Mac is about to face, the consequences of it going wrong. It's a lot of pressure for me, and I'm not even really involved.

"I want to know," I decide.

He nods. "The three of us have been working together for a few years now. There's someone we report to called the General. He's sort of our behind-the-scenes guy; he sends us the info on the job and takes a cut when we get the payout. We don't take every job—I mentioned before that we like to do our own research and make sure these guys are as bad as they seem."

"Do you ever get jobs that are kids or women?"

He cuts me a look. "Sometimes."

"Do you take them?"

"The 'kid' was 17, but he was into some real heavy shit—wanted by the Italians for stealing from the Don and fucking his wife. We tried scaring him straight, told him to disappear. He didn't, and someone else took the hit. No kids since."

"And women?"

He sits back and laces his fingers over his lower abdomen. "Yes, I've killed women. One who helped her husband sell other women in human trafficking rings. A group of women stealing infants from poorer countries and selling them in the US. The head of the board of a pharmaceutical company who was responsible for covering up dumping practices that poisoned the drinking water in an entire city—it killed 43 people."

I cover my mouth in horror. There are so many fucking terrible people in the world.

"Women are capable of atrocities. It's not as... frequent or obvious as it sometimes is with men, but I don't have some strict moral code that says no women at all, if that's what you were hoping to hear."

I chew on my lip. It isn't what I wanted to hear, but it's also self-consistent enough with the moral code he'd mentioned before that it makes sense at least. "If I can live with the other killing, I suppose I can live with that," I say. "So, this General gets you the jobs; you decide if you're going to do it. Then what?"

"Then we take them out. In this case, Rossi has men under him that would just assume control of the operation if he disappears, so we need to make sure we take care of them, too. And since there's a shipment of weapons already here in the country, we want to try to avoid those falling into the wrong hands."

I nod, looking down at my stew. I roll a carrot from one side to the other. "What would have happened if I hadn't interrupted you that night?"

"I never would have... um..." The uncharacteristic way he flounders for words makes me cock my head in surprise, but he recovers a second later. "I wouldn't have fumbled the shot. Rossi was on his way to the warehouse, but he was warned—the guy I missed had time to call or text him that they were under attack. If it had all gone according to plan, we would have gotten Rossi, his inner circle and the weapons shipment at once."

I wince. "I'm sorry."

"I'm not. It's why you're here now, and I'm a selfish enough bastard that I like that outcome too much to regret what happened to get here."

I feel my face heating and curse how easily I blush. But the fact that Mac is willing to damn the consequences just to know me? Yeah, I'm fucking swooning. "For what it's worth, I don't regret it either."

He smiles. "It's worth a hell of a lot to me," he says softly, then inhales, preparing for the next part of the story. "They moved their shipment out of the warehouse to a storage unit on the other side of town. I was watching the unit in the hopes that Rossi would show eventually, but he never did. So, we had to pivot. We've been keeping watch at his house to try to get eyes on him—so far, no luck. He's slippery."

"And what's happening tomorrow night?"

"Rossi sold the weapons, so the contents of that unit are going to change hands at midnight tomorrow night. We're still hoping he'll show for the sale."

"And then what? Everyone there dies?"

Mac nods.

I chew my lip. "That's the part where you lose me."

He tilts his head, an unspoken question.

"I get that Rossi is going to die, and based on what you told me about him, I don't think I'll be too torn up about it. But can you tell me for sure that everyone else deserves it, too? You did your due diligence, like you said, and everyone who will be there tomorrow night fits into that same bad-guy box?"

"Most people there will either see the money exchange hands or move boxes full of illegal guns and explosives. They're not really innocent in the situation."

"What if someone else is there, just accessing their unit and they're in the wrong place at the wrong time? Or what if someone gets dropped off by a driver, and he's just some guy who works for a ride-share app to make ends meet so he can support his family?"

He has the good grace to look uncomfortable when he says, "Leaving witnesses is... not how we normally do things."

I push away my bowl and sit back in my chair to look him hard in the eye. "I'd never think to tell you how to do what you do. All I'm saying is, if you'd made the same decision that night, I wouldn't be here right now. Am I the only one who deserves to live in spite of what I stumbled into?"

He sits with that, and doesn't reply. But it was mostly rhetorical anyway.

When I move to start upstairs, I pause in the doorway with my hand outstretched. He smiles at me and motions to the sink. "You go ahead; I'm going to do the dishes. I'll be up in a little bit. Don't start without me. Actually, wait, do. Just don't come without me."

I laugh and head to the bedroom. As I go, I replay our conversation, and I'm left with nothing but nervous apprehension—for the bystanders, for him.

For the danger he's in.

For the danger he *is*.

26

MAC

Why does it have to be zero-sum?

What would have happened if I hadn't interrupted that night?

I never would have... fallen in love.

I can't believe I almost told her I love her.

I can't believe I'm about to try to convince my team to change the plan for tomorrow night because she makes me feel like I could do better. Could be better.

This oughtta be interesting.

I knock on Wes's door and push it open after his affirmative noise. He's shoving chips into his mouth, washing them down with an energy drink, and his eyes are glued to his screen. "What's up, Mac?"

"Team meeting about tomorrow night. Can you get Dimitri on video?"

Wes nods, sets the bag of chips on the far edge of the desk—I know because it's out of the view of the cam—and pulls up the app on his screen. Dimitri answers on the second ring.

His face is barely illuminated by the brightness of his screen as he holds his phone up. The car is dark around him. Some flickering streetlights in the background show an empty cul-de-sac. It's not where I'd pick to do surveillance—a lone occupied car in an otherwise empty street tends to make people take notice, especially in the burbs—but Dimitri has his own ways. I know for a fact it's much closer to the house than where I've been parking. He does like to be closer to the action.

"Any sign of Rossi?" I ask.

"The house is quiet. Interior camera feed is quiet. No movement in the main living room, back door, or garage."

Wes sighs. "That's the issue with borrowing the feed on cameras already in someone's house. They never put them in the places they spend most of their time—bedroom, toilet, kitchen."

"I think we all know that the likelihood of Rossi showing tomorrow is low. We're not even sure if he's still in Jersey, right?"

Wes brings up a window on his other screen and types in a few things that show up as green typeface on a black background. It's real Matrix-looking shit. "No hits on his passport or license, so he hasn't flown commercial—not much of a shocker, there. Could still have chartered something private. But a car registered to him went through an EZ pass lane through Pennsylvania. No pictures of the driver, so it might have been his wife.

"I'm getting the camera access to his other homes. California just came through, still working on Colorado and Florida. He's smart, or someone who works for him is—they used different security companies. It's been a real pain in my arse."

"If he does not show, we have our backup plan," Dimitri says. "Neutralize the team, blow the unit."

The backup plan does take care of most of our problems, admittedly. But an explosion that destroys the unit and all the weapons will easily destroy most of the storage facility, and Eleanor is right—there's no way to plan for everything. Any person in the wrong place will be a casualty.

"Yeah, but we know guys like him. If after tomorrow night, he has no weapons, nothing to sell, and all his top guys are dead, he might just disappear and slip away. And he has enough money that—if he's smart—we'll never find him."

"Okay, get to the point, James," Dimitri says impatiently.

"I think we need a new Plan B. If the deal doesn't draw him out, we're going to have to do it." I inhale and turn to Wes. "How many times have you had to remove Dimitri's picture from that site?"

"Three, now."

Dimitri rolls his eyes and mutters something in Russian. I catch the word for "persistence."

"I think at this point, it's pretty clear that he thinks Dimitri is a threat, and I think we can use that. They think Big D's after the weapons, so let's go after the weapons. If we steal the shipment and D takes credit for it, I think it will piss him off enough to actually go on the offensive. And if we leave just enough of his men alive, he'll feel safe enough to show his face and have something to prove to them."

Wes sits back, tapping his fingers on the glass top of the desk as he thinks. "He's got an ego; we know that much. Wounding it could be the trick."

Dimitri's jaw grinds. He doesn't like the idea, but he didn't turn it down flat, so he doesn't hate it either. "If we take the guns, the buyer will be out for blood. Rossi will be out for blood."

"That's kind of the point."

"Anger could make him unpredictable," Dimitri argues. "Or, the buyer may try to kill him, thinking he crossed them twice."

"Double crossed," Wes corrects.

"That is what I said."

"It's a risk," I agree. "We can probably figure out how to take care of the buyer, though. What do you think, Wes?"

Wes cuts me a look. He doesn't like to appear to be taking sides; he likes to be the impartial one who weighs the decisions based on logic. "I think... I've been nervous that we'd drive Rossi underground tomorrow night. I think it could work, but I'm not the one whose face is plastered all over fucking Craigslist for assassins."

"Yes, that is me. And I do not like it. It is too big a change, too last minute, too many factors out of our control."

"Well, let's figure out how to control them. We still have time. You've got nowhere to be tonight, right?" I ask with a grin. Dimitri would never admit to it, but I know he gets bored the same as anyone else on surveillance duty. And nighttime watch is especially bad. "Let's start with how we'd steal the weapons and work out from there."

Dimitri looks thoughtful. "For this, I might have an idea. But it is more work for Wesley."

Wes cracks his knuckles and grins. "I could do with a challenge."

It's hours before we're done, but in the end, we have a plan—divert the truck, kill the drivers, stash the weapons and I'm on cleanup. I'm cool with it, since it's still mostly my idea. Wes is excited—he's a creature of chaos at heart, so he loves any time he gets to hack a public office. Dimitri is comfortable with the plan, which is the most we ever really get from him.

Wes has a long night ahead of him, so he follows me out of the office to head into the kitchen for another energy drink. I'm headed upstairs. But before we part ways in the foyer, he clears his throat.

"Dimitri wouldn't think to ask why—the reason you gave for wanting to change the plan makes sense to him. But I have been wondering."

"What?"

"If you're doing this for civilian casualty #4."

I shake my head. "I don't know what that means."

"It's what she called herself once," Wes glances up the stairs. "I don't think it's a coincidence that you chose to save her, and now you want to minimize fatalities."

"Maybe not," I shrug.

"This is not an accusation. I simply find it interesting. She's interesting, or rather, having an interesting effect."

"So, what, you just want to show me you're smart enough to have figured out she had something to do with this?"

"No..." he shakes his head and sighs. "Forget it."

I'm a dick. And probably too fucking sensitive on the subject of Eleanor. "Wait, no, tell me."

"We could all do with a fresh perspective now and again, and I think it got too easy to treat people's lives as obstacles," he begins slowly, seeming to choose his words. "I think it's good that she is pushing you—us, by extension—to reexamine the sacrifices we're willing to make. But she cares, James. Too much, maybe. If we did anything other than kill people for a living..."

I cross my arms. "She's... We're coming to terms."

"Maybe you are. But I don't think you're looking ahead, and I think that's a mistake. It won't work if you don't decide to make it work. You can't strong-arm this one and hope it goes your way—both of you have to engineer it."

As much as I want to pummel him for it, he's right. "I'm on it."

"Good. I like her. And I like her for you. I want her to... stay, whatever that means. And only a little bit because she's keeping us all fed."

I nod and start my ascent as he gives me a smile of commiseration and heads for the kitchen.

My girl is asleep. I hadn't really expected her to stay awake, and if she had her phone, I would have texted that I was held up. She's kicked off her covers and is lying on her stomach, one leg crooked up, both arms under the pillow. I sit in the chair across the room, watching her body rise and fall with her even breathing.

I just bought us a little more time; it'll put off the inevitable for another few days, maybe a week—as long as it takes Rossi to try to hit back after the attack on his ego. But Wesley is right. As per fucking usual.

I've been actively avoiding thinking about what happens after tomorrow night. After Rossi is gone. After I have to...

What do I have to do? Leave her? That's not fucking happening. Make a choice, then? Why does it have to be zero-sum?

She makes a soft sound in her sleep and my cock almost instantly hardens. It's a breathy noise, almost a moan. She shifts on her stomach, straightening her leg and pulling the pillow closer.

"Mac," she whispers.

I freeze. I can see her clearly in the darkness—my pupils adjust very quickly—but her head is tilted so I don't know if her eyes are open. She didn't sound awake.

She makes that same moaning noise again, and I'm done. She's asleep, and if she's dreaming, it's about me. I bet she's even still wet from getting primed before falling asleep. She's always wet by the time I touch her. It drives me fucking crazy.

Silently, I stalk over to the bed. Once I'm standing over her, I pull off my shirt. The noise it makes as it hits the floor is a low rustle of fabric. My pants are next. I shift my weight onto the bed incrementally, so the mattress doesn't move too much, and get into position slowly until I'm kneeling with her legs trapped under me.

Up on my knees, the view is spectacular. I can see her cream-colored, pale skin in the moonlight, the way her tank top has shifted in her sleep and is revealing most of a hard nipple, the way her shorts have ridden up and that she's not wearing underwear...

Bending slightly, I reach forward and gently move the shorts aside. Yup, they're soaked. She's soaked. I run my finger where her lips come together, relishing in the slick, wet heat of her.

Fuck, I need her.

I know that even now, as it sits undisturbed and turned off in our safe, her phone has a saved incognito tab with a filthy little story about a girl getting fucked by a home invader while she's asleep. I know that rape fantasies are common, just like I know that fantasy is the key word there. When we discussed our fantasies, this scenario didn't come up specifically, but she did admit she particularly likes being taken, feeling out of control.

And it just so happens that I love taking it from her.

I spit in my hand and palm myself, rubbing it along the hard length. Then, I line myself up and drop to my hands, which puts me only an inch or so above her. I feel her body jolt as she wakes up underneath me from the disturbance, and I slide my arms up next to hers to hold her wrists.

"Don't be scared. I'm just going to fuck this tight little pussy, darlin'," I say into her ear.

"What?" The sleep-fueled confusion is heavy in her voice. "Mac?"

I nudge the tip of me against her entrance, and she breathes in sharply. "Gonna fuck it because I can. Because it's mine. Right, baby?" I ask, showcasing willpower of fucking steel, not just ramming right in. I still want to give her one more chance to kick me off before I penetrate.

"Mac," she sighs and presses back against me. "I was dreaming that you were here..."

That's good enough for me. I curl forward, sliding in easily. She cries out at the feel, and I grit my teeth. It's so fucking good. Her body is warm and loose from sleep; her cunt is tight and hot. It hugs my cock, envelops it, sucks it as I pull back. Even more than usual with her legs together like this.

She wriggles a little in my grip, trying to hug the pillow closer, and as closely pressed as we are, it jostles my body too. She moans, dragging in breaths that are musical and needy. Between those sweet noises and the added tightness of this position, it's almost too much.

"Look at you, taking it like such a good girl," I grit out into her ear. She whimpers.

"Mac... it's so deep, I'm so full..."

I release her wrists to get better leverage, pulling up a little to thrust harder. "You like me using you like this? Using this pussy?" I ask through my teeth, my breath coming faster now.

"Yes," she moans back immediately. "I love it. Please use me... it's yours."

My dick twitches on its own, independent of the thrusting, and I nearly blow, hearing the words on her lips. *Yes. Fuck yes. Mine.*

"After I'm done, I'm going to leave my cock inside you all night. Can't let any of that cum go to waste; gotta plug it up."

Her cry is louder this time, a mixture of shock and pure arousal as my words hit home and turn the dial up on the stimulation in a way she wasn't expecting. I pick up the speed, unable to speak as my muscles strain to match pace with my desire. I chase the orgasm, falling headfirst into it as it catches me off guard. My vision flashes red and white in the dark. I feel my whole body tense, and I spill myself deep into her.

As the feeling passes, I let my hips slow to a languid pace, fucking the cum back into her. She's still breathing heavily, still writhing under me, still fucking me back as much as she can, like a desperate little thing. I know she hasn't come yet.

"You want to come too, darlin'?" I ask.

"Yes," she whines, adding as an afterthought, "please."

"You know I love it when you beg, but you can do better than that," I taunt.

"Please, please... I need to come. Please, can I come?"

Goddamn, my dick is already getting hard again. There's just something about how much she wants it, the intensity, the lack of shame. I start moving, thrusting gently, shallowly. Her pussy is a damn vise, gripping me so tight in spite of the extra lubrication inside her. Knowing that she's full of my cum, that she's going to take another load...

I reach for her breast, the one mostly hanging out of her shirt, and pull the pajama top down. She gasps as I grab it, massage it, roll the tip between my fingers. I kiss the shell of her ear as I do, licking along the curve of it the way I want to lick that tight bud between her legs. Focusing on her helps keep the second orgasm at bay for now, and I do love the way she responds to it all.

There's no way for me to get to her clit from this position, so I rear back and sit on my knees. I give the round globe of her ass a little smack, and she jolts. "Move your leg up, baby, like how it is when you sleep."

Our legs switch positions so I'm between hers. Staying a bit more upright, I'm not completely surrounding her like before, but I can still fuck her nice and deep and reach around her leg in the space by her hip to give her exactly what she needs to get off. She's so wet—so many fluids—my fingers glide over the nerves there. She grinds against my hand, using my fingers for her pleasure much the same way I'm using her pussy for mine.

I rub circles, letting her hip movements set the pace, and find a good counter rhythm with my own hips. It's amazing how slick that smooth skin can become, almost slippery, and so firm. It's pulsing with desire. She cries out and pushes hard against my fingers. I feel her clench around me, and I have to grit my teeth against my own creeping orgasm. She rides it out, wailing in her pleasure, lost to the world around her.

She's still shaking when she begs, "No more."

Some nights, I don't let her decide that. Tonight, I want to come inside my girl again, pull her into my arms, and sleep with my cock warm between her legs all night. So, I move my hand away from her overstimulated clit, and use it to grab that perfect handhold below her waist to give myself leverage. I thrust hard, enjoying the feeling of bottoming out, and after a few more minutes I'm succumbing to the pleasure again. My balls tighten—the second load is usually smaller—and my skin prickles. This time, there's a roaring in my ears, and my thighs start shaking with the effort of holding myself up over her.

With a final grunt, I relax onto her, rolling off to the side before giving her my full weight. I hook my arm around her waist to pull her with me. She wriggles to settle in, and I close my eyes, exhausted and satisfied.

27

MAC

<hr>

I'm left with the satisfaction of a well-executed plan

That's it. That's the last box. The rolling door of the truck comes down, closing in $500 million of heavy weaponry.

I tap the bud in my ear. "No sign of him," I say.

"I'm watching the house and traffic. I've got nothing," Wes agrees with me.

"Fuck," Dimitri says. *"Okay. Plan B. Is the truck loaded?"*

"Just about to leave," I say, watching the driver move around to the front.

"I will move into position. Wesley, lead them to us."

"Roger."

The line goes dead. We all have our tasks. Wesley diverts the truck to their waiting trap, and he and Dimitri take care of the drivers and escort and stash the shipment in an old warehouse just purchased through a shell corporation. I take out most, but not all, of Rossi's men left at the scene. So now, I just have to wait for my shot and hope it comes before they go their respective ways.

I stare through the scope and see the faces I've been memorizing from a combination of surveillance photos and mugshots. Nice of them to crowd together like that for me. Phil Beasley, Karthik Uman, Owen Johnson, Alec Putnam. Rossi's top brass. Grigori Folson is missing, which isn't surprising, as he's Rossi's right hand.

The other men in the group are not on my list, but I do recognize some of them as lower-ranking members of his crew. They're the ones who've never shot a man in the kneecap for information, or weighed down a body bag before tossing it in the river. They're the ones who don't know what's really going on behind their paycheck. The night shift security guard for the storage facility is with them, too—likely just shooting the shit because he's bored at work.

These are the people my girl doesn't want me to kill. So, I won't.

I inhale, line up my shot, and blow the breath out slowly and controlled as I squeeze the trigger. Before anyone in the group registers the kill shot to the back of Karthik's head that makes it explode, spraying everyone around him with red, I recover from the kickback and fire off another that catches Phil right between the eyes. Alec's head moves, his face splattered with Karthik's blood and brains, eyes wide with confused horror, and my last shot isn't dead center because he turns. Still deadly, blowing out the whole front of his face from the side.

It's Owen's lucky night. He gets to be the one to describe to his boss the horror of seeing everyone around him die violently, and the unparalleled fear of not knowing where the threat is coming from.

Pride swells at three—well, two and a half—perfect shots, just as all hell breaks loose in front of my eyes. Owen and the remaining low-level soldiers draw their own weapons as they scatter. The security guard shakes, locked in place in his fear, and I watch the wet spot grow down the leg of his pants.

"Keep it together, Harry," I mutter to him. He's just a rented warm body, a former high school jock with a taser gun. But he's got protocol to follow—he should be running back to the office and calling the real police. We want that dirty cop, McCloskey, to know.

My heart rate is barely altered as I calmly pack everything into the Corolla. The nervous excitement that used to make my hands shake for hours ran out a long time ago, and now I'm left with the satisfaction of a well-executed plan and a dull buzz that runs throughout my body. At least I've never had to deal with the Sniper's High—the feeling some of us get that instant you see someone's head explode into a fine red mist. It's a God complex thing, knowing you can choose who lives and who dies. It makes you want to just keep shooting, they say.

The trees shield my movements, and the wet fallen leaves make gentle shushing noises under my feet. I've got another stop before I can go home to my girl. Based on Grigori's habits, I know where he'll be, and I want to see if my hunch is right. After this kind of attack, Rossi needs to be informed. But if Rossi isn't around, Owen will go to Grigori, and McCloskey will be the one to break it to the big boss.

Before I head back, I take another moment to look in on the chaos. Owen is trying to organize the few guys left to check a perimeter, all the while trying not to look at the bodies, now missing significant chunks of their heads.

He's on the phone—it's a toss-up whether it's Grigori or McCloskey. Or maybe even Felix. I wouldn't be surprised if he double-dips and plays both sides. Everyone needs a fixer now and then, and he's discreet enough that Rossi would never know that last week Felix took a job to dispose of the body of someone on his payroll.

It's not a long drive to Eleanor's apartment building, though I do park a block away and slip through the alleys in the dark to get to the back door. The building has dim lighting in the stairwell at night when it's fully occupied, and it leaves me feeling exposed, so I take the stairs two at a time.

The apartment is full of stale, undisturbed air and the sickly rotting scent of trash that should have been taken out last week. Well, she did leave in a hurry, and my request for Felix was just to pack things, not take care of the trash.

Luckily, she doesn't have anything that needs care, like plants, or pets...

Oh, wait. What was that thing she mentioned the first time we met? She was worried about the chemicals because it was alive... I open the fridge and see the jar of white goo. Yeah, that's it. Whatever it is, it looks disgusting, so I check to make sure the lid is tight before shoving it into my pocket.

The view of The Lucky Goat from her window is pretty good, though the angle could be better to really see in—my field of view is narrow. But beggars can't be choosers, and spying from a dark apartment is better than being out on the street at 1 AM, or trying my luck with another unit on the first floor.

The binoculars in my other pocket are enough. I can see just well enough through the grimy windows to spot Grigori at the end of the bar. Some time passes. He nearly finishes his drink, then he lifts his phone to his ear. Suddenly, as if something electrocutes him, he straightens and jumps up. The stool falls behind him, and the bartender and the only other patron of the bar at this hour swivel around to look at him.

Noticing the attention he's drawing, he aggressively says something into the phone and starts pulling on his coat. When he busts through the door of the bar, I am tempted to open her window to hear. But he's across the street, and I doubt his voice would carry.

He fumbles with his keys, dropping them in a pile of gray snow on the street corner, unlocks his car with a flash of the headlights and climbs in.

So, Grigori knows now, and he's likely headed to the crime scene. If he doesn't get a DUI on the way.

The question is, where's Rossi?

28

ELEANOR

But now the reckoning is here

It has to have been 10 minutes since I last looked at the clock, right? I mean, I got lost in my thoughts for at least that long, and it feels like it's been a fucking eternity. I spit out the thumbnail I just chewed off and let my knees fall to the sides. I can't stand it anymore. I look.

12:21 AM.

It's been three minutes.

Ugh! Fuck this.

I jump out of bed and head down to the kitchen. I need to chop something. Or bake.

The problem with baking is that it's too precise—too recipe driven—and I don't have anything memorized well enough that I wouldn't need my phone. And the problem with a perfectly diced mirepoix is that it's busy work. It gives me something to do with my hands, but isn't mindful enough that my brain shuts off. But it's better than nothing, even if I'm still sick with worry and doubt and questions without answers and no way to contact anyone.

So, mirepoix it is.

The next time I look up, it's 12:47 AM. Mac still isn't back, but I'm sure that whatever he set out to do is done. People are... dead.

But how many? And is he all right? Fear knots in my stomach.

No. I have to assume he's okay. It's the only way I'll get through the night.

But then what if he is okay, and they got their guy? What happens now? Like... is this... is it done? Do I go back to...

My chest tightens, and I have to hold back tears.

I put down the knife and curse the onions, wiping under my eyes.

For a moment there, I really thought I was doing a good job of not getting too far ahead of myself. Or living in a world that doesn't actually exist; one where I get to stay here, be here with Mac, and feed these guys—who I genuinely, really like—forever.

I told myself shit like "it'll just be easier to use the closet instead of trying to live out of the suitcase" and, "it's really more economical to buy the 25-pound bag of flour, I'm sure I'll get through it." But really, I've been making decisions based on the assumption that I'll be staying. That this doesn't have to end.

And days ago, this conclusion still felt like an infinite amount of time away. I didn't have to think about it yet. But now the reckoning is here, and I'm so emotionally invested that I'm going to be completely crushed by it.

I toss a thick-bottomed pot on the stove and start cooking the carrots, onions, and celery. It may be 1 AM, but it's never too late—early?—for a pot pie.

The pie crust is just coming together when I hear the front door open and a deep laugh fill the foyer. It echoes off the marble, sounding right next to me in the kitchen. I drop the dough and walk towards the hallway.

"—and then it's really just a matter of a password cracking program and enough juice. Any lag might have lost us the truck."

"What is this, false modesty? It does not suit you," Dimitri says with a scoff. It almost sounds like a joke.

Wesley's low chuckle sounds. "Well, what about that road closure sign? Stroke of genius—"

They stop as I step into the opening between the double stairs. Wesley is hanging his coat, his back to me, and Dimitri is toeing off his boots. A bruise is forming on his jaw, purple and swollen, and blood has dripped and dried into a crusty line under one of his nostrils.

"You are still awake," Dimitri observes. He's looking at me cautiously, like a horse he doesn't want to spook.

"Where's Mac?" I look between them and don't miss the glance they exchange. "Oh my God... Is he—" Why is there suddenly no air in this room?

"He's fine," Wesley says, stepping forward and grabbing my hand. "Calm down, Eleanor. Breathe. We spoke with him on the phone not long ago. He'll be along."

I force in a deep breath. Wesley really does have kind eyes, and I find it easy to believe the things he says. I nod. "Okay."

He squeezes my hand, then lets go. He opens his mouth to say something else, but looks down and makes a face. "What's on your hands?"

"Oh, flour."

He claps his palms together, wiping them against each other and scattering some of what transferred to his skin. "Let's get back into the kitchen, hmm? Perhaps a little washing up?"

"No, I'm... uh, making a pie crust."

Dimitri snorts at that, and Wesley glances over his shoulder with an expression meant to silence. Dimitri raises his eyebrows and disappears into the powder room by the entrance. I hear the water come on and assume he's cleaning up the blood.

"Well, let's get you a drink then. Fancy some bubbles?"

When I'd go back to the counter and pick my dough back up, he ushers me towards the table. Moving fluidly through the kitchen, he grabs two champagne flutes that are so strangely shaped I know they cost a fortune. There's a small drink refrigerator built into the cabinetry under the island, and he pulls out a bottle that's been chilling on its side.

"So... it went well?" I broach. "Seems like maybe it went well. You guys were in a good mood."

"It did."

"And Mac wasn't with you? He was... somewhere else, I suppose."

"Ah, you didn't know. Your reaction makes sense." He pops the top as he sits down on the opposite side of the corner next to me. "Yes, we had different parts to play, so he was at another location."

His expression is pure focus as he expertly tilts the glass and fills it slowly enough that he doesn't even have to wait for the bubbles to subside. I feel the tension easing out of my shoulders at his unbothered demeanor—he's so calm. He clearly thinks there's nothing to worry about.

"It was quite the reaction, Eleanor."

I bite my lip. "I've been a bit"—*out of my damn mind*—"worried."

He regards me over the top of his champagne flute. "Didn't you speak with him beforehand about what was going to happen tonight?"

I wince at his gently reproving tone and accept the flute. After a quick sip that tickles my nose and prickles my tongue, I shake my head. "Not really. But it's my fault. Mac says he'd tell me anything I ask, I just... I didn't ask."

"You don't want to know," he guesses.

"I didn't." It's part agreement, part correction. Because I'm kicking myself for it now.

My second sip is more of a gulp, but the bubbles start to go to my head, and warmth spreads across my face, starting from my nose.

"That was not the fearful look of a woman who didn't ask for details because she doesn't care."

"It's not why I didn't ask," I say softly. "I do care."

"I know," he says, just as softly.

There's a world of understanding in his look, and I get the sense that he really does know. He knows that I don't just mean that I care about the mission, or about Mac. He knows how torn I am, how much my heart aches. Maybe he even knows how scared I am about what's going to happen next.

"I don't know what to do." Normally, I'd call Mel. It's what sisters are for. Sure, sometimes they talk at you for an hour, but they're always there when you need someone to listen to you, too.

"Do you want some advice?" he asks, spinning the flute from the base of the stem.

For some reason, that makes me smile—asking for consent before trying to help. "Sure."

"Someone wise once said, 'It won't work if you don't decide to make it work; you have to engineer it.'"

I nod because it's good advice and I can't fault its truth, then I frown. "Who said that?"

"Someone wise. Don't worry about it. My point is, you can't do this by halves. You are either part of our world or you're out of it. And trust me, the easier way is to just get out. But..." he pauses, takes another sip, and smiles at me, "if you're up for the challenge, you may find that the benefits outweigh the drawbacks."

I finish my glass—damn, these flutes are small—and he reaches over to refill it for me. "That's assuming he even wants me to be part of this world."

He chuckles. "Sounds like that's the first conversation you need to have with him, then."

"Maybe." I take another sip and reach for the bottle to read the label. I don't recognize it, and it's not French, like I was expecting. "This is really good."

"My brother always said that a man ought not to have too many vices, but good champagne makes life worth living," he says poetically, looking at the fine bubbles rising up the side of the glass.

"So was your brother the one who said the thing about engineering a relationship?"

There's a beat, and he takes a sip to hide a smile. Then, a car door slams closed outside, just audible in the silence of the kitchen. "Ah, there he is. See? I told you he was right behind us," Wesley says. He tops me off one last time and stands, picking up the half-full bottle, then his drink from the base of its thin stem. "I'll leave you two."

"Wesley?"

"Yes, love?"

"Thanks for waiting with me. And for the champagne."

He lifts his glass in a "cheers" kind of acknowledgment.

I wasn't even aware I had the capacity for so many feelings at once. I take a drink from my glass to give myself something to do as they all come swirling in like the wind through the open front door. I'm debating rising from the table—now that I'm calmer and the first glass of too-quickly consumed champagne has gone to my head, it feels less urgent to meet him in the foyer—when he comes into the kitchen.

Mac's smile for me is exhausted, but warm. "I just followed my nose. What are you still doing up, darlin'?"

"Waiting for you," I reply truthfully. I lift the glass. "And having a drink with Wesley."

"Oh? Where'd he go?"

"Back into his office. They got back a bit before you; he told me you were okay."

He grabs a beer from the fridge and moves to join me at the table. "We usually all have a drink together when we get back from a successful mission. Guess this one's not quite over yet, though."

I perk up a little. "It's not?"

The cap of his drink twists off with a little hissing noise. "Not yet. We didn't get him, but we set something in motion to." He motions to the mess still sitting on the counter with his index finger extended from his grip around the bottle. "What's all this?"

"Nervous cooking," I say with a laugh. "I'm glad you're home safe."

"Me too." He sits in the chair Wesley vacated, and pats his knee. "Come here, I want to hold you."

I put the flute down on the table. "Mac," I begin hesitantly. "I'm really not a lap girl."

He shakes his head. "Give me your foot, then. I just need my hands on you."

There's a flash of excitement low in my belly at that, then I register the words. He sounds uncharacteristically uneasy. I shift my chair back and around the corner of the table so I can better face him.

"Are you okay?" I ask, lifting my bare foot slowly and placing it on his knee.

He slides his fingers under the arch, and I have to bite back a giggle—it's maybe the only place on my body I'm ticklish. He starts squeezing, and holds out his other hand like he wants me to give him my right foot, too. So, I do. My core starts pounding—another Pavlovian response to being slightly open, spread, and near him.

But it occurs to me that he's being almost a little... distant. He didn't just come right for me when he entered the room. Usually, he grabs me from behind, or drops a kiss on my upturned mouth even before he says hello.

And he only further confirms my suspicions as he avoids my eye when he says, "I know tonight was different from when I killed that guy in the steam room. I wasn't sure you'd let me touch you again, knowing what I did."

My head whips up from its slight downward tilt, as I'd been watching his huge hands dwarf my perfectly normally sized feet. I'm shocked at the admission, then contrite. That's my fault. I made him feel that way. "I'm sorry."

He shakes his head. "I didn't say it to make you apologize. And you shouldn't apologize for not being okay with what I do."

I inhale, take a sip of the champagne to center myself, and prepare to dive into Wesley's advice. No doing this by halves. "Tell me what happened. I want to know."

He eyes me, searching my face, then resumes his careful kneading of the arches of my feet. "Rossi is in hiding, so we have to try to draw him out. We got control of the weapons shipment; it's sitting in a warehouse where no one would ever think to look. It's going to really piss off the buyer, and Rossi will hopefully take it personally. Well, the stealing and what I did. I stayed behind after the truck left to... send a message."

I know what that means. "And how many people did you—"

"Three. And all of them were Rossi's top guys. Real scumbags."

I raise my brows. "Only three?" then, realizing how that sounded, I make a face. "I mean—"

"I know what you mean. Yeah, only three. I left the others."

A chill shoots up my spine. He left witnesses? "Why?" it comes out barely above a whisper. I'm so afraid of the answer, and I'm not even really sure why.

His hands travel up from my feet. Still using a stiff massaging motion, he slides under my heels and circles my ankles. "Because I could. Because someone reminded me that I held people's lives in my hands and that I have a choice not to become a monster."

I swallow hard, surprised to find my throat thick with emotion. "I didn't say all that," I choke out.

He smiles a little, and it's an odd expression—the corners of his lips still point down. "You did, just not using those exact words."

It suddenly feels like my skin is too small for my body—I'm soaring, flying towards him and somewhere above us both, reveling in the feeling of importance and worth. His fingers anchor me, though, as they dig into my calves. He finds a tight spot, applies pressure, and I bite down on a moan.

My head is so full of thoughts, each one vying to be the first one on my lips. What comes out is, "I was so afraid tonight. I was afraid you'd get hurt—"

"I'm usually pretty far from the action," he says, releasing one of my calves to take a drink from his beer. "I still have to be on my game and secure my spot, but I'm not in as much danger as Dimitri is, for example."

That actually does calm some of the swirling panic. "I was also afraid," I inhale and throw back the rest of the glass for courage, "that you'd succeed."

He grimaces. "I know you don't like—"

"No, wait, let me... I meant because if Rossi is dead, there's no more reason for me to stay here." I chance a look up and find him staring at me, eyes intense. His fingers stop moving. "I'm just... um... I mean, can we just pretend like it doesn't have to end?"

"You want to pretend?"

"I don't want to think about everything else."

"Everything else?"

"Like what happens when I leave? You don't live here; you're renting. You probably move all over, and even if you did want to bring me along, I can't imagine that's a good idea for either of us..." I trail off, hoping he'll jump in and let me off the hook. He doesn't, so I clear my throat. "Let's just pretend like we're going to figure it out and make it work. Let's pretend like there isn't a time limit. Okay?"

He resumes rubbing my legs with a secret little smile on his lips. "Eleanor, let me ask you something. Do you want to figure out how to make it work?"

I bite my lip. More than anything. The worst emotion I had in that awful mixed bag was the paralyzing fear that I'd have to give him up. There's still this insidious worry that he's going to tire of me eventually, and leave me at some point... But that future heartbreak can be future Eleanor's problem.

"Yes."

"Then that's what we'll do." His tone is final. Decided. "Come on, it's late."

He finishes his beer while I clean up my mess, and we climb up the stairs and into bed. For the first night since we started being intimate, we don't have sex. We just lay there, cuddled, holding each other. And the wall I'd started trying to build around my heart comes crumbling back down.

29

MAC

———◆◇◆———

Date stuff

She stirs as I sit on the bed, fully dressed, putting on my watch. I tug the covers up higher over her back, and she opens her eyes, blinks slowly, and smiles. My body responds instantly to the soft, sweet look, humming with warmth and energy. I lean down to kiss her temple.

"What time is it?" the rasp of sleep is thick in her voice. She clears her throat.

"Early. I have to go check on a few things. But I want you to be ready to go tonight at 9 PM."

The relaxation disappears from her expression, and she lifts up off the pillow. "Go?"

"We're going on a date."

She falls back down, rolling a little to face me better. A tentative smile lifts the corners of her mouth. "A... date? Like, outside the house? Around... other people?"

I reach out and trace the line of her lovely neck, down her shoulder. "We're going to try to make this work, right? Well, couples go out on dates. So, we're going to a restaurant—a good one. It's some new place, the Rouge something—"

Her eyes go wide. "Rouge Elephant? You got a reservation at Rouge Elephant?!"

"I know a guy." I give myself a metaphorical pat on the back at her excitement.

"Chef Robert couldn't get a reservation there for his anniversary," she says with a chuckle. "He was so pissed that he completely changed the menu to prove we could do Vietnamese fusion, too. We couldn't."

"I'm sure *you* could," I say.

She grins and flips onto her back, lifting her arms over her head in a stretch that pulls her shirt tight against her breasts. I lock eyes with the little nubs of her nipples poking through the pajama top. "I assume if we're going out, it's safe enough?"

"We think so. For this, anyway."

Still no sign of him in the 36 hours since we struck. Rossi is somewhere licking his wounds and planning his next move. Logic—and lack of activity—indicates he's at another of his homes.

I specifically selected the time and location for dinner to minimize the risk. She's unlikely to see anyone she knows at an expensive, fancy restaurant far from the center of Ulysses late on a Tuesday.

"If it's safe, can I have my phone back? I'd like to look up the menu at some point today."

"I ordered you a new one; it'll get here tomorrow. Wes is going to set it up for you."

She sits up at that. "What? Why? I don't need a new phone—"

"Because you need a way to get ahold of me so you're not worried like you were the other night, but Wes still thinks it's better if you don't use your old phone. We'll transfer your contacts and everything once this is all over." And it'll satisfy that deep, possessive animal inside of me to know that—at least for a little while—mine will be the only contact she has.

"I... I shouldn't take it—it's too generous—but you're talking like it's already done, so I suppose there isn't much point in protesting?"

I shake my head.

"Then, thank you."

After a quick kiss, I'm out the door. I drive to the crime scene first, and I'm not at all surprised to see that the police tape has been removed. The bodies disappeared after about six hours—two guys in official uniforms bagged and tagged them while Officer McCloskey took all the witness statements and his partner spoke to CSI.

I'm not particularly worried about what the law will find. It'll be obvious, even to the mayor's nepo-hire for coroner, that a long-range rifle was responsible for the shooting. But I trust McCloskey to do what he can to bury as many details as possible—they were moving a storage unit full of illegal weapons, after all.

Then, it's off to the Rossi residence for another long day of fucking nothing. The local cable company comes for maintenance on some of the buried lines, but no one else even drives down his street. 7 PM rolls around eventually, and Dimitri relieves me so I can go get ready for my date.

I don't see her in our room, but I know she was just here from the steam in the air and the heaviness of her scent. I'm running a little behind, so I shower quickly and throw on the jacket, button down and slacks I already picked out. As I'm dressing, it occurs to me that I didn't consider what she'd wear. Or if she had anything to wear...

Not a problem, evidently. She's waiting for me in the foyer, and she's in one of those little black dresses, as they call them.

"How do I look?" she asks, all nervous energy. "I was surprised the dress was packed—it's, like, the only nice thing I own—and it's not quite seasonally appropriate, but I couldn't wear leggings to the Rouge Elephant."

I have to school my expression, because I think it's what's making her anxious. She looks fucking hot; she just looks... well, too fucking hot. There's definitely a little too much skin showing for the cold weather, and those legs look longer than normal in her heeled ankle boots. I have to swallow the demand that she go put on those leggings she mentioned.

"You look amazing, baby."

She grins, and it's so happy and relieved that I feel like an ass. I should have bought her something. Something expensive. Something worthy of her. Something with a fucking floor-length skirt.

"You look amazing, too."

I hold out my arm and place my hand on her lower back to lead her out to the car. This place is the kind of deal with a dress code, so I decide to take Wes's rented Mustang to fit in better—he cares a bit more about horsepower and a bit less about being seen since he usually ends up leaving in the van anyway. I open her door, then trot around to my side. The car starts up with a satisfying purr.

As we get onto the highway, I settle my hand on her knee and—just barely—resist the urge to slide it up between her legs. The skin of her thigh is freshly shaved, smooth, and so soft and warm. "So, tell me some things about yourself."

"Some things?" she repeats with a laugh, looking down at my hand covering her knee. I can tell she likes it. "Like what?"

"Childhood, family, how you got into cooking. Tell me things. Date stuff."

She inhales and turns her head to stare at the passing streetlights and dark scenery behind them. "Start at the beginning, huh? Okay, well, I grew up around here. I've got an older sister. She was always my best friend growing up..." she trails off with a laugh, "but I was her younger sister, so I wasn't her best friend, ya know?"

I don't, but I don't say that. The thought of anyone having her as an option and not picking her is baffling. "Your parents?"

"They're still together; they did the Jersey thing and moved down to Florida for their retirement. No income tax," she says, like that explains why someone would move so far from their daughter, who clearly needs a little more help and support. "They were around when I was little, but we're not super close. They just… I don't know. Mel's always been the one who needs attention. I always felt like I had to fight to be seen."

"No wonder you have a praise kink—you were ignored as a child."

Her jaw drops, and she turns to face me. "You… what… Excuse me! Did you just casually turn my whole self-image on its head?"

"As adults, we often want what we didn't get as children." I chuckle and give her knee a squeeze. "Go on."

She narrows her eyes at me. "Okay, but I don't know how I'm supposed to just keep living my life after that revelation. Um, let's see, you asked how I got into cooking? I guess the same way people get interested in things. I was praised for being good at it early on," she says with a smirk, letting me know she's teasing. "I was told I had a good palate and a good nose, but really it fit into this interesting cross section of wanting to experiment and enjoying the process. I find it soothing and challenging. But then I got a job in a kitchen."

"And now you don't?"

"Now I… I'm too tired to enjoy the process most of the time. Kitchens are high energy, high emotion, stressful, even a little dangerous with the fire and knives and all that," she says, laughing. "It feels silly to say, knowing the relative dangers of our professions."

"So, you don't like working in a restaurant kitchen, but that doesn't mean you don't like cooking," I say.

"No, you're right. I've always kind of thought it would be nice to get a private chef type of gig. More freedom, be my own boss, manage the expectations of like four people instead of forty per hour."

"That does sound better," I agree. "You're hired."

She laughs—like I was kidding—and shifts in her seat to point both knees my way. I take full advantage and move my hand to grab the outside of the other leg. Now they're pressed against the center console, as close to me as possible.

"I guess it's why I haven't been all that worried about losing my job. Maybe it'll be the kick in the ass I need."

We chat about the restaurant next, and she admits she never did look up the menu. She starts talking about the different types of fusion food and the ideas she has for different combinations. She's so animated, so passionate. And even though she cares about food way more than I ever will, I appreciate passion.

Two people don't need the same interests to be compatible; they both just need to care enough to pay attention while the other person talks about theirs.

The restaurant is a standalone building set back from a main thoroughfare that connects adjacent areas of generational wealth. The architecture has Asian influences, making it feel like the whole place was designed around the type of restaurant it is.

Its distance from Ulysses proper was part of the appeal, and it's not so far from the house that we can't make a quick retreat if we need to. I park near the back, open her door and lace our fingers as we walk across the lot. As Eleanor is craning her neck, taking in the two-story ceiling with skylights, I catch a flash of green hair at the hostess stand.

Fuck.

"Reservation? Oh, it's you. Mr. No-Smell Flowers," the green-haired girl says, her voice switching over to a purr halfway through, after the surprise of seeing me subsides. She leans forward a little over the stand, letting her eyes drop slowly in an obvious perusal.

"Hello," I say, aiming for distant but polite. I felt rather than saw Eleanor's head snap around when the girl spoke. "Two at 9 PM under Thomas."

The green-haired girl's eyes cut to Eleanor. At whatever look they exchange, she smirks a little, and looks down at her seating chart. "Sure, you and your sister can follow me."

"She's my date," I correct, but the girl has already grabbed two menus and taken off through the loud restaurant.

Eleanor glances at me. "Friend of yours?" she asks lightly. She's trying not to make it too obvious, but I can hear the edge of jealousy.

"Nope." I guide her forward with a hand at the small of her back.

Our table is towards the back, with a view of the open kitchen, tucked between some tropical plants and an indoor pond. "There's fish!" Eleanor points out to me in a low but excited voice, pointing down at the koi weaving through the lily pads.

The hostess hands us the burgundy cloth menus with Rouge Elephant embossed in gold after we sit. "Can I get you anything?" she asks me—only me—leaning over the table and giving me a view down her shirt that I pointedly ignore. "Maybe a drink while you wait for your server?"

I clear my throat and press my lips together at Eleanor's displeased expression. "I'm all right. But maybe for my girlfriend? You want anything, darlin'?" I extend my hand across the table to her.

Her expression is pure gratification as she reaches forward and places her fingers in my palm. She smiles at me, which turns slightly more spiteful when she looks at the hostess. The girl's eyes have dropped to our intertwined hands, and her lips have flattened to a line.

"Is there anything you recommend?" Eleanor asks, obviously enjoying the girl's newfound discomfort. Gotta say, jealous Eleanor is really turning me on.

"Uh, people like our lychee martini." The green hair gets a flip and, though she moves to turn towards Eleanor, she doesn't look right at her.

"Sounds delicious; I'll have that."

"Someone will be right with you." With one last glance my way, she leaves.

"Girlfriend?" Eleanor asks, cocking her head.

I chuckle, lifting her hand to my lips. "Doesn't feel like quite the right word, does it? I thought about calling you Mrs. Thomas, but that's not my name and that finger doesn't have my ring." Yet.

Her chest heaves a huge breath, and her cheeks turn pink as she retracts her hand. "Wait, Thomas? That was my grandfather's name. Did you—"

I grin and pick up the menu. "So, what do we have here?"

With a little tinkling laugh, Eleanor opens her own book and stares down. After a minute or so, she sighs. "It all sounds so amazing. I would seriously order everything on this menu—it's going to be really hard to choose."

A few minutes later, our waiter comes to the table. He makes some small talk, takes our drink orders, and I hand him my menu. "We'll just have one of everything."

Eleanor's mouth pops open. "Wh—" she starts, staring at me blankly.

The server is dumbfounded, too. "Really?"

I just nod.

"Any allergies? Special requests?"

I look at Eleanor, and, still making a surprised face, she shakes her head. The waiter grins. "So cool, I can't wait to tell the Chef. I'll have the appetizers out as they're ready."

He leaves, and I sit back in my chair. Her surprise has melted into something else, and she's biting her lip as she looks at me. "You're spoiling me."

"That's the plan. I do love spoiling my girl."

She shifts on her chair and, between that and her face flushing, I realize that she's getting a little turned on. "I guess I just thought I was too... um, unremarkable?"

I laugh and lean forward in my chair so she'll still hear me when I lower my voice. "Eleanor, are you trying to ask for a spanking?"

"Maybe?" she bites her lip again and looks down.

"See, that's the problem with bratting," I shake my head. "You think you can say the right thing and get me to do what you want, but you're playing with fire. Me? I don't like brats. I like good girls who do what they're told. So, the more infractions, the harsher the punishment. It's only a gentle warning the first time."

She inhales sharply and glances around, checking to ensure that no one is close enough to hear. She leans forward, mirroring me, and this time when the dip in a dress presents me with a perfect, deep view of cleavage, I look. The roundness of her breasts spilling out the middle of a black lace bra is hypnotic. "How do I ask for a spanking, then?"

I groan, barely resisting the urge to pull her in. Especially when I feel her foot on my calf, rubbing up and down. "You say, 'Mac, have I been a good girl?' and you let me decide if you deserve it."

I watch her work the swallow down her throat and lick her lips. "Mac, have I been a good girl?"

My dick twitches, and I grin. "Absolutely fucking not." It's going to be torture, sitting three feet from her and not touching her, and I decide I need her to feel it too, even when she's overwhelmed by what is sure to be an incredible meal. "But you can do something to help your case. Take your panties off and give them to me."

"What, here?" Her eyes go wide, and she sits back. She glances to the side that's open to the rest of the restaurant, then down at the long tablecloth obscuring both of our legs, assessing the likelihood that someone will see her do it.

"Right here, right now. Better decide quickly, too. The appetizers will probably start coming out soon."

It only takes her another heartbeat to choose. She wriggles in the seat, trying to keep her movements subtle and not jostle the table. The cloth moves over her lap, and she curves her back as her hands slide the material down her legs.

"Ma'am, your martini." Someone different than our waiter steps around the plants and deposits a frosty glass in front of Eleanor.

Her face has drained of color other than the two bright red spots at the top of each cheek. "Thanks," she whispers, sounding caught and mortified.

I grab his attention so she can finish her task, wherever she's paused in it. "Excuse me? I'll take one of those too; it looks good. Though I don't need the lychee at the bottom. Can you do that?"

"Of course, Sir."

"Hey, don't I know you from somewhere?"

"Um... I don't think so..."

"Sure. You're Billy's kid, right?"

"No, sorry. You've got me mixed up with someone else."

I shrug, seeing Eleanor is finished. "My mistake."

She straightens just as he turns around and nods at her before leaving. I chuckle, then feel the press of something at my crotch. When I look down, her boot is between my legs, and the black lace panties are hooked around the toe. "I'm impressed," I admit, grabbing the fabric and stuffing it into my pocket.

"I don't think he saw. Oh God, that was almost so bad," she groans. "But also... kind of hot?"

I laugh, and after a second, she joins me.

90 minutes, 16 delicious dishes, and several almost-sexual moans of pleasure from Eleanor later, we both sit back with our hands on our stomachs, too full for another bite.

"I have to admit, I was a little concerned when the fifth entrée came out. Luckily, it's a fancy place, so the menu is small. And I forgot what a bottomless pit you are," she says, eyeing the mostly empty plates on the table. "I'm honestly a little bummed there isn't any cassoulet left. I wanted to try to recreate the spice blend."

"Order another to go," I say simply, with a shrug.

"Oh my God, I can't," she says. That flush is creeping towards her ears, exacerbated by the rich food and alcohol. She glances up as the waiter comes to clear the table, thanking him.

"Everything was fantastic, and you did a great job," I tell him as he piles empty plates. "We'll take the check when you get a minute."

When I look back up, Eleanor is smiling at me. The heat in her eyes hasn't disappeared all evening, but it's shifted a bit. "What?"

"Coming from someone who's worked in the service industry, you can tell a lot about someone from how they treat waitstaff. Sometimes people come into the restaurant and act like they were never taught manners, but you're polite and kind—you gave him a compliment on his service... I just, I would have noticed and I would have appreciated it. I do appreciate it. Thank you for dinner. This was truly amazing—by far the best date I've ever been on."

Pride swells in my chest. "First of many. I'm going to use the restroom, be right back."

She nods and sits back in her seat.

The bathrooms are down a short hall from the kitchen, and catch some of the echoing noise from it. Pots clanging, people shouting, water rushing... it sounds like pure chaos, and I'm not terribly surprised it grates on Eleanor.

I do my business, wash my hands, and step through the door, just as someone passes by the end of the hallway, headed back through the kitchen doors. I have to steel myself not to react as another man approaches the bathroom and I move out of his way.

That looked a lot like Owen Johnson.

I walk quickly, my stomach dropping as I do. If that was Owen, this isn't good. I glance out into the dining room and see Eleanor staring at the pond. The tables have started really clearing out for the night with the kitchen closing soon, and a quick sweep of the room confirms that there's no imminent threat to her.

So, I follow him into the kitchen. I pull out my phone and shoot off a text to Dimitri, then push through the swinging doors. They open into the heart of the kitchen, with a line of cooks in all white barely visible behind stainless steel shelves in front of me, and a long stretch curving to the left, leading to an external door. That door is swinging shut.

"Whoa! Hey, you can't be back here," says a short woman in all black, taking out an earbud with one hand and holding a filthy mop in the other.

"Oh, I'm sorry," I say, giving her a charming smile as I hold up my phone. "But did a man just come through here? I think he dropped this."

She glances at the phone, then points towards the door. "He just went out that way." She puts her earbud back in and resumes pushing the dirty water on the floor back and forth in front of her.

I trot towards the door and open it cautiously, aware that I don't know what the back of this suburban building opens up to. It's dark, the only light coming from the very back of the parking lot on my left, but I can make out a man disappearing around the other corner. A plume of smoke from his lit cigarette follows him as he goes.

I creep behind him when he clears the side, and I know he won't be able to see me. I have to avoid some lingering snow piles and trash on the pavement, and tuck my head down in my shirt so the steam of my breath doesn't give me away. I pause to listen.

"—can't believe he's still keeping his fucking dinner date."

"Fuck off, man, it's dinner with the mayor; Boss couldn't cancel."

"Yeah, but with all that shit that went down Sunday night? It was a fucking massacre. Frank's right—we should be out there, finding those fuckers—"

Fuck. Three of Rossi's men—two who either weren't there or I let live. And they're not just here; they're sweeping the place, keeping guard. There's really only one thing that means. Rossi is here.

I need to get back to the table. I need to get Eleanor the fuck out of here. I glance down to fire off one more text to Dimitri, looping Wes in, too.

"What the fuck do we have here?"

Sometimes, you don't get a choice for your next move. Sometimes, it chooses you.

30

ELEANOR

I know instantly I've done the wrong thing. Again.

I spin the empty martini glass on the table in front of me and look back towards the bathrooms again. The check is sitting in the little burgundy booklet in the middle of the table, and our waiter is hanging out at the bar, staying close by to ensure his tip isn't affected by how quickly he turns over our payment. It's times like this that I really miss not having a phone. I could use a little endless scroll right now to not look so pathetic and alone at a table, waiting for someone to come back and pay.

For the millionth time, I smooth down the sides of my skirt. I know the dress is long enough that I don't have any bare, tender skin touching the fine upholstery, but I'm still a little nervous that it'll flip up when I stand, for no other reason than it would be mortifying to accidentally show the whole restaurant my ass. It's been so much fun having this dirty little secret with Mac all throughout dinner, though.

The bar is across the restaurant from where I'm standing, but I can still see pretty clearly. Our waiter turns as someone approaches, straightens and jerks a thumb in my direction. I try studiously to avoid what I assume will be the hostess coming back to hurry us along.

Green-haired bitch... openly flirting in front of me, calling me his sister... I'm really not a fan of suddenly being so territorial; it makes me feel a little crazy. It's never happened to me before.

I feel a presence come stand next to the table, and I look up. It's not the hostess.

He's a handsome man, lanky and probably about 5'11". It's hard to tell, since his face is unlined, but there are more than a few silvers among the straight black hair, so I'd put him in his early 40s. And his apron says Executive Chef in scrawling embroidery above his name—Anh.

"I had to come meet the table that ordered the whole menu!" he says with a warm smile, grabbing the back of Mac's empty chair and leaning on both his hands. "How was your meal?"

I feel more than a little starstruck. The executive chef at Rouge Elephant is at my table? He may not be a celebrity, but I know how good you have to be and how hard you have to work to get where he is. "It was all so amazing," I gush. Then, knowing he'd probably want to know, I add, "My favorite was definitely the cassoulet."

His eyes widen. "Really? I'm pleased to hear it. It's a new addition, and it got some... mixed reviews from the staff, but it's a favorite of mine, too."

"Maybe the use of those lovely warming spices might have thrown people off who were expecting something more traditional?" I suggest. "What was that blend? I got coriander, star anise, cinnamon, white pepper, soy, obviously... and cloves, maybe?"

His grin widens. "I'm impressed. My sous chef couldn't pick out the cloves. You got it exactly; you only missed the palm sugar."

I feel my cheeks heat, for the like millionth time tonight. "I'm—I was at Bistro Jacques. Now more like a... private chef."

"Ah, now it makes sense—you've worked in a restaurant. I admit that I was surprised that anyone would order the whole menu with no modifications."

"Only someone who knows what a hassle it is, I guess." ...and who's had a plate thrown at her head for it? "That and I know how much goes into planning a dish—it should be enjoyed as you've designed it."

"From your lips to the customers' ears. If only I could convince—"

"Chef!" a deep, booming voice cuts through Chef Anh's soft baritone. He straightens and turns his entire body when he sees who it is; his smile smooths into a mask of pleasant politeness, and he holds his head a little higher.

A heavy hand is placed on my shoulder, and I stiffen at the familiarity of a stranger who says, "Sorry for the interruption," in the tone of someone not sorry enough not to do it.

A man I don't recognize comes to give Chef Anh an aggressive hand-shake. He's got an air of old white guy confidence to go with his shock of gray hair and expensive suit. "Mr. Mayor," the chef says with a nod of greeting.

"So good to catch you on my way in. Don't think you've met my associate, Jay Rossi?"

In what is possibly the least smooth move anyone could possibly execute when they need to stay quiet and unnoticed, I gasp, then choke on air. I'm coughing, reaching for my almost-empty water, as Jay Rossi himself strides up next to the mayor and gives the chef his own my-dick-is-small handshake.

Rossi glances at me as I try to quell the cough, hiding my face as best I can behind the glass. He looks just like the smiling picture on the side of bus stop benches and building signs. He's tall and in good shape, if a little thick around the middle with age. His thinning hair is combed back and looks wet, that way middle-aged Jersey businessmen do to make it look like they've got more. I can smell him from here—though, that might also be the mayor—and the cloud of expensive cologne around him is so thick that it nearly gags me.

He'd intimidate me even if I didn't know who he was and what he does—but I do. And it gives him a sinister vibe that I can't be sure actually exists or is in my head. That perfectly cut suit, Italian leather loafers, and gold jewelry were bought with the lives of the people whose names get added to In Memoriams or disappear like they never existed.

The mayor goes on talking, and I try to be as small as possible as I get my breathing under control. Meanwhile, my heart is racing, and it's making my whole body feel super weird—like quivering Jello.

"—and we can't wait to see what you've got in store for us tonight!" the mayor finishes with a hearty laugh.

"Of course," Chef Anh replies, his face that same polite mask. "Still gluten-free?"

When Chef Anh's eyes cut to me, mirth sparkling there due to our recent shared commiseration, the mayor follows his look. Then Rossi does.

"Er, yes," the elderly man replies, squinting a little at me.

I've never wanted to be able to disappear more in my life. Not in 8th grade, when I was changing for gym, and Jessica Hill loudly pointed out my first period stain. Not when my mother told the sales associate that the white prom dress I'd picked out made me look like a "chunky bride." Not even when I tripped off the bottom step of the bus and four full bags of groceries ripped and everyone watched as I chased a rolling tomato into the street. It's just not possible to chase things into the street with dignity.

"I'm sorry, I don't know if we've met, Miss..." the mayor—*the mayor*—says to me, turning bloodshot blue eyes to scan me head to toe.

"Wilson." It just pops out of my mouth. Fuck. I should have lied. It never occurred to my unconscious brain to lie about my name. I've never done it before.

Then I glance at Rossi, and I know instantly I've done the wrong thing. Again. He hides it quickly, but there's a flash of recognition.

"Well, I should be getting back to the kitchen. Enjoy your meal, and thanks for coming in tonight," Chef Anh says, directing his nod first to the mayor and then to me.

The three men part, the mayor leading Rossi away, and I try to swallow the bile climbing into my throat. I watch out of the corner of my eye as

Rossi and the mayor sit at a table across the restaurant, and Rossi brings out his phone. He starts tapping away.

My stomach roils; all that rich food is not sitting nearly so well anymore.

This is bad. This feels bad. I need to get out of here.

I look down at the little red book with our check. I can practically feel our waiter's eyes on me, so sneaking away is hardly an option now—especially since Chef Anh came out here to talk to me. I feel pretty confident that if confronted about skipping out on the check, I'd burst into terrified tears and make a complete spectacle of myself.

I feel completely paralyzed, completely unsure of what to do. At least we're in public, so it's not like Rossi has many moves either... right?

I don't know. I don't know!

Fuck. Where is Mac?

31

DIMITRI

───◆◇◆───

I would never kill someone for so little, either.

911 Rossi's Men @ Rouge Elephant

The text from James has enough information and alarm that I am breaking my rule about driving the speed limit in suburban areas. The police in these places have nothing to do but watch for traffic violations, and it is something too easily avoided to be stupid about. But the situation will occasionally warrant the breaking of a rule.

I park near the entrance, pausing in my car. The exterior is calm, and well-enough lit from the streetlamps on the main road that I can see there are no dangers lurking between buildings. Trees line the back of the lot, shielding it from a neighborhood behind.

I exit my car and look through the large glass windows that serve as exterior walls—so cold, so impractical, but quite helpful in this application—on my way to the entrance. It is late, so many of the tables are empty, but I do spot Eleanor. Her back is to me, but I recognize the color of her hair and the curves of her back.

I do not see James, nor do I see any of Rossi's men. I must assume James is handling the problem elsewhere. And if that is the case, I know the priority is to remove Eleanor from the situation.

I climb the steps and enter through the glass doors, blowing past the welcome stand—or whatever it is Americans call the dining gatekeepers—and stalk to her table. It is only when I place a hand on her shoulder and her wide, fearful eyes turn to me that I realize something else is going on.

"Eleanor. Come, now," I say. I see James's jacket on the chair across from her and lay it over my arm.

"We can't—the check," she says, grabbing a long, thin, red booklet sitting in the center of the table.

I heave a sigh. "How much?" I grind out, pulling my wallet from my back pocket.

"Um, $800 I think?"

"You think?" I snap, pulling out bills.

"$800."

I learned a very long time ago to carry plenty of cash of whatever currency is local. I always have enough in my wallet to bribe an official, buy an old car, or—apparently—pay for my team member and his woman's ridiculously expensive dinner. I toss down enough to cover the meal and stand over her protectively as she gathers her coat.

"Rossi is here," she says quietly to me. I can tell she is trying to be subtle.

Fuck. I should not have come in without doing a full sweep of the building. That is on me. "Where?" I reply, matching her tone.

"Um, directly behind you. He keeps looking over here, but I don't think he's seen your face. Maybe if you cheat this way as we walk out, he won't..."

A strange sensation spreads through my chest at this small woman's concern for me. I am not certain how much she knows of the situation, but I doubt that James told her of my picture being posted in hitman forums. Which means she does this for me because she is inclined to protect those around her. Which means that she is foolish, that she does not recognize her own weakness, that she will likely make poor decisions that do not prioritize her own safety... and that she must be defended at all costs.

I move as she recommended, keeping my body diagonal to where she said he is sitting—it protects her from his view as much as me. We are nearly at the door when I glance into the reflection in the window and see him.

These fucking ridiculous windows. Almost as bad as a mirror. Rossi has seen my face.

I grab Eleanor's upper arm and pick up the pace, pulling her with me. As we step onto the lot, I see a car parking in the very back and curse. Grigori Folson stands from the driver's side, and another man I do not recognize slams the passenger door.

My eyes cut to Eleanor. What do I do with her?

I release her arm and grab the base of James's coat to find the lump that means he does not have his car keys on him, wherever he is. I paid enough attention driving in to know that Wesley's rented convertible is not near where Grigori has parked, so I hand the keys to her quickly, before Grigori and his backup see her.

"Go to your car and leave the keys on top of the back passenger wheel for James. Then go to the silver SUV over there and wait for me. Stay low, out of sight."

"Why? Where's Mac?" she asks.

"I do not know, but we have to leave now. Go!"

She rushes off to do as I instructed, and her lack of hesitation, at least, shows good sense.

It is ridiculous. James allows Grigori Folson to live, and he creates an enormous pain in my ass. Now I must also try to save the woman. This place is reasonably empty, true, but it is public. That is why I cannot make an attempt on Rossi's life now—not while he eats with that old, corrupt man they made the mayor. I do not have enough knives on me, and I will not leave witnesses.

Related to that, I need to take care of these two men in a way that the people behind the restaurant in their homes will not hear or see. The only stroke of good fortune is that being in an area this conspicuous means I do not need to concern myself with guns.

Grigori Folson is not a small man—thugs for crime lords hardly ever are—but still I am larger. His partner is about the same size, so I know I can handle both at once. My gunshot graze is now barely a scratch, and I have my full range of motion back.

I grip a knife in each hand and thumb them down my palm until they are in optimal position. Bloodlessly would be the better way to do this, but silently is most important. I trot along the side of the building, keeping my movements big enough and being loud enough to attract their notice. I know they see me when they change course, cutting across the pavement and heading right for me.

I slip around the back of the building—well away from all those fucking windows—and catch the man who is not Grigori Folson off guard. He was closer, or he was the faster runner—whichever the reason, he rounds the corner first and gets a throwing knife to the throat. He chokes on his scream of pain and terror, blood spilling down his neck and through the fingers he automatically tries to use to hold the wound closed.

He stumbles back, falling against Grigori, who shouts, "What the fuck?"

I throw the other knife, but Grigori is quick or lucky, because he moves the other man in front of him at the precisely wrong moment. A second knife joins the first in his friend's throat. His body falls to the ground, and Grigori charges me. I could grab more knives, but my backups are in less accessible areas, and he is coming in fast.

His gun is barely up at chest height when I kick it from his grasp. It flies from his hand, landing several feet away. I let my leg's momentum carry me around and plant that foot on the ground so I can deliver a donkey kick with my other. He staggers backwards, though he keeps his balance and does not fall all the way down. The force of my blow makes his body immediately empty his lungs. His breath is knocked out, and he gasps for air, unable to make his diaphragm work. But he recovers more quickly than I expected.

This man clearly has training, because he comes at me with no fear and plenty of confidence.

Which is a shame for him because I have more training. And I can tell he is left-handed.

Fists drawn, he throws a punch from the left that I duck to the side to avoid. While his fist is still outstretched, I bring my arm up to grip his wrist in the crook of my elbow, and come across my body with my left hand. It is my weaker arm, but the windpipe is surprisingly fragile for something so important.

My blow does not land because he blocks it, hitting my arm away. He jerks backwards, and I release him.

Enough of this.

He punches twice, and I dodge, avoiding the contact as I fall into a kneel to grab another knife from my ankle holster. The next attack is a kick, aimed at my chest and meant to take advantage of my lower position, but I catch his leg with an uppercut, landing the knife in the back of his knee. He cries out, but I jump up and slam into his chest with my shoulder, sending him flying backwards. He collapses onto the ground, and I jerk the knife from his knee, grip one hand around his mouth to keep him quiet and shove the blade into his eye socket for quick brain death.

I waste no more time. I have already lost precious moments, and more men could show up at any time. My right hand is slippery with blood, but that is the nice thing about black. I wipe it as best I can on my dark shirt, then place it in my pocket so no one will see the red staining as I walk back to the car.

Fuck. Two bodies. I cannot leave them; this area is open enough that someone is bound to walk by within the next hour or so. And I have no way to know who will find them first—if I could guarantee it was Rossi, that would be another story. But there is enough blood spilled to make anyone who comes across it call the police, even without bodies.

I need to cover my ass, and I do not have time to scrub a crime scene. There is nothing else to do. We have to take the bodies with us.

I force a slow pace as I walk back towards my car. I picked a poorly lit area to park on purpose, but Eleanor's wide eyes as she takes in the sight of me tell me that I need to stick to the shadows. "Get in," I say, unlocking and sliding into the driver's side.

She slams her door and grabs for the belt.

"Wait, I need your help with something." James may kill me for this if it ends up scarring her, but it will be much faster with her assistance.

I drive at a reasonable speed around to where the bodies are, and pull up next to them. She glances out the window and gasps. "Are they—"

"Dead, yes. They were coming to kill me, and probably you. I need your help to lift them into the trunk. Can you do this?"

Her face screws up like she is going to cry, but she does not. She just swallows and nods.

I hope she does not throw up. All it will do is leave more DNA at the crime scene.

"Grab his feet," I say, pointing to the closer body with two of my knives in his throat. I open the door of the trunk and lean down to slide my arms under his pits. "Lift with your legs," I instruct, then am surprised when she manages before I finish the sentence.

Together, we get him into the trunk, rolling him forward to make more room, and move to the other. Her face is red with exertion, and her expression is grave, but she makes no complaints. When the second body is in the car, I close the trunk.

When she takes a few steps past the passenger door, I open my mouth to warn her to hold her stomach, but watch her stoop and pick something up off the ground. She turns, holding it up from the barrel.

Son of a goat. I am almost as surprised at myself as I am at her—I forgot the gun.

She does have good sense. I nod to her. "Good, bring it."

With so much blood pumping and adrenaline from the fight, it is difficult to keep to the speed limit. But with two bodies in the back of the vehicle and blood drying to a burnt red color on my hand, I will not risk anything. I set the cruise control to 42 mph.

When I am satisfied she is not hyperventilating, I pull out my cell and dial Wesley. He answers before the first ring finishes. "What's going on?"

"I need you to find and wipe all footage at the restaurant and parking lot. James and I were never here."

"Time frame?" I can already hear typing in the background.

"When did you arrive?" I ask Eleanor. She is staring, unblinking, at her legs, and then I notice the smears of red against her pale skin.

"Eleanor," I say, trying to be gentle.

She looks up, dazed.

"When did you arrive at the restaurant?"

"Um... our reservation was... 9 PM. I think we got here just before that." She swallows hard, audibly.

I do not need to repeat it back to Wesley—he has excellent hearing. "She's all right?" he asks.

I glance at her. "Probably. Has James checked in?"

"Not yet. Dimitri... what the bloody hell happened?"

I sigh. "Rossi was there."

"Fuuuuck."

"I will be home in 20 minutes." I end the call.

"Has he heard from Mac?" she asks me, her brows lifting in the middle in distress.

"No, but I am not worrying. James was the one who texted me to come to the restaurant," I say. I do not explain that he did not mention Rossi, just his men. "Rossi arrived after you had finished?"

Her lips flatten, and she nods. Now she stares at the gun she is holding in both hands. I reach over and take the weapon, stashing it in the middle compartment.

"And you knew it was him?" I ask. She nods again, and I have to choke down a growl of frustration. I hate nonverbal answers, especially when I am driving and cannot safely look. "Tell me what happened. Now. Speak."

She grimaces at my clipped tone, but I cannot take it back. "We finished dinner, and Mac went to the bathroom. While he was gone, the chef came to our table. The mayor walked in and saw him there and stopped to say hello and Rossi was with him. He..." Her lower lip trembles a bit, and she bites down on it. "He knew who I was, I think. Or, he recognized me, maybe."

I curse him inside—stupid little goat man. I wish I could have killed him tonight. "Why did you stay?"

"What?"

"You understood the danger?" I ask, gratified and confused when she nods stiffly. "Why did you not leave the table?"

She shifts uncomfortably on her seat. "I didn't know what to do, and I had no way to contact any of you guys. I thought Mac was coming back. And I," she pauses, chewing briefly on her lip, "didn't have any money. We ordered everything on the menu and a super nice bottle of wine—"

I curse aloud this time. Of all the stupidity in the world... "Do you think being polite is more important than being alive?"

"I know, I know. Now that I say it out loud, it was so dumb." She grimaces. "I'm sorry."

"Do not be sorry. Learn."

"Our waiter would have had to pay our bill," she says sadly, as if not done proving her point. Which is no point at all, in my opinion.

I scoff. "You think he would kill you for $800?"

"What? No."

"No," I agree. "It would have been your life for his $800, so it is basically as I said. I would never kill someone for so little, either. Your death would be worth more than that."

"That's the... weirdest nice thing anyone's ever said to me. At least, I think it was nice."

I do not completely understand her meaning, so I choose to ignore it. "You need a cell phone."

She blows out a frustrated breath, crossing her arms over her chest. "Yeah. You're telling me."

Her anger placates me, proving she will not begin crying quite yet. "Yes, I just did."

"No, I meant... never mind." She fists the hem of her dress with both hands and pulls the skirt down over her knees. "Thank you for coming to get me. I hope I didn't... I hope you can still get him."

"As do I." I can see from the edge of my vision that she has started shaking. That will be the shock. I reach forward and blast the heat, though I know it will dry my eyes. "When we get home, have a big glass of water, then take a long, warm shower and put your clothes in the machine that cleans them."

"The washing machine?"

"That is what I said."

32

MAC

—◆○◆—

I'll... owe you one.

I tense my stomach, hardening the abdominals in preparation for another hit. The other two guys holding my arms against the brick wall tighten their grips as the fist comes flying my way. I grunt, doubling over as far as I can as the pain radiates through already-sore muscle tissue and skin.

They didn't buy my "just out for a smoke" routine, likely a by-product of being on edge from nearly becoming a casualty at the "storage unit massacre." Their words.

"Why were you spying?" Owen barks at me, leaning down to get closer to my ear to say it. The proximity forces his beer breath up my nose. "Who sent you?

Owen is strong, but his aim is shitty, and it's obvious that his hand is starting to hurt. So far, I've taken a hit to the jaw and two to the large intestine. No serious damage. But a shot to the kidneys, or solar plexus—Dimitri's favorite—would have knocked the wind out of me and is normally enough pain to scare someone into talking. Interrogation is often more about fear than it is about pain.

It makes me doubt that Owen usually gets his hands dirty, and from the way his elbows flare out I know he can't hide a punch. He strikes me as more of a bullet to the knee kind of guy. Lucky for me, this area is too suburban for gunshots, and Owen is at least that smart. Also smart enough to have both guys holding me back.

"I swear I don't know what you're talking about!" I say, forcing a groan. "Please, I've got a wife and kids—"

Sure, they didn't believe me at first, but they're not used to anyone sticking to their story after a beating. Most people they beat up probably haven't gone through mandatory torture and interrogation training.

Owen's eyes narrow at me and he steps back, rubbing the knuckles on his right hand. "Frank, take his wallet. See what kind of ID he's got."

I've been trying to figure out a way out of this. My priorities are, in order, to get out alive, to get out unidentified, to learn whatever I can from these chuckleheads, and to leave at least one of them alive as my witness—otherwise, our plan to draw out Rossi was for nothing. But I don't carry ID on me, for obvious reasons, and I'm sure it will seem suspicious enough to put the last two priorities at risk.

So far all I've learned is that Rossi is either here or coming here, and is having dinner with the mayor. I'm not too surprised that they're meeting so late. The mayor probably takes Rossi's money and looks the other way about permitting and various minor infractions. He's just a local official—sure, he's at the very top, but his days are filled with meetings and proposals and budgets. He can help Rossi, but there's only so much he can do for him.

But I don't think I'm going to get some kind of serious insight into Rossi's inner workings, and my opportunity to listen just came to an end. So, it's time to act. Frank is on my left, pressing his body weight into my forearm. When he shifts to the side and reaches down with one hand to access my back pocket, I make my move.

I lift my knee into his groin as he turns towards me, and I let my foot land heavily on his instep. When he staggers back, howling and clutching his dick, I yank my left hand around and use it to help Bad Guy #3's head get acquainted with the brick. It makes a loud crunch, likely his nose, and he pulls back enough that I can get my right hand free.

Owen hits me from behind just as I start pulling back, and the impact against the brick wall rattles my teeth. He's quick; I'm quicker. I clip him in the nose with my elbow and spin. He's right there with a 1-2-hook, one of the most standard boxing attacks, so I know about where he is in his hand-to-hand training.

I get my guard up around my face, allowing the blows to land on the backs of my vertical forearms, and move my right arm to the side to block the hook. When the next combo starts, I tuck my chin after the second impact and snake out with my right cross. It's all about that invisible hit landing clean—they can't see your fist coming if your elbows are tucked and you don't wind up.

Cheek shot, swinging left hook to the chest, low kick to the knee and Owen is down, can't catch a breath and has a concussion.

But by now Frank has recovered, and he comes at me. He places a hand on each shoulder, pushing me back against the wall, and I grab his coat from behind. Before he can get his arm up to my neck, I grip the material and shove. It gives me the momentum to flip him over my leg, and he falls hard on his back on the pavement.

I land on my knee as I sense an approach from behind, and #3 hits me on the chin as I turn, which spins me. I fall onto my arm, and kick out behind his leg, taking his legs out from under him. He cracks his head against the brick on his way down and lies unmoving.

Frank is coming to his feet, but I'm crouching by the time he lunges again. He's got a mini keg in his hands—likely something he found on the ground—and he swings it at my head, but I duck into the opening the large overhead swing creates and jab my fist into his kidney twice as he passes. He drops the keg with a dull thwang, and staggers away, clutching his side. Then he throws me a look over his shoulder and makes a break for it.

"Fuck," I mutter. I'm up and I catch him in a few steps, before he can clear the corner, and I wrap my arm around his neck from behind and spin us both, sending him crashing into Owen.

They both go down in a heap, and I deliver two sharp enough kicks to their heads that it's lights out. They're not dead—though I have my doubts about #3, there's a substantial pool of blood under him—but I've done it enough to know that a kick that hard to the face will probably knock them out for hours.

I cross my arms as I consider my next move. I could leave them here like this. Except for the dead one, obviously. The other two would wake eventually, limp to a hospital to be treated for serious concussions. No bodies, no crime scene. But dead men tell no tales, and they don't give descriptions of the guy that jumped them to their boss.

But really, what would they say? If they remember anything at all in spite of the head trauma, they could give my height, build, a rough description of my face... As long as Wesley wipes the video footage of anything that may be around, they're not likely to actually find me. It may send Rossi into hiding, thinking someone else is after him, but so might killing the rest of his men.

As a sniper, close-range killing isn't my specialty. And even the black-market type of silencers do not make guns silent. At most, you shave off 50 dB, which still brings the shot to about the level of a vacuum cleaner. And I don't like how out in the open we are. I'd have three bodies to take care of and a potential crime scene. I can't exactly take them with me—there's barely enough trunk space in a Mustang to fit a suitcase. There is a dumpster 10 yards away that's a viable option, but the time it would take to drag three grown men one by one and hoist them over the side leaves me too open for discovery.

I pocket the phones, wallets and the three guns I find. #3's name is—was, he's starting to go cold—John Powell. Unfortunately, he is going into the dumpster tonight. If anyone comes across two men passed out, they'll call for an ambulance. They can't find a dead body, too.

When I'm done, I take a pause to catch my breath, then keep circling around the building, looking inside for Eleanor. The table where we were sitting is empty, and I breathe a sigh of relief. I keep scanning, stopping short of walking into any light streaming out through the large windows, and find Rossi at a table with the mayor, over by the bar. And me without my rifle.

I turn around and retrace my steps, knowing that continuing around the front of the structure puts me near the road, under street lamps, and well within view of any remaining patrons.

I pull out my phone from the three new acquisitions so I can look casual to anyone who might notice me now. A quick scroll catches me up—some worried messages from Wes wanting to know what's going on, and a few from Dimitri.

Dimitri

She is secure.

Every cell in my body is screaming at me to get in my car and drive home. But this isn't finished; I still have a problem. There's a body in the dumpster and two men passed out. My mind goes to Felix, but then I pause.

What if I made my problem into Rossi's problem?

What kind of man has the mayor and police force in his pocket? One who works outside the law. One who prefers delegation. One who doesn't like getting his hands dirty. One who thinks he can buy his way out of problems because he has more important things to do.

That's the kind of man who uses a cleaning service.

I hope I'm right about this.

Owen wears a large diamond stud in his ear. I reach down and tear it from his lobe, and the move jostles his head, but doesn't wake him. As I come around the side of the building, I have to avoid a new, fresh pool of blood that I had nothing to do with.

There are only about a dozen cars in the lot, and most of them are low-to mid-tier sedans that probably belong to staff. Of the cars left, it's not hard to pick out which one belongs to Rossi—the pearly white Escalade with a license plate that reads KING J. I use the diamond to carve TRASH into his window, then leave the earring stuck into the front of the driver's handle.

I head for the Mustang. I left my keys in my coat pocket and my coat at the table. I can't exactly walk back inside and ask if they found it. I'm rumpled, probably blood-splattered, and I definitely look like I've been in a fight. But if I were a betting man, I'd bet on Dimitri every time. And I find the key fob on top of the back right tire.

It's only when I'm sitting behind the steering wheel that I finally take a full inhale, which my stomach protests heavily. But there's no time to catalog injuries. I have to get back to my girl. She needs me. She's probably terrified, confused...

I place the key in the ignition and my foot on the brake. Then, I stop.

My urgency and panic around Eleanor is clouding my judgment. Dimitri got Eleanor out, and I'm sure by now she's home safe. But my blood is pounding so loudly in my head, and the need to get my hands on her—to prove to myself that she's in one piece—is so overwhelming that I'm not thinking clearly.

I need to stay. I need to watch to make sure he takes the bait and finds his men—both to know if we're going to have trouble with the police and if he takes it as the message it was intended to be. I need to follow his car back to where he's staying, since he's clearly not at his home.

Eleanor or the job. The job or Eleanor.

No. That's the wrong way to think about this. The job is what is going to help Eleanor. It's not *or*, it's *both*. I can't protect her without finishing this.

I put the car in gear and ease out of the parking lot, driving straight across two lanes to park across the street at the edge of the pharmacy's lot. From here, I'll be able to see him exit the restaurant and follow him.

It plays out like a fucking movie scene. Rossi and the mayor exit the building, clapping each other on the back, and the mayor places the end of a cigar into his mouth to chew on. Once he reaches his door, Rossi goes still, his back to me as he stares down at his window. The mayor circles around, sees it, and tilts his head back to laugh.

I smirk at that. I'd been going for subtlety, the "could have been a mistress" approach, in the very slim chance I'd gotten the wrong car. I know Rossi recognizes the earring, though—he pockets it instead of tossing it aside and turns his head. With one more handshake and a firm pat on the shoulder accompanied by a conciliatory expression, the mayor saunters off, getting into the back of the car that stops at the entrance to pick him up.

Rossi watches him go, the lines of his shoulders taut. As soon as the dark SUV turns off the lot, Rossi turns on his heel and heads for the back of the building. He stops and peers into the window of a black coupe on his way, and I make a note of the make and model. It's probably Owen's.

He disappears from my line of sight for about a minute, and when he comes back around, he's red-faced and talking on the phone. What I wouldn't give for a bug right now.

I've got to follow this hunch. I start my car as Rossi gets into his, and I speed dial Felix.

"Yo."

"Felix. I need your help."

There's a laugh. "Another favor? You are suddenly very bad at your job, *amigo*."

"It's just information this time."

"Knowing me is becoming very expensive for you."

I roll my eyes and navigate out onto the main street, leaving a car between me and Rossi's SUV. "Just let me know if you get a cleanup request at Rouge Elephant. I'm not asking who; I just want to know *if* you were called."

Felix runs his mouth sometimes, but he doesn't ask questions—not ones he expects answered, anyway. It's why he's still in business. But I can hear the curiosity in his voice when he says, "You know I don't give out information about clients."

Fuck. This is not a good idea. I could just ask him to clean the scene for me, but knowing if Rossi asked him to do the same is worth more to me. It tells us a lot about his connections. It also tells me a little more about Felix himself. And I can't stick around to see if his team is the one that shows—I won't recognize them anyway, and I'll lose my chance to follow Rossi.

"I'll... owe you one."

There's a long silence—though it's probably only a few seconds—and a low laugh. "No shit?"

I turn onto the same street Rossi did. "One favor, something that doesn't put me or mine in danger, you feel me?"

"Done. Okay, I got the call like 30 fucking seconds ago. A cold one and two for the ER. I've got guys there in about two minutes."

"Thanks, Felix."

"Does this mean we're actually cleaning up after you? Not that I'm opposed to some double dipping, especially when it means I get paid and a sharpshooter in my pocket."

"Is the answer to that question what you want as your favor?" I shoot back.

The answering chuckle this time is a much darker sound. Ominous. "Definitely not. I'm going to save that one for a rainy day, huh, *amigo*?"

Yup. Bad idea. "Talk to you later, Felix."

"Don't lose my number."

As Rossi drives further into suburbia, I have to put more distance between us. So much that I almost miss the driveway he turns down. I drive right past it, but catch sight of the back of the white SUV before the garage door closes fully.

That's odd. A house in this neighborhood never showed on his financials. I send a pin of the address to the group chat as the lights in the house come on, proving he's moving through the rooms that lead out from the garage.

Time to head for home. I can't be away from her any longer. The desperation grows the closer I get. It adds lead to my foot, making me blow through a few stop signs. I barely get the key out of the ignition before I'm up the front steps and inside.

"Eleanor!" I bellow, slamming the front door behind me.

But it's Dimitri's face I see coming around the corner. He's sliding leather gloves onto his hands and has a roll of trash bags tucked under his arm. He takes one look at me and moves between me and the stairwell. "Stop, James. You cannot go to her like this."

I'm seconds from hitting him with the fist my hand just formed when he stepped in front of me. I'm not even thinking rationally about why Dimitri would try to come between us; I only know that nothing is going to keep me from her a second longer.

"The fuck I can't."

"My brother, stop! Listen to me. You will scare her. She is already frightened, fragile. And you are wearing the blood of several other men."

As he approaches and lays a hand on my shoulder, I inhale and follow his gaze down to my shaking fist. With a jerking motion, I open my palm. Was I really going to hit him?

His voice is uncharacteristically understanding. "Wash your face. Calm your eyes. She needs you, but not like this."

I grumble a little at that—suddenly he's some sort of expert on what she needs?—but go to do as he recommends. When I look in the mirror,

I understand. My face is splattered, and there's a dried patch at the corner of my mouth from some kind of internal bleeding. My knuckles are bruised, and the skin is broken and colored with more than just my own blood. My jacket is torn at both shoulders, and my light-colored shirt is ripped and stained. My eyes are wide, wild, angry.

I remove my jacket and splash water on my face, using the hand towel to scrub anything remaining.

When I emerge, Dimitri is gone. Judging from his outfit, he was taking care of some of his own dead bodies. I immediately connect the dots. The large pool of blood at the restaurant...

Well, luckily there's a cleaning crew on it.

I climb the stairs two at a time until I'm on the third floor. The door is closed, but light is spilling out from underneath. She likes to sit in the middle of the bed, but she's not there this time. I hear the shower running.

It doesn't even occur to me to knock, and it makes me feel like a chump when she startles at the sound of the door opening. She's sitting on the floor of the shower, naked, and the water is falling on her back like rain. The steam is thick, so I know she's been in there a while.

"Mac? I... I think there's something wrong with me."

Oh, hell.

I don't bother with my clothes—I step into the shower.

33

ELEANOR

This is what gets the tears?

"Is it—are you hurt?" he asks in an urgent tone.

"No. I couldn't... I can't cry. Aren't—don't people cry when they're scared? Or when they see..." I shiver, remembering the pale skin and sightless eyes of those two men. And the knives... covered in so much blood...

I didn't expect him to come into the shower. And I could barely see him through the glass doors with the steam and running water, so I didn't expect him to look so beat up. But he doesn't give me a chance to get a good look at the bruises or bloodstains. He sits on the floor next to me, pulls me into his lap, tucks my head under his chin, and drapes my legs over his.

"Shh." He sweeps a hand up and down my back in a comforting gesture. "I'm so sorry, baby. I'm so sorry."

I swallow and shake my head. Why is he sorry? I flatten my hand against his chest, watching as the water beads against my skin and slides down towards my arm. The warmth of the shower helped with the shivering at first, and it felt so good that I didn't want to get out. I'm probably using up all the hot water. I'm the one who should be sorry—

No, I shouldn't. What a weird thought.

God, I feel so weird. Like I'm going to float away.

"You're hurt?" I ask, trying to tilt my head back to see. I thought I'd caught the outline of bruising and swelling on his jaw. He hugs me tighter, not letting me pull back.

"Not badly."

"Good. That's... good," I whisper. I feel like I have to tell him, like I need to confess. If their whole mission is screwed up now, it was my fault. "I was so stupid, Mac."

"Shh," he repeats gently.

"I saw him—Rossi—and I stayed at the table because we hadn't paid... Dimitri had to come in to get me... God, I was so dumb. I should have left."

"Eleanor, stop. I know you were scared. You didn't know what to do, and I wasn't there. I'm so sorry. It's all my fault, baby. I should never have taken you out."

"You didn't know that would happen," I argue.

"It's no excuse. Your safety is my responsibility."

I wipe the water out of my eyes—tap, not tears—and blink. The declaration warms me from the inside in a way the hot water hasn't been able to touch, but it doesn't really make much sense. I'm an adult; my safety is my own responsibility. Sure, he knows more about the dangers than I do in this particular situation, but he can't feel responsible for the stupid choices I make.

"Why?" I ask.

He doesn't say anything, so I tilt back and look up at him. I'm not surprised to find the intensity in his features but a little taken aback by the level of it.

"Because I..." his eyes flick back and forth between mine. "I care about you. And I got you into this."

I feel my lips stretch and part a little. He cares about me. It feels ridiculous that this is the first thing that's broken through the weird, cold numbness. "I care about you, too."

He smiles and winces, then I see the swelling on his jaw. I trace it gently, skimming the area with the very tips of my fingers. "What happened?"

What he tells me is surely the abridged version, but I appreciate that there are enough details that I'm sure he didn't leave out anything important. I shift away to make room so I can unbutton his shirt, and hiss in sympathy at the blue skin—that's going to make a colorful bruise tomorrow. I take his hand and examine the cuts on his knuckles.

Finally, I feel ready to leave the heat. I stand awkwardly, and shut the main valve. He's out of the shower and holding open a towel for me before I can offer him my hand up, and I have to contain a smile at the sight of him trying to help me dry myself while he's making a puddle on the floor. I let him wind it around me, then watch as he drops his sopping clothes before getting one for himself.

The sight of his toned ass makes me look away and busy myself with giving my hair a rough towel dry. It feels wrong to be lusting after him when he's injured.

I grab his clothes—which, wet, weigh a ton—from the floor for him and deposit them on top of mine in the washer, and crank it. Dimitri told me to wash my dress, but I'd waited for him.

"Go sit on the bed," I instruct him as I turn to rifle around in the supply baskets in the closet. I know I saw some first-aid supplies. At his quizzical head tilt, I explain, "I'm going to put antibiotic ointment on your hand and bandage it."

His answering smile is tender. "Darlin', you don't have to—"

"It's not a request," I say, lifting my chin, echoing his words when he first applied the medicated psoriasis cream for me. Even though I'm not sure I'm even capable of the same amount of confidence he had when he said it, it feels like the right thing to say.

He steps towards me and brushes his lips against mine. There's no real heat to it; it's more of a thank you, and he goes to do as I asked.

When I exit the bathroom, I see that he's stretched out on the bed. His towel is still tucked around his waist, and he's slightly upright against the padded headboard. I expect him to move over to make room for me to sit, but he doesn't. He looks at me and gestures to his outstretched legs. "You know what I'm going to ask. Darlin', I need this. For once—"

I cut him off by climbing up next to him, balancing myself against his chest for as long as it takes to throw my knee over his legs, and settling back onto my heels. He's been injured tonight, but he knows his limitations. He won't let me hurt him. I am careful of the area on his stomach where he was hit, though.

His towel is against my bare skin, and I can feel every movement underneath me. It's almost distractingly arousing, but I try to focus. He needs this.

His left hand grips my hip, and he presents his right for my inspection. I uncap the ointment and lay the roll of gauze on the bed next to me until I need it. "What happens now? With Rossi and everything?"

He inhales and watches my fingers move gently over the broken skin. I keep glancing up, expecting a wince or some sort of indication of pain. There is none.

"It's a bit of a waiting game. Most of his men are dead now, so he may retreat. At least we have some idea of where he is, though."

"Do you think he's been staying in that house you followed him to all along?"

"Possibly. Wes will need to do a little digging on that property—it didn't show in our initial search under his name, and we also checked properties registered to his wife and kids. We might have missed one he bought for another family member or something."

I screw the cap back on the ointment and lay it on the bed next to us. The gauze is next, and I break open the sterile seal. He holds his hand up, wearing a patient expression, as I try to find the end of the roll. "Why do you think he was there with the mayor? Especially so late—so close to closing."

"He's probably in Rossi's pocket. Bribes, that sort of thing."

I consider that as I start carefully winding the white fabric loosely around his hand. "It's weird. I didn't even recognize the mayor, but I knew immediately it was Rossi."

"It's not that strange—lots of people don't follow local politics."

"I guess," I allow. I don't follow local politics that closely, but I'm pretty sure I could pick out our Attorney General, and the office of Mayor is at least that important. "It just seems strange to me. Rossi's face is everywhere—bus stops, billboards, stuff like that—and the mayor's isn't. It's like he doesn't want us regular people to know who he is."

"He may not. If people know who he is, they'll ask for things. I'm sure he's just coasting—running unopposed and taking money under the table."

I tuck the end of the gauze into the wrapping I made, and Mac drops his bandaged hand to my hip, gripping loosely. I let my gaze settle onto the outline of trauma on his stomach. My lower lip quivers, so I press it against the top one as I run my fingers gently over the ridges of his abdomen.

"It's okay," he assures me, covering my hand with his uninjured one. "It's a little sore, but it doesn't really hurt."

"*You,*" I correct. "It doesn't hurt *you.* It would hurt me. And that makes me wonder what happened to you that being punched in the stomach doesn't even register."

"It's not worth wondering about."

I look up, aghast. "How can you say that? Someone was trying to cause pain! To k-kill you—" All of a sudden, my eyes fill with tears. It surprises me so much that I gasp.

Mac sits up, wrapping a thick arm around my back and cupping my cheek with the other. "Hey, no. Baby, stop. There's no real damage."

But I'm rattled. This is what gets the tears? Not the dead men, or the blood, or the fear, or the worry… It's the thought that Mac was hurt, that he's been hurt so bad in the past that he barely perceives it, and that he's so unbothered by it that I know he's accepted that it will happen again in the future? The ache that makes in my chest is deep, stealing my breath.

I slide both hands to frame his face, lean forward and kiss him, tasting the salt of my tears. I meant for it to just be emotional—an apology for whatever he's been through, an assurance that I feel for him, a promise of some kind that I can't even identify—but his hand slides to the nape of my neck and he deepens it. I feel his cock hardening under me, pressing the soft towel harder against where all the heat and need is pooling, and I can't help myself as I rock against it.

Realizing what I'm doing, I pull back, shocked at myself. But with a growl, he fists the terry cloth at my hip and yanks it, jerking the whole thing to the ground before I can grab onto it. My hands drop to his chest as he flexes a thick arm and uses his grip in my hair to bring me back in.

I allow myself to pour what I'm feeling into him because it feels so good to let it go. Fear, anger, horror, dread, cowardice, self-loathing, everything becomes a spiral of passion and yearning that he takes from me and gives back to me as only more heat. Raw lust zings through me, bringing a rush of moisture, readying my body.

I have to tear myself away this time. "Wait, but you're all bruised," I protest.

"Not being inside you is what hurts."

He bends his neck, dropping his head at the same time that he grabs my breast. Taking the sensitive peak into his mouth, he swirls his tongue around it and the skin tingles, hardening painfully. I cry out, letting my head fall back, and he repeats the action on the other nipple. I stroke his soft, still damp hair as he teases me with the pleasure-pain that sets my body on fire.

His left arm snakes down, winding under my ass and lifting me slightly. Then his towel is open. This time when I lower my pussy against him, it's only searing, unyielding flesh against me. I moan as I roll my hips, rubbing the length of him through my lips.

His torso falls back a few inches, resting against the headboard again. "Ride me, baby. Take what you need. Give me that beautiful body."

The tip of his cock against the hardened, pulsating center of my desire is almost enough to get me there. But I need him inside me more than I need to come. I rise on my knees and reach down to align his head with my entrance. Then I slide down slowly.

We both make long noises of hunger and satisfaction as I sink onto him. I barely maintain the presence of mind to make sure his noises aren't also edged with the wrong kind of pain. They're not. On his face is nothing but lust and awe. I lean forward, pressing against his chest and needing my lips on his as I start slow movements with my legs and pelvis.

He answers me with an all-consuming longing that matches my own. We kiss, exploring each other's mouths, as our bodies rock together. He's unbelievably deep inside me, each small motion nudging him to the very end of what I have to give. It's like being glued to someone, not allowing an inch of space between us. I feel like I'd crawl inside him if I could.

I break away when the need for air and more pressure gets the better of me. He takes both breasts, squeezing then rubbing rough thumbs over my nipples, and I find a rhythm that gives us both a little more. More impact and stimulation and pleasure.

"I was really scared when you were gone," I say, letting the emotions well in my throat and spill out however they want. Now that we're so connected again, it doesn't feel as hard to do.

"I know. Never again. I'm never leaving you like that again."

"Never again," I moan. "Mac, you feel so good."

"Fuck me, baby," he urges. "Use me to feel good."

I almost argue—that's not what this was supposed to be about—but a wave of pleasure crashes down over my shoulders as my fingers find my clit. His hand—the injured one—pinches my nipple, and I cry out.

"Mac, please—"

"Do it, come for me. My good girl."

Between the gentle friction of my fingers exactly where and how I like, the not-so-gentle pressure of his cock deep inside me, and the words—the reminder that I'm his—I'm done. The orgasm barely builds before I'm tumbling over the peak. The pleasure is extraordinary, shooting out from where our bodies are connected and, for a brief moment, my senses get all mixed up. It fills every limb of my body with color. It feels loud.

I open my eyes and see nothing but so much tenderness as he watches me come down from my high, I almost lose it again. His abdomen is tensing, forcing his hips and cock up inside me as much as he can, prolonging the pleasure. I fold forward to kiss him again and rise.

"Okay, now you come for me."

I set a steady pace, up and down, enjoying the feeling as much as I enjoy watching him fall apart under me. His eyes are locked where his cock sinks in and out as I ride him. I'm not sure what kind of dirty talk he really likes, since he's usually the one instigating, but I do know a few things he likes to hear...

"It's all for you. Only you."

His eyes fly up to meet mine, wide and surprised, like he's checking if I'm serious. "Eleanor—"

"Yours," I promise. "Yours, yours, yours, yours."

I barely make it all the way back up and down before his body is tensing under me. His mouth opens wide as his head goes back, though the sound that escapes is choked. His legs jerk underneath me, his fingers dig hard into my hips, and every muscle in his chest and abs comes into stark relief. God, he is stunning.

He finishes, and I can feel the effect of gravity on our mixed fluids as I climb off and fall to my side next to him. I'm a little sore, tired, and drunk on pleasure, the way only really intense sex makes you.

"I didn't think I could come if I was on the bottom," he says as he turns towards me.

"Have you never before?" At his shake of the head, I smile. "I do like being on top, but I have to admit that I love being under you."

He grins and settles his hand in the valley of my waist. "Then don't be surprised if that's how you wake up in a few hours."

Even though we just did all that, my body instantly responds to it. I feel my nipples prickle and my sex pulsate. "My favorite way to wake up."

34

MAC

Who meets for dinner on a Tuesday at 10:30 PM?

After I wake in the morning, I lie there and listen to her even, shallow breathing for a while. My dick is hard, like it usually is when I wake, and I'm sorely tempted to recreate the dream I was having, but I doubt she'd appreciate regaining consciousness in surprise bondage. She needs to rest anyway.

Instead, I slip out of bed, toss on enough clothes so I won't catch any shit for my nudity or hard-on, and head downstairs. I leave the gauze wrap in place, in spite of the fact that I don't really need it since the wounds aren't oozing, because it reminds me of her. It reminds me that she cares enough to want to help heal me; that she soothes me.

I smile, remembering the way she handled my wounds. I like how tender she was with me. No one else does that, which could have something to do with my chosen profession. But somehow her gentle treatment isn't emasculating, like I thought it would be. If anything, it makes me feel stronger, more manly. It's an addictive feeling.

Like I needed another reason to be addicted to her.

Wes is in his cave, as per usual, staring at his screen with a pensive frown.

"Hey man, what did you find?"

He glances at me, then sits back. "Nice face."

I scrub my jaw where I know the skin has turned black and blue. I can feel the puffiness that tells me it's still a bit swollen, but something being tender to the touch doesn't faze me anymore unless something is broken. "I'm thinking of going into modeling, but you wouldn't know anything about that, ugly mug like yours."

He grins. "Let me get Dimitri on a call. Go get some coffee and an ice pack."

"Where is he?"

"At the address you sent us. It was purchased 25 years ago by Lucy Silvie. It took some digging—life was so much more offline 25 years ago—but I found her. Get this—she's Kevin Anderson's former mistress."

"The mayor?"

"None other."

I mull that over as I walk out of the room. Why would Rossi be staying at the mayor's former mistress's house? Are they having an affair? Does the mayor know?

The fancy espresso machine gets to work on my drink—so loudly it sounds like it's trying to achieve liftoff—as I nuke some of the egg muffin things Eleanor baked us. I cram them into my mouth, fist the coffee in one hand and the ice pack in the other. I hear the noise that means the call is starting up as I close the office door behind me.

"Well, he is definitely in there. He sits in the living room in an open bathrobe. That is a sight I cannot unsee," Dimitri kicks us off immediately.

It's hard to believe we finally know where he is. It's even harder to believe he's somewhere so unprotected. Why stay in a random suburban two-bedroom when you have a home like a palace with armed guards? Clearly, he wasn't expecting to be followed, or for anyone who might be after him to find the connection to the mayor.

"Thanks for getting Eleanor out of there last night," I say as I pull a chair around to sit next to Wes. He rolls to the side to make room.

Dimitri jerks a nod, his acknowledgement of my thanks. "I read your message that explained what happened after you left the table. You should know that Grigori and one other are dead. They arrived just as we were leaving."

I nod. "I figured it was something like that. I'm sure the cleanup crew brought enough bleach."

Dimitri huffs a little sound of amusement that's basically like his version of a laugh. "It is what they are paid to do. What have you found, Wesley?"

Wes taps a few keys, bringing up a browser. "He definitely thinks it was all Dimitri—the weapons and the row at Rouge Elephant. They upped the reward significantly."

"Let him think this," Dimitri says dismissively.

Wes glances at me, and his lips flatten. "I've got worse news. He also thinks Eleanor is involved—Dimitri's accomplice, maybe."

When he brings up the ad, I stiffen. There's an image from the restaurant, slightly fuzzy from a long zoom in dim lighting, with about half of Eleanor's face as Dimitri rushes her out. His back is to the camera. I scan the ad and curse when I see the last line.

...and information on the whereabouts of Eleanor Wilson, 28, Caucasian female, last known address in Ulysses, NJ.

My blood boils, even as a cold kind of fury settles in my chest. He's going to put out a hit on my girl? "He's a dead man."

"*Da.* That is the job," Dimitri reminds me dryly.

"At least it's not an APB," Wes says, like it's some kind of consolation. "It tells us they still aren't doing anything above board."

The mention of possible police intervention scratches at something in the back of my brain. Something Eleanor said. Why wouldn't a man like him—up for reelection—plaster his face everywhere, unless it was easier for him if people don't know what he looks like?

I sit back and cross my arms. "I've got a question. Who meets for dinner on a Tuesday at 10:30 PM?"

"Someone who doesn't want to be seen with their company," Wes suggests with a shrug. "They don't want people to know about their connection because Rossi's buying the mayor off?"

"That's what I thought, too. But if you had the mayor in your pocket—you go to dinner, he takes your money, gets some building permits pushed through, some petty crime expunged, lets you stay in his safe house—why wouldn't you just go to the cops to track Dimitri down?"

"And say what?" Wes asks.

I shrug. "Anything. He broke in, he assaulted him, he stole something... My point is, the reason doesn't matter if cops are going to do it anyway as a favor to the mayor. Surely it would be easier for Rossi if he could get some help from law enforcement, especially since he knows Dimitri is still local, and he's got at least one guy on the force under his thumb."

Dimitri frowns into the middle distance. "Police do have resources that would be valuable in the search."

"And a mayor is effectively in charge of local police."

"Why go underground if you don't have to?" Wes asks, thinking aloud. "It's expensive."

"And discreet." I adjust my ice pack to take a sip of my coffee while I think. "Rossi hires cleaners, which means he doesn't want to get the police involved. For a guy like him, that probably means he doesn't want his name or any of his associates on the record. But if he could just get the mayor to look the other way, why wouldn't he?"

"So, there's no record of it," Dimitri says. "Or, the mayor would not want to help with this for some reason, perhaps."

"Maybe the mayor answers to someone, and it looks suspicious if he's too involved in police matters," Wes suggests.

I shake my head. "Locally, the mayor only answers to taxpayers. No one above him is even around to notice any excessive involvement with local law enforcement."

"So, Rossi does not want to involve the mayor in these affairs. We still do not know why," Dimitri declares.

"I just... have a hunch. What if we were wrong, and it's not just Rossi? Let's look into the mayor—follow the money. How much does a public servant like him make?"

Wes blows out a breath. "Before bribes? $100K at most."

"Does he live a $100K a year life? Or, does he make large deposits in offshore accounts?"

Wes grins. "I'll find out."

"It does not change that we still know Rossi is involved. And now we know where he is hiding, and it can finally be a simple matter of your rifle from 500 yards," Dimitri goes on.

"Not if the mayor will keep up this operation after Rossi is dead," I argue. I'll never be able to leave Eleanor here if I know the mayor of her town was in bed with a weapons smuggler. Especially not now that her picture has been in this forum, even for a minute. She'll either have to move or come with me—another option that's being taken from her. "Give Wes some time, see what he can dig up."

"I can't take too long. Now that he thinks Eleanor is involved, the clock is ticking on her family being put at risk."

Dimitri grinds his jaw. "Fine. But I will be taking the day watch again."

"Fine." I should have known that would be his stipulation. "How's that new cell phone coming?"

Wes grabs it off the edge of the desk. "Got it here. I'll give it to her when she gets up."

I stand, draining the last of my coffee. "You mean when she gets down here. She's about to be up, but she won't be coming down for a while yet, if you know what I mean—"

Wes groans, and Dimitri disconnects the call with a resentful, "Of course we know what you mean."

"Lucky sod," Wes mutters as I leave the room.

She's still asleep when I return to the room, and looking so peaceful, my erection prompts a heated internal debate. The softer side of me wins, and I grab my sneakers on the way back out of the bedroom to work off some of this energy the solitary way.

35

ELEANOR

I can't believe I said the quiet part out loud.

"You've got your standard on-the-lam package—no social media and email is blocked for now. Use this app for chats, Mac's already loaded as your top contact, but Dimitri and I are in there as well. The Internet is okay, but a smart girl like you knows not to leave a footprint, yeah? Don't sign in to anything, no contacting friends or family, no comments, no interactions."

I nod furiously, hand outstretched. I haven't touched a phone in what feels like ages. But as Wesley lays the top-of-the-line model in my palm, I'm hit with nothing but anxiety about breaking it, and disappointment because all I want to do is show it off to Harrison.

Oh, well. At least it will help me stay connected to Mac while he's gone at night. I'm already dreading going to sleep in that big bed alone tonight. And since he's resting for the day in preparation for having to be awake all night, it's another day spent occupying myself. With him on night-surveillance, we won't get days together, and we won't get to lay together in our post-coital exhaustion. The pillow talk was always my second favorite part of the night.

I look down appraisingly at the phone. At least my workouts won't be in silence anymore. That was getting a bit boring.

The day slips away from me as I putter around the kitchen, preparing and then refilling the empty containers of pelmeni with what's in the freezer. I get a workout in, mindlessly browse for recipe inspiration and do a search on everyone I care about that I haven't talked to. Mac said no signing into anything and socials are out, so I'm left scanning titles from articles about college achievements for any sign that something might have happened to them more recently.

Mac comes down into the kitchen at 6:30, with just enough time to eat dinner before heading out. He's ruffled and scrubs his eyes like he didn't sleep well. I'm not hungry yet, but I sit next to him as I slide the plate in front of him. Steak, baked potato, broccoli—filling and satisfying.

He smiles in appreciation. "Thank you, darlin'."

"Are you going to kill him?" I ask. He chokes on his first bite of steak, probably at the abruptness, and I wince. "Sorry—"

Eyes watering, he coughs and reaches for his water. "It's fine."

"I just thought since you know where he is now and everything up until this point has really just been about killing him, right? So, I figured tonight's the night?"

He shakes his head and pounds his chest with a fist. With a final cough, he settles. "No, not tonight. We're keeping an eye on him while we check on another lead."

I frown at the lack of details—that's new. "A lead you won't tell me about?"

"I'll tell you if it checks out." He looks down and starts sawing off another piece of meat. "I don't want to share suspicions with you if you have to live here when the job is done. I wouldn't want to bias your future interactions with people by scaring you about them."

I swallow in a throat that has just gone thick. Right. The after. When I stay here—where I live—and Mac leaves. "Makes sense," I say. I hear the smallness of my voice, but Mac apparently doesn't over the sound of his knife against the steak.

"But now that we know where Rossi is, we're just keeping tabs on him. Making sure we don't lose him again. And meanwhile, Wes is following a money trail, following up on our lead."

I shake myself out of it. *Focus on the now, Eleanor.*

No use getting two steps ahead of myself. I have him right now, right in front of me—that's where I need to be.

Mac finishes his dinner—in a significantly better mood after some food, I might add—and pulls me in for a kiss before heading out. After feeding Wesley, then myself, then Dimitri, I clean the kitchen and wander back downstairs to watch a movie. The projector situation is just as intimidating as the speakers in the gym, but now I have the internet in the palm of my hand to look up the instructions.

I've already decided to try to stay awake as late as possible. I can't completely shift my waking hours because I tried working nights once, and it made me sick, but the restaurant has me up until 1 or 2 AM most of the time anyway. What's a few more hours?

The restaurant. It was so easy to use the past tense when talking to Chef Anh about it. So easy to let myself think of eight years there as part of an old life.

I pop in an action movie—one with a lot of fight scenes—and picture Mac as the protagonist, fighting off three guys at once. I bet he could. I bet he'd look badass doing it, too. So I text him.

> How many grown men do you think you could fistfight at once?

It takes him a few minutes to get back to me.

> Probably max 5 or 6, depending on skill level.

My eyes widen, and I glance up at the screen. The actor is making it look easy, but I know how highly choreographed it is. I also don't feel like Mac's bragging.

> Okay, but how about toddlers?

20. Easily.

20?! But they bite!

But they're basically babies. They wouldn't know how to organize against me.

How many if they could organize?

There's a pause, and I can picture his face as he considers. As he gives my ridiculous question enough thought to give a reasonable answer.

Probably 12.

I laugh and set my phone down. After a minute, it buzzes again.

What about you?

I'd never fight a toddler! What a horrible thing to ask.

There's another pause, where his typing bubble appears and then disappears.

I miss you.

I inhale heavily and put my phone back down. It feels kind of like something is sitting on my chest and I can't get the whole breath in. I focus on the movie, but I've seen it already. So, I change it to something else I've already seen, hoping this one will keep my attention better. I probably shouldn't be surprised when it doesn't. I wake on the couch after the credits have ended and decide to put myself to bed.

Hours later, I wake in the middle of a bad dream. I sit up, chest heaving, and check the clock. 7:23. It's probably too late in the morning to fall back asleep, but maybe if I lie in bed, it will come back. After a visit to the bathroom, that is.

I hear the bedroom door close as I'm washing my hands, and my heart does a little flip in my chest. Mac's back.

"Hi," I say, smiling at him. The light spilling through the blackout curtains gives the room a strange light quality, like dark daylight.

He comes immediately to me and drops a kiss onto my lips. I eagerly go up on my toes to meet him halfway. "I was expecting to find you asleep," he says, rubbing my bare upper arms. "That goodnight text came late—or, early, I guess."

"I decided to stay up; I got all out of whack with bedtimes the past couple weeks. But it'll be good to be back on roughly the same schedule for when I go back to the restaurant. If I still have that job anyway…"

He tilts his head at me, then goes to sit on the bed to remove his shoes. "I thought you didn't want to work in the restaurant."

I love how well this man listens. I also love watching the veins in his large hands as he unlaces his black combat boots. "I think that realization was just the first step. I'd like to have any business I start already turning a profit before I leave a steady paycheck."

He nods, but his face is impassive, so I can't really tell if he has any opinions on that. "That's a safe way to do it. Do you have a timeline in mind?"

I shrug as he stands and starts working his belt. "Being in business for myself is something I can start doing anytime. I just have to really go after it. It'll probably mean longer days for a little while—two jobs, getting my name out there—but it'll be worth it for something I like better."

He meets my eye, then starts unbuttoning his shirt in the front. "It's your call, of course. But you're not going back to that apartment, that's for sure. You're going to live in another building, one with better security and a doorman—"

"I can't afford that," I point out with a laugh. What a nice thought, though. "I'm not quite paycheck to paycheck. I'm… weekend trip to new cell phone. It's not a comfortable way to live."

"I'll pay for it."

"And what, I'll be some kind of kept woman?" I laugh again, even as my stomach flops over. It sounds a little more forced to my own ears this time. "You're sweet, but if you're not in my life, I need to have the apartment I can afford with the job I've got—"

"What the hell makes you think I'm not going to be in your life?" The lightness is gone, and his brows have snapped together. His fingers have stopped unbuttoning, and his posture has become rigid.

I falter. I hadn't really meant to say that part out loud. "Oh, um..."

"Eleanor," he says, his tone a warning. "What about anything that's happened here has given you any indication I intend to let you go when this is over?"

"I... uh..."

He takes a step towards me. "I thought we agreed to make this work. Didn't we? Don't you want to?"

My mouth has gone dry, and my heart is racing. Distractingly, it's part fear and part desire, as the aggression in his steps towards me has me remembering back to when we first got together—when he was all wild passion and possession. Heat blooms in my face and moves under my skin, directly to my core.

I fall back. "Yes, of course—"

"Then why did you just say I won't be in your life?" he demands.

"I... you just said earlier that I would be staying here after the job is done, and I know you won't be... It's not like you meant we were going to be living together."

"That's exactly what I meant, Eleanor."

"What?" I stop as the bathroom door presses against my back. "You just said *I* wasn't going back to my apartment, that *I* was going to live somewhere with a doorman. You never said 'we.' It didn't sound like you were planning on joining me."

He doesn't say anything for a few seconds, just breathes audibly through his nose and stares down at me. His chest brushes against mine, and I feel cornered. "*We're* going to live in an apartment building with a doorman."

Hope, and a lifting sense of joy fills my body. He's making plans for a life with me? He has been all this time? "Really?" I breathe.

But he doesn't share my newfound happy relief. His hand comes up to circle my neck, and I feel my eyes go wide. His voice is that low, dangerous tone that sends a shiver up my spine. "You seem to have forgotten something very important, darlin'. I think you need a reminder."

My breath catches. I think I know where he's going with this, but... I really, really want to be right. "Does that mean... I haven't been a very good girl, Mac?"

His eyes drop to my lips, and I lick them. He releases me and takes a step back. "No, you have not. Go stand by the bed."

My entire pussy contracts, spasming. I look down towards the floor as I wind around him, shuffling over to the corner at the foot of the bed.

"Take off your shorts."

I hook the waistband in my thumbs and pull down, and I'm bared to him as he sits on the edge. I know that even if I were wearing underwear, it would also be coming off now.

"Shirt."

I lift it up, and it joins my shorts on the floor. He stares at my naked body from his position sitting on the bed. He radiates power, from his posture to his expression to the fact that he's still almost fully clothed. And the submission I feel in being silently stared at while I have my eyes lowered is unreal—I'm almost shaking from the erotic fear and excitement.

Just as the silence starts to feel heavy, the palpable tension in the air making me shift from foot to foot, he speaks. "You're going to lie across my lap. I want your ass," he points to his left thigh. "Right. Fucking. Here."

Nervous, but unbelievably turned on, I move to kneel on the mattress. I shuffle forward, then go onto my hands so I can crawl over his lap instead of falling into place. I'm so aware of my nudity as I lie across the fabric covering his legs.

I flinch as his hand comes to rest on the bare skin of my ass, but he just rubs the area and I have to bite my lip to keep in the moan. His fingers are so firm, so strong. His other arm lies across my lower back, and I feel like I'm strapped in. I don't know what to do with my hands, so I keep them pressed into the mattress on either side of my head.

"Eleanor, what do you think I mean when I say you're mine?"

I falter because I wasn't really expecting a question, and suddenly, a sharp noise resounds around us. I jump, mostly in surprise, and an instant later, there's a stinging sensation on my ass. I hiss.

"Do you think I say things like that lightly—that I don't mean it?"

"No," I whisper, then jolt as a blow lands on my other cheek. The stinging sensation brings heat to the surface of the skin.

"No," he agrees. "Do you think I mean that you're mine for a little while, as long as this job takes?"

"No?" I repeat, but that one is a little bit of a fib. That is sort of what I was expecting to happen. Maybe we'd try for a little while, but invariably...

Smack. I squeal this time, wiggling under his arm from the force of his hand against skin that's already received an impact. It's starting to pulsate.

"No. Do you think I just toss aside the things that are important to me?"

"No."

I tense, trying to be ready for his hand this time. I'm so wet I can feel it on my inner thighs, and I know it's only a matter of time before he sees it. *Smack!* That's the second hit to my left cheek. I whimper.

"No." His hand comes down, but gently, kneading the skin and making me squirm on his lap. "Do you think you're important to me?"

I falter again. But this time, no spank lands.

"So help me, Eleanor, if the answer to that question isn't 'yes,'" he warns.

"I don't know," I whisper. I feel a tear prickle at the bottom of each eye, stinging the lids.

Instead of another hit, I feel his fingers brush my pussy lips. "You don't know?" he asks in a low voice I almost have to strain to hear.

I rock my hips back, wanting some more pressure in a desperate way. "I don't know, yes, I guess. I... don't know how I could be important to someone like you."

"Someone like me?" he repeats, his voice thick with bewilderment. "Hold on. As much as I love staring at your ass, I think I need to see your face for this one."

A surprised laugh spills from my lips as he helps me up off his lap, up to my knees. I sit back on them for an instant, long enough to see the question in the slash of his eyebrows. Then, it feels like too damn much. I climb down off the bed and grab the blanket I fold and lay across the end of the mattress every morning.

He stands, takes a step towards me, and stops when I move to retreat away. "What do you mean, Eleanor? Hey, talk to me."

I can't believe I said the quiet part out loud. I wasn't supposed to let the insecurities out—those stay in a tiny box that I locked away and labeled "fake it 'til you make it" to fool myself.

"You're..." I tilt my head, letting my eyes rove over his body. "You're brave and strong and charismatic... I'm not like you."

He smiles a little at me. "I think they call that a complimentary fit, darlin'."

"Stop, I'm being serious."

"So am I," he counters easily. "I don't want someone like me. You see brave and strong; I see hardened and jaded. You see charisma—thanks for that, by the way, I like it—but the truth is, lies come easy to me and charisma is really just another manipulation."

I must look unconvinced, because he extends his arm. "Come here."

I take the outstretched hand hesitantly, but he doesn't bring me back to the bed. He leads us over to the corner of the room next to the closet, which has a long mirror that leans against the wall aesthetically. He stands behind me, making me face both of our reflections. He places his lips on the side of my neck, and I watch as the hair on the top of his head blocks both of our faces. I close my eyes, not wanting to see how we look next to each other like this—where I can't hide at all.

"We're very different," he murmurs against my skin. "And I think that's what made me so crazy about you to begin with, but that doesn't mean you're not brave or strong or charismatic."

He moves to the other side of my neck, and I let my head tilt to the side to make room as a soft sigh escapes my lips. "You are brave—you feel for people, you open your heart and you care, and that's one of the bravest things I can think of. I'm not brave like that. And you're strong. You've been making it on your own all this time, chasing a dream and pivoting when it didn't work out; that takes incredible strength of will. And charisma? You've got Wes and Dimitri wrapped so tightly around your little finger, I'm honestly a bit jealous."

I'm barely daring to breathe, not wanting to miss a single word, but at that I do laugh a little.

"You make me better. I'm just trying not to make you worse."

My eyes fly open, and I meet his in the mirror. "What? You could never—you wouldn't. You amaze me, Mac."

"Eleanor, I love you."

A breath breaks in my throat. He loves me? *He loves me?* I try to turn—I don't want to see his face reflected; I want the real thing—but he stops me with both hands on my waist.

"The only reason I haven't said it before is because I know it's early and I didn't want to scare you off. I want you to know that I'm going to try to deserve you." One of his hands comes around the front of me, finding where the edges of the blanket overlap, and disappears inside. "Now, watch yourself. Watch how beautiful you are when you come apart for me."

My mind is swimming.

He loves me.

I shake my head as I feel his fingers find the hot, wet center of me. "No."

He stills.

I stare at his handsome face in the mirror, and I'm momentarily speechless. I feel completely overwhelmed. I'm desperate for this man, who's already given me so much, then gave me his love without the expectation of reciprocation. And even after that declaration, he'd just keep giving if I let him. But I don't want it—not like that.

I don't want soft and sweet. I don't want him to give. I want to be the one to give.

"Take me—take what's yours. Right now." I let go of the blanket, and it slides down my body, tickling the fine hairs.

"Fuck," he moans, and I hear the noise of a zipper.

"Please, Mac. Fuck me. I want it hard. I need it."

"Lean forward, grab the sides," he orders, his voice labored and urgent.

I shout as he enters me before I even get my hold positioned right between the mirror and walls. Hands digging into my waist, he bottoms out in the first stroke and pulls back, giving me no time to adjust. It's hard, just like I asked, and frantic. My breasts bounce with the force of his thrusts.

"Open your eyes," he grits out between thrusts. "Look at us."

I didn't even realize I'd closed them. But our gazes lock in the mirror, and it intensifies everything tenfold. I adjust my grip as the mirror starts rattling, and lock my elbows so my arms won't wobble. My jaw drops, and the breathy noises come out deeper, more guttural.

He pulls back, swapping speed for depth, and each press of the hard head of his cock against my cervix draws a cry from my lips. I keep my focus on him, even when the edges of my vision haze in the pleasure. His nostrils flare as his breaths come out on a low grunt, and every muscle I can see in his arms and chest and neck and shoulders is taut and straining. Suddenly, I kind of love doing this in front of the mirror because of the view it gives me—I can see that he's taking with everything he has.

His need is so wild, so addictive. I squeeze, contracting my muscles inside, wanting to grip him tighter. "You're so good. So deep, it's fucking amazing."

"Fuck, you're tight. I'm not going to last," he groans, his brows coming down low.

"Yes, do it—come," I say.

I can't touch my clit, not while I'm propped up like this and supporting his weight at the apex of each thrust. But his balls are hitting me just so in this position that it's actually making me wonder if I'll be able to get off without the clitoral stimulation for once. His cock is definitely hitting the right spot inside of me... but I'm not close enough to see if penetration will get me there if he's nearly finished.

"You're going to come with me."

He reaches around, and I spread my legs a little wider to give him access. "I love how you touch me," I bite out. "I love how you feel inside me."

"I love you," he replies to that, starting a gentle strumming across my clit.

I open my mouth to say it too, but hold back. I'm not sure why. "Make me come," I urge instead. "Make me yours."

"You are mine."

The motion of his fingers against the almost raw nerve endings is as soothing as it is stimulating—it's like the pressure they provide turns the painful edge the need had become into a lever that starts cranking something low inside my belly. It creeps up with each contrasting brush of his fingers and thrust of his cock until I'm panting and prickled all over with sweat.

"Come now."

I fall apart instantly, though whether it's because I knew he wanted it or he could tell that it was just about to happen anyway, it's impossible to know. His shout of release rings in my ears, even though I'm miles away, and when I come back into my body everything is shaking. His arm comes up, weaving through my breasts to firmly plant a hand over my sternum, and he lifts me back against him. He turns my head to the side and kisses me slowly, thoroughly.

When I can trust my legs again, I turn in his hold and wrap my arms around his neck, never breaking the kiss. We stay connected like that until we both come down from the orgasm, with tender licks and nibbles and the taste of each other. I pull back, letting my hands trail down the sides of his shirt, then sneaking inside so I can press them against his lower back under the fabric.

"I still owe you another spanking for that comment about *someone like me.*"

When I look up, I see that he's staring at my ass in the mirror. I smile and nuzzle against his chest. I can still vaguely feel the pounding heat on my skin. "I'll take a rain check."

36

MAC

⚬

I can't believe I'm considering this.

"Yeah, he's not take-a-couple-of-bribes-a-year rich. And he's definitely not public-servant rich."

Dimitri whistles as Wes shares his screen. "That's a lot of money."

"Could it be generational? Inheritance?" I ask.

Wes shrugs. "I looked back a few generations, and his family has money, but that only accounts for maybe 10% of this. It's hard to know for sure, but this might actually have been the family business—his father, who was also briefly the mayor here, received irregular, large lump sums that he started funneling offshore in the 90s."

I blow out a breath and lace my fingers behind my head as I lean back in my chair. "So, Mayor Anderson is probably in on the weapons scheme. That explains why Rossi wouldn't go to the cops. If he works for or with Anderson, he wouldn't want to go running to him to clean up every mess, not when it makes him look incompetent and he's got his own contacts."

Wes nods and stands as he drains the rest of his energy drink. "And if he is in on it, this just got a lot more fucking complicated. We can't just assassinate a public official. It draws media attention. Higher authorities of law, like the FBI... that sort of thing."

Dimitri sighs. "*Here* you cannot."

Wes and I exchange a look. Dimitri is so tight-lipped about his past, I collect the factoids like breadcrumbs, and I know Wes does, too.

"What the bloody hell is going on in Russia?" Wes asks as he goes to the built-ins on the wall of the study and opens one of the bottom cabinets, revealing a safe and a mini fridge.

"A blanket of snow hides many sins."

I snort, and Wes straightens, new drink in hand. "That was fucking poetry, mate."

Dimitri hmmphs.

"When did you get a mini-fridge?" I ask.

Wes cracks the drink and takes a sip, finishing with a little *ahh*. "Day before yesterday. I'm all about peak efficiency."

"I know you've got short legs, but it's only like 40 steps to the kitchen. What's that, like, half a mile for you—"

"Can we get back to the job?" Dimitri mutters some colorful Russian insults under his breath—*penis from the mountains*. That's new. "The money alone is not proof, but it is strong evidence. We need something more concrete that ties Anderson to the sale, or to this business with Rossi."

"That's going to be tricky. All those weeks of research and his name never even came up once. If he's in this, he's well-hidden," Wes points out.

Dimitri scratches his chin, the noise rasping against his stubble even through the call. "I have an idea, but James will not like it."

"I already don't, just from that lead-in."

Dimitri lifts a brow, and goes on, "Our problem is that we do not know for sure the mayor's involvement and, if he is involved, we do not know what he knows."

"That about sums it up," Wes acknowledges.

"If we kill Rossi, and it actually has been the mayor's operation this whole time, we lose. Even though Rossi is the job. Agreed?"

"Agreed," Wes says.

I'm done with the buildup. "Quit edging us and tell us your idea."

"We should use the cop. Eleanor could—"

"No."

At Dimitri's sigh, Wes nudges me. "Unless you've got one locked and loaded, let's hear his idea out."

"I'm not putting the woman I love in danger," I say.

"I am not suggesting this is what we do," Dimitri snaps. "Well, not really."

"The woman you love?" Wes says slyly.

"Yes, it was obvious he loves her. Focus! It is like being a goat herder sometimes," Dimitri mutters. "This cop came to Eleanor to ask for information about me weeks ago. Now they think that we are connected because Rossi saw us together at the restaurant. So, she can offer this cop information about me to get a meeting, then we can use him to determine how involved the mayor is. And you can be there; you can ensure no harm comes to her."

I grind my jaw. I hate the thought of Eleanor being anywhere near that dirty cop. Or Rossi. Or the mayor. Or any of this.

"Think about it. Rossi is in hiding. All his men are dead, other than Owen Johnson, who is in the coma—"

"A coma," Wes pipes in.

"That is what I said. The mayor's part in this has eluded us so far, so he is likely not directly involved by design. This officer is the last connection we know of between them and a good opportunity for us. Perhaps the last we will get."

"I don't want her involved," I say, rubbing my eyes.

"Eleanor is involved, my friend. She has been for many weeks now."

"But if she does this, we can't know how McCloskey will react or what he'll do. What if he goes right to Rossi, or tries to arrest her on some bullshit charges? She'll be in danger."

Wes catches my eye. "So, we do what we do best—we make our plan, we control the variables. His hands are tied, too; he won't arrest her for the same reason Rossi never reported Dimitri to the police. It's really not a bad idea, Mac."

I sigh. There are ways we could protect her—mic her up, be in her ear and coach her on what to say, be there in person. The cop hasn't seen my face, or Wesley's... "I can't believe I'm considering this."

"You are considering it because you are a reasonable man and you know we are very good at what we do," Dimitri says, not bothering to hide his satisfaction. "You know we take precautions so no one on the team gets hurt—this would now include Eleanor."

Truthfully, I did know that. He's come a long way from thinking of her as collateral damage. "Okay, but we let her decide if she wants to help."

"A given," Wes says. Dimitri rolls his eyes, but nods.

"And if we do this, we finish it—one fell swoop. It needs to be soon, and we'll need a trap, or something foolproof, so there's no time for it to escalate."

"I agree," Dimitri says.

Wes leans forward in his chair. "Then we don't have time to do anything clever with costumes or—"

"Costumes?" Dimitri repeats, appalled.

"Disguises," Wes amends with a little laugh. "The easiest way to know they're working together for sure would be just to get them together and let them dig their own grave."

Dimitri shakes his head and leans forward, like he's checking something out the window of his car. "It will be difficult to draw Rossi out. He is very... comfortable. He only goes outside for the mail—everything is delivered and he works from the house office, taking calls in his underpants."

I consider that. "So... we need to rattle him?"

"It would not hurt. He is safe in this house, he believes, but I think our original assessment is correct and he would react if provoked. Especially if he thought it was me, and he thought he could be close to catching me."

I stand, "One second. I think I know what we can use."

I head to the kitchen, listening to Wes and Dimitri lapse into work-adjacent conversation that isn't more planning they'd need to catch me up on. I head to the freezer to grab the paper bag I tucked in the back of an empty drawer, and toss it on the table in front of Wes when I get back to the office.

"We'll send him this. Taunt him."

Wesley unrolls the bag, glances inside and calmly rolls the bag back up, just a bit more green around the gills. "Bloody hell," he murmurs to himself, making a face.

"What is it?" Dimitri wants to know.

"You might have warned me!" Wes snaps at me, heated. It's interesting to see; he's normally so unflappable.

"What is it?" Dimitri repeats, louder.

"Fucking eyeballs," Wes growls, wiping his hand on his pants, then grimacing when he realizes that if there was something on his hand, now it's on his pants.

"Whose?" Dimitri presses, pure curiosity.

"Rossi's fixer from the steam room—the one who pretended to be a detective."

"Why do you even have them?" Wes prompts, still sounding miffed.

I shrug. "He saw her in a towel."

Dimitri smiles his approval, likely both at the bloody-yet-fitting nature of the vengeance and the idea to gift them to our favorite weapons smuggler. "This could work."

Wes opens a drawer of his desk and grabs a container of wet wipes. "Troglodytes," he mutters, giving his hands and then the desk in front of him a thorough scrub as I remove the bag with a laugh.

"So, we need Rossi to think Dimitri is within his grasp, and we need the mayor to have a reason to seek Rossi out." Wes starts tapping his fingers against the glass, a deep-in-thought gesture. He grimaces. "Honestly, Dimitri would be the best for that—he could play them off each other, and we'd know how involved the mayor is by whether or not he recognizes him."

"I cannot be in two places at once," Dimitri observes.

But Wes's eyes have narrowed, and he's staring at my jaw. "You know, you both have a bruise in almost the exact same spot..." he points to his jaw, like we needed a reminder of where.

Dimitri and I look at each other. His is a bit more advanced in healing, more of a brown than my fresh purple one. But I can see where Wes is coming from. When using distinguishing facial features to describe someone, people hardly ever think to comment on what color the bruise was, just the existence of it and its location.

And while Dimitri and I aren't exactly twins, we do have roughly similar builds that I could pad out with a thick jacket, and a hat pulled down over our eyes would hide most of his largest scar that I don't share...

"I think I have an idea..."

37

ELEANOR

What in the holy hell and whole world...

I wake to a text from Mac, my phone buzzing on the bed next to me and scaring me out of my half-conscious snoozing with the noise that's been so absent from my life lately. The clock tells me it's a little after noon, so I've been asleep for about four hours.

> Hey baby. Come to Wes's cave when you wake up.

I set the phone face down next to me and give my whole body one of those toe-curling stretches. I can feel all the tightness in my abs and obliques and inner thighs that reminds me of exactly how I spent my early morning. And I'm very sore.

The soreness on my ass, on the other hand, is only skin deep.

God, anytime he wants to try to spank the self-doubt out of me again, I will happily submit.

I hop in the shower, since Mac's text didn't sound particularly urgent, and put on some soft clothes in preparation for spending another day in paradise. Some people in my position would probably have gone stir crazy by now, but I'm finding that I genuinely enjoy my day spent planning and cooking, feeding these guys, and doing whatever I feel like in soft pants that have a drawstring.

Padding down to the first floor, I hang a right where I'd normally go left towards the kitchen and approach Wesley's study. I don't make a habit of being on this side of the first floor—even though it has all the other rooms for entertainment purposes; I hate feeling like I might bother him. He's always typing furiously or talking to someone through his headset in a low voice.

"All I'm saying is, as far as nicknames go, The Exterminator isn't bad," I hear Mac arguing from the room at the end of the hall.

"Like, 'I'll be back, but you won't'?" Wesley laughs.

Feeling a little silly because it's open, I knock on the door. Wesley is reclining back in his office chair, arms crossed, facing Mac, who's got his torso turned, leaning with his elbow over the back of his. Mac jumps up when he sees me and comes around the desk. He meets me with a kiss, and grabs the other chair to start dragging it around.

"Morning, darlin'. Do I need to ask how you slept?" he says with a wink.

I can sense Wesley's eyes on us, so my face starts heating involuntarily. It feels like I'm a teenager, kissing my boyfriend in front of my parents. "So good it's not morning anymore," I say. "What's up—what did you need me for?"

"Hang on just a tick, I'll get Dimitri back..." Wesley says, leaning forward and pressing a few keys.

Mac gestures to the chair that puts me between him and Wesley, facing all the screens. I feel a little like I'm entering a cockpit, or Batman's secret lair where he watches all of Gotham. This many screens is honestly overwhelming—I don't even know where to look.

Suddenly, Dimitri's angry face fills the screen. "I was just about to take a piss, must you—" he cuts himself off, seeing me.

"Hi," I say to him, waving a little awkwardly at the camera.

His scowl softens. "Hello, Eleanor," he says, much more gently.

"This is about the job—Rossi?" I guess, glancing side to side. I push my chair back a little so I can have all three of them in my view at the same time. "I'll help however I can."

Mac places a hand on my leg and gives it a little squeeze that shoots right to my nipples, tightening them. I hope that the desire he sparks—even from such an innocent touch—never fades.

"We'll get to that," he says. "First, some questions about the other night, in the restaurant, when Rossi and the Mayor showed up. As much as you can remember, can you walk us through exactly what happened?"

"Um, sure. So, you left, and I was sitting there, and the executive chef came by to chat. We were talking about... um, substitutions being annoying to deal with in the kitchen and the mayor interrupted. He put his hand on my shoulder, like to say sorry for interrupting—" Mac makes a low grumbling noise of disapproval, for which I shoot him a private kind of smile. "He shook hands with the chef, and was saying, like, he was looking forward to the meal. He asked if Chef Anh had met his business partner, Jay Rossi—"

"Business partner? That's the exact phrase he used?" Mac asks.

I falter. "Uh..."

"Not, 'my friend'? Or, restaurateur, or something like that?"

"No, it was definitely business-y. I remember because they were both wearing suits, and I thought it made sense because they looked like they were coming from some kind of meeting. Maybe he said associate?"

Wesley and Mac look at each other.

"Associate implies something different than partner, but either way he's stressing a business connection," Mac is pointing out to Wesley, who's nodding thoughtfully. He turns back to me. "What happened after that?"

"Um... Chef Anh said something that was kind of an inside joke with me and kind of at the mayor's expense, so he turned to look at me for the first time. Asked my name." I look down, feeling my cheeks heat. "I gave it... I didn't think to lie—"

"That is not important. Go on," Dimitri interrupts impatiently. For some reason, the fact that he's the one that says it relieves my guilt more than Mac or Wesley might have. Maybe it's because Dimitri has never sugarcoated anything he's said to protect my feelings, so I know he really means that this thing I thought was a massive fuckup is not important.

"Rossi looked at me, too, and I think he recognized my name."

"Did the mayor?" Wesley asks.

"I don't think so," I shake my head. "If he did, he hid it really well."

"Then what?"

"They... walked to their table. Rossi kept looking at me."

"And the mayor?"

"His back was to me, so I'm not sure, and at that point I was trying to hide my face. It looked like they were there to have some sort of meeting. And that was kind of it until Dimitri showed up to rescue me... I'm going to go out on a limb here and guess that the mayor is that lead you were following up on?" I say to Mac.

Mac nods and leans forward to take my hand. "Baby, we need your help."

Mac goes on to explain what they need—with some interjections from Wesley and taciturn silence from Dimitri—and dread slowly fills my stomach like lead weights. I shoot up out of the chair and walk around the back of it, like putting it between us will somehow protect me from the idea.

"What in the holy hell and whole world makes you think I'm the right person to do this?" I explode.

"McCloskey already knows you, and it is likely he will underestimate you," Dimitri says. "He will not be as threatened by a woman."

"But I'm literally the worst liar. When you saw me do it the first time, you said, and I quote, that I needed to 'work on my face,'" I remind Mac, accusatory.

"We'll be there, helping you," Mac says.

"I'm not what the kids would call 'cool under pressure.'"

"Kids don't say that," Wesley pipes in helpfully.

I cut him a glare, then return my attention back to Mac. "I don't think on my feet well when I'm afraid."

"No one does. And you won't have to. We'll be there, helping you," Wesley repeats Mac's sentiment.

Mac stands and circles his chair. He lays his hands on my shoulders and leans his head down to catch my eye. "Remember when I tackled you and tied you up, then you watched me shoot a bunch of bad guys?"

Wes hides a smile.

I scratch my elbow and scoff. "If this is your way of trying to convince me that I'll be able to keep a cool head, you picked the wrong example."

"But you did keep a pretty cool head," he argues.

"I was terrified! I thought I was going to die!"

"James will be with you; you will be safe," Dimitri says.

"That's not what I'm worried about. If Mac's there, I know I'll be safe," I say.

His chest physically puffs a little at that, and he grins at me. "Fuckin' A, baby."

"I'm..." I trail off and lift my eyes to Mac's. I can see his confidence, like it's an extension of him, and I wonder if it really extends to me. He wouldn't suggest it if he didn't think it would work. "You really think I can do it?"

He tips my chin up using his finger. "I know you can, darlin'."

I inhale and chew on my lip. If I'm really being honest with myself, I knew my part in this wasn't quite over. Not after what happened at the restaurant. "Okay. What do you need me to do?"

"Brilliant," Wesley exclaims, as Dimitri says, "Good girl," which earns him a sharp look from Mac.

"Okay, come sit back down," Mac says, taking my hand and leading me back to the desk. "Once we get started, there's no going back, and it's all going to go really fast. But it's the best shot we're going to get. So, I'm going to go over what we're going to do, and if you have questions, ask them. Okay? It's important that you understand what's going to happen and feel comfortable with your part in it."

I nod.

About an hour, a bajillion questions, and a mini panic attack later, Wesley is handing me an untraceable cell phone. Dimitri dropped the video call before they really got into explaining the plan, so I know he's probably already getting started with what he has to do.

"Wes and I are right here," Mac says. It's probably the sixth time he's had to console me with that.

Wesley slides the legal pad where he's been jotting out a little script for me. "Remember, it's all right if you sound scared," he says. "It'll help sell it."

"Ulysses County Sheriff's Office," says the voice that answers the phone on the non-emergency line. She has a thick Jersey accent and sounds bored.

"Um, is Officer McCloskey there?"

"Sure, hon. Who's calling and what's this about?"

Wes coaches my next words, mouthing them silently to me. "He, uh... came to my door a couple weeks ago. I have some information for him about the person he's looking for."

Wesley gives me a thumbs up.

"Okay, name?"

Wes underlines where he's written NO LAST NAME on the paper.

"Eleanor."

"Okay, hold please."

Some standard waiting music comes on the line, and I let out the rest of the breath I somehow managed to keep inside my lungs while talking. Mac rubs my back. This is the easy part, though. I can get through a phone call—it's the meet-up that's really going to test how strong my stomach is.

"McCloskey," a deep, gruff voice barks. I jump a little, because I was expecting the woman to come back on the line.

"H-hi," I stammer, then wince. Not a super strong start, there. Mac taps the page, where he's crossed off the NO on his previous instructions. "It's Eleanor Wilson."

"Where the hell have you been?" he asks, though his voice is lowered now. I think I hear him getting up and shutting his door. "You haven't been seen in weeks; we assumed you skipped town. You're going to be in huge trouble—"

"Officer, I *am* in trouble," I read. I have to really try not to let it leak into my voice, but I'm beyond impressed that not only did Mac and Wesley predict he'd immediately go on the offensive, but Mac actually guessed the exact words he'd use. "I'm really scared. I need your help."

"Why? What's going on?"

"It's the Russian... I can't say over the phone. But please... meet me. Maplewood Park in an hour?"

"How do I know this is legit? Not some kind of trap?"

Wes taps the part of the page where he wrote IF HE'S SUSPICIOUS. "Um... you can pick the spot in the park?"

There's a bit of silence, and I swear I hear the faint sound of typing, like he's looking it up. "The double bench by the swing set, on the side that faces the parking lot. I'll be there in an hour and a half."

Mac nods. "Okay," I agree.

"But if you're wasting my time or—"

Mac points to END IT. So, I hang up on him, mid-sentence.

Wes is all smiles, which makes me tentatively pleased. "I think that went well! Our Eleanor's a natural."

Yeah, if you call having a racing heart, shaking hands and feeling like I want to throw up being a natural at something...

"And now we know he's trying to be a strong man. Coming out the gate with threats, trying to keep her off balance."

Wes checks his watch. "And what a prat, making her wait a half hour when—for all he knows—she's scared for her life."

"He was just giving himself more time to scope everything out beforehand. He'll be there as soon as he can, so we have to move," Mac says.

I stand and head upstairs with Mac—both of us have to change into outside clothes, though his is the all-black, kickass ensemble of someone trying not to be noticed, and I just have to put on jeans. I mentally repeat the plan to myself like a mantra, in an effort to calm my nerves.

As soon as we're both dressed, he stops me with my hand on the doorknob. "Before we do this, I need you to know you can still back out—you can still say no. I know we just spent hours planning and drilling into you what to say and do... but this is not a risk you have to take, okay?

"Because we can try to control for everything that might go wrong, and believe me, darlin', we are trying. But in the end, there's always the possibility that something happens that we didn't expect. Someone doesn't show up who's supposed to, someone acts in a way you couldn't predict... someone comes back to a fumigated building for a medication."

"What kind of dummy would do that?" I laugh, and he smiles in response. "So, what do you do?"

"There's no way to plan for everything. Sometimes you've gotta think on your feet and try to minimize the consequences."

I nod. "I think, deep down, I knew that. And I'm not going to lie to you—that scares me. But what's going on in my city scares me. What Rossi does scares me. The thought of not having a life with you here scares me..." I bite my lip and meet his eyes, blazing with something that feels a lot like love. "I'm not saying I want to be the fourth musketeer or anything, but I think I can step up to protect what's mine."

His expression is grave. Instead of answering me, he sweeps me into his arms, holds me close to his chest, and presses his mouth down on mine.

"Thank you for helping us. Thank you for trusting me. Thank you for being brave."

I inhale a shaky breath through my nose, trying not to let his kind words go straight to my tear ducts. I'm struck with the knowledge that I would do anything for him, truly, and it also scares me—a little too much to say out loud. It's a different fear than the paralysis of not knowing what to say on the phone; it's one my fight-or-flight response learned from life beating me down.

I feel the corners of my mouth lift just enough to be considered a smile and nod at him. "Let's finish this."

38

MAC

And the Oscar goes to...

Since the van already has all the equipment, we just remove the decals and park it in a few streets down from the park. Eleanor takes deep, calming breaths as we mic her up and give her the rundown on the equipment she's wearing. We talk her through this part of the plan again, and I grab the tube of psoriasis cream I'd stuck in my pocket last minute on our way out. She seems to take comfort in the small contact as I rub it into the skin I noticed she's been scratching.

She puts the earpiece in and fluffs her hair down, covering it after with a hat so she remembers not to tuck her hair behind her ears. "How does this work again?"

Wes is all business, in his element. He's dressed in his winter running getup: black spandex with reflectors and a bright jacket. "You can turn it on now. All you have to do is tap the earpiece, and we'll be able to hear you. If you tap it again, you close the line on your end. Works the same way on the other side—like a call, but the other person doesn't have to pick up."

"My hair won't accidentally turn it off, will it? That happens sometimes with earbuds."

Wes smiles indulgently at her inexperience. "No, it won't. If it does get tapped accidentally, act like you're fixing your hair or something and just hit it again. You remember your story?"

"Yeah." She taps her ear, and her breathing picks up a little. "Okay. How much longer?"

I check my watch. It's almost 4:00 on a weekday and the warmest day in February so far, even with the overcast sky. A preliminary sweep of the area showed us that the park is relatively full—parents with children, people using the wide paved trail for exercise and walkers holding leashed dogs. It settles me—McCloskey won't try anything here. At most, he's got someone he trusts in plainclothes as backup, but that's why Wes and I are here.

"Whenever you're ready. I'm going to head out first, then I'll let you know if it's safe."

She nods. "I'm ready. Let's get this over with."

Wes grins and stands, ducking in the low back of the van. "Chin up, love. It'll be over before you know it."

"Pick a different nickname," I growl to him as he slides open the van door.

He laughs and disappears behind the closed door.

Eleanor and I sit in somewhat tense silence, waiting for Wes to come back online. It doesn't take long. *"He's here. A few spots over from the bench, ducked down and watching everyone like a hawk—like he can't quite remember what she looks like. I don't see any obvious backup. No one's just sitting with a leashed dog, and every buggy's got a baby."*

"So, I should go?" she asks me.

"Yeah, go ahead."

She surprises me by leaning in towards me before I could do the same thing and brushing her lips against mine. "For luck."

I grin and smack her ass lightly, mindful that it may be a bit sore. "You don't need it."

As she leaves the van, we hear Wes again. *"Eleanor, sit on the far side of the bench. It'll mean that he has to turn his back to the car to face you when you talk."*

"Okay."

It's weird hearing her voice in my ear like this—I'm so used to Wes or D's deep tones.

I'm the last out of the van, and I lock it since I'm not coming back. Wes's mustang is in a street spot about a block away from the park, and I climb inside. From this vantage, and with my scope, she's in my field of vision, and McCloskey will be, too. If he tries anything, I won't fucking hesitate. I don't care that it's still daylight, and the park is full of kids.

I see her sit on the bench and nervously shuffle her hands under her thighs, like she's sitting on them for warmth and restless with nervous energy. McCloskey watches her for a few minutes.

"Incoming. 30 yards east," I tell her as he gets out of his car.

"Mac," she grinds out through lips that barely move. *"I am not some kind of tactical mastermind or ship captain."*

"What?"

"Which way is east?" she hisses.

Wes guffaws.

"It's to your left. You're doing great, darlin'."

McCloskey walks up to her, and I see her body language change instantly. She straightens, pulls out her hands, and clasps them in her lap. He sits facing forward, and she turns her body slightly to mimic his posture. She did that without anyone telling her to. Good girl.

"You wanted to meet?" he asks, gruff.

"We don't have much time," she says. *"He doesn't know I'm here."*

"The Russian?"

She nods. *"I told him I was meeting a friend at the park."*

"Good. That's what we are, right?" The suggestion is as greasy as his hair.

"I hope so," she says, her voice wavering. She hands him the piece of folded-up paper. Her hand shakes in the air between them, and she

immediately snatches it back when he gets his fingers around it. *"Give this to the mayor,"* she says, just like we practiced.

Predictably, McCloskey opens the paper immediately. *"An address? What is this?"*

Her eyes dart around, and I want to kiss her. She's doing such a great job. *"It's what he's been looking for,"* she whispers.

"Who? The Russian?"

She shakes her head. *"Your boss."*

For that one, I might kiss her. We told her to be vague, but that's perfect. Let McCloskey decide who he thinks she means.

"You're just giving me this?" he asks her. *"Why?"*

I speak clearly, knowing she's not going to be able to speak and listen to me at the same time. But this is as good a time as any for her to take a moment to reply. "Okay, baby, Wes is almost there. Don't make eye contact with him. Remember when the mayor interrupted you with the chef? Pretend like he's interrupting you the same way. You don't need to say anything to him, but look kind of put out. Like, frown."

"I—" she starts.

I watch Wes place his hand on the bench by McCloskey's shoulder and bend over to reach for his shoe. *"Aw, crap!"*

McCloskey tenses and turns in his seat, shooting him a glare over the back of the bench. *"Hey, buddy, we're having a conversation here."*

"Oh, my bad," Wes says, his British accent gone. *"Just... got a damn rock in my shoe."*

With McCloskey's attention on Wes's face, he doesn't notice or feel the small listening device being planted under the collar of his jacket in the back. For her part, Eleanor's face is pale, and her eyes are firmly on her hands in her lap.

"Got it," he says, holding up a pebble with a triumphant grin. It's our signal—the bugging was a success—and he takes off at his easy jogging

pace, like nothing even happened. I start the car and ease out of my spot in the minimal traffic, taking a right at the end of the block.

"Well?" McCloskey asks. *"Tell me why I should believe you, Miss Wilson."*

Anger flashes at the disdainful tone he uses when he says her name. Makes me want to carve out his voice box. "He's just trying to intimidate you, to remind you he knows your full name. Do the answer we practiced that'll get his sympathy, about not wanting to be involved," I tell her as I park a block away.

A second later, I hear her. *"He's... a bad man. You have to believe me; I didn't mean to get mixed up in this. I want to help, but I... I don't want to die."*

I grin. "Good job. Now, look past his head, look surprised and say you have to go. If he tries to stop you, start making a scene and he'll let you go."

She executes it nearly perfectly—her gasp is maybe a bit overdramatic. *"I have to go!"*

"Wait! Who is he? What's his name?" McCloskey demands.

"He's the Ghost," she stage-whispers.

There's a beat of stunned silence on the line at her improv, then Wes chuckles. *"And the Oscar goes to..."*

Okay, yeah, now she's getting a bit too dramatic. Better get her out of there now, before she goes any further off book. I hear her power walking away, but there's no sound of shuffling or further cries from McCloskey, so I take it she didn't have to resort to making a scene.

"Good job. Hang a right at the end of the block. Slow down and turn around, like you're making sure you're not being followed. If you see him, pretend you didn't. Don't make eye contact."

"I'm almost there," she says a second later. *"He's like 20 feet behind me. He didn't duck behind a car fast enough, so I saw him, and he's definitely following me."*

"Good girl. Go into the alley on your left and try to look casual about it."

"Try to look casual," she repeats, scoffing. *"My heart is fucking racing. I don't think I can do that."*

"You're almost there. I'm in the Mustang. Get in."

She's breathless as she slams the door behind her. "Is he still there?"

"Running back to his car, I think. You did so good, baby. We're almost done. Almost there."

I put the car in gear. The Mustang was a fully intentional choice—one of the easiest cars to pick out on the street, which is a good thing for the old cop who thinks he's being sly, following us. I wait a few seconds, then ease out onto the main street slowly and go just above the speed limit.

Officer McCloskey is old school—he uses the two-cars-between rule of thumb. Luckily for us, Officer McCloskey isn't old school enough to want to hold the phone, so he makes and takes the calls on his car's Bluetooth. Wes's bug broadcasts his voice to both of our ears.

"Ulysses Sheriff's office," comes the voice we both recognize from earlier.

"Hey, Irene."

"Oh, hi, Chris," she says, mustering up quite a bit more enthusiasm.

"Can you get me some info on this address?" He rattles off what's written on the paper.

"Uh... sure. Hold on a sec." There's some slow typing and clicking. *"Looks like a warehouse a couple counties over."*

"A warehouse?" McCloskey repeats, his tone heavily confused.

"Yeah..." She laughs sharply. *"Kind of a shitty one, too. I just pulled it up on Maps. I went out that way once with my niece to a pumpkin patch. It's all farms out there."*

"Who owns it?"

"Uh... hold on a sec. These ancient computers... Ha! Some guy named Ivan Ivanokov. Is that really someone's name, you think?"

"Yeah... Okay, thanks," he says slowly, not laughing at what I'm sure Wes thought was fuckin' hilarious. *"Do me another favor while you're at it? Have Bill run me a plate."* He gives the mustang's license plate.

"Okay, I'll have him call you."

"Great, thanks, hun."

"I live to serve."

He hangs up on her, and waits a little. We're almost at the hotel when he makes another call.

"What happened with the girl?" comes Rossi's voice immediately. He sounds pissed.

Eleanor and I exchange a look.

"Uh, we just met. She was real scared, shifty. Looked like she got in his car—I'm following them now."

"What did she say?" he asks slowly, enunciating each syllable in a condescending tone.

I inhale. Now we find out if he's Rossi's man through and through or if that little tidbit about the warehouse was enough for the seed of doubt Eleanor planted with the mayor's name to take root.

"She said she wants to help us."

"I don't give a fuck about her or what she wants. Did you get anything about the Russian? A name? Fucking anything?"

"Like I said, she was real shifty. I think they're definitely together, and I got the sense she's not there by choice—maybe she's important to him?"

Rossi makes a thinking noise. *"Hmm, if she is, we can use her. You're on them now?"*

"Yup. Pulling into the Tipward Hotel, looks like. Want me to nab him?"

"No," Rossi is quick to say. *"He's got something of mine, and it's fucking personal now. I'm going to rip his fucking balls off and make him eat 'em. You stay on him; call me immediately if he moves."*

"Okie doke." They hang up, and McCloskey mutters, *"asshole..."*

Eleanor's laugh is more a sound of relief, though edged with some worry. I have to echo the sentiment. So far, so good, but we're not out of the woods yet.

The room I was staying in before all the shit went down that day in the steam room still has a do not disturb sign on the door. I cringe, not really remembering the state of it and hoping I didn't leave anything in the trash that's now rotting. Fortunately, I tend to take the important stuff with me when I leave my hotel rooms for the day, but that does mean I haven't been back to check.

As per usual, as long as someone is paying the bill, the hotel doesn't care about whether the room is being used. Everything is untouched, and there is a slight smell from the dirty takeout containers, but the heat was turned way down, so it could be worse.

Once inside, I look immediately to the window and check that the gauzy first layer of curtains is still the only one closed. It is, so I turn on all the lights and move to stand by the window.

"Okay, slight change of plan," I say, gesturing wildly. Her eyes follow the exaggerated movements of my arms and widen at how little they match my calm tone. "Come stand over here and move around like we're having a fight. I'm going to pretend to hit you."

Her frown is curious, but her attention is on the room around us, on the unmade bed and the bag of clothes on the ground. "Why?"

"Gotcha," McCloskey says, proud of himself for finding the bait I laid out for him.

"He thinks I'm Dimitri, and this will help convince him that you're working against Dimitri because you're scared. We're playing into the big, scarred Russian thug image."

"I heard that," Dimitri says dryly.

"Hey, man," I say brightly, pointing at Eleanor and shaking my fist dramatically. "How'd it go?"

"Rossi got the package. He vomited. It was disgusting. I am at the mayor's office now, waiting for my meeting."

"Sounds good. Eleanor and I are at the hotel room, McCloskey's outside. He called the precinct and looked up the address, but didn't tell Rossi about the note. Wes?"

"I'm en route to the warehouse."

Eleanor looks at me, hope shining in her eyes. "I can't believe you're pulling this off."

"*We're* pulling this off," I correct, fisting my hands on my hips and pacing away from her. "Now come over here and look like you're arguing back."

She moves into place and throws her hands out to the side. "Like this? I feel silly."

"That was fine, but now keep it small so it looks like you're trying to calm me. After a few seconds, I'm going to spin around and make it look like I'm backhanding you. I am not going to hit you, so try not to flinch prematurely. But snap your head to the side and lift your hand to hold your cheek like it hurts. Okay?"

"Got it."

"My right hand is coming around and going to come at your right cheek on three. Not going to hit," I remind her, knowing full well how hard it is to pretend to get hit without practicing. "One, two, three."

Our performance is clunky, but apparently our cop buys it. *"Whoa,"* we hear him mutter. *"Scumbag..."*

"It's so weird that we can hear him but he can't hear us," Eleanor observes a bit breathlessly, holding her cheek. "I keep thinking I have to whisper."

"Turn away from me," I instruct, then address her comment, "I know, it used to make me really nervous that something would go wrong, and they'd be able to hear us, too. Wes explained to me that those bugs aren't made with a speaker, only a mic."

"That does make me feel a little bit better."

"Okay, now we're going to make up." I walk to her, lay my hand on her shoulder, and press into her when she turns. My body instantly responds, not caring that we're acting. Blood fills my cock at the instant heat in her gaze and rapid intake of breath. I slide my hand into her hair and hold her head in place.

She moans a little against my lips, and her hands slide up my arms.

"Jesus, if you're going to do that, at least mute yourselves," Wes complains into our ear.

"Even the scumbag's rakin' 'em in. I can't catch a fuckin' break..." McCloskey thinks he remarks to himself with a sigh.

"I think we're good at this," she says with a little smile.

I lift my brows at her. "Are you having fun?"

"Depends on how far we can go to convince him we're making up," she says, a little mischievous sparkle in her eye.

I kiss her again, not caring that Wes and Dimitri are getting an earful of my tongue in her mouth, and back her up towards the bed.

"Fuck this," McCloskey says.

We all hear his car start up.

"He's on the move," Wes informs us all.

39

WESLEY

I really hate having my hands tied like this.

I lock the chain around the fence door and climb back into the van's driver seat, just as the cold rain starts falling. It would look too suspicious for the vehicle to be on the side of the road, or anywhere else nearby, so I park in the rear of the warehouse. The fields around are flat, and other than a patch of trees on the opposite side of the road, the nearest tall thing is a house, only just visible half a mile away from its lit windows in the dark.

If anyone does manage to get through the fence, hopefully I've arrived early enough for the engine to cool. It's got bulletproof glass, so at least that isn't a concern. Any light in the back can be shut off at a second's notice, and I won't be making any noise, so I should avoid attention. This rain is perfect, in fact, creating a dry spot that sells the image of an abandoned van in the back of a warehouse parking lot.

The warehouse itself is only about 20,000 square feet, small for this kind of thing in America, I've gathered. And it's in a state of disrepair that makes it nondescript—it's not shiny new, but the roof is intact and the rust staining the paint on the cinderblocks hasn't eaten through any key features. The windows are high, giving a good illusion of privacy, and the rolling door in the front was big enough to drive that lorry straight through.

After a quick walk-through of the building, confirming that the lorry—truck, Mac is always saying, *truck*—is exactly where we left it, I settle into the back of the van and open up my laptop. We have video visuals inside the warehouse already, something I set up before we left half a billion dollars of high-grade weaponry in a low-security warehouse in New Jersey. Because it's so dark in there, the nighttime vision upgrade was critical.

The picture casts a greenish light into the back of the van, and I settle into my seat. I reach into the bin under the makeshift desk and produce a bag of jerky that Mac forgot about.

A message pops up in my secure Internet Relay Chat, or IRC. Normally I ignore it when I'm on a job, but it is going to take McCloskey at least a quarter hour to get here from the hotel.

> mermaidav: heard you're looking for info on a certain mayor

I grin and type back. This could tie up nicely.

> SpyderMan: Fresh meat. Who gave you my contact?

> mermaidav: vinny

> SpyderMan: Send it.

> mermaidav: no freebies

> SpyderMan: Vinny sent you? Then I know he told you how it works. Intel, then $.

> mermaidav: fine. don't stiff me… i know where you type

I laugh and send her my email for the tip. The *her* is part assumption, part deduction—I've never met a man with mermaid in the username. I'm not ruling it out; it's just the most likely scenario.

Just as the email comes through, I spot headlights down the road. It's not a back road, but traffic has been slim, so I watch as it approaches. The car slows, then comes to a screeching halt, nearly missing the entrance to the car park. After a wide turn that rolls over some of the grass, the car drives around the front, and I lose eyes on it.

I pull up the cameras and split the screen into six. There are two outside, one that gets a south-east visual and one that gets the north-west sides. The four inside are basically pointing in from each corner of the rectangular building.

I watch McCloskey park facing the chain-link fence. He keeps up a pretty steady stream of nervous babbling to himself—standard stuff, like, "what the fuck is this place," and "looks pretty empty." He's a bit too thick around the middle to consider trying to scale the fence, and a little too nervous to think about trying to break the chain. He goes to the door on the side by the fence, tries it, and finds it unlocked.

Just how I left it for him.

Gun drawn forward in one hand and police-issued torch in the other resting on top, he creeps through the building, about as silently as a hunting house cat. I can hear his ragged breath, and I wonder how long it's been since he was really in the field.

Deciding he's alone in the echoing silence and dark, he tucks his gun in his holster and winds through the racks, empty of everything except stacked pallets on the ground. He comes around into the large open space and notices the truck.

"He found it, and he's approaching," I tell the others.

I get no response. From Dimitri, it's nothing less than I'd expect, though from Mac... As much as I'm not particularly opposed to a bit of adrenaline-fueled fun, it would be remarkably poor decision making on Mac's part to act on those fuck-or-kill urges we all get. We're in the literal thick of things.

"You've gotta be shitting me," McCloskey says as he pulls open the right trailer door.

I don't have the correct angle to see into the truck, but I can see McCloskey shine his light into the bed. I also see his jaw drop.

Awkwardly, he uses the foothold under the doors and pulls himself into the truck, disappearing into the 50-foot steel box filled with crates of stolen weapons.

Now begins the true nail-biting portion of the evening.

"Come on... take the bait," I urge him, moving closer to the screen, like it's going to help me see through the solid metal walls.

I hear the sound of plywood lids being lifted and dropped, and some surprised laughter that turns gleeful the further he gets into the truck. *"No fucking way,"* he mutters. *"No fucking way!"*

Here it is. Our crossroads, thanks to the unknown that is McCloskey. We couldn't be sure how much he knows—if he knows about the smuggling and selling, if he ever saw these weapons, if he ever learned they were missing...

But any corrupt cop of reasonable intelligence, confronted with a truck full of illegal goods, would likely go one of two ways. If he's Rossi's man, he's going to call his boss back and let him know what he's discovered. If he's Anderson's, he's going to the mayor with this.

If he calls Rossi, we follow one response plan. If he calls Anderson, we go with the other.

I see a faint light spill out the back of the truck and hear him lift the phone to his ear. The voice that picks up is faint, only really audible from the utter silence in the room and the amplification provided by the metal box he's standing in.

Rossi asks, *"They on the move?"*

"No, they're probably still there, fucking." McCloskey sounds relaxed. In control.

"Probably? The fuck you mean, proba—"

"I found 'em. The crates. Still on the truck and everything."

There's a beat of silence, then Rossi's greedy voice, *"No shit? Where are you, I can be right there—"*

"Yeah, it's not gonna be like that, Jay. I'm thinking this info is worth a little more to you than that."

"You motherfucker."

"I could call Mayor Anderson, give him my location, if you want—"

"No," Rossi hurries to say. *"That's... not a good idea."*

"That's what I thought. It's a lot of guns, Jay. What're they worth to you?"

"What do you want?" Rossi growls.

McCloskey pauses, perhaps reveling in the moment. *"You're a smart guy; you can recognize an opportunity, right? Well, I want in—this operation you're running with the mayor? I'm part of it now. You and Anderson are gonna make me the Chief. I know you're the logistics guy and he's got the contacts. But I'll be the law, and we can split the profit as equal partners."*

There's silence on the other end, as Rossi marinates in his own anger. So, McCloskey tries to reason with him. *"Think about it—how much easier would your life be with the Chief of Police protecting you? Protecting us."*

"Fine. We'll make it happen. Now, where are you?"

McCloskey laughs, a cruel but gleeful sound. *"No, no, no. Why would I give up my leverage like that, Jay? Make it happen, then I'll tell you."*

"It's going to take some time to—"

"Not my problem."

"Those guns are—"

"What's that sound? The sound of Pete Harris retiring early and Mayor Anderson asking me to be the new Chief of Police?" McCloskey lets it hang, and when Rossi says nothing, he finishes with, *"Make it happen, Jay."*

I sit back in my chair as McCloskey hangs up. *Fuck.* McCloskey's officially a complication. I didn't know that tosser had it in him. I really thought he was going to prove to be the mayor's man, not throw us a third option and try to ransom the weapons back to Rossi, which makes Dimitri's bait for the mayor a moot fucking point. We need the mayor to find them here. I need the mayor to find them here.

"Erm... Did you all hear that?" I ask, a little dumbfounded.

"Yeah," Mac sounds as stunned as I feel.

I rub my eyes. "This is why I hate when the plan is reacting to the decisions of other people," I grumble. "How are we going to get Rossi here if McCloskey isn't going to give up his location?"

"We pivot," Mac says, predictably. *"He dies tonight. Dimitri moves forward to lay the trap for the mayor. I'll go to his safe house and take my shot; you guys handle the mayor and McCloskey."*

I curse as the cop's head pokes out of the back of the trailer and he looks around, like he's making sure he's still alone. "I think he's probably going to try to move the truck, or come back with something to move the crates. He won't just leave it here, now that it's his leverage to get what he wants if he thinks Dimitri will come for it."

"Then handle him," Dimitri replies simply. *"I will be there in 30 minutes—40 if there are complications. Send me the documentation we discussed."*

I tap my earpiece to effectively mute myself and take a few seconds for an angry reaction. Once I'm under control, I get back on the line and shoot off the email to Dimitri. With a sigh, I pull the burner phone out of my pocket, and send off the text to the FBI tip line. I really hate having my hands tied like this.

I creep inside using the much quieter and well-oiled back door. I can see the torch waving around inside the back of the truck, and hear McCloskey's delighted noises, like he's a kid on Christmas. Likely, he's deciding what he wants to keep for himself. Because he's blithely unaware, he doesn't hear me as I move towards the opening at the back of the truck. Only the right door is hanging open, so I use the left to shield me while I get ready.

"Hands up," I say, shining my high-powered torch into his face.

From his position bent over a box, McCloskey freezes, and spins slowly, squinting against my light, then lifting his hands as he spots the gun. He's still got his cell phone in his grasp. I'll be needing that so he doesn't call for help.

"Phone," I say. "Kick it over."

He looks up at the cell in his hands, gauging his move. I know he has his weapon tucked in his holster, but I don't care too much about that. As long as he doesn't...

He throws the phone at me and goes for his gun. The phone clatters noisily on the ground, and I duck to the right, under the door, coming around the other side of it. I push it with all my might. It swings closed, the sound of metal against metal resounding in the cavernous room, and he bangs into it just as I get the latch in place, locking him inside.

"Fuck!" he screams. "Let me the fuck out of here! I'm the Chief of Police!"

I laugh. "Not yet!"

"Who the fuck are you? What do you want? I've got money!"

I leave him yelling and cursing in the truck as I walk back towards the van. When I get back in front of the screen and see McCloskey's car in one of the frames, I curse again. I've got to get rid of that so no one sees. He's still got his keys with him, but I've got an internet connection and several kinds of tools available to me. Time to learn how to hot-wire a car...

40

DIMITRI

I am the Ghost

The kind lady receptionist tells me it is my turn and the mayor will see me now. I have made a note of all cameras, and cheat my face away from them as she leads me towards the office. I have already removed my earpiece, as I do not need anyone else in my head while I do this.

"Thank you," I say to her. "I will see myself in from here."

She gives me a brief flash of a smile, trying to conceal the tightness of fear in her eyes I have come to expect, then disappears down the hall. She is young, and since I am not yet dead, I take a moment to appreciate the curve of her generous hips as she walks away. But now, I do not need witnesses to his reaction to my face, whatever it may be.

I enter without knocking, briefly taking stock of the wall of windows facing a retention pond, the filing cabinets lining the wall, and expensive furnishings that certainly were not standard government issue. I get all the way to the chairs in front of his oversized desk before he swivels around. He freezes.

"Pete, let me call you back..." Mayor Anderson says into the receiver of the phone.

We stare at each other for a second, and I track the very slow, purposeful movements of his arms as they move down to his lap, then slip under the top drawer. I sit back, as if I have no cares, though I keep my muscles tense so I am ready to move as quickly as I may need to.

"I hear you have been looking for me," I say.

He frowns, posturing as if he has no fear, but his eyes dart to the closed door behind me, giving him away. He feels trapped, cornered. But it is not my fault that weaker men are often intimidated. "Pal, I got no clue who you are."

"Oh? Is that why you are going for the gun under your desk?" I ask, making a guess.

His arms stop moving as his brows snap down, then his smiling mask slowly falls. He brings the gun up and levels it at me across the table, keeping it low and close to his body. "You're the Russian that Rossi's been looking for."

I shrug, not looking at the barrel. This is not my first time at the wrong end of a gun. What terrified me as a boy does not as a man. "I cannot deny this. I have come here about a certain... shipment that went missing."

"What the fuck are you talking about?" When I sigh and lean forward, it spooks him enough for him to lift the gun. "Hey, stay right where I can see you or I'll fucking shoot."

He will not. Not with so many witnesses still in the building. Still, he would like for me to think he would. "You can shoot me, but then you will never find those weapons."

His face is so expressive I have to wonder how he has managed to keep his dirty businesses a secret all this time. I watch the confusion, then internal debate, then anger cross his features so clearly that it is like he is narrating it aloud.

"I don't know what you're talking about," he lies, letting his hand holding the gun drop to rest on the tabletop. "What is this, some cheap attempt at blackmail?"

Years of training and I know my face does not so much as flinch as Mayor Anderson confirms my suspicions. He did not say as much, but I know it to be true. No innocent man would lower his gun as he asks if I am trying to blackmail him. "Rossi is trying to pin it on me, but I did not steal your shipment."

"Okay, so, you didn't do anything. Fine, thanks. Get the fuck out and don't let the door hit ya."

"I did not say I do not know where they are." I glance down at the phone in my hand and send him the information from Wesley. "Open your email."

He transfers the gun to his left hand and rolls his chair a few inches to the right to wake his computer. I can see the screen light up in the reflection that the glass windows make behind him. More glass. What an idiotic design choice. Everyone can see your business.

"What is this... a warehouse?"

"Rossi's warehouse. Now, ask yourself, as I did, what would a smart businessman—a property manager and buyer of good investments—want with a warehouse in the middle of nowhere? Especially one purchased right before the weapons went missing?"

Anderson looks at me, assessing for a moment, then turns back to the screen. He uses the wheel on his mouse to scroll through what I assume is paperwork that looks totally legitimate. Wesley is thorough.

"I don't know anything about any weapons, pal. But if I did... what, I'm supposed to believe you're telling me this out of the kindness of your heart?"

I laugh, and the deep sound fills the room. "My heart has no kindness."

"So?"

"Currently, I am the Russian that Rossi is looking for. I think instead I can be the Russian who is a friend of the mayor, yes? And the mayor helps his friends, I think."

I let the threat and suggestion suspend between us. The mayor slowly puts the gun away. "I think I like to know who my friends are."

I stand. "I am the Ghost," I say, using the name Eleanor created for me. I like it.

49

ELEANOR

Minimizing the consequences

I scramble off the bed where I was sitting cross-legged in the middle while Mac tried to pace his hard-on away. I'm not 100% sure what the implications of what I just heard are, but I know that things have officially detoured from the plan we discussed. "So, Rossi isn't going to the warehouse?" I ask.

"McCloskey was supposed to tell him where it was. Or the mayor. We didn't figure he'd pull a power play—he seemed like such a yes-man to me. Mid-mission is never a good time for the reminder that people can surprise you."

"Why did you need Rossi to go there?" I ask.

Mac grabs his keys off the dresser in front of the small TV. "It was just the fastest, cleanest way to understand Mayor Anderson's involvement. It's okay; there's always another way. We're still cleaning up this mess tonight."

My hat and coat are the only items of clothing I've removed, so it's not hard to be ready to leave. I start forcing my arms through the sleeves as I follow. "What do we do now?"

He moves towards the door. "We get you somewhere secure and I'm going to hopefully catch him at his safe house—"

"I want to come with you."

He turns his head to eye me, hand on the knob. "It's better if we get you somewhere that you'll be safe until it's all over—"

"But time's a factor, right? If Rossi leaves and you don't know where he is, you lose him? I don't want that to happen just because you felt like you had to keep me out of the action. I want to come. I'll stay hidden, maybe in the back seat or something? Although maybe that will look suspicious... I'll have to defer to you on that—"

He cuts me off by reaching up and cupping my cheek. "Baby, it's not that I don't want you there; it's that I don't want you to have to see this—it's not going to be like what you saw me do last time. It's probably going to be gross."

I cover his hand with mine. I appreciate his instinct to protect me, but I feel like I've come pretty far since that first terrifying night we met. It would also be nice to see it for myself, so when I invariably start having stress nightmares about Rossi, I'll be able to console myself with the fact that I saw him die.

"I don't know. I'm feeling kind of... extraordinary. I want to see how it ends."

He grins at me. "All right. Let's go."

Mac leads me out the door after glancing up and down the hall to make sure it's empty. We hurry towards the stairs, and I notice he's got one hand tucked under the back of his jacket, likely positioned near a gun. It makes me feel immensely safer, all of a sudden, and it hits me that's an unusual reaction for me around guns.

The stairwell is empty, so we descend the two flights, and it puts us just around the corner from the main lobby. I realize my heart is racing from how hard I have to breathe to feel like I'm getting air. It's like the two stories we just climbed were up, not down. But it's probably a by-product of anxiety over how sneaky we must look, pressed against the wall as Mac peers into the lobby.

"There are cameras in the corners of the ceiling," he says, pointing to some obelisk-looking things above our heads. They don't blend well, but I suppose they're not really supposed to. "I don't want them to have us on tape, leaving at the same time, just in case. I'll head out the back door. After I go, wait a few seconds and then go out the front. I'll come around to pick you up. Got it?"

I nod solemnly.

From my position against the wall, I watch Mac stroll across the lobby, looking down at his phone and seeming like he hasn't got a care in the world. I nearly sigh—I doubt I'll manage to make it look quite that effortless, though I guess I could pretend to look at my phone too... As the door closes behind him and I start mentally counting to five, something flashes in the corner of my eye.

It's Rossi.

My stomach drops.

I know from his face that he saw Mac. And he's going after him... And from the way he's reaching for his own back waistband, he's got a gun, too.

Fuck! I freeze halfway between shooting forward and staggering back in shock. For a second, I'm paralyzed with fear for the man I love. I have to do something! Mac's in danger. He didn't see Rossi, doesn't know he's there...

Something Mac said earlier echoes in my head.

There's no way to plan for everything. Sometimes you've gotta think on your feet and try to minimize the consequences.

And I know what I need to do.

I need to protect my Mac.

So, I walk forward into the lobby, right into a stand of pamphlets with local attractions. It topples to the floor loudly, sending papers flying. Rossi glances over his shoulder at the noise and does a double take as we lock eyes.

"Eleanor, what was that? What are you doing?" comes Mac's frantic voice in my earpiece.

"Minimizing the consequences."

Rossi stops, turning towards me with a bewildered expression, so I do the most conspicuous thing I can think of—I run. I dart towards the front doors.

"Ma'am? Sir?" the receptionist calls in her high, girlish voice after Rossi.

I know he's behind me—I can hear his heavy footfalls. But I'm out the door, almost to the parking lot. Maybe I'll be able to beat him to the street...

I feel a grip around my hair just as my foot hits the asphalt. He yanks me back painfully, and it brings tears to my eyes. I yelp.

"Well, well, well. Eleanor Wilson," Rossi mutters into my ear. He gives a sharp tug that draws another pained cry from my lips. "Isn't it just my lucky fucking day?"

"No!" Mac roars, and I swear I hear it in stereo, in my earpiece and muffled in the night air, from the inside of a car around the back of the building.

"Sir? What are you—Oh my God. Let her go! I'm calling the police!" It's the scared teenage receptionist—my hero.

"Don't hurt me!" I breathe between gulping inhales, labored from the fear and exercise. I reach back to hold on, trying to relieve the burning pain in my scalp. "Ah! I... I know where the guns are!"

"Do you?" he growls, his tone all at once condescending and cruel.

"I'll tell you—"

"No, you'll show me." He shoves me forward, using his grip in my hair, ripping some of it clean out of my skull as I struggle to maintain my balance. His car is the first one parked on the left, a handicapped spot. He opens the driver's door and shoves me in.

"I will fucking shoot you if you run."

He slams the door and hustles around to the passenger's side. When he sits in the seat, he's pointing a gun right at me.

My body erupts in chills of déjà vu. I back up in the seat, putting some distance between me and the barrel. My whole body starts to shake with cold fear.

Rossi waves the gun at me. "Hands on the wheel, foot on the brake. Quickly." As I comply, he sticks the key into the ignition and shifts the car into gear. "Drive."

"Eleanor, stay calm. Just do what he says. I'll tell you how to get to the warehouse," comes Wesley's soothing voice. I've never been so glad to hear anyone's voice in all my life. I'm not alone. They're going to be here with me the whole time.

I have to stop myself from nodding along in understanding. Rossi can't know about the earpiece. Luckily, it's on my left side.

"I'm going to fucking kill him; I'm shooting him from here—"

"Mac, no! Witnesses!" This time, Wesley's voice is a bit more frantic.

A tear slips down my cheek, and I start the car. I feel even more helpless, hearing his helplessness.

"Then I'll run him off the road."

"James, she is the one driving," Dimitri reminds. *"If Rossi thinks you are following him, he may harm her."*

Bile climbs in the back of my throat. I whimper.

"Take it offline, you're distracting her," Wesley snaps. Then, his tone lowers back to that calm, 911-dispatcher level. *"Turn left out of the lot, love."*

"What's the address?" Rossi barks at me, grabbing his phone from his pocket.

I repeat after Wesley.

From the corner of my eye, I see Rossi pull it up in his maps app, then look at the place in street view. "A warehouse. Should have known... If you go anywhere other than here, I'll shoot you. If you drive at any speed other than the fucking limit, I will shoot you. If you try to get the attention of any cops or other cars... you get the deal, right?"

I swallow and nod. I come to a stop at a light. "C-can I put on my seatbelt?" Just in case we get rammed by a Mustang...

"No," he says quickly. "In fact..." He leans forward in his seat and drops the glove compartment door. As he rifles around, I see papers, a gun, a length of rope and a knife... your standard bad-guy car emergency kit. He pulls out the roll of duct tape. "Hands together at the top."

"Just do what he says, love. It'll keep him calmer," Wesley instructs. *"He's much less likely to hurt you if you do what he says."*

Shaking, I pull my wrists together at the top of the wheel, and Rossi winds several lengths of duct tape around them. I whimper at the tightness, and how it cuts into my skin and prevents proper blood movement through my hands.

Rossi clicks his own belt and faces me, phone still out in front so he can ensure I'm taking the correct path. "So, how'd a fat, ugly bitch like you get caught up in all this?"

I wince. It makes sense—he's a bully, so the first thing that occurs to him to do is tear me down. Good thing for me, I've pretty much internalized the fact that my body size is one of the least interesting things about me. But we're so off script, I have no idea what to say...

"He's insulting you to maintain the upper hand—don't let him get to you. Tell him you didn't know what you were getting caught up in. Give him the same speech you gave McCloskey. And go south on 539."

I say the words; I make the turn onto the state route.

"Who is he? What's his name?" Rossi asks.

I inhale a few times, listening to Wesley's story and memorizing the unfamiliar word. "His name is Sergei Ivanov. He's... New York *Bratva*."

"Fuck. I knew it. I haven't done shit to any New York *Bratvas*. Why's he trying to kill me?"

"H-he wants your territory, your contacts."

"Fuck," Rossi curses again.

"Good job, love. He believes you," Wesley says. *"Your exit is in five miles."*

"So, you're what? His little American piece? You?" Rossi asks, looking pointedly at my body. "It must be true what they say—low self-esteem makes you cunts great in the sack."

"Don't listen to him, baby." It's Mac this time, and I almost choke on my relief. *"I'm tailing you; you're not alone."*

"I bet you'd take my dick up your ass real easy, wouldn't you, sweetheart?" Rossi goes on, his demeaning jeering in sharp contrast to Mac's gentle endearments.

"He's just trying to scare you, love," Wesley says.

"Maybe I'll give it a shot. Make him watch. Bet you'd like that, huh?" Rossi taunts.

"I am going to cut his puny penis off his body," Dimitri grinds out.

"You're doing so good, darlin'," Mac bites out, his tone full of rage and terror that he's desperately trying—and failing—to hide from me.

I feel another tear well in my eye—not because Rossi's words particularly hit home, but because they're all listening. Nothing wrong with enjoying anal, if you ask me. But these three dangerous killers are all unwitting witnesses to Rossi's attempt at humiliation, and they're outraged for me. It makes me feel exposed somehow, but also fills my heart with appreciation for them.

I need to show them he's not getting to me—that I'm not scared of him or his soon-to-be severed penis.

"He's going to kill you," I murmur quietly, with all the conviction I'm feeling. I don't care if I should or shouldn't have said it, because the way his eyes widen for just a fraction of a second—showing that on some level he doubts his handle on the situation—is enough to soothe me.

"Fuckin' A," Mac agrees.

"He can try," Rossi replies flippantly. "Which *Bratva* is he? There's, like, 20 in New York."

Wesley feeds me my next line. "Um, I'm not sure. I think he's from Brooklyn?"

"Brooklyn? Fuck," Rossi mutters, and blows out an angry breath. He pulls his phone out and starts tapping away, writing a text or an email. Unhelpfully, he doesn't narrate it, but I'm grateful for the respite from his attention.

A few minutes later, Wesley pipes in, *"Take the next left. The warehouse is a couple miles down, only building in the middle of a bunch of fields. Home stretch, love."*

"How did Ivanov know about the sale?" Rossi asks, finally looking up from his phone and glancing around us at the low, flat fields. He turns over his shoulder to check that we're not being followed.

I glance in the rearview mirror, trying again to see any sign of Mac. I don't, not even a car. This road is straight and flat, so I have no idea how he could be anywhere near me. The thought fills me with dread.

"I don't know," I say after Wesley confirms it.

"Yeah, not surprised. 'Eleanor Wilson' doesn't sound very Russian. You're just a dumb cunt that fucked the wrong guy, aren't you?"

"Yeah... That's it, up there," I say, gesturing ahead to the dark, flat building.

"Go past and pull off on the side of the road up there."

I do as he instructs, leaving my hands on the wheel and foot on the brake as the car eases to a stop. He puts the car in park and takes the keys. The rain is drizzling around us, bringing a chill in the night air, and I can see the breath of my scream as he pulls me from the driver's seat by my hair.

"Shut the fuck up," he says, smacking my temple with the butt of his gun.

I fall back a step, landing against the back door of the car. It dazes me, my ears are ringing, and the pain sets in slowly, in waves that coincide with my heartbeat. Then I groan, the ache growing into something pointy and stinging.

Mac yells something I can't discern, and Rossi is gripping the back of my neck with harsh fingers that dig into my skin. He forces me towards the building, and I stumble along.

"Eleanor, I'm right here with you. I'm at the warehouse too, okay?" It's Wesley again. *"You need to bring Rossi inside, through that big open door just beyond the chain-link fence. There's a truck just inside the entrance; that's where the guns are. But it's dark in there, and there are plenty of racks in the back half—if you can get away, you may be able to lose him."*

"Where are the guns?"

"The truck is inside," I tell Rossi, repeating Wesley's instructions. "Um, there's a fence over there—"

"Why is the bay door open?" he asks suspiciously.

"I don't know," I say, letting a sob bleed into my voice as the pain settles into a pounding headache. "Maybe someone got here first."

"McCloskey," Rossi growls. He shoves me forward, using his grip on my neck for leverage, and shoves the unyielding metal into my back. "Walk. Go ahead of me."

I trudge along through the wet grass that seeps into my sneakers and makes my toes freezing cold. We approach the fence, and he pauses. I can see a broken chain with a padlock still attached to two ends—someone cut it. The arm is flipped up, and the door is a few inches ajar. He shoves me forward again through the opening. I keep my taped hands low, looking around wildly and trying not to trip over my own feet because my limbs feel strange and loose, like I don't have total control over them.

We move towards the open rolling door, and the first thing I see is the truck Wesley mentioned. Rossi pushes me inside and looks around. It's very quiet, and very dark.

"How do we close this?"

"Eleanor, do not *let him close the door,"* Mac says. *"I need it open."*

Suddenly, there's a banging noise, and we both startle. It sounds like it's coming from the back of the truck, like someone is inside hitting the walls. "Help! Let me out!" comes a muffled voice from inside. "I promise I won't tell anyone anything!"

"McCloskey?" Rossi says, like he doesn't quite believe it. He gestures to me to go forward until I'm just past the truck and he can get to the handle.

He lifts the latch and pulls the door open, immediately training his gun into the opening. "Boss! Thank God! How did you find..." McCloskey trails off as he sees me about an arm's reach from Rossi. "You little bitch!"

"Funny, I was going to call you the same thing," Rossi rasps, aiming the gun at McCloskey. "It's 'Boss' again now, huh?"

"She's playing us, Jay."

"Is she?" Rossi scoffs sarcastically. "I know that, you idiot. She's still with the Russian, and he's still a pain in my ass. I'm gonna use her, like I planned."

"But we've got the guns now! Look, it's all in here!"

Rossi stretches his neck, following the movements as McCloskey shines the flashlight around at the crates and boxes around him. The state of it looks like someone has recently been rifling through it—lids are off, packaging material covers the floor. "That's not all of it."

"It's not?" Wesley says faintly.

"It's not?" McCloskey echoes him.

"Where are the other six crates?" Rossi asks.

McCloskey turns his accusatory stare on me. "They must have moved some of it... I'm telling you, she's setting us up! She's the one that gave me this address, told me to tell Kevin..."

Rossi's face darkens, and McCloskey falls back a step as his drains of color. Well, he certainly said the wrong thing. "What?" Rossi growls. "You told Anderson—"

"Shit. This is going to be bad. Eleanor, start slowly moving away," Wesley instructs.

Before I can even try, the lights come on and everyone is blinded. I cover my eyes, lowering my head. Rossi staggers and throws his free arm over his face, the one holding the gun.

When the stars clear from my vision and it doesn't hurt too much to look up, I can see that it's the mayor, standing in the bay door, flanked by two big guys.

"Told me what?" The mayor glances at me, lifts a brow, then turns his attention to Rossi. "I didn't want to believe it. Even when I saw your car, I thought to myself… no. No way. Not Jay Rossi. Not my business partner of five years. He couldn't be trying to cut me out."

"I'm not!"

"And yet, here you are. And here they are," the mayor gestures to the crates inside the truck.

The two guys on either side of the mayor lift the big guns they're carrying and point them directly at Rossi and McCloskey. I'm close enough to Rossi that it probably won't take too much to shoot me, too—just a slight shifting of their aim.

Oh shit. Wesley wasn't kidding. This is going to be bad.

I take a slow step back and whisper, "I love you, James Mackenzie."

42

MAC

No shot I've ever made has been more important than this one.

Laying in the field, on my stomach, I'm transported back to a time where heat was the enemy instead of cold, and sand stuck to my face instead of whatever wet leaves are waving around in this clear-cut field. Every sniper in our unit had his preferred distance for a kill shot. With a gun small enough to be mistaken for a close-range shot, mine happens to be 100 meters. It's a good enough distance that staying low on this side of the road meant that Mayor Anderson and his goons never saw me when he rolled up to the warehouse just a minute after Rossi and Eleanor walked through the fence.

I close my eyes, center myself, focus on a deep inhale. I have one chance at this. There are too many guys, too many guns, too many factors. I have one chance, and five quick shots to make. If I don't recover from the recoil fast enough, and they start shooting, Eleanor is very likely to catch a bullet in the crossfire. Or if I miss, and she's standing so close to Rossi...

Nope. Not going there. I don't miss.

The mayor is part of this. He'll die. His guys have guns pointed way too close to my girl, so they'll die, too. McCloskey will die for calling her a bitch. In fact, I may shoot him in the stomach so he's in agony for a little while, too.

Rossi? He's last. He's going to be pissing himself in fear, then he's going to bleed out from the blown-out hole where his dick used to be. He's going to be fucking riddled with lead in all the peak pain places—kneecaps, mid-thigh, stomach. I bet I can even get the bullet right through his femur without hitting the femoral artery, which will cause the muscles to contract and send him into a world of the worst pain a human can endure.

They're almost squared up in my shot, but a strong gust of wind kicks up and I curse and wipe the drizzling rain from my forehead. Wind makes a huge difference in shots at a distance, and everyone's a giant clusterfuck in there. Mayor Anderson and his two guys are silhouettes in the bright warehouse lights, and I can see straight into the back of the truck where McCloskey is elevated—he's probably the easiest target.

"I love you, James Mackenzie."

My heart kicks me in the ribs. Did she just...

"It was McCloskey," Rossi accuses. *"He wants Chief of Police, tried to blackmail me for it. He was probably going to try to sell our shipment right out from under—"*

"What?" comes the horrified voice of McCloskey—and his face matches the tone. *"I didn't—"*

The mayor calmly points the handgun he's got at McCloskey and pulls the trigger. Eleanor's scream fills my ears, the sound of her fear making my stomach turn over, as McCloskey staggers back into the trailer and falls on his ass, clutching the fabric that's blooming with red on his chest.

"Shh, honey," Anderson says to my girl. *"I can see from the duct tape that you're about as thrilled to be here as I am, but I'll shoot you, too, if you don't shut the fuck up."*

I grind my jaw. He won't get the chance.

"She's the Russian's girlfriend," Rossi explains. *"He's behind it all; we can use her—"*

"Maybe I'm confused here—is it the Russian, or was it McCloskey?"

Rossi's bluster is gone, and now he's just a scared, cornered deer.

"Not answering is the wrong answer, Jay," Anderson says. *"Now, the Russian will die because I don't need the* Bratva *in my business. But McCloskey died because he picked the wrong side. That's you, Jay. You're the wrong side."*

"Kevin, I wouldn't—"

"I saw the sales records for this warehouse. I know it's yours. What I don't know is why you thought you'd get away with it. You thought I was just going to let you steal from me?"

I see the instant Rossi knows what's going to happen—that Mayor Anderson isn't going to listen to his version of the truth—and he starts bringing up his own weapon to make a feeble attempt to strike first.

"Dive, Eleanor! Under the truck!" I yell frantically.

I'll thank whatever god I need to that she reacts quickly. She's almost under the truck when I take out the gunman on my left, who was closest to her. Simultaneously, Rossi gets a shot in Mayor Anderson's shoulder. Anderson spins from the impact, going down, and the other gunman fires off towards Rossi.

Rossi is hit in the chest, and he fires another shot, missing the gunman entirely. If I weren't so fucking pissed, I'd laugh at how poor his aim is. I get the gunman through the temple as he turns to help his boss.

Anderson is clutching his arm, but Rossi is back up with a hand pressed to his pec. No blood is leaking through his fingers.

Fuck. He's got on a vest.

He takes a few steps forward, approaching Anderson on the ground. He stands over the older man, who's writhing and trying to get his gun back up in position.

"I never needed you anyway."

He fires off a few rounds, and Mayor Anderson stops moving.

Then, like he realizes the other gunmen were taken care of by someone that wasn't him, Rossi turns on a dime and dives. Too late, the bullet I fired off lands somewhere in the cinderblock wall 500 feet behind where

Rossi was standing. When I recover from the recoil, and find him again, he's dragging Eleanor to her feet, and using her as a shield. He has his gun pointed at her face from the side.

I see red. Every thought of torture flies out the window—he dies now.

"Show yourself, Ivanov!" Rossi shouts into the darkness beyond the warehouse, in my general direction. I can hear his elevated voice clearly in the still night air. *"I will fucking shoot her!"*

Generally speaking, I have enough confidence in my ability to know that if two men are 500 meters away, standing a foot apart, the one that I wanted to hit is the one with the bullet in his brain. Which is not to say that I've never missed, only that it's been a while.

But no shot I've ever made has been more important than this one. She is... She's everything to me. Three inches too far left, and I hit her. An overcorrection to the right to ensure I don't hit her might go too wide and he'll fire off in fear.

"Mac?" Wes prods. *"You good?"*

I breathe in and out. In and out. I have to get out of my head.

"You want me to try to hit him from the side? I am almost in position—"

"No," I say to Dimitri. "If he sees you, he's definitely going to shoot."

"You've got this, mate."

"Eleanor, on the count of three, I want you to drop to the ground. I know he's got your hair, and it's going to hurt, but it'll surprise him, and you'll be out of the way of my shot. I promise you I will not miss. Blink twice if you understand."

A terrified expression fills her face, but she blinks twice in rapid succession.

"One..." I see her tense, and I press the gun into the right spot against my chest. "Two..." Her knees go soft, and she brings up her hands to be in place to catch her fall as I place my finger on the trigger.

"I swear I will shoot her—" Rossi shouts.

"Three."

She drops, I shoot, and the hole forms right through his eye. First, there's a dark round spot as his eye blows out the back of his head, then red pours out, falling down his face and squirting from the wound.

And I'm up, leaving everything where it is in the middle of the field, sprinting for the warehouse. Dimitri has just finished cutting the tape off her wrists when I come running up. We lock eyes, and the relief shining there makes my chest hurt. But as I get close, opening my arms for her to run into, she reaches up and slaps me in the face.

"'Drop to the ground on three so I don't shoot you'?" she shrieks at me. "You asshole!"

Wes chokes on a laugh as Dimitri hides a smile by turning around completely.

"Never do that again, James Mackenzie," she hisses, poking me in the sternum.

In spite of the slight sting in my cheek, I grin. "Tell me you love me again and it's a deal," I say, not letting her get a single word out as I cover her mouth with mine.

She clutches me desperately, and the blood pounds in my veins for her—I'm so fucking happy to have her in my arms again, it makes me want to bend her over Rossi's dead body. Maybe we'll leave the *fucking in front of corpses* thing for another day...

"I hate when they monologue and try to get the last word," Dimitri mutters, looking down at the bodies with his lip curled.

"'You're the wrong side, Jay,' and 'I never needed you anyway,'" Wes mimics. "What a pair of muppets."

Eleanor breaks away and laughs at Wes's terrible impression, and it's a wet noise. She sniffles, wipes under her eyes, and I pull her close to drop a kiss on the top of her head.

"The Feds are coming?" I ask.

Wes nods. "Whenever they get off their arses and dispatch someone to check the tip. My guess is sometime tomorrow morning."

"We could just leave them for the Feds," Dimitri—all practicality—shrugs. "They shot each other. Maybe we take these two." I watch him toe the body of the man I shot in the back of the head and point at the other.

A Federal CSI tech would definitely be able to determine that the trajectory the bullet took through the body and the way the body landed means a shot from behind. And I'll be long gone, and so will every trace of me, but the point is to remain off the radar. And a highly accurate sniper going after civilians tends to get you on the radar.

"I'm going to go get my gear. You have your SUV; you can grab these two, right?"

Dimitri sighs and rolls his eyes. "Yes, fine, go. We will clean up."

"We?" Wes repeats, full of false outrage. "Oh, I just remembered I... don't want to do that."

"Doing things you do not want to do builds character," Dimitri argues, bending down and lifting the torso of the first man into a sitting position.

"Are you saying I'm not enough of a character already? I thought I was just some *penis from the mountains*. That insult is my new favorite, by the way. Even better than when you call us goat testicles."

As they continue to quip back and forth—well, Wes quips and Dimitri meets each sarcastic comment at face value—I grab Eleanor's hand and pull her after me. I want to have her closer than this. I'd try to carry her if I thought she'd let me, but I'll settle for this small contact. For now.

"Are you okay, darlin'? How's your head?"

"It stings, but the pounding is mostly gone. I don't think I'm concussed or anything; I feel okay. Well, mostly..."

"You sure? You're shaking and your heart is racing."

"No," she says, and it's so raw and honest that it makes me grimace. "I never want to do anything like that. Ever. Never again."

"So, not the career change you were looking for, I take it?"

She shivers, but smiles a little at me. It's watery, but it's a start. "I think I'll stick to *torch* guns and *chef* knives being my only weapons."

I chuckle.

We reach the spot where my gear is still spread out on the ground. I was in a hurry when I set it up, so it's not meticulous. It does make cleanup easier, though. I start unscrewing parts and laying them in my cases. She stands watching me, trying to figure out if there's some way she can help but finding none.

"What about whoever Rossi sold those guns to originally?" she asks. "The one who you stole the weapons from? Won't they be, like, mad and try to come find them?"

I smile because she's got good instincts and asks good questions. "That's why we tipped off the Feds. No one will come looking; they'll be in evidence lockup."

"And they won't find anything else? I feel like in shows, they always find hair or blood at the scene of the crime and that's how they catch who did it. Except we're not the bad guys in this scenario... or are we? My moral compass is way out of whack."

When I stand, I catch her chin in my hand and scan her face. I seethe, seeing the red-purple mark on her temple that has a thin line of dried blood in the middle. "I wish I could have shot him how I planned." I tap my ear to reconnect the line and tell Wes and Big D, "Make sure you clean Rossi's gun. He broke the skin."

"Already handled."

"How were you going to do it?" she asks lightly, tilting up her chin.

I raise an eyebrow. "You really want to know?"

"As long as it was going to be painful... I think I do."

I nearly groan as the blood rushes to my cock at her husky tone. Bloodthirsty Eleanor is a new kind of filthy delight.

43

ELEANOR

Alive is right—it's the perfect description for how this feels.

Is it normal to be this horny after something so... appalling? Because the sight of Mac's tight ass sticking out of the trunk of the car has me feeling some kinds of ways and one of them is completely disgusted with myself. I just saw people die. Violently. I've probably got blood all over me—I can see the tiny droplets on my hands from the spray Rossi's head created.

And yet, I'm so wet, and that ache deep inside me that wants to be filled with his cock is growing steadily more urgent at an alarming rate.

I watch as Mac stows the cases with all the neat little perfectly shaped cutouts in foam for the pieces of his gun in the back of the mustang. He didn't let me carry anything over from the field, but he does let me hand him the bag he set down so he could open the trunk.

"Give me your earpiece." He holds out his hand, and mine joins his in the small protective box, and goes into his pocket.

I head for the passenger seat as Mac closes the back door. I know I'm shaken, and my brain keeps flashing me horrific images that make me cringe. But I'm also... I think Mac would say, juiced. My senses feel sharp, my emotions are heightened, my limbs feel warm and loose like after my warm-up for a workout.

He gets in and starts the car. The purr of the engine fills me with calm, and we're leaving the now-dark warehouse behind. I hope I never see it again.

"I can't believe how incredible that shot was," I muse.

"Thank you, darlin'." He sounds proud.

"Right through the eye, from all the way out in that field. Just... wow. I had no idea how good you were."

"Oh, I think you've known how good I am, just not about that," he says, winking at me.

I smile.

As Mac speeds along the empty road, I watch the dark, unidentifiable shadows pass out the window. It's so empty out here. Only the faint light from farmhouses breaks up the dark scenery, set back from the road so far you almost can't see them.

I turn back to look at Mac, and he glances back at me, eyes lingering for half a second on the painful spot on my face.

The little lighted mirror in the visor shows me the damage Mac seems so upset about. "I can't believe I'm alive and relatively unharmed," I say, gingerly prodding the broken skin at my temple. Frankly, even though I had full faith in Mac, I'm also in disbelief that I'm still alive. I've never come so close to death.

"Honestly, you were incredible, baby. You kept so calm."

I swallow and close the visor. I eye him, letting my gaze drop to his pants. He doesn't notice because he's focused on the dark road, but I think I can see a bulge. It's just hard to tell from the dark and the angle.

I bite my lip. "So, what you're saying is... I was a very good girl?"

The car swerves a hair as he looks over at me, face full of shock. But he recovers quickly, and his hand goes to my knee. "A very, very good girl."

I grin—pure gallows humor—as the phrase *shooting my shot* enters my head and I lean towards him. I let my hand trail down his hard abdomen, relishing in how the muscles ripple under it, and find the top of his pants. The button is open with a skillful flick, and the zipper comes down.

I unbuckle myself and shift in my seat to get the right angle to lower my face into his lap.

"What are you—" he starts, cutting himself off as my hand finds him through the hole in his boxers and curls around the hot, pulsating length of him. He's already half-hard. Then I hear the thunk of his head falling back against the headrest and a low, "fuuuuuck."

I get my mouth around the tip, swirling my tongue and tasting his salty desire. His legs tense, and the motion of the car changes, making my body rock towards the steering wheel as he slows down. I try taking him deeper in my mouth, but the car stops, and his gentle hands on my cheek and jaw lift me.

I sit back. "Why did you stop? I wanted to—"

He cuts me off with his rough fingertips against my lips. His hand moves quickly, cupping my jaw and holding my chin. "As much as I want a blowjob in this car, I very much want to shoot my load deep inside that pretty pussy while you look me in the eye and tell me you love me. Stay right there."

He unbuckles and shoots out of his seat, slamming the door and jogging around the front of the car. I laugh, seeing his purposeful face and state of half-undress flash through each headlight. In the second or so it takes him to reach me, I look around, assessing. We're off the road but facing it, tucked between some trees. Pretty secluded.

When my door opens, I turn towards him, and he practically lifts me out of the car. His mouth fuses to mine, and I meet him back with the same desperate energy as he guides me sideways to the back of the Mustang. It's a low car, and when he pushes me against the trunk, my ass hits the shelf in such a way I know it's going to be a really good height for what we're about to do.

My skin prickles in the cold, but the fire underneath is all-consuming. I press into him, needing more contact, and my nipples strain in my bra. He gets my jeans undone, but we hit a snag as I try stepping out. I pull away, trying to get my sneaker through the leg-hole the wrong way.

"I fucking hate jeans!" he shouts into the night air, making me giggle and shush him. "It's only skirts or dresses from now on. We're gonna need easy access, baby."

I laugh and hold on to his shoulders as I kick off my shoes. "I thought you didn't like anyone seeing what's yours?"

"Long skirts. Like, Amish-long."

I laugh again, knowing he's kidding.

Shoes gone, jeans gone, underwear gone, the wet ground seeps into my socks but I couldn't care less as he lifts me the inch or so onto the car. It's freezing against my ass, and I tilt my hips with a little shriek so my bare pussy doesn't touch anything so cold, but he's right between my legs. He grips me under the thighs, and it makes my torso fall backwards onto the steep slant of the back window.

"Ready, baby?" he asks, strained.

"Do it!" I cry loudly. I need it so badly I don't think I could stand even a second of teasing.

His cock feels unbelievable, all hard, thick, silky steel. And the heat is a searing contrast to the temperatures all around me. I lock my legs behind him as he fully seats himself inside me and we both groan hoarsely.

His chest comes down over me, and his hand rests on my neck as he starts pumping his hips. I grab his shirt, balling it in my hands, and bring him down to mash my lips into his. It limits the arc of his thrusts, but it feels so good I don't care. I have his cock deep inside, his lips against mine, his hand around my throat, and it feels so fucking right.

He pulls back, and I release him and move my arms down under my knees to help hold them up.

The first thing I can make out in the darkness is the whites of his eyes. The headlights and brake lights have extinguished from their time delay, and it's just the two of us with the brightness of a cloudy night. I can smell him all around me—his rich scent, his breath, even the coppery edge of blood—and it blocks out all awareness of where we are.

"I love you," I whisper, then whimper as his cock nudges the deepest part of me.

"Say it again," he urges, thrusting forward harshly.

"I love you, Mac."

"Again." Hard thrust.

"I love you," I moan, screwing up my face as his hips take over and he pounds into me in a frenzied, determined way.

"Oh, fuck, Eleanor, I love you so fucking much." He reaches between us, and his fingertips find my clit in an easy, practiced move. They slide against the slick skin, and his fingers tighten around my throat. "You want to come on my cock like this, baby?"

"Yes," I moan. "I needed you so bad. I want you to make me come."

He laughs, and it turns into a groan as I squeeze around him. "Were you as fucking"—he changes his rhythm, snapping his hips roughly—"hot for me as I was for you? Did all that fear turn you on?"

"Yes! Oh God, I... I thought there was something wrong with me."

"Not wrong—fuck—never wrong. It's natural, baby. Adrenaline... feeling alive... fuuuck. You feel so fucking good."

I have to agree. The motion of his fingers against me is perfect, and that coupled with his cock pressing inside me so hard and fast, and the sharp cold of the night air reminding me of where we are, what we're doing... It feels so wild and freeing. *Alive* is right—it's the perfect description for how this feels.

I grab around his forearm, clutching it like a lifeline as the pressure builds in my abdomen. "Mac—" I whine.

"That's it, baby. You can do it. You can come for me. Come for me, come with my cock inside you on the back of this car in the middle of the fucking woods. Come knowing that you're safe with me, that I've got you... I've got you. Look at me."

I meet his eye and scream my love for him as loud as I want. I feel like I'm blown apart at the seams, shattering and shooting out into the cloudy sky, landing somewhere among the dark, bare tree branches. My body convulses, shivering against the cold and with the intensity of the electrical pulses of my nerves. His fingers push me higher, just as I would normally fall back down, and his eyes refuse to release mine.

"Keep coming, that's it, squeeze my cock. Take my cum..."

A half-whined, half-sobbed, "Mac," is all I'm capable of as the shaking in my body turns even more intense.

He releases my throat and clit to use both hands for leverage on the sides of the car, fucking me harder than I can ever remember being fucked. Each thrust and retreat moves me up and down the glass window until he's hammering too fast for gravity or friction to keep up.

I cry out just as it becomes too much, and he lets out a choked groan. His cock is warm in me, but his cum feels different—warmer, maybe—and I swear I notice as I'm suddenly even more full of him.

As we both come down, panting harshly, I become suddenly aware of how cold my legs are, and how much my thighs burn with the effort of keeping them up. I let them fall, which drags my body down the cool metal. It tilts my hips back down, so his cock naturally slips out a bit, and I feel the trickle of his sperm follow.

"You're amazing," he murmurs, helping me sit up and slide off the car.

I tilt my head up for his cold, sweaty, sloppy kiss that lights the fire right back in my pussy every time. I love how full of emotion it is, like I can taste how much he wishes he didn't have a refractory period. Like he wants me all the time.

"Right back atcha, sharpshooter."

44

ELEANOR

◄━◆━►

*It's just part of being in love with a dangerous man,
I guess.*

"Well, it's official. I'm unemployed."

I toss the phone onto the top of the box I just finished taping up. I had some missed calls in the first half of my "vacation" that petered off as time went on. I assumed, but needed to actually call in to hear from the owner, Jack, that Bistro Jacques no longer employs me.

The only real shame is that I didn't get to quit first.

"Perfect. More time to work on your business," Mac says, shrugging in his customary no-worries-everything-works-out way.

We're packing up my apartment, putting my stuff in storage until we find a place to stay. Mac stands, grunting with the effort of lifting the box he swore could hold the weight of my food processor *and* blender. He stacks it on top of the others near the door. He's been equally as silly about the crates full of all my cookbooks, thinking a 60-pound box is no big deal. But I suppose I only have myself to blame because I wouldn't let him hire a moving company, nor would I let Dimitri or Wesley help. It's seriously only going to take the two of us a couple of hours.

I've been pretty full of emotions the whole time. I can't put my finger on why I'm so sad. Objectively, this is a happy event. Mac and I are going to live together in the mansion until the lease runs out, then we're going to live in one of the fancy buildings in the city with a pool and a well-appointed gym. And a doorman, obviously.

And obviously, I'm beyond thrilled about it. I'm so excited to start my life with him and have him around and all to myself, I can barely stand it sometimes.

So, why does it feel like there's a hole in my chest?

"Eleanor?"

I whirl, my guard coming up a little at the use of my name and not an endearment.

He's holding the silver frame with the grainy picture of me in the middle of the target circle. He must have found it nestled in among the other photos on my shelf, wedged in between the one of me and Mel as kids and the one of my parents at the beach.

"You kept it?" he asks.

"Yeah," I say, plucking it from out of his hands and hugging it protectively to my chest.

His eyes narrow. "You said it was creepy. 'Really fucking creepy,' if memory serves."

"Yeah, but you're the one who took it. And gave it to me."

"So, let me get this straight," he says, taking a heavy step towards me. Grinning ear to ear, I back away a step. "You didn't keep it because it's a picture of yourself."

I shake my head as he advances, and I retreat. I don't have far to go; the couch is right behind me.

"You kept it because I gave it to you."

The backs of my thighs hit the armrest, and I tilt my head up towards him. "Yup."

His hand slides up my arm, over my shoulder, around my throat. "Even though you think it's creepy."

I inhale sharply. "Well, *you're* creepy. And the creepy gifts, the stalking, being chased and cornered with a hand on my throat..." His lips twitch and his fingers flex, just a hair. "It's just... part of being in love with a dangerous man, I guess."

He kisses me then, and I melt into him. Just as I feel the stirrings, there's the sound of a door closing down the hall, and we're both reminded that mine is open. I can tell from the distance and direction that it wasn't Harrison, and my heart sinks a little since I still haven't seen him yet.

I texted him as soon as I was allowed, and after some invented explanation and apologies, he forgave my radio silence and revealed that he hadn't been spending much time in his apartment either since he got together with Stacey. We both expressed happiness for each other and promised to get together soon for lunch.

Melissa wasn't so easily mollified, but I found out that Wesley had sent her an additional two emails during my time offline to keep her calm. Apparently, she'd called the police in Ulysses for a wellness check on me (that McCloskey apparently blocked) and bought a plane ticket to come out and see for herself that my apartment was empty. If nothing else, it's nice knowing she cares that much, though I feel awful for making her worry.

It's going to take a few more trips to get the rest of my stuff to the car, and I don't look forward to the weighted treks down the stairs, but I like taking an active part in the ending of something like this. Because that's what it is—the end of a phase. The start of a new one, sure, but this apartment served me for a long time, and it feels like saying goodbye to a friend.

Suddenly, I realize exactly why I'm so emotional.

Mac is instantly at my side again, running his hands over my upper arms. I'm so grateful for him—he's been such a rock. "Are you crying, darlin'? Why?"

"Because it's sad. I can't believe it's over. This is the real end, right? Everyone goes their separate ways? Except for us, obviously."

Mac's lips twitch. "Obviously."

"But like, Wesley and Dimitri... they're never coming back, right? They have no reason to. And I just..." I sniffle. "I like them. I liked cooking for them. I liked this weird little life we had."

He brings me in close and kisses the top of my head. "Me too."

I like that he doesn't try to console me, or fix it, or change the subject. He sits with me in my small moment of mourning and lets us both feel it. When I pull away, he gives my arms another rub and goes to grab the top box off the stack he created. I follow.

"Come on, let's go home. I've got something I want to try with you."

"Oh?" I ask curiously.

"I bought a pair of handcuffs just for the occasion."

I inhale sharply and look at him with wide eyes. I swear all the blood in my body is currently pounding an urgent Morse code message in my clit.

His grin is nothing short of salacious. "You like that, huh?"

To distract myself, I grab a box and follow him out the door, kicking it closed behind me. "How... how do you always know exactly what I want?"

"I had your phone, remember? I looked at your incognito tabs."

I stop dead, nearly dropping the box on my toes. I scowl at him. "Well, that explains why it's kind of felt like you had cheat codes to my deepest fantasies."

He grins. "Forgive me?"

"On one condition. I want to see what kind of stuff you watch."

"Told you I'd make you worse," he laughs.

I shake my head and turn towards him as he holds the door at the top of the stairs open for me. "Oh, I don't think that makes me worse. It just makes me... more like you. You know, the creepy, obsessive type. Now you go first; I want to watch you walk away."

45

MAC

Why don't we stay?

At 7 PM sharp, I'm the first to the kitchen table, and I crack my beer while I wait for the other two. Wes pings us that he'll be right in, and Dimitri reads it but doesn't offer the same courtesy. I know he's just getting dressed after his shower.

A few minutes later, Dimitri greets me with a curt nod and heads to the freezer, where his prized bottle of flavorless booze chills on its side. He grabs a lowball glass and joins me. His pour is heavy-handed; the only time I see him drink more than a few shots is when we celebrate finishing a job, but I've never seen him drunk. I'm pretty sure that at his size he can put it away.

Wesley enters seconds later and crosses right to the drink fridge.

"Why did Eleanor burst into tears when she came into my office earlier?" Wes asks.

"Obviously it was something you said," Dimitri assumes, taking a gulp and turning his head to the side slightly as the only indication of the burning liquid traveling down his throat.

Wes joins us and pops the cork on a bottle of champagne, tilting his glass and pouring it ⅔ of the way. "You think I'd still have my tongue if Loverboy thought something I said upset her?"

Dimitri raises an eyebrow and looks my way. "Perhaps no," he says, tone full of approval.

"She's just sad—doesn't want this to end. She keeps saying she's going to miss the two of you... can't imagine why, though."

Wes smiles before taking his first sip. "She's a proper sweetheart."

"Enough discussion of women," Dimitri says. "Did the FBI find the guns?"

Wes nods. "I've got an ear on the chatter, making sure they reach the right conclusions about the bodies. The mayor's death won't stay quiet much longer. A day at most is my guess." He pauses, then asks, "What happened to the rest of the crates, Dimitri? The truck had all 24 when we parked it in that warehouse."

"I split the shipment for safekeeping," Dimitri replies nonchalantly. "I left some guns and the explosives in case we decided we did want to blow up the warehouse."

"What happened to the rest?" Wes asks, taking a sip.

Dimitri cocks his head at Wes's interest. "They are taken care of. You are concerned that I have these weapons now, or that you do not know where they are?"

It's an open challenge, and I frown, looking between them. What is this all about?

Wes places his glass back down and twists it from the base of the stem. "I think they all should have gone into evidence lockup. Anyone paying close attention will know the FBI didn't seize it all, like Rossi's original buyer."

"The buyer will likely assume Rossi decided to separate and sell off smaller pieces. But he is dead and they cannot kill him again, so I do not think we will have to deal with them."

"So, where are they?" I ask the obvious question.

Dimitri cuts me a look. "I have them locked away somewhere very safe. There may come a time when we can use them, and we will be glad they are not all in federal storage. You trust me, *da*?"

I sit back with a shrug. "Good enough for me."

Wes presses his lips together and, after a second, nods his head thoughtfully. "You're the one who's always on about good communication. Would have been nice to know you did it. That's all."

"I agree," I say. It does irritate me that Dimitri went off on his own and did something without us, but I don't have much of a leg to stand on with that one. "Not that it really impacted our plan in the end, but it could have caused an issue if the mayor hadn't shown when he did."

"True," Dimitri agrees. "I promise not to do this kind of thing again. We must all trust each other, yes?"

I don't miss the way he looks at Wes when he says it, though whether it's because Wes didn't confirm that he trusted Dimitri when I did or that there's something else brewing, I'm not sure. I should keep an eye on this.

"Absolutely," Wes answers without pause this time, satisfying Dimitri.

"Speaking of trust..." I pivot, dispelling the tense moment. "McCloskey said something about Anderson being the one with the contacts. Isn't it weird that we only got Rossi's name?" I say, taking a swig and looking at Wes. I don't know what his connection really is with this man we call the General.

"I think it's much more curious that we followed Rossi for weeks and never caught wind of Anderson's part in it," Wes says with a sigh. "I don't like feeling like I've lost my edge."

"We must learn from this error," Dimitri decides. "We probably should start bugging their homes."

Wes rolls his eyes. "It's an infringement—"

"Oh, you think so?" Dimitri interrupts with a scoff. "So much more invasive than murdering them?"

"It's not just the target that lives in a home. There are usually innocents there, too, and that's an infringement of their right to privacy. Mac, back me up."

I hold up my hands, thinking about how I'd handled Eleanor's right to privacy. "You really don't want me weighing in on this one."

"So, where will everyone go next?" Dimitri asks, finishing his glass of vodka. He reaches for the bottle to pour another.

"I was thinking of staying until the lease runs out," Wes says, looking towards me. "If I'm not intruding in the love nest, that is…"

My grin is wry. "You have as much right to stay here as me. You, too, if you're not trying to rush off," I tell Dimitri.

He shrugs. "I am not in a rush. I can stay until the next job brings us somewhere else. It would be good, too, to keep a close eye on the FBI while they work on the investigation into the mayor's death."

"And after that?" I ask, taking another swig.

He shrugs.

I sit back, considering it. Ever since Eleanor revealed how sad she was to be leaving Wesley and Dimitri, it got me thinking. "Why don't we stay? In this house. All of us. It can be our headquarters or something. The house is for sale, right?"

Dimitri and Wes exchange a surprised look. Then, Wes's eyes dart from side to side as he considers it seriously. Dimitri just shakes his head and downs another shot.

"We'd have to give this place a serious security upgrade," Wes says, his entire body perking up at the prospect.

Dimitri turns on him. "You are considering this? When the next job comes in, you know we need to drop everything at a moment's notice—"

"We can carpool," Wes points out helpfully. "And the fiber optic situation is way better here than in a lot of other places we've been."

Dimitri narrows his eyes at Wes, like his words are some kind of betrayal. "It is too crowded in this city," he decides.

"It's easier to be anonymous in a crowd."

"Not when you live in the most ostentatious house on the block."

My lips twitch—not much I can argue with on that point. "This place has, like, 10 acres; we'll never even see our neighbors. Plus, every other rich son of a bitch around here has their own staff of personal security." I rub my fingers together between our faces. "Money talks loud enough that no one asks any questions, right?"

"Hide in plain sight, I say." Wes takes a delicate sip of his champagne.

Judging from the look on his face, though, our surly Russian friend is still not convinced. "You're telling me you like living out of shitty motels?" I press.

Dimitri crosses his arms. "You cannot get away from shitty motels in this line of work," he argues.

"Yeah, but this can be home base. Somewhere to return to that's central so we're all close if something happens."

"Just think, somewhere permanent you can get your fancy custom knives delivered," Wes goads.

I sit back with a grin. When Wes gets on board enough to start helping make my point, it's all over. Dimitri never stands a chance in two against one. Unless he's got a knife.

"We can each have our own floor if you want. No danger of seeing anyone else's junk. Dibs on the top floor," I add quickly.

Wes sighs dramatically. "Of course the sniper wants the best view."

I shrug, unapologetic.

Dimitri's face is lost in thought as he reaches for his glass. "It is a risk," he says gravely. "Someone could more easily take out all of us if they find out we are in the same place."

"Leave that to me," Wes pipes in. "I'll make sure none of our names are on it. And how much do you want to bet one of these rich twats already has the requests in the proper channels to make this a no-fly zone?"

"I will not take that bet," Dimitri adds, humor sparkling in his eye. It's dry, but at least he's showing he understands the humor, even if he still can't bring himself not to meet it with austerity. Progress.

"So, it's settled? We've got a home base?"

"I suppose you will want her to live here, too?" Dimitri cocks a brow at me.

"Kind of implied. She goes where I go."

Wes's lips twitch. "Just try not to shake the chandeliers."

"No promises," I laugh, then turn to Dimitri. His approval is moot—either she stays or the whole thing is off and I'm keeping the house for myself. "That okay by you?"

"She does know how to make pelmeni," he says thoughtfully. "I will consider this. It is not so bad of an idea to have a base of operations while we work together. Though I agree with Wesley—you must learn to reign in your impulses. I will not live in a sex house."

Wes chokes on his champagne, and even I find his phrasing more entertaining than offensive.

"You think I could not hear you? You are only one floor away, and sound travels," he adds, making a face. "Though I suppose the two of you have... calmed down."

Wes chimes in with a shit-eating grin, "Yeah, trouble in paradise already?"

I roll my eyes, but my hands tense in warning. "I'd just like to remind you both that turnabout is fair fuckin' play. If you ever manage to build yourself some kind of fuckable computer," I nod at Wes, "or if you find someone to melt that icicle in your chest," I direct to Dimitri, "I'm going to be right there. I can't wait to give y'all the same shit you've been giving me."

"I do not have an icicle in my chest," Dimitri scoffs. "Though I have a story of a man who was impaled that way and the police could not figure out what happened to the murder weapon because—"

"It melted," Wes and I finish in unison.

Dimitri scowls. "You have heard this story?"

"Urban legend, big guy," I say, leaning forward and clapping him on the shoulder. "Everyone's heard that story."

"It is not an urban legend," Dimitri retorts. "His name was Leonov. Icicles are too slippery to get a proper grip, but a fortuitous weapon choice, as it turned out."

Wes and I glance at each other, and I feel my jaw fall slack. "Are you saying... you..." I scoff. "No way."

"You do not believe that I did it?" Dimitri asks, his brow lifting. "Hmm. Good."

Wes and I exchange a hard look. He shakes his head. "No way," he says, echoing my sentiment.

With a laugh about the enigmatic nature of hitmen, I raise my beer between us. Dimitri hits it with the bottom of his lowball, and the delicate clink of Wes's champagne flute has me rolling my eyes.

"You're such a fancy little boy," I mutter.

"A fancy little boy who knows your social security number, so don't test me."

I grin and look between them. For once in my life, I feel like I've really got everything.

My team. My friends. My brothers.

And my woman.

46

MAC

Some time later...

I hear raised voices in the kitchen, so I pick up the pace and hustle down the stairs. I find Dimitri with his back to me, waving a receipt at Eleanor, who is calmly peeling potatoes over the sink built into the marble island. Her eyes meet mine, and she smiles warmly.

Dimitri looks over his shoulder and, seeing it's me, turns and waves the receipt at me. His face is red, like he's been working himself up for a little while now. "James, control your woman."

"I'm trying, but she keeps getting out of the handcuffs."

Dimitri plows over me as I catch the blush settling across Eleanor's cheeks. "She spent $45 on a bottle of olive oil! A small bottle of olive oil."

"Oh, let it go, you control freak. I didn't hear you complaining last week when you went for seconds of that olive oil cake," she replies primly.

He glares at her and storms out of the room. Then, from the hallway we hear him call, "You had better make another cake!"

She chuckles to herself and resumes peeling the potato in her hand.

My heart bangs around in my chest, seeing my woman so at home, so in her element, and so easily handling the anger of a lethal killer who literally made a man piss himself in fear yesterday.

"Eleanor, will you marry me?"

She looks up and smiles and teases, "Took you long enough."

Acknowledgements

First of all, thank YOU for picking up my book.

Thank you so much to my supportive family and friends. For putting up with countless cover revisions and discussions about plotlines.

Dana, you're the best line editor a gal could ask for! Thank you for being my biggest fan.

Thank you, Ben, my love, for being my sounding board and lending both your ear and your learned perspective. I know this isn't your genre and you'll never see this, but it needs to be said.

Thank you to the members of countless Facebook groups for motivation, weighing in on blurbs and art, and helping me find my way in this indie publishing journey.

Every ARC reviewer is a rockstar. I'm serious. Thank you so much.

About the Author

L.M. Whiteley writes dark, steamy romance with morally gray male main characters, relatable female main characters, obsessive love and hard-won happily-ever-afters. *Eyes in the Shadows* is her debut novel.

When she's not writing, she can be found cooking, gardening, gaming, playing outside with her friends or letting book boyfriends written by other fantastic indie authors ruin her.

Blog posts, signed copies of the books, and links to all socials can be found on her website: http://lmwhiteley.com

<u>Loved the book?</u>

The best way to support indie authors is by leaving a review!

Please consider rating and reviewing *Eyes in the Shadows* on **Amazon** and **Goodreads**.

Scan this code for the Goodreads page:

Scan this code for the Amazon page:

Stay Obsessed

Join the newsletter for exclusive content, sneak peeks, and bonus scenes:
http://lmwhiteley.com/contact-me/

Follow L.M. Whiteley on social media:

Instagram [@LMWhiteleyauthor]|
TikTok [@LM.Whiteley]|
Facebook: [@LMWhiteleyauthor]
Website: [http://lmwhiteley.com]